THE FIRST CHRONICLES OF DRUSS THE LEGEND

'We all die. You . . . me . . . Druss. The measure of us all
is established by how we live.'

By David Gemmell

DAVID GEMMELL

THE FIRST CHRONICLES OF DRUSS THE LEGEND

www.orbitbooks.net

ORBIT

First published in Great Britain in 1993 by Legend Books
Reprinted by Orbit in 1998
This paperback edition published in 2012 by Orbit

5 7 9 11 12 10 8 6

A CIP catalogue record for this book
is available from the British Library.

ISBN 978-0-356-50142-0

Typeset in Sabon by Hewer Text UK Ltd, Edinburgh
Printed and bound by Clays Ltd, St Ives PLC

Papers used by Orbit are from well-managed forests
and other responsible sources.

MIX
Paper from
responsible sources

FSC
www.fsc.org   FSC® C104740

Orbit
An imprint of
Little, Brown Book Group
Carmelite House
50 Victoria Embankment
London EC4Y 0DZ

An Hachette UK Company
www.hachette.co.uk

www.orbitbooks.net

Druss the Legend is dedicated with great love and affection to the memory of Mick Jeffrey, a quiet Christian of infinite patience and kindness. Those privileged to know him were blessed indeed. Goodnight and God bless, Mick!

Contents

Contents

Introduction

Druss was really the first of my heroes. He was based on a child's idealised view of his stepfather.

Bill Woodford became my stepfather in 1954. He changed my life in so many ways. Probably the best example of this came soon after he married my mother. I was six years old and had terrible dreams of vampires coming to drink my blood. I don't know why these dreams occurred, but I still recall the terror of them. My mother took me to see specialists who assured me that vampires didn't exist, but the dreams continued.

One night, as I awoke screaming, Bill came into the room. I told him there was a vampire coming for me. He said: 'I know, son. I saw it. Broke its neck. Won't have no vampires in my house.' I never dreamt of vampires again.

Druss was Bill writ large.

After the publication of *Legend* in 1984, I wrote a prequel called *Druss the Legend*. The publishers rejected it on two counts. Firstly, as a young man, Druss was too similar to Conan, invincible and deadly, and, secondly, all of his early tales were recounted in *Legend* and this robbed the prequel of surprise.

So I moved on, writing other stories. Over the years more and more fans wrote asking for earlier tales of Druss. I talked it over with editors and test-readers. Would it sell? We couldn't decide.

Then I gave an interview to a journalist from a science fiction publication. In it I said I was considering a new Druss novel.

The response was overwhelming. Letters were coming in from all over the world asking when it would be published.

This answered the question as to whether it would sell.

Which was not enough for me. The real question was whether I could overcome the lack of surprise.

At a convention in 1990 I asked a fan, who knew *Legend* so well he could quote passages verbatim, what he could remember about Druss's early life. He said: 'He loses Rowena, sets off to track her down, finds her then takes part in the Battle of Skeln. He also becomes known as the Silver Slayer among the Sathuli and Deathwalker among the Nadir.' He then also listed other characters mentioned by Druss in *Legend* – Sieben the Poet, Ekodas, Bodasen and Gorben the prince who became a king.

My heart sank. 'No point in you reading the prequel then,' I said. 'You know it already.'

'I know *what* he did, but I'd love to read *how*,' he told me.

'I'd like to find *that* out myself,' I said.

It was a real joy to walk the hills with Druss again. So much so that some years later I added a third story to the series, *Legend of Deathwalker*. God willing there will be one more before Druss is finally laid to rest.

Book One

Birth of a Legend

Prologue

Screened by the undergrowth he knelt by the trail, dark eyes scanning the boulders ahead of him and the trees beyond. Dressed as he was in a shirt of fringed buckskin, and brown leather leggings and boots, the tall man was virtually invisible, kneeling in the shadows of the trees.

The sun was high in a cloudless summer sky, and the spoor was more than three hours old. Insects had criss-crossed the hoof-marks, but the edges of the prints were still firm.

Forty horsemen, laden with plunder . . .

Shadak faded back through the undergrowth to where his horse was tethered. He stroked the beast's long neck and lifted his sword-belt from the back of the saddle. Strapping it to his waist he drew the two short swords; they were of the finest Vagrian steel, and double-edged. He thought for a moment, then sheathed the blades and reached for the bow and quiver strapped to the saddle pommel. The bow was of Vagrian horn, a hunting weapon capable of launching a two-foot-long arrow across a killing space of sixty paces. The doeskin quiver held twenty shafts that Shadak had crafted himself: the flights of goose feather, stained red and yellow, the heads of pointed iron, not barbed, and easily withdrawn from the bodies of the slain. Swiftly he strung the bow and notched an arrow to the string. Then, looping the quiver over his shoulder, he made his way carefully back to the trail.

Would they have left a rearguard? It was unlikely, for there were no Drenai soldiers within fifty miles.

But Shadak was a cautious man. And he knew Collan. Tension rose in him as he pictured the smiling face and the cruel, mocking eyes. 'No anger,' he told himself. But it was hard, bitterly hard. Angry men make mistakes, he reminded himself. The hunter must be cold as iron.

Silently he edged his way forward. A towering boulder jutted from the earth some twenty paces ahead and to his left; to the right was a cluster of smaller rocks, no more than four feet high. Shadak took a deep breath and rose from his hiding-place.

From behind the large boulder a man stepped into sight, bowstring bent. Shadak dropped to his knee, the attacker's arrow slashing through the air above his head. The bowman tried to leap back behind the shelter of the boulder, but even as he was dropping Shadak loosed a shaft which plunged into the bowman's throat, punching through the skin at the back of his neck.

Another attacker ran forward, this time from Shadak's right. With no time to notch a second arrow Shadak swung the bow, lashing it across the man's face. As the attacker stumbled, Shadak dropped the bow and drew his two short swords; with one sweeping blow he cut through the neck of the fallen man. Two more attackers ran into view and he leapt to meet them. Both men wore iron breastplates, their necks and heads protected by chain mail, and they carried sabres.

'You'll not die easily, you bastard!' shouted the first, a tall, wide-shouldered warrior. Then his eyes narrowed as he recognised the swordsman facing him. Fear replaced battle lust – but he was too close to Shadak to withdraw and made a clumsy lunge with his sabre. Shadak parried the blade with ease, his second sword lancing forward into the man's mouth and through the bones of his neck. As the swordsman died, the second warrior backed away.

'We didn't know it was you, I swear!' he said, hands trembling.

'Now you do,' said Shadak softly.

Without a word the man turned and ran back towards the trees as Shadak sheathed his swords and moved to his bow. Notching an arrow, he drew back on the string. The shaft flashed through the air to punch home into the running man's thigh. He screamed and fell. As Shadak loped to where he lay, the man rolled to his back, dropping his sword.

'For pity's sake don't kill me!' he pleaded.

'You had no pity back in Corialis,' said Shadak. 'But tell me where Collan is heading and I'll let you live.' A wolf howled in the distance, a lonely sound. It was answered by another, then another.

'There's a village ... twenty miles south-east,' said the man, his eyes fixed on the short sword in Shadak's hand. 'We scouted it. Plenty of young women. Collan and Harib Ka plan to raid it for slaves, then take them to Mashrapur.'

Shadak nodded. 'I believe you,' he said, at last.

'You're going to let me live, yes? You promised,' the wounded man whimpered.

'I always keep my promises,' said Shadak, disgusted at the man's weakness. Reaching down, he wrenched his shaft clear of the man's leg. Blood gushed from the wound, and the injured warrior groaned. Shadak wiped the arrow clean on the man's cloak, then stood and walked to the body of the first man he had killed. Kneeling beside the corpse, he recovered his arrow and then strode to where the raiders had tethered their horses. Mounting the first, he led the others back down the trail to where his gelding waited. Gathering the reins, he led the four mounts back out on the trail.

'What about me?' shouted the wounded man.

Shadak turned in the saddle. 'Do your best to keep the wolves away,' he advised. 'By dark they will have picked up the scent of blood.'

'Leave me a horse! In the name of Mercy!'

'I am not a merciful man,' said Shadak.

And he rode on towards the south-east, and the distant mountains.

1

The axe was four feet long, with a ten-pound head, the blade flared and sharp as any sword. The haft was of elm, beautifully curved, and more than forty years old. For most men it was a heavy tool, unwieldy and imprecise. But in the hands of the dark-haired young man who stood before the towering beech it sang through the air, seemingly as light as a sabre. Every long swing saw the head bite exactly where the woodsman intended, deeper and deeper into the meat of the trunk.

Druss stepped back, then glanced up. There were several heavy branches jutting towards the north. He moved around the tree, gauging the line where it would fall, then returned to his work. This was the third tree he had tackled today and his muscles ached, sweat gleaming on his naked back. His short-cropped black hair was soaked with perspiration that trickled over his brow, stinging his ice-blue eyes. His mouth was dry, but he was determined to finish the task before allowing himself the reward of a cooling drink.

Some way to his left the brothers Pilan and Yorath were sitting on a fallen tree, laughing and talking, their hatchets beside them. Theirs was the task of stripping the trunks, hacking away smaller branches and limbs that could be used for winter firewood. But they stopped often and Druss could hear them discussing the merits and alleged vices of the village girls. They were handsome youths, blond and tall, sons of the blacksmith, Tetrin. Both were witty and intelligent, and popular among the girls.

Druss disliked them. To his right several of the older boys were sawing through the larger branches of the first tree Druss had felled, while elsewhere young girls were gathering deadwood, kindling for winter fires, and loading them to wheelbarrows to be pushed down-hill to the village.

At the edge of the new clearing stood the four workhorses, hobbled now and grazing, waiting for the trees to be cleaned so that chain traces could be attached to the trunks for the long haul into the valley. Autumn was fading fast, and the village elders were deter-mined that the new perimeter wall would be finished before winter. The frontier mountains of Skoda boasted only one troop of Drenai cavalry, patrolling an area of a thousand square miles. Raiders, cattle thieves, slavers, robbers and outlaws roamed the mountains, and the ruling council in Drenai made it clear they would accept no responsibility for the new settlements on the Vagrian borders.

But thoughts of the perils of frontier life did not discourage the men and women who journeyed to Skoda. They sought a new life, far removed from the more civilised south and east, and built their homes where land was still free and wild, and where strong men did not need to tug the forelock nor bow when the nobles rode by.

Freedom was the key word, and no talk of raiders could deter them.

Druss hefted his axe, then thundered the blade into the widening notch. Ten times more he struck, deep into the base of the trunk. Then another ten smooth, powerful strokes. Three more axe-blows and the tree would groan and give, wrenching and tearing as she fell.

Stepping back he scanned the ground along the line of the fall. A movement caught his eye, and he saw a small child with golden hair sitting beneath a bush, a rag doll in her hand. 'Kiris!' bellowed Druss. 'If you are not out of there by the time I count to three I'll tear off your leg and beat you to death with the wet end! One! Two!'

The child's mouth dropped open, her eyes widening. Dropping her rag doll she scrambled clear of the bush and ran crying from the forest. Druss shook his head and walked forward to retrieve the doll, tucking it into his wide belt. He felt the eyes of the others on him, and guessed what they were thinking: Druss the Brute, Druss the Cruel – that's how they saw him. And maybe they were right.

Ignoring them, he walked back to the tree and hefted his axe.

Only two weeks before he had been felling a tall beech, and had been called away with the work almost completed. When he returned it was to find Kiris sitting in the topmost branches with her doll, as always, beside her.

'Come down,' he had coaxed. 'The tree is about to fall.'

'Won't,' said Kiris. 'We like it here. We can see for ever.'

Druss had looked around, for once hoping that some of the village girls were close by. But there was no one. He examined the huge cleft in the trunk; a sudden wind could cause the trunk to topple. 'Come down, there's a good girl. You'll be hurt if the tree falls.'

'Why should it fall?'

'Because I've been hitting it with my axe. Now come down.'

'All right,' she said, then started to climb down. The tree suddenly tilted and Kiris screamed and clung to a branch. Druss's mouth was dry.

'Quickly now,' he said. Kiris said nothing, nor did she move. Druss swore and, setting his foot to a low knot, levered himself up to the first branch. Slowly and with great care he climbed the half-felled tree, higher and higher towards the child.

At last he reached her. 'Put your arms around my neck,' he commanded. She did so, and he began the climb down.

Half-way to the ground Druss felt the tree shudder – and snap. Leaping clear he hugged the child to him, then hit the ground, landing awkwardly with his left shoulder slamming into the soft earth. Shielded by his bulk, Kiris was unhurt, but Druss groaned as he rose.

'Are you hurt?' asked Kiris.

Druss's pale eyes swung on the child. 'If I catch you near my trees again, I shall feed you to the wolves!' he roared. 'Now begone!' She had sprinted away as if her dress was on fire. Chuckling at the memory now, he hefted his axe and thundered the blade into the beech. A great groan came from the tree, a wrenching, tearing sound that drowned out the nearby thudding of hatchets and the sawing of boughs.

The beech toppled, twisting as it fell. Druss turned towards the water-sack hanging from a branch nearby; the felling of the tree signalled the break for the midday meal, and the village youngsters gathered in groups in the sunshine, laughing and joking. But no one approached Druss. His recent fight with the former soldier Alarin had unsettled them, and they viewed him even more warily than before. He sat alone, eating bread and cheese and taking long, cool swallows of water.

Pilan and Yorath were now sitting with Berys and Tailia, the daughters of the miller. The girls were smiling prettily, tilting their heads and enjoying the attention. Yorath leaned in close to Tailia, kissing her ear. Tailia feigned outrage.

Their games ceased when a black-bearded man entered the clearing. He was tall, with massive shoulders and eyes the colour of winter clouds. Druss saw his father approach, and stood.

'Clothe yourself and walk with me,' said Bress, striding away into the woods. Druss donned his shirt and followed his father. Out of earshot of the others, the tall man sat down beside a fast-moving stream and Druss joined him.

'You must learn to control that temper, my son,' said Bress. 'You almost killed the man.'

'I just hit him . . . once.'

'The *once* broke his jaw and dislodged three teeth.'

'Have the Elders decided on a penalty?'

'Aye. I must support Alarin and his family through the winter. Now I can ill afford that, boy.'

'He spoke slightingly of Rowena and I'll not tolerate that. *Ever*.'

Bress took a deep breath, but before speaking he lifted a pebble and hurled it into the stream. Then he sighed. 'We are not known here, Druss – save as good workers and fellow villagers. We came a long way to be rid of the stigma my father bequeathed our family. But remember the lessons of his life. He could not control his temper – and he became an outcast and a renegade, a bloodthirsty butcher. Now they say blood runs true. In our case I hope they are wrong.'

'I'm not a killer,' argued Druss. 'Had I wanted him dead, I could have broken his neck with a single blow.'

'I know. You are strong – you take after me in that regard. And proud; that I think came from your mother, may her soul know peace. The gods alone know how often I have been forced to

11

swallow my pride.' Bress tugged at his beard and turned to face his son. 'We are a small settlement now, and we cannot have violence among ourselves – we would not survive as a community. Can you understand that?'

'What did they ask you to tell me?'

Bress sighed. 'You must make your peace with Alarin. And know this – if you attack any other man of the village you will be cast out.'

Druss's face darkened. 'I work harder than any man. I trouble no one. I do not get drunk like Pilan and Yorath, nor try to make whores of the village maids like their father. I do not steal. I do not lie. Yet they will cast *me* out?'

'You frighten them, Druss. You frighten me too.'

'I am not my grandfather. I am not a murderer.'

Bress sighed. 'I had hoped that Rowena, with all her gentleness, would have helped to calm that temper of yours. But on the morning after your wedding you half-kill a fellow settler. And for what? Don't tell me he spoke slightingly. All he said was that you were a lucky man and he'd like to have bedded her himself. By all the gods, son! If you feel you have to break a man's jaw for every compliment he pays your wife, there won't be any men left in this village to work at all.'

'It wasn't said as a compliment. And I can control my temper, but Alarin is a loud-mouthed braggart – and he received exactly what he deserved.'

'I hope you'll take note of what I've said, son.' Bress stood and stretched his back. 'I know you have little respect for me. But I hope you'll think of how Rowena would fare if you were both declared outcast.'

Druss gazed up at him and swallowed back his disappointment. Bress was a physical giant, stronger than any man Druss had ever known, but he wore defeat like a cloak. The younger man rose alongside his father.

'I'll take heed,' he said.

Bress smiled wearily. 'I have to get back to the wall. It should be finished in another three days; we'll all sleep sounder then.'

'You'll have the timber,' Druss promised.

12

'You're a good man with an axe, I'll say that.' Bress walked away for several paces, then turned. 'If they did cast you out, son, you wouldn't be alone. I'd walk with you.'

Druss nodded. 'It won't come to that. I've already promised Rowena I'll mend my ways.'

'I'll wager she was angry,' said Bress, with a grin.

'Worse. She was disappointed in me.' Druss chuckled. 'Sharper than a serpent's tooth is the *disappointment* of a new wife.'

'You should laugh more often, my boy. It suits you.'

But as Bress walked away the smile faded from the young man's face as he gazed down at his bruised knuckles and remembered the emotions that had surged within him as he struck Alarin. There had been anger, and a savage need for combat. But when his fist landed and Alarin toppled there had been only one sensation, brief and indescribably powerful.

Joy. Pure pleasure, of a kind and a power he had not experienced before. He closed his eyes, forcing the scene from his mind.

'I am not my grandfather,' he told himself. 'I am not insane.' That night he repeated the words to Rowena as they lay in the broad bed Bress had fashioned for a wedding gift.

Rolling to her stomach she leaned on his chest, her long hair feeling like silk upon his massive shoulder. 'Of course you are not insane, my love,' she assured him. 'You are one of the gentlest men I've known.'

'That's not how they see me,' he told her, reaching up and stroking her hair.

'I know. It was wrong of you to break Alarin's jaw. They were just words – and it matters not a whit if he meant them unpleasantly. They were just noises, blowing into the air.'

Easing her from him, Druss sat up. 'It is not that easy, Rowena. The man had been goading me for weeks. He wanted that fight – because he wanted to humble me. But he did not. No man ever will.' She shivered beside him. 'Are you cold?' he asked, drawing her into his embrace.

'*Deathwalker*,' she whispered.

'What? What did you say?'

13

Her eyelids fluttered. She smiled and kissed his cheek. 'It doesn't matter. Let us forget Alarin, and enjoy each other's company.'

'I'll always enjoy your company,' he said. 'I love you.'

Rowena's dreams were dark and brooding and the following day, at the riverside, she could not force the images from her mind. Druss, dressed in black and silver and bearing a mighty axe, stood upon a hillside. From the axe-blades came a great host of souls, flowing like smoke around their grim killer. *Deathwalker!* The vision had been powerful. Squeezing the last of the water from the shirt she was washing, she laid it over a flat rock alongside the drying blankets and the scrubbed woollen dress. Stretching her back, she rose from the water's edge and walked to the tree line where she sat, her right hand closing on the brooch Druss had fashioned for her in his father's workshop – soft copper strands entwined around a moonstone, misty and translucent. As her fingers touched the stone her eyes closed and her mind cleared. She saw Druss sitting alone by the high stream.

'I am with you,' she whispered. But he could not hear her and she sighed.

No one in the village knew of her Talent, for her father, Voren, had impressed upon her the need for secrecy. Only last year four women in Drenan had been convicted of sorcery and burnt alive by the priests of Missael. Voren was a careful man. He had brought Rowena to this remote village, far from Drenan, because, as he told her, 'Secrets cannot live quietly among a multitude. Cities are full of prying eyes and attentive ears, vengeful minds and malevolent thoughts. You will be safer in the mountains.'

And he had made her promise to tell no one of her skills. Not even Druss. Rowena regretted that promise as she gazed with the eyes of Spirit upon her husband. She could see no harshness in his blunt, flat features, no swirling storm-clouds in those grey-blue eyes, no hint of sullenness in the flat lines of his mouth. He was Druss – and she loved him. With a certainty born of her Talent she knew she would love no other man as she loved Druss. And she knew why . . . he needed her. She had gazed through the window of his soul and had found there a warmth and a purity, an island of tranquillity set in a sea of roaring violent emotions. While she was with him Druss was tender, his turbulent spirit at peace. In her company he smiled. Perhaps, she thought, with my help I can keep him at peace. Perhaps the grim killer will never know life.

'Dreaming again, Ro,' said Mari, moving to sit alongside Rowena. The young woman opened her eyes and smiled at her friend. Mari was short and plump, with honey-coloured hair and a bright, open smile.

'I was thinking of Druss,' said Rowena.

Mari nodded and looked away and Rowena could feel her concern. For weeks her friend had tried to dissuade her from marrying Druss, adding her arguments to those of Voren and others.

'Will Pilan be your partner at the Solstice Dance?' asked Rowena, changing the subject.

Mari's mood changed abruptly, and she giggled. 'Yes. But he doesn't know yet.'

'When will he find out?'

'Tonight.' Mari lowered her voice, though there was no one else within earshot. 'We're meeting in the lower meadow.'

'Be careful,' warned Rowena.

'Is that the advice of the old married woman? Didn't you and Druss make love before you were wed?'

'Yes, we did,' Rowena admitted, 'but Druss had already made his pledge before the Oak. Pilan hasn't.'

'Just words, Ro. I don't need them. Oh, I know Pilan's been flirting with Tailia, but she's not for him. No passion, you see. All she thinks about is wealth. She doesn't want to stay in the wilderness, she yearns for Drenan. She'll not want to keep a mountain man warm at night, nor make the beast with two backs in a wet meadow, with the grass tickling her ...'

'Mari! You really are too frank,' admonished Rowena.

Mari giggled and leaned in close. 'Is Druss a good lover?'

Rowena sighed, all tension and sadness disappearing. 'Oh, Mari! Why is it that you can talk about forbidden subjects and make them seem so . . . so wonderfully ordinary? You are like the sunshine that follows rain.'

'They're not forbidden here, Ro. That's the trouble with girls born in cities and surrounded by stone walls and marble, and granite. You don't feel the earth any more. Why did you come here?'

'You know why,' said Rowena uneasily. 'Father wanted a life in the mountains.'

'I know that's what you've always said – but I never believed it. You're a terrible liar – your face goes red and you always look away!'

'I . . . can't tell you. I made a promise.'

'Wonderful!' exclaimed Mari. 'I love mysteries. Is he a criminal? He was a book-keeper, wasn't he? Did he steal some rich man's money?'

'No! It was nothing to do with him. It was me! Don't ask me any more. Please?'

'I thought we were friends,' said Mari. 'I thought we could trust one another.'

'We can. Honestly!'

'I wouldn't tell anyone.'

'I know,' said Rowena sadly. 'But it would spoil our friendship.'

'Nothing could do that. How long have you been here – two seasons? Have we ever fought? Oh, come on, Ro. Where's the harm? You tell me your secret and I'll tell you mine.'

'I know yours already,' whispered Rowena. 'You gave yourself to the Drenai captain when he and his men passed through here on patrol in the summer. You took him to the lower meadow.'

'How did you find out?'

'I didn't. It was in your mind when you told me you would share a secret with me.'

'I don't understand.'

'I can see what people are thinking. And I can sometimes tell what is going to happen. That's my secret.'

'You have the Gift? I don't believe it! What am I thinking now?'

'A white horse with a garland of red flowers.'

'Oh, Ro! That's wonderful. Tell my fortune,' she pleaded, holding out her hand.

16

'You won't tell anyone else?'

'I promised, didn't I?'

'Sometimes it doesn't work.'

'Try anyway,' urged Mari, thrusting out her plump hand. Rowena reached out, her slender fingers closing on Mari's palm, but suddenly she shuddered and the colour faded from her face.

'What is it?'

Rowena began to tremble. 'I . . . I must find Druss. Can't . . . talk . . .' Rising, she stumbled away, the washed clothes forgotten.

'Ro! Rowena, come back!'

On the hillside above, a rider stared down at the women by the river. Then he turned his horse and rode swiftly towards the north.

Bress closed the door of the cabin and moved through to his work room, where from a small box he took a lace glove. It was old and yellowed, and several of the pearls which had once graced the wrist were now missing. It was a small glove and Bress sat at his bench staring down at it, his huge fingers stroking the remaining pearls.

'I am a lost man,' he said softly, closing his eyes and picturing Alithae's sweet face. 'He despises me. Gods, I despise myself.' Leaning back in his chair he gazed idly at the walls, and the many shelves bearing strands of copper and brass, work tools, jars of dye, boxes of beads. It was rare now for Bress to find the time to make jewellery; there was little call for such luxuries here in the mountains. Now it was his skills as a carpenter which were valued; he had become merely a maker of doors and tables, chairs and beds.

Still nursing the glove, he moved back into the hearth room.

'I think we were born under unlucky stars,' he told the dead Alithae. 'Or perhaps Bardan's evil stained our lives. Druss is like him, you know. I see it in the eyes, in the sudden rages. I don't know what to do. I could never convince father. And I cannot reach Druss.'

His thoughts drifted back – memories, dark and painful, flooding his mind. He saw Bardan on that last day, blood-covered, his enemies all around him. Six men were dead, and that terrible axe was still slashing left and right . . . Then a lance had been thrust into Bardan's throat. Blood bubbled from the wound but Bardan slew

17

the lance wielder before falling to his knees. A man ran in behind him and delivered a terrible blow to Bardan's neck.

From his hiding-place high in the oak the fourteen-year-old Bress had watched his father die, and heard one of the killers say: 'The old wolf is dead – now where is the pup?'

He had stayed in the tree all night, high above the headless body of Bardan. Then, in the cold of the dawn he had climbed down and stood by the corpse. There was no sadness, only a terrible sense of relief combined with guilt. Bardan was dead: Bardan the Butcher. Bardan the Slayer. Bardan the Demon.

He had walked sixty miles to a settlement, and there had found employment, apprenticed to a carpenter. But just as he was settling down, the past came back to torment him when a travelling tinker recognised him: he was the son of the Devil! A crowd gathered outside the carpenter's shop, an angry mob armed with clubs and stones.

Bress had climbed from the rear window and fled from the settlement. Three times during the next five years he had been forced to run – and then he had met Alithae.

Fortune smiled on him then and he remembered Alithae's father, on the day of the wedding, approaching him and offering him a goblet of wine. 'I know you have suffered, boy,' said the old man. 'But I am not one who believes that a father's evil is visited upon the souls of his children. I know you, Bress. You are a good man.'

Aye, thought Bress as he sat by the hearth, a good man.

Lifting the glove he kissed it softly. Alithae had been wearing it when the three men from the south had arrived at the settlement where Bress and his wife and new son had made their homes. Bress had a small but thriving business making brooches and rings and necklets for the wealthy. He was out walking one morning, Alithae beside him carrying the babe.

'It's Bardan's son!' he heard someone shout and he glanced round. The three riders had stopped their horses, and one of the men was pointing at him; they spurred their mounts and rode at him. Alithae, struck by a charging horse, fell heavily, and Bress had leapt at the rider, dragging him from the saddle. The other men hurled themselves from their saddles. Bress struck left and right, his huge fists clubbing them to the ground.

As the dust settled he turned back to Alithae . . .

Only to find her dead, the babe crying beside her.

From that moment he lived like a man with no hope. He rarely smiled and he never laughed.

The ghost of Bardan was upon him, and he took to travelling, moving through the lands of the Drenai with his son beside him. Bress took what jobs he could find: a labourer in Drenan, a carpenter in Delnoch, a bridge-builder in Mashrapur, a horse-handler in Corteswain. Five years ago he had wed a farmer's daughter named Patica – a simple lass, plain of face and none too bright. Bress cared for her, but there was no room left for love in his heart for Alithae had taken it with her when she died. He had married Patica to give Druss a mother, but the boy had never taken to her.

Two years ago, with Druss now fifteen, they had come to Skoda. But even here the ghost remained – born again, it seemed, into the boy.

'What can I do, Alithae?' he asked.

Patica entered the cabin, holding three fresh loaves in her arms. She was a large woman with a round pleasant face framed by auburn hair. She saw the glove and tried to mask the hurt she felt. 'Did you see Druss?' she asked.

'Aye, I did. He says he'll try to curb his temper.'

'Give him time. Rowena will calm him.'

Hearing the thunder of hooves outside, Bress placed the glove on the table and moved to the door. Armed men were riding into the village, swords in their hands.

Bress saw Rowena running into the settlement, her dress hitched up around her thighs. She saw the raiders and tried to turn away but a horseman bore down on her. Bress ran into the open and leapt at the man, pulling him from the saddle. The rider hit the ground hard, losing his grip on his sword. Bress snatched it up, but a lance pierced his shoulder and with a roar of anger he twisted round and the lance snapped. Bress lashed out with the sword. The rider fell back, and the horse reared.

Riders surrounded him, with lances levelled.

In that instant Bress knew he was about to die. Time froze for him. He was the sky, filled with lowering clouds, and smelled the new-mown grass of the meadows. Other raiders were galloping through the settlement, and he heard the screams of the dying villagers. Everything they had built was for nothing. A terrible anger raged inside him. Gripping the sword, he let out the battle-cry of Bardan.

'Blood and death!' he bellowed.

And charged.

Deep within the woods Druss leaned on his axe, a rare smile on his normally grim face. Above him the sun shone through a break in the clouds, and he saw an eagle soaring, golden wings seemingly aflame. Druss removed his sweat-drenched linen headband, laying it on a stone to dry. Lifting a waterskin, he took a long drink. Nearby Pilan and Yorath laid aside their hatchets.

Soon Tailia and Berys would arrive with the haul-horses and the work would begin again, attaching the chains and dragging the timbers down to the village. But for now there was little to do but sit and wait. Druss opened the linen-wrapped package Rowena had given him that morning; within was a wedge of meat pie, and a large slice of honey cake.

'Ah, the joys of married life!' said Pilan.

Druss laughed. 'You should have tried harder to woo her. Too late to be jealous now.'

'She wouldn't have me, Druss. She said she was waiting for a man whose face would curdle milk and that if she married me she would spend the rest of her life wondering which of her pretty friends would steal me from her. It seems her dream was to find the world's ugliest man.'

His smile faded as he saw the expression on the woodsman's face, and the cold gleam that appeared in his pale eyes. 'Only jesting,' said Pilan swiftly, the colour ebbing from his face.

Druss took a deep breath and, remembering his father's warning, fought down his anger. 'I am not ... good with jests,' he said, the words tasting like bile in his mouth.

'No harm done,' said Pilan's brother, moving to sit alongside the giant. 'But if you don't mind my saying so, Druss, you need to develop a sense of humour. We all make jests at the expense of our . . . friends. It means nothing.'

Druss merely nodded and turned his attention to the pie. Yorath was right. Rowena had said exactly the same words, but from her it was easy to take criticism. With her he felt calm and the world had colour and joy. He finished the food and stood. 'The girls should have been here by now,' he said.

'I can hear horses,' said Pilan, rising.

'They're coming fast,' Yorath added.

Tailia and Berys came running into the clearing, their faces showing fear, their heads turning towards the unseen horsemen. Druss snatched his axe from the stump and ran towards them as Tailia, looking back, stumbled and fell.

Six horsemen rode into sight, armour gleaming in the sunlight. Druss saw raven-winged helms, lances and swords. The horses were lathered and, on seeing the three youths, the warriors shouted battle cries and spurred their mounts towards them.

Pilan and Yorath sprinted away towards the right. Three riders swung their horses to give chase, but the remaining three came on towards Druss.

The young man stood calmly, the axe held loosely across his naked chest. Directly in front of him was a felled tree. The first of the riders, a lancer, leaned forward in the saddle as his gelding jumped over the fallen beech. At that moment Druss moved, sprinting forward and swinging his axe in a murderous arc. As the horse landed the axe-blade hissed over its head, plunging into the chest of the lancer to splinter his breastplate and smash his ribs to shards. The blow hammered the man from the saddle. Druss tried to wrench the axe clear, but the blade was caught by the fractured armour. A sword slashed down at the youth's head and Druss dived and rolled. As a horseman moved in close he hurled himself from the ground, grabbing the stallion's right foreleg. With one awesome heave he toppled horse and rider. Hurdling the fallen tree, he ran to where the other two youths had left their hatchets. Scooping up the first he turned as a raider galloped towards him. Druss's arm came back, then snapped forward. The hatchet sliced through the air, the iron head crunching into the man's teeth. He swayed in the saddle. Druss ran forward to drag him from the horse. The raider, having dropped his lance, tried to draw a dagger. Druss slapped it from his hand, delivered a bone-breaking punch to the warrior's chin and then, snatching up the dagger, rammed it into the man's unprotected throat.

'Look out, Druss!' yelled Tailia. Druss spun, just as a sword flashed for his belly. Parrying the blade with his forearm, he thundered a right cross which took the attacker full on the jaw, spinning him from his feet. Druss leapt on the man, one huge hand grabbing his chin, the other his brow. With one savage twist Druss heard the swordsman's neck snap like a dry stick.

Moving swiftly to the first man he had killed, Druss tore the felling axe clear of the breastplate as Tailia ran from her hiding-place in the bushes. 'They are attacking the village,' she said, tears in her eyes.

Pilan came running into the clearing, a lancer behind him. 'Swerve!' bellowed Druss. But Pilan was too terrified to obey and he ran straight on – until the lance pierced his back, exiting in a bloody spray from his chest. The youth cried out, then slumped to the ground. Druss roared in anger and raced forward. The lancer desperately tried to wrench his weapon clear of the dying boy. Druss swung wildly with the axe, which glanced from the rider's shoulder and plunged into the horse's back. The animal whinnied in pain and reared before falling to the earth, its legs flailing. The rider scrambled clear, blood gushing from his shoulder and tried to run, but Druss's next blow almost decapitated him.

Hearing a scream, Druss began to run towards the sound and found Yorath struggling with one raider; the second was kneeling on the ground, blood streaming from a wound in his head. The body of Berys was beside him, a blood-smeared stone in her hand. The swordsman grappling with Yorath suddenly head-butted the youth, sending Yorath back several paces. The sword came up.

Druss shouted, trying to distract the warrior. But to no avail. The weapon lanced into Yorath's side. The swordsman dragged the blade clear and turned towards Druss.

'Now your time to die, farm boy!' he said.

'In your dreams!' snarled the woodsman. Swinging the axe over his head, Druss charged. The swordsman sidestepped to his right – but Druss had been waiting for the move, and with all the power of his mighty shoulders he wrenched the axe, changing its course. It clove through the man's collarbone, smashing the shoulder-blade and ripping into his lungs. Tearing the axe loose, Druss turned from the body to see the first wounded warrior struggling to rise; jumping forward, he struck him a murderous blow to the neck.

'Help me!' called Yorath.

'I'll send Tailia,' Druss told him, and began to run back through the trees.

Reaching the crest of the hill he gazed down on the village. He could see scattered bodies, but no sign of raiders. For a moment he thought the villagers had beaten them back . . . but there was no movement at all.

'Rowena!' he yelled. 'Rowena!'

Druss ran down the slope. He fell and rolled, losing his grip on the felling-axe, but scrambling to his feet he pounded on – down into the meadow, across the flat, through the half-finished gates. Bodies lay everywhere. Rowena's father, the former book-keeper Voren, had been stabbed through the throat, and blood was staining the earth beneath him. Breathing hard, Druss stopped, and stared around the settlement square.

Old women, young children and all the men were dead. As he stumbled on he saw the golden-haired child, Kiris, beloved of all the villagers, lying sprawled in death alongside her rag doll. The body of an infant lay against one building, a bloodstain on the wall above showing how it had been slain.

He found his father lying in the open with four dead raiders around him. Patica was beside him, a hammer in her hand, her plain brown woollen dress drenched in blood. Druss fell to his knees by his father's body. There were terrible wounds to the chest and belly, and his left arm was almost severed at the wrist. Bress groaned and opened his eyes.

'Druss ...'

'I am here, Father.'

'They took the young women.... Rowena ... was among them.'

'I'll find her.'

The dying man glanced to his right at the dead woman beside him. 'She was a brave lass; she tried to help me. I should have ... loved her better.' Bress sighed, then choked as blood flowed into his throat. He spat it clear. 'There is ... a weapon. In the house ... far wall, beneath the boards. It has a terrible history. But ... but you will need it.'

Druss stared down at the dying man and their eyes met. Bress lifted his right hand. Druss took it. 'I did my best, boy,' said his father.

'I know.' Bress was fading fast, and Druss was not a man of words. Instead he lifted his father into his arms and kissed his brow, hugging him close until the last breath of life rasped from the broken body.

Then he pushed himself to his feet and entered his father's home. It had been ransacked – cupboards hauled open, drawers pulled from the dressers, rugs ripped from the walls. But by the far wall the hidden compartment was undiscovered and Druss prised open the boards and hauled out the chest that lay in the dust below the floor. It was locked. Moving through into his father's workshop, he returned with a large hammer and a chisel which he used to pry off the hinges. Then he took hold of the lid and wrenched it clear, the brass lock twisting and tearing free.

Inside, wrapped in oilskin, was an axe. And such an axe! Druss unwrapped it reverently. The black metal haft was as long as a man's arm, the double heads shaped like the wings of a butterfly. He tested the edges with his thumb; the weapon was as sharp as his father's shaving-knife. Silver runes were inscribed on the haft, and though Druss could not read them he knew the words etched there. For this was the awful axe of Bardan, the weapon that had slain men, women, and even children during the reign of terror. The words were part of the dark folklore of the Drenai.

Snaga, the Sender, the blades of no return

24

He lifted the axe clear, surprised by its lightness and its perfect balance in his hand.

Beneath it in the chest was a black leather jerkin, the shoulders reinforced by strips of silver steel; two black leather gauntlets, also protected by shaped metal knuckle-guards; and a pair of black, knee-length boots. Beneath the clothes was a small pouch, and within it Druss found eighteen silver pieces.

Kicking off his soft leather shoes, Druss pulled on the boots and donned the jerkin. At the bottom of the chest was a helm of black metal, edged with silver; upon the brow was a small silver axe flanked by silver skulls. Druss settled the helm into place, then lifted the axe once more. Gazing down at his reflection in the shining blades, he saw a pair of cold, cold blue eyes, empty, devoid of feeling.

Snaga, forged in the Elder days, crafted by a master. The blade had never been sharpened, for it had never dulled despite the many battles and skirmishes that filled the life of Bardan. And even before that the blade had been in use. Bardan had acquired the battleaxe during the Second Vagrian War, looting it from an old barrow in which lay the bones of an ancient battle king, a monster of Legend, Caras the Axeman.

'It was an evil weapon,' Bress had once told his son. 'All the men who ever bore it were killers with no souls.'

'Why do you keep it then?' asked his thirteen-year-old son.

'It cannot kill where I keep it,' was all Bress had answered.

Druss stared at the blade. 'Now you can kill,' he whispered.

Then he heard the sound of a walking horse. Slowly he rose.

2

Shadak's horses were skittish, the smell of death unnerving the beasts. He had bought his own three-year-old from a farmer south of Corialis and the gelding had not been trained for war. The four mounts he had taken from the raiders were less nervous, but still their ears were back and their nostrils flaring. He spoke soothingly to them and rode on.

Shadak had been a soldier for most of his adult life. He had seen death – and he thanked the gods that it still had the power to stir his emotions. Sorrow and anger vied in his heart as he gazed upon the still corpses, the children and the old women.

None of the houses had been put to the torch – the smoke would be seen for miles, and could have brought a troop of lancers. He gently tugged on the reins. A golden-haired child lay against the wall of a building, a doll beside it. Slavers had no time for children, for they had no market in Mashrapur. Young Drenai women between the ages of fourteen and twenty-five were still popular in the eastern kingdoms of Ventria, Sherak, Dospilis and Naashan.

Shadak touched heels to the gelding. There was no point in remaining in this place; the trail led south.

A young warrior stepped from one of the buildings, startling his horse which reared and whinnied. Shadak calmed it and gazed upon the man. Although of average height he was powerfully built, his huge shoulders and mighty arms giving the impression of a giant. He wore a black leather jerkin and helm and carried a fearful axe. Shadak glanced swiftly around the corpse-strewn settlement. But there was no sign of a horse.

Lifting his leg, Shadak slid from the saddle. 'Your friends leave you behind, laddie?' he asked the axeman. The young man did not speak but stepped out into the open. Shadak looked into the man's pale eyes and felt the unaccustomed thrill of fear.

The face beneath the helm was flat and expressionless, but power emanated from the young warrior. Shadak moved warily to his right, hands resting on the hilts of his short swords. 'Proud of your handiwork, are you?' he asked, trying to force the man into conversation. 'Killed many babes today, did you?'

The young man's brow furrowed. 'This was my . . . my home,' he said, his voice deep. 'You are not one of the raiders?'

'I am hunting them,' said Shadak, surprised at the relief he felt. 'They attacked Corialis looking for slaves, but the young women escaped them. The villagers fought hard. Seventeen of them died, but the attack was beaten off. My name is Shadak. Who are you?'

'I am Druss. They took my wife. I'll find them.'

Shadak glanced at the sky. 'It's getting dark. Best to start in the morning, we could lose their trail in the night.'

'I'll not wait,' said the young man. 'I need one of your horses.'

Shadak smiled grimly. 'It is difficult to refuse when you ask so politely. But I think we should talk before you ride out.'

'Why?'

'Because there are many of them, laddie, and they do have a tendency to leave rearguards behind them, watching the road.' Shadak pointed to the horses. 'Four lay in wait for me.'

'I'll kill any I find.'

'I take it they took all the young women, since I see no corpses here?'

'Yes.'

Shadak hitched his horses to a rail and stepped past the young man into the home of Bress. 'You'll lose nothing by listening for a few minutes,' he said.

Inside the building he righted the chairs and stopped. On the table was an old glove, made of lace and edged with pearls. 'What's this?' he asked the cold-eyed young man.

'It belonged to my mother. My father used to take it out now and again, and sit by the fire holding it. What did you want to talk about?'

27

Shadak sat down at the table. 'The raiders are led by two men – Collan, a renegade Drenai officer, and Harib Ka, a Ventrian. They will be making for Mashrapur and the slave markets there. With all the captives they will not be able to move at speed and we will have little difficulty catching them. But if we follow now, we will come upon them in the open. Two against forty – these are not odds to inspire confidence. They will push on through most of tonight, crossing the plain and reaching the long valley trails to Mashrapur late tomorrow. Then they will relax.'

'They have my wife,' said the young man. 'I'll not let them keep her for a heartbeat longer than necessary.'

Shadak shook his head and sighed. 'Nor would I, laddie. But you know the country to the south. What chance would we have of rescuing her on the plains? They would see us coming from a mile away.'

For the first time the young man looked uncertain. Then he shrugged and sat, laying the great axe on the table-top, where it covered the tiny glove. 'You are a soldier?' he asked.

'I was. Now I am a hunter – a hunter of men. Trust me. Now, how many women did they take?'

The young man thought for a moment. 'Perhaps around thirty. They killed Berys in the woods. Tailia escaped. But I have not seen all the bodies. Maybe others were killed.'

'Then let us think of thirty. It won't be easy freeing them.'

A sound from outside made both men turn as a young woman entered the room. Shadak rose. The woman was fair-haired and pretty, and there was blood upon her blue woollen skirt and her shirt of white linen.

'Yorath died,' she told the young man. 'They're all dead, Druss.' Her eyes filled with tears and she stood in the doorway looking lost and forlorn. Druss did not move, but Shadak stepped swiftly towards her, taking her in his arms and stroking her back.

He led her into the room and sat her at the table. 'Is there any food here?' he asked Druss. The young man nodded and moved through to the back room, returning with a pitcher of water and some bread. Shadak filled a clay cup with water and told the girl to drink. 'Are you hurt?' he asked.

She shook her head. 'The blood is Yorath's,' she whispered. Shadak sat beside her and Tailia sagged against him; she was exhausted.

'You need to rest,' he told her gently, helping her to rise and leading her through the building to a small bedroom. Obediently she lay down, and he covered her with a thick blanket. 'Sleep, child. I will be here.'

'Don't leave me,' she pleaded.

He took her hand. 'You are safe . . . Tailia. Sleep.' She closed her eyes, but clung to his hand, and Shadak sat with her until the grip eased and her breathing deepened. At last he stood and returned to the outer room.

'You were planning to leave her behind?' he asked the young man.

'She is nothing to me,' he said coldly. 'Rowena is everything.'

'I see. Then think on this, my friend: suppose it was you who had died and it was Rowena who survived hiding in the woods. How would your spirit feel if you saw me ride in and leave her alone in this wilderness?'

'I did not die,' said Druss.

'No,' said Shadak, 'you didn't. We'll take the girl with us.'

'No!'

'Either that or you walk on alone, laddie. And I do mean *walk*.'

The young man looked up at the hunter, and his eyes gleamed. 'I have killed men today,' he said, 'and I will not be threatened by you, or anyone. Not ever again. If I choose to leave here on one of your stolen horses, I shall do so. You would be wise not to try to stop me.'

'I wouldn't *try*, boy, I'd do it.' The words were spoken softly, and with a quiet confidence. But deep inside Shadak was surprised, for it was a confidence he did not feel. He saw the young man's hand snake around the haft of the axe. 'I know you are angry, lad, and concerned for the safety of . . . Rowena. But you can do nothing alone – unless of course you are a tracker, and an expert horseman. You could ride off into the dark and lose them. Or you could stumble upon them, and try to kill forty warriors. Then there'll be no one to rescue her, or the others.'

29

Slowly the giant's fingers relaxed, the hand moving away from the axe haft, the gleam fading from his eyes. 'It hurts me to sit here while they carry her further away.'

'I understand that. But we will catch them. And they will not harm the women; they are valuable to them.'

'You have a plan?'

'I do. I know the country, and I can guess where they will be camped tomorrow. We will go in at night, deal with the sentries and free the captives.'

Druss nodded. 'What then? They'll be hunting us. How do we escape with thirty women?'

'Their leaders will be dead,' said Shadak softly. 'I'll see to that.'

'Others will take the lead. They will come after us.'

Shadak shrugged, then smiled. 'Then we kill as many as we can.'

'I like that part of the plan,' said the young man grimly.

The stars were bright and Shadak sat on the porch of the timber dwelling, watching Druss sitting beside the bodies of his parents.

'You're getting old,' Shadak told himself, his gaze fixed on Druss. 'You make me feel old,' he whispered. Not in twenty years had a man inspired such fear in Shadak. He remembered the moment well – he was a Sathuli tribesman named Jonacin, a man with eyes of ice and fire, a legend among his own people. The Lord's champion, he had killed seventeen men in single combat, among them the Vagrian champion, Vearl.

Shadak had known the Vagrian – a tall, lean man, lightning-fast and tactically sound. The Sathuli, it was said, had treated him like a novice, first slicing off his right ear before despatching him with a heart thrust.

Shadak smiled as he remembered hoping with all his heart that he would never have to fight the man. But such hopes are akin to magic, he knew now, and all men are ultimately faced with their darkest fears.

It had been a golden morning in the Delnoch mountains. The Drenai were negotiating treaties with a Sathuli Lord and Shadak was present merely as one of the envoy's guards. Jonacin had been mildly insulting at the dinner the night before, speaking sneeringly of Drenai sword skills. Shadak had been ordered to ignore the man. But on the following morning the white-robed Sathuli stepped in front of him as he walked along the path to the Long Hall.

'It is said you are a fighter,' said Jonacin, the sneer in his voice showing disbelief.

Shadak had remained cool under the other's baleful stare. 'Stand aside, if you please. I am expected at the meeting.'

'I shall stand aside – as soon as you have kissed my feet.'

Shadak had been twenty-two then, in his prime. He looked into Jonacin's eyes and knew there was no avoiding confrontation. Other Sathuli warriors had gathered close by and Shadak forced a smile. 'Kiss your feet? I don't think so. Kiss this instead!' His right fist lashed into the Sathuli's chin, spinning him to the ground. Then Shadak walked on and took his place at the table.

As he sat he glanced at the Sathuli Lord, a tall man with dark, cruel eyes. The man saw him, and Shadak thought he glimpsed a look of faint amusement, even triumph, in the Lord's face. A messenger whispered something in the Lord's ear and the chieftain stood. 'The hospitality of my house has been abused,' he told the envoy. 'One of your men struck my champion, Jonacin. The attack was unwarranted. Jonacin demands satisfaction.'

The envoy was speechless. Shadak stood. 'He shall have it, my Lord. But let us fight in the cemetery. At least then you will not have far to carry his body!'

Now the hoot of an owl brought Shadak back to the present, and he saw Druss striding towards him. The young man made as if to walk by, then stopped. 'I had no words,' he said. 'I could think of nothing to say.'

'Sit down for a moment and we will speak of them,' said Shadak. 'It is said that our praises follow the dead to their place of rest. Perhaps it is true.'

Druss sat alongside the swordsman. 'There is not much to tell. He was a carpenter, and a fashioner of brooches. She was a bought wife.'

'They raised you, helped you to be strong.'

'I needed no help in that.'

'You are wrong, Druss. If your father had been a weak or a vengeful man, he would have beaten you as a child, robbed you of your spirit. In my experience it takes a strong man to raise strong men. Was the axe his?'

'No. It belonged to my grandfather.'

'Bardan the Axeman,' said Shadak softly.

'How could you know?'

'It is an infamous weapon. Snaga. That was the name. Your father had a hard life, trying to live down such a beast as Bardan. What happened to your real mother?'

Druss shrugged. 'She died in an accident when I was a babe.'

'Ah yes, I remember the story,' said Shadak. 'Three men attacked your father; he killed two of them with his bare hands and near crippled the third. Your mother was struck down by a charging horse.'

'He killed two men?' Druss was astonished. 'Are you sure?'

'So the story goes.'

'I cannot believe it. He always backed away from any argument. He never stood up for himself at all. He was weak . . . spineless.'

'I don't think so.'

'You didn't know him.'

'I saw where his body lay, and I saw the dead men around it. And I know many stories concerning the son of Bardan. None of them speaks of his cowardice. After his own father was killed he tried to settle in many towns, under many names. Always he was discovered and forced to flee. But on at least three occasions he was followed and attacked. Just outside Drenan he was cornered by five soldiers. One of them shot an arrow into your father's shoulder. Bress was carrying an infant at the time and according to the soldiers he laid the babe behind a boulder, and then charged at them. He had no weapon, and they were all armed with swords. But he tore a limb from a tree and laid into them. Two went down swiftly, the others turned and fled. I know *that* story is true, Druss, because my brother was one of the soldiers. It was the year before he was killed in the Sathuli campaign. He said that Bardan's son was a black-bearded giant with the strength of six men.'

'I knew none of this,' said Druss. 'Why did he never speak of it?'

'Why should he? Perhaps he took no pleasure for being the son of a monster. Perhaps he did not relish speaking of killing men with his hands, or beating them unconscious with a tree branch.'

'I didn't know him at all,' whispered Druss. 'Not at all.'

'I expect he didn't know you either,' said Shadak with a sigh. 'It is the curse of parents and children.'

'You have sons?'

'One. He died a week ago at Corialis. He thought he was immortal.'

'What happened?'

'He went up against Collan; he was cut to pieces.' Shadak cleared his throat and stood. 'Time for some sleep. It'll be dawn soon, and I'm not as young as I was.'

'Sleep well,' said Druss.

'I will, laddie. I always do. Go back to your parents and find something to say.'

'Wait!' called Druss.

'Yes,' answered the swordsman, pausing in the doorway.

'You were correct in what you said. I wouldn't have wanted Rowena left in the mountains alone. I spoke in . . . anger.'

Shadak nodded. 'A man is only as strong as that which makes him angry. Remember that, laddie.'

Shadak could not sleep. He sat in the wide leather chair beside the hearth, his long legs stretched out before him, his head resting on a cushion, his body relaxed. But his mind was in turmoil – images, memories flashing into thoughts.

He saw again the Sathuli cemetery, Jonacin stripped to the waist, a broad-bladed tulwar in his hands and a small iron buckler strapped to his left forearm.

'Do you feel fear, Drenai?' asked Jonacin.

Shadak did not answer. Slowly he unstrapped his baldric, then lifted clear his heavy woollen shirt. The sun was warm on his back, the mountain air fresh in his lungs. *You are going to die today*, said the voice of his soul.

And then the duel began. Jonacin drew first blood, a narrow cut appearing on Shadak's chest. More than a thousand Sathuli onlookers, standing around the perimeter of the cemetery, cheered as the blood began to flow. Shadak leapt back.

'Not going to try for the ear?' he asked conversationally. Jonacin gave an angry growl, and launched a new attack. Shadak blocked a thrust, then thundered a punch to the Sathuli's face. It glanced from his cheekbone, but the man staggered. Shadak followed up with a disembowelling thrust and the Sathuli swayed to his right, the blade slashing the skin of his waist. Now it was Jonacin's turn to jump backwards. Blood gushed from the shallow wound in his side; he touched the cut with his fingers, staring down amazed.

'Yes,' said Shadak, 'you bleed too. Come to me. Bleed some more.'

Jonacin screamed and rushed forward but Shadak sidestepped and clove his sabre through the Sathuli's neck. As the dying man fell to the ground Shadak felt a tremendous sense of relief, and a surging realisation. He was alive!

But his career was ruined. The treaty talks came to nothing, and his commission was revoked upon his return to Drenan.

Then Shadak had found his true vocation: Shadak the Hunter. Shadak the Tracker. Outlaws, killers, renegades – he hunted them all, following like a wolf on the trail.

In all the years since the fight with Jonacin he had never again known such fear. Until today, when the young axeman had stepped into the sunlight.

He is young and untrained. I would have killed him, he told himself.

But then he pictured again the ice-blue eyes and the shining axe.

Druss sat under the stars. He was tired, but he could not sleep. A fox moved out into the open, edging towards a corpse. Druss threw a stone at it and the creature slunk away . . . but not far.

By tomorrow the crows would be feasting here, and the other carrion beasts would tear at the dead flesh. Only hours ago this had been a living community, full of people enjoying their own hopes and dreams. Druss stood and walked along the main street of the

34

settlement, past the home of the baker, whose body was stretched out in the doorway with his wife beside him. The smithy was open, the fires still glowing faintly. There were three bodies here. Tetrin the Smith had managed to kill two of the raiders, clubbing them down with his forge hammer. Tetrin himself lay beside the long anvil, his throat cut.

Druss swung away from the scene.

What was it for? Slaves and gold. The raiders cared nothing for the dreams of other men. 'I will make you pay,' said Druss. He glanced at the body of the smith. 'I will avenge you. And your sons. I will avenge you all,' he promised.

And he thought of Rowena and his throat went dry, his heartbeat increasing. Forcing back his fears, he gazed around at the settlement.

In the moonlight the village still seemed strangely alive, its buildings untouched. Druss wondered at this. Why did the raiders not put the settlement to the torch? In all the stories he had heard of such attacks, the plunderers usually fired the buildings. Then he remembered the troop of Drenai cavalry patrolling the wilderness. A column of smoke would alert them, were they close.

Druss knew then what he had to do. Moving to the body of Tetrin he hauled it across the street to the meeting hall, kicking open the door and dragging the corpse inside, laying it at the centre of the hall. Then he returned to the street and began to gather, one by one, all the dead of the community. He was tired when he began, and bone-weary by the finish. Forty-four bodies he placed in the long hall, making sure that husbands were beside wives and their children close. He did not know why he did this, but it seemed right.

Lastly he carried the body of Bress into the building, and laid it beside Patica. Then he knelt by the woman and, taking the dead hand in his own, he bowed his head. 'I thank you,' he said quietly, 'for your years of care, and for the love you gave my father. You deserved better than this, Patica.' With all the bodies accounted for, he began to fetch wood from the winter store, piling it against the walls and across the bodies. At last he carried a large barrel of lantern oil from the main storehouse and poured it over the wood, splashing it to the dry walls.

As dawn streaked the eastern sky, he struck a flame to the pyre and blew it into life. The morning breeze licked at the flames in the doorway, caught at the tinder beyond, then hungrily roared up the first wall.

Druss stepped back into the street. At first the blaze made little smoke, but as the fire grew into an inferno a black column of oily smoke billowed into the morning sky, hanging in the light wind, flattening and spreading like an earth-born storm cloud. 'You have been working hard,' said Shadak, moving silently alongside the young axeman.

Druss nodded. 'There was no time to bury them,' he said. 'Now maybe the smoke will be seen.'

'Perhaps,' agreed the hunter, 'but you should have rested. Tonight you will need your strength.' As Shadak moved away, Druss watched him; the man's movements were sure and smooth, confident and strong.

Druss admired that – as he admired the way that Shadak had comforted Tailia in the doorway. Like a father or a brother might. Druss had known that she needed such consolation, but had been unable to provide it. He had never possessed the easy touch of a Pilan or a Yorath, and had always been uncomfortable in the company of women or girls.

But not Rowena. He remembered the day when she and her father had come to the village, a spring day three seasons ago. They had arrived with several other families, and he had seen Rowena standing beside a wagon helping to unload furniture. She seemed so frail. Druss had approached the wagon.

'I'll help if you want,' offered the fifteen-year-old Druss, more gruffly than he had intended. She turned and smiled. Such a smile, radiant and friendly. Reaching up, he took hold of the chair her father was lowering and carried it into the half-built dwelling. He helped them unload and arrange the furniture, then made to leave. But Rowena brought him a goblet of water.

'It was kind of you to help us,' she said. 'You are very strong.'

He had mumbled some inanity, listened as she told him her name, and left without telling her his own. That evening she had seen him sitting by the southern stream and had sat beside him. So close that he had felt remarkably uncomfortable.

'The land is beautiful, isn't it?' she said.

It was. The mountains were huge, like snow-haired giants, the sky the colour of molten copper, the setting sun a dish of gold, the hills bedecked with flowers. But Druss had not seen the beauty until the moment she observed it. He felt a sense of peace, a calm that settled over his turbulent spirit in a blanket of warmth.

'I am Druss.'

'I know. I asked your mother where you were.'

'Why?'

'You are my first friend here.'

'How can we be friends? You do not know me.'

'Of course I do. You are Druss, the son of Bress.'

'That is not knowing. I ... I am not popular here,' he said, though he did not know why he should admit it so readily. 'I am disliked.'

'Why do they dislike you?' The question was innocently asked, and he turned to look at her. Her face was so close that he blushed. Twisting, he put space between them.

'My ways are rough, I suppose. I don't ... talk easily. And I ... sometimes ... become angry. I don't understand their jests and their humour. I like to be ... alone.'

'Would you like me to go?'

'No! I just ... I don't know what I am saying.' He shrugged, and blushed a deeper crimson.

'Shall we be friends then?' she asked him, holding out her hand.

'I have never had a friend,' he admitted.

'Then take my hand, and we will start now.' Reaching out, he felt the warmth of her fingers against his calloused palm. 'Friends?' she asked with a smile.

'Friends,' he agreed. She made as if to withdraw her hand, but he held it for a moment longer. 'Thank you,' he said softly, as he released his hold.

She laughed then. 'Why would you thank me?'

He shrugged. 'I don't know. It is just that . . . you have given me a gift that no one else ever offered. And I do not take it lightly. I will be your friend, Rowena. Until the stars burn out and die.'

'Be careful with such promises, Druss. You do not know where they might lead you.'

One of the roof timbers cracked and crashed into the blaze. Shadak called out to him. 'Better choose yourself a mount, axeman. It's time to go.'

Gathering his axe, Druss turned his gaze towards the south. Somewhere out there was Rowena.

'I'm on my way,' he whispered.

And she heard him.

3

The wagons rolled on through the first afternoon, and on into the night. At first the captured women were silent, stunned, disbelieving. Then grief replaced shock, and there were tears. These were harshly dealt with by the men riding alongside the wagons, who ordered silence and, when it was not forthcoming, dismounted and leapt aboard the wagons dealing blows and brutal slaps, and issuing threats of whip and lash.

Rowena, her hands tied before her, sat beside the equally bound Mari. Her friend had swollen eyes, both from weeping and from a blow that had caught her on the bridge of the nose. 'How are you feeling now?' Rowena whispered.

'All dead,' came the response. 'They're all dead.' Mari's eyes gazed unseeing across the wagon, where other young women were sitting.

'We are alive,' continued Rowena, her voice low and gentle. 'Do not give up hope, Mari. Druss is alive also. And there is a man with him – a great hunter. They are following us.'

'All dead,' said Mari. 'They're all dead.'

'Oh, Mari!' Rowena reached out with her bound hands but Mari screamed and pulled away.

'Don't touch me!' She swung round to face Rowena, her eyes fierce and gleaming. 'This was a punishment. For you. You are a witch! It is all your fault!'

'No, I did nothing!'

'She's a witch,' shouted Mari. The other women stared. 'She has powers of Second Sight. She knew the raid was coming, but she didn't warn us.'

'Why did you not tell us?' shouted another woman. Rowena swung and saw the daughter of Jarin the Baker. 'My father is dead. My brothers are dead. Why did you not warn us?'

'I didn't know. Not until the last moment!'

'Witch!' screamed Mari. 'Stinking witch!' She lashed out with her tied hands, catching Rowena on the side of the head. Rowena fell to her left, into another woman. Fists struck as all around her in the wagon women surged upright, lashing out with hands and feet. Riders galloped alongside the wagon and Rowena felt herself lifted clear and flung to the ground. She hit hard, the breath knocked out of her.

'What is going on here?' she heard someone yell.

'Witch! Witch! Witch!' chanted the women.

Rowena was hauled to her feet, then a filthy hand caught her by the hair. She opened her eyes and looked up into a gaunt, scarred face. 'Witch, are you?' grunted the man. 'We'll see about that!' He drew a knife and held it before her, the point resting against the woollen shirt she wore. 'Witches have three nipples, so it's said,' he told her.

'Leave her be!' came another voice, and a horseman rode close alongside. The man sheathed his knife.

'I wasn't going to cut her, Harib. Witch or no, she'll still bring a pretty price.'

'More if she is a witch,' said the horseman. 'Let her ride behind you.'

Rowena gazed up at the rider. His face was swarthy, his eyes dark, his mouth part hidden by the bronze ear-flaps of his battle helm. Touching spurs to his mount the rider galloped on. The man holding her stepped into the saddle, pulling her up behind him. He smelt of stale sweat and old dirt, but Rowena scarcely noticed it. Glancing at the wagon where her former friends now sat silently, she felt afresh the terrible sense of loss.

Yesterday the world was full of hope. Their home was almost complete, her husband coming to terms with his restless spirit, her father relaxed and free from care, Mari preparing for a night of passion with Pilan.

40

In the space of a few hours it had all changed. Reaching up, she touched the brooch at her breast ...

And saw the Axeman her husband was becoming. *Deathwalker!* Tears flowed then, silently coursing down her cheeks.

Shadak rode ahead, following the trail, while Druss and Tailia travelled side by side, the girl on a bay mare, the young man on a chestnut gelding. Tailia said little for the first hour, which suited Druss, but as they topped a rise before a long valley she leaned in close and touched his arm.

'What are you planning?' she asked. 'Why are we following them?'

'What do you mean?' responded Druss, nonplussed.

'Well, you obviously can't fight them all; you'll be killed. Why don't we just ride for the garrison at Padia? Send troops?' He swung to look at her. Her blue eyes were red-rimmed from crying.

'That's a four-day walk. I don't know how long it would take to ride – two days at the least, I would think. Then, if the troop was there – and they may not be – it would take them at least three days to find the raiders. By then they will be in Vagrian territory, and close to the borders of Mashrapur. Drenai soldiers have no jurisdiction there.'

'But you can't do anything. There is no point to this pursuit.'

Druss took a deep breath. 'They have Rowena,' he said. 'And Shadak has a plan.'

'Ah, a plan,' she said derisively, her full-lipped mouth twisting in a sneer. 'Two men with a plan. Then I suppose I am safe?'

'You are alive – and free,' Druss told her. 'If you want to ride to Padia, then do so.'

Her expression softened and she reached out, laying her hand on Druss's forearm. 'I know you are brave, Druss; I saw you kill those raiders and you were magnificent. I don't want to see you die in some meaningless battle. Rowena wouldn't want it either. There are many of them, and they're all killers.'

'So am I,' he said. 'And there are fewer than there were.'

'Well, what happens to me when they cut you down?' she snapped. 'What chance will I have?'

He looked at her for a moment, his eyes cold. 'None,' he told her.

Tailia's eyes widened. 'You never liked me, did you?' she whispered. 'You never liked any of us.'

'I have no time for this nonsense,' he said, touching heels to the gelding and moving ahead. He did not look back, and was not surprised when he heard the sound of her horse galloping off towards the north.

A few minutes later Shadak rode up from the south. 'Where is she?' asked the hunter, letting go of the reins of the two horses he was leading and allowing them to wander close by, cropping the long grass.

'Riding for Padia,' answered Druss. The hunter said nothing for a moment, but he gazed towards the north where Tailia could be seen as a tiny figure in the distance. 'You'll not talk her out of it,' Druss said.

'Did you send her away?'

'No. She thinks we are both dead men, and she doesn't want to risk being taken by the slavers.'

'That's a hard point to argue with,' agreed Shadak. Then he shrugged. 'Ah well, she chose her own road. Let us hope it was a wise one.'

'What of the raiders?' asked Druss, all thoughts of Tailia gone from his mind.

'They rode through the night, and are heading due south. I think they will make camp by the Tigren, some thirty miles from here. There is a narrow valley opening on to a bowl-shaped canyon. It's been used by slavers for years – and horse thieves, cattle stealers and renegades. It is easily defensible.'

'How long until we reach them?'

'Some time after midnight. We'll move on for two more hours, then we'll rest and eat before switching horses.'

'I don't need a rest.'

'The horses do,' said Shadak, 'and so do I. Be patient. It will be a long night, and fraught with peril. And I have to tell you that our chances are not good. Tailia was right to be concerned for her safety; we will need more luck than any two men have a right to ask for.'

'Why are you doing this?' asked Druss. 'The women are nothing to you.' Shadak did not reply and they rode in silence until the sun was almost at noon. The hunter spotted a small grove of trees to the east and turned his horse; the two men dismounted in the shade of several spreading elms beside a rock pool.

'How many did you kill back there?' he asked Druss as they sat in the shade.

'Six,' answered the axeman, taking a strip of dried beef from the pouch at his side and tearing off a chunk.

'You ever kill men before?'

'No.'

'Six is . . . impressive. What did you use?'

Druss chewed for a moment, then swallowed. 'Felling-axe and a hatchet. Oh . . . and one of their daggers,' he said at last. 'And my hands.'

'And you have had no training in combat?'

'No.'

Shadak shook his head. 'Talk me through the fights – everything you can remember.' Druss did so, Shadak listened in silence, and when the axeman had finished his tale the hunter smiled. 'You are a rare young man. You positioned yourself well, in front of the fallen tree. That was a good move – the first of many, it seems. But the most impressive is the last. How did you know the swordsman would jump to your left?'

'He saw I had an axe and that I was right-handed. In normal circumstances the axe would have been raised over my left shoulder and pulled down towards the right. Therefore he moved to his right – my left.'

'That is cool thinking for a man in combat. I think there is a great deal of your grandfather in you.'

'Don't say that!' growled Druss. 'He was insane.'

'He was also a brilliant fighting man. Yes, he was evil. But that does not lessen his courage and his skills.'

'I am my own man,' said Druss. 'What I have is mine.'

'I do not doubt it. But you have great strength, good timing and a warrior's mind. These are gifts that pass from father to son, and

43

on through the line. But know this, laddie, there are responsibilities that you must accept.'

'Like what?'

'Burdens that separate the hero from the rogue.'

'I don't know what you mean.'

'It comes back to the question you asked me, about the women. The true warrior lives by a code. He has to. For each man there are different perspectives, but at the core they are the same: *Never violate a woman, nor harm a child. Do not lie, cheat or steal. These things are for lesser men. Protect the weak against the evil strong. And never allow thoughts of gain to lead you into the pursuit of evil.*'

'This is your code?' asked Druss.

'It is. And there is more, but I shall not bore you with it.'

'I am not bored. Why do you need such a code to live by?'

Shadak laughed. 'You will understand, Druss, as the years go by.'

'I want to understand now,' said the younger man.

'Of course you do. That is the curse of the young, they want it all now. No. Rest a while. Even your prodigious strength will fail after a time. Sleep a little. And wake refreshed. It will be a long – and bloody – night.'

The moon was high, and a quarter full in a cloudless sky. Silver light bathed the mountains, rippling on the river below, making it seem of molten metal. Three campfires burned and Druss could just make out the movement of men in the flickering light. The women were huddled between two wagons; there was no fire near them, but guards patrolled close by. To the north of the wagons, around thirty paces from the women, was a large tent. It gleamed yellow-gold, like a great lantern, shimmering shadows being cast on the inside walls; there was obviously a brazier within, and several lamps.

Shadak moved silently alongside the axeman, beckoning him back. Druss edged from the slope, returning to the glade where the horses were tethered.

'How many did you count?' asked Shadak, keeping his voice low.

'Thirty-four, not including those inside the tent.'

'There are two men there, Harib Ka and Collan. But I make it thirty-six outside. They have placed two men by the river-bank to prevent any of the women trying to swim to safety.'

'When do we go in?' asked Druss.

'You are very anxious to fight, laddie. But I need you to have a cool head down there. No baresark warfare.'

'Do not concern yourself about me, hunter. I merely want my wife back.'

Shadak nodded. 'I understand that, but now I want you to consider something. What if she has been raped?'

Druss's eyes gleamed, his fingers tightening on the axe haft. 'Why do you ask this now?'

'It is certain that some of the women will have been violated. It is the way of men such as these to take their pleasures where they want them. How cool do you feel now?'

Druss swallowed back his rising anger. 'Cool enough. I am not a baresark, Shadak. I know this. And I will follow your plan to the last detail, live or die, win or lose.'

'Good. We will move two hours before dawn. Most of them will be deeply asleep by then. Do you believe in the gods?'

'I never saw one – so no.'

Shadak grinned. 'Neither do I. It puts praying for divine help out of the question, I suppose.'

Druss was silent for a moment. 'Tell me now,' he said at last, 'why you need a code to live by.'

Shadak's face was ghostly in the moonlight, the expression suddenly stern and forbidding. Then he relaxed and turned to gaze down at the camp of the raiders. 'Those men down there have only one code. It is simple: *Do what you will is the whole of the law*. Do you understand?'

'No,' admitted Druss.

'It means that whatever their strength can obtain is rightfully theirs. If another man holds something they desire they kill the other man. This is right in their minds; this is the law the world offers – the law of the wolf. But you and I are no different from them, Druss. We have the same desires, the same perceived needs. If we are attracted to a woman, why should we not have her, regardless

45

of her opinions? If another man has wealth, why should we not take it, if we are stronger, deadlier than he? It is an easy trap to fall into. Collan was once an officer in the Drenai lancers. He comes from a good family; he took the Oath as we all did, and when he said the words he probably believed them. But in Drenan he met a woman he wanted desperately, and she wanted him. But she was married. Collan murdered her husband. That was his first step on the road to Perdition; after that the other steps were easy. Short of money, he became a mercenary – fighting for gold in any cause, right or wrong, good or evil. He began to see only what was good for Collan. Villages were there merely for him to raid. Harib Ka is a Ventrian nobleman, distantly related to the Royal House. His story is similar. Both lacked the Iron Code. I am not a good man, Druss, but the Code holds me to the Way of the Warrior.'

'I can understand,' said Druss, 'that a man will seek to protect what is his, and not steal or kill for gain. But it does not explain why you risk your life tonight for women you do not know.'

'Never back away from an enemy, Druss. Either fight or surrender. It is not enough to say I will not *be* evil. It must be fought wherever it is found. I am hunting Collan, not just for killing my son but for being what he is. But if necessary I will put off that hunt tonight in order for the girls to be freed; they are more important.'

'Perhaps,' Druss said, unconvinced. 'For me, all I want is Rowena and a home in the mountains. I care nothing about fighting evil.'

'I hope you learn to care,' said Shadak.

Harib Ka could not sleep. The ground was hard beneath the tent floor and despite the heat from the brazier he felt cold through to his bones. The girl's face haunted him. He sat up and reached for the wine-jug. You are drinking too much, he told himself. Stretching, he poured a full goblet of red wine, draining it in two swallows. Then he pushed back his blankets and rose. His head ached. He sat down on a canvas stool and refilled his goblet.

What have you become? whispered a voice in his mind. He rubbed at his eyes, his thoughts returning to the academy and his days with Bodasen and the young Prince.

'We will change the world,' said the Prince. 'We will feed the poor and ensure employment for all. And we will drive the raiders from Ventria, and establish a kingdom of peace and prosperity.'

Harib Ka gave a dry laugh and sipped his wine. Heady days, a time of youth and optimism with its talk of knights and brave deeds, great victories and the triumph of the Light over the Dark.

'There is no Light and Dark,' he said aloud. 'There is only Power.'

He thought then of the first girl – what was her name, Mari? Yes. Compliant, obedient to his desires, warm, soft. She had cried out with pleasure at his touch. No. She had pretended to enjoy his coarse lovemaking. 'I'll do anything for you – but don't hurt me.'

Don't hurt me.

The chill winds of autumn rippled the tent walls. Within two hours of enjoying Mari he had felt in need of a second woman, and had chosen the hazel-eyed witch. That was a mistake. She had entered his tent, rubbing at her chafed wrists, her eyes large and sorrowful.

'You intend to rape me?' she had asked him quietly.

He had smiled. 'Not necessarily. That is your choice. What is your name?'

'Rowena,' she told him. 'And how can it be my choice?'

'You can give yourself to me, or you can fight me. Either way the result will be the same. So why not enjoy the lovemaking?'

'Why do you speak of love?'

'What?'

'There is no love in this. You have murdered those I have loved. And now you seek to pleasure yourself at the expense of what dignity I have left.'

He strode towards her, gripping her upper arms. 'You are not here to debate with me, whore! You are here to do as you are told.'

'Why do you call me a whore? Does it make your actions more simple for you? Oh, Harib Ka, how would Rajica view your actions?'

He reeled back as if struck. 'What do you know of Rajica?'

'Only that you loved her – and that she died in your arms.'

'You are a witch!'

47

'And you are a lost man, Harib Ka. Everything you once held dear has been sold – your pride, your honour, your love of life.'

'I will not be judged by you,' he said, but he made no move to silence her.

'I do not judge you,' she told him. 'I pity you. And I tell you this: unless you release me and the other women, you will die.'

'You are a seer also?' he said, trying to mock. 'Are the Drenai cavalry close, witch? Is there an army waiting to fall upon me and my men? No. Do not seek to threaten me, girl. Whatever else I may have lost I am still a warrior and, with the possible exception of Collan, the finest swordsman you will ever see. I do not fear death. No. Sometimes I long for it.' He felt his passion ebbing away. 'So tell me, witch, what is this peril I face?'

'His name is Druss. He is my husband.'

'We killed all the men in the village.'

'No. He was in the woods, felling timbers for the palisade.'

'I sent six men there.'

'But they have not returned,' Rowena pointed out.

'You are saying he killed them all?'

'He did,' she told him softly, 'and now he is coming for you.'

'You make him sound like a warrior of legend,' said Harib uneasily. 'I could send men back to kill him.'

'I hope you do not.'

'You fear for his life?'

'No, I would mourn for theirs.' She sighed.

'Tell me of him. Is he a swordsman? A soldier?'

'No, he is the son of a carpenter. But once I dreamt I saw him on a mountainside. He was black-bearded and his axe was smeared with blood. And before him were hundreds of souls. They stood mourning their lives. More flowed from his axe, and they wailed. Men of many nations, billowing like smoke until broken by the breeze. All slain by Druss. Mighty Druss. The Captain of the Axe. The *Deathwalker*.'

'And this is your husband?'

'No, not yet. This is the man he will become if you do not free me. This is the man you created when you slew his father and took me prisoner. You will not stop him, Harib Ka.'

He sent her away then, and ordered the guards to let her remain unmolested.

Collan had come to him and had laughed at his misery. 'By Missael, Harib, she is just a village wench and now a slave. She is property. *Our* property. And her gift makes her worth ten times the price we will receive for any of the others. She is attractive and young – I'd say around a thousand gold pieces' worth. There is that Ventrian merchant, Kabuchek; he's always looking for seers and fortune-tellers. I'll wager he'd pay a thousand.'

Harib sighed. 'Aye, you are right, my friend. Take her. We'll need coin upon our arrival. But don't touch her, Collan,' he warned the handsome swordsman. 'She really does have the Gift, and she will see into your soul.'

'There is nothing to see,' answered Collan, with a harsh, forced smile.

Druss edged his way along the river-bank, keeping close to the undergrowth and pausing to listen. There were no sounds save the rustling of autumn leaves in the branches above, no movement apart from the occasional swooping flight of bat or owl. His mouth was dry, but he felt no fear.

Across the narrow river he saw a white jutting boulder, cracked down the centre. According to Shadak, the first of the sentries was positioned almost opposite. Moving carefully Druss crept back into the woods, then angled towards the river-bank, timing his approach by the wind which stirred the leaves above him, the rustling in the trees masking the sound of his movements.

The sentry was sitting on a rock no more than ten feet to Druss's right, and he had stretched out his right leg. Taking Snaga in his left hand, Druss wiped his sweating palm on his trews, his eyes scanning the undergrowth for the second sentry. He could see no one.

Druss waited, his back against a broad tree. From a little distance to the left came a harsh, gurgling sound. The sentry heard it too, and rose.

'Bushin! What are you doing there, you fool?'

Druss stepped out behind the man. 'He is dying,' he said.

49

The man spun, hand snaking down for the sword at his hip. Snaga flashed up and across, the silver blade entering the neck just below the ear and shearing through sinew and bone. The head toppled to the right, the body to the left.

Shadak stepped from the undergrowth. 'Well done,' he whispered. 'Now, when I send the women down to you, get them to wade across by the boulder, then head north up into the canyon to the cave.'

'We've been over this many times,' Druss pointed out.

Ignoring the comment, Shadak laid a hand on the younger man's shoulder. 'Now, whatever happens, do not come back into the camp. Stay with the women. There is only one path up to the cave, but several leading from it to the north. Get the women moving on the north-west route. You hold the path.'

Shadak faded back into the undergrowth and Druss settled down to wait.

Shadak moved carefully to the edge of the camp. Most of the women were asleep, and a guard was sitting by them; his head was resting against a wagon wheel, and Shadak guessed he was dozing. Unbuckling his sword-belt, he moved forward on his belly, drawing himself on his elbows until he reached the wagon. Slipping his hunting-knife from the sheath at his hip, Shadak came up behind the man – his left hand reached through the wheel, fingers closing on the sentry's throat. The knife rammed home into the man's back; his leg jerked once, then he was still.

Moving back from beneath the wagon, Shadak came to the first girl. She was sleeping close to several other women, huddled together for warmth. He clamped a hand over her mouth and shook her. She awoke in a panic and started to struggle.

'I am here to rescue you!' hissed Shadak. 'One of your villagers is by the river-bank and he will lead you to safety. You understand? When I release you, slowly wake the others. Head south to the river. Druss, the son of Bress, is waiting there. Nod if you understand me.'

He felt her head move against his hand. 'Good. Make sure none of the others make a noise. You must move slowly. Which one is Rowena?'

'She is not with us,' whispered the girl. 'They took her away.'

'Where?'

'One of the leaders, a man with a scarred cheek, rode out with her just after dusk.'

Shadak swore softly. There was no time for a second plan. 'What is your name?'

'Mari.'

'Well, Mari, get the others moving – and tell Druss to follow the original plan.'

Shadak moved away from the girl, gathered his swords and belted them to his waist. Then he stepped out into the open and strolled casually towards the tent. Only a few men were awake, and they paid little heed to the figure moving through the shadows so confidently.

Lifting the tent-flap he swiftly entered, drawing his right-hand sword as he did so. Harib Ka was sitting on a canvas chair with a goblet of wine in his left hand, a sabre in his right. 'Welcome to my hearth, Wolf-man,' he said with a smile. He drained the goblet and stood. Wine had run into his dark, forked beard, making it shine in the lantern light as if oiled. 'May I offer you a drink?'

'Why not?' answered Shadak, aware that if they began to fight too soon the noise of clashing steel would wake the other raiders and they would see the women fleeing.

'You are far from home,' remarked Harib Ka.

'These days I have no home,' Shadak told him.

Harib Ka filled a second goblet and passed it to the hunter. 'You are here to kill me?'

'I came for Collan. I understand he has gone?'

'Why Collan?' asked Harib Ka, his dark eyes glittering in the golden light.

'He killed my son in Corialis.'

'Ah, the blond boy. Fine swordsman, but too reckless.'

'A vice of the young.' Shadak sipped his wine, his anger controlled like an armourer's fire, hot but contained.

'That vice killed him,' observed Shadak. 'Collan is very skilled. Where did you leave the young villager, the one with the axe?'

'You are well informed.'

51

'Only a few hours ago his wife stood where you now stand; she told me he was coming. She's a witch – did you know that?'

'No. Where is she?'

'On her way to Mashrapur with Collan. When do you want the fight to begin?'

'As soon as . . .' began Shadak, but even as he was speaking Harib attacked, his sabre slashing for Shadak's throat. The hunter ducked, leaned to the left and kicked out at Harib's knee. The Ventrian crashed to the floor and Shadak's sword touched the skin of Harib's throat. 'Never fight drunk,' he said softly.

'I'll remember that. What now?'

'Now tell me where Collan stays in Mashrapur.'

'The White Bear Inn. It's in the western quarter.'

'I know that. Now, what is your life worth, Harib Ka?'

'To the Drenai authorities? Around a thousand gold pieces. To me? I have nothing to offer – until I sell my slaves.'

'You have no slaves.'

'I can find them again. Thirty women on foot in the mountains will pose me no problem.'

'Hunting is not easy with a slit throat,' pointed out Shadak, adding an extra ounce of pressure to the sword-blade, which pricked the skin of Harib's neck.

'True,' agreed the Ventrian, glancing up. 'What do you suggest?' Just as Shadak was about to answer he caught the gleam of triumph in Harib's eyes and he swung round. But too late.

Something cold, hard and metallic crashed against his skull.

And the world spun into darkness.

Pain brought Shadak back to consciousness, harsh slaps to his face that jarred his teeth. His eyes opened. His arms were being held by two men who had hauled him to his knees, and Harib Ka was squatting before him.

'Did you think me so stupid that I would allow an assassin to enter my tent unobserved? I knew someone was following us. And when the four men I left in the pass did not return I guessed it had to be you. Now I have questions for you, Shadak. Firstly, where is the young farmer with the axe; and secondly, where are my women?'

Shadak said nothing. One of the men holding him crashed a fist against the hunter's ear; lights blazed before Shadak's eyes and he sagged to his right. He watched Harib Ka rise and move to the brazier where the coals had burned low. 'Get him outside to a fire,' ordered the leader. Shadak was hauled to his feet and half carried out into the camp. Most of the men were still asleep. His captors pushed him to his knees beside a campfire and Harib Ka drew his dagger, pushing the blade into the flames. 'You will tell me what I wish to know,' he said, 'or I will burn out your eyes and then set you free in the mountains.'

Shadak tasted blood on his tongue, and fear in his belly. But still he said nothing.

An unearthly scream tore through the silence of the night, followed by the thunder of hooves. Harib swung to see forty terrified horses galloping towards the camp. One of the men holding the hunter turned also, his grip slackening. Shadak surged upright, head-butting the raider who staggered back. The second man, seeing the stampeding horses closing fast, released his hold and ran for the safety of the wagons. Harib Ka drew his sabre and leapt at Shadak, but the first of the horses cannoned into him, spinning him from his feet. Shadak spun on his heel to face the terrified beasts and began to wave his arms. The maddened horses swerved around him and galloped on through the camp. Some men, still wrapped in their blankets, were trampled underfoot. Others tried to halt the charging beasts. Shadak ran back to Harib's tent and found his swords. Then he stepped out into the night. All was chaos.

The fires had been scattered by pounding hooves and several corpses were lying on the open ground. Some twenty of the horses had been halted and calmed; the others were running on through the woods, pursued by many of the warriors.

A second scream sounded and despite his years of experience in warfare and battle, Shadak was astonished by what followed.

Alone, the young woodsman had attacked the camp. The awesome axe shone silver in the moonlight, slashing and cleaving into the surprised warriors. Several took up swords and ran at him; they died in moments.

But he could not survive. Shadak saw the raiders group together, a dozen men spread out in a semicircle around the black-garbed giant, Harib Ka among them. The hunter, his two short swords drawn, ran towards them yelling the battle-cry of the Lancers. 'Ayiaa! Ayiaa!' At that moment arrows flashed from the woods. One took a raider in the throat, a second glanced from a helm to plunge home into an unprotected shoulder. Combined with the sudden battle-cry, the attack made the raiders pause, many of them backing away and scanning the tree line. At that moment Druss charged the enemy centre, cutting to left and right. The raiders fell back before him, several tumbling to the ground, tripping over their fellows. The mighty blood-smeared axe clove into them, rising and falling with a merciless rhythm.

Just as Shadak reached them, the raiders broke and fled. More arrows sailed after them.

Harib Ka ran for one of the horses, grabbing its mane and vaulting to its bare back. The animal reared, but he held on. Shadak hurled his right-hand sword, which lanced into Harib's shoulder. The Ventrian sagged, then fell to the ground as the horse galloped away.

'Druss!' shouted Shadak. 'Druss!' The axeman was pursuing the fleeing raiders, but he stopped at the edge of the trees and swung back. Harib Ka was on his knees, trying to pull the brass-hilted sword from his body.

The axeman stalked back to where Shadak was waiting. He was blood-drenched and his eyes glittered. 'Where is she?' he asked the hunter.

'Collan took her to Mashrapur; they left at dusk.'

Two women emerged from the trees, carrying bows and quivers of arrows. 'Who are they?' asked Shadak.

'The Tanner's daughters. They did a lot of hunting for the village. I gave them the bows the sentries had with them.'

The tallest of the women approached Druss. 'They are fleeing into the night. I don't think they'll come back now. You want us to follow them?'

'No, bring the others down and gather the horses.' The axeman turned towards the kneeling figure of Harib Ka. 'Who is this?' Druss asked Shadak.

'One of the leaders.'

Without a word Druss clove the axe through Harib's neck. 'Not any more,' he observed.

'Indeed not,' agreed Shadak, stepping to the still-quivering corpse and pulling free his sword. He gazed around the clearing and counted the bodies. 'Nineteen. By all the gods, Druss, I can't believe you did that!'

'Some were trampled by the horses I stampeded, others were killed by the girls.' Druss turned and stared out over the campsite. Somewhere to his left a man groaned and the tallest of the girls ran to him, plunging a dagger into his throat. Druss turned back to Shadak. 'Will you see the women get safely to Padia?'

'You're going on to Mashrapur?'

'I'm going to find her.'

Shadak laid his hand on the young man's shoulder. 'I hope that you do, Druss. Seek out the White Bear Inn – that's where Collan will stay. But be warned, my friend. In Mashrapur, Rowena is his property. That is their law.'

'This is mine,' answered Druss, raising the double-headed axe.

Shadak took the young man's arm and led him back to Harib's tent where he poured himself a goblet of wine and drained it. One of Harib's linen tunics was draped over a small chest and Shadak threw it to Druss. 'Wipe off the blood. You look like a demon.'

Druss smiled grimly and wiped his face and arms, then cleaned the double blades.

'What do you know of Mashrapur?' asked Shadak.

The axeman shrugged. 'It is an independent state, ruled by an exiled Ventrian Prince. That's all.'

'It is a haven for thieves and slavers,' said Shadak. 'The laws are simple: those with gold to offer bribes are considered fine citizens. It matters not where the gold comes from. Collan is respected there; he owns property and dines with the Emir.'

'So?'

'So if you march in and kill him, you will be taken and executed. It is that simple.'

'What do you suggest?'

'There is a small town around twenty miles from here, due south. There is a man there, a friend of mine. Go to him, tell him I sent you. He is young and talented. You won't like him, Druss; he is a fop and a pleasure-seeker. He has no morals. But it will make him invaluable in Mashrapur.'

'Who is this man?'

'His name is Sieben. He's a poet, a saga-teller, and he performs at palaces; he's very good as a matter of fact. He could have been rich. But he spends most of his time trying to bed every pretty young woman who comes into his line of vision. He never concerns himself whether they are married or single – that has brought him many enemies.'

'Already I don't like the sound of him.'

Shadak chuckled. 'He has good qualities. He is a loyal friend, and he is ridiculously fearless. A good man with a knife. And he knows Mashrapur. Trust him.'

'Why should he help me?'

'He owes me a favour.' Shadak poured a second goblet of wine and passed it to the young man.

Druss sipped it, then drained the goblet. 'This is good. What is it?'

'Lentrian Red. Around five years old, I'd say. Not the best, but good enough on a night like this.'

'I can see that a man could get a taste for it,' Druss agreed.

4

Sieben was enjoying himself. A small crowd had gathered around the barrel, and three men had already lost heavily. The green crystal was small and fitted easily under one of the three walnut shells. 'I'll move a little more slowly,' the young poet told the tall, bearded warrior who had just lost four silver pieces. His slender hands slid the shells around the smooth barrel top, halting them in a line across the centre. 'Which one? And take your time, my friend, for that emerald is worth twenty golden raq.'

The man sniffed loudly and scratched at his beard with a dirty finger. 'That one,' he said at last, pointing to the centre shell. Sieben flipped the shell. There was nothing beneath it. Moving his hand to the right he covered a second shell, expertly palmed the stone under it and showed it to the audience.

'So close,' he said with a bright smile. The warrior swore, then turned and thrust his way through the crowd. A short swarthy man was next; he had body odour that could have felled an ox. Sieben was tempted to let him win. The fake emerald was only worth a tenth of what he had already cheated from the crowd. But he was enjoying himself too much. The swarthy man lost three silver pieces.

The crowd parted and a young warrior eased his way to the front as Sieben glanced up. The newcomer was dressed in black, with shoulder guards of shining silver steel. He wore a helm on which was blazoned a motif of two skulls on either side of a silver axe. And he was carrying a double-headed axe. 'Try your luck?' asked Sieben, gazing up into the eyes of winter blue.

'Why not?' answered the warrior, his voice deep and cold. He placed a silver piece on the barrel head. The poet's hands moved with bewildering speed, gliding the shells in elaborate figure eights. At last he stopped.

'I hope you have a keen eye, my friend,' said Sieben.

'Keen enough,' said the axeman, and leaning forward he placed a huge finger on the central shell. 'It is here,' he said.

'Let us see,' said the poet, reaching out, but the axeman pushed his hand away.

'Indeed we shall,' he said. Slowly he flipped the shells to the left and right of the centre. Both were empty. 'I must be right,' he said, his pale eyes locked to Sieben's face. 'You may show us.' Lifting his finger, he gestured to the poet.

Sieben forced a smile and palmed the crystal under the shell as he flipped it. 'Well done, my friend. You are indeed hawk-eyed.' The crowd applauded and drifted away.

'Thank you for not exposing me,' said Sieben, rising and gathering his silver.

'Fools and money are like ice and heat,' quoted the young man. 'They cannot live together. You are Sieben?'

'I might be,' answered the other cautiously. 'Who is asking?'

'Shadak sent me.'

'For what purpose?'

'A favour you owe him.'

'That is between the two of us. What has it to do with you?'

The warrior's face darkened. 'Nothing at all,' he said, then turned away and strode towards the tavern on the other side of the street. As Sieben watched him go, a young woman approached from the shadows.

'Did you earn enough to buy me a fine necklace?' she asked. He swung and smiled. The woman was tall and shapely, raven-haired and full-lipped; her eyes were tawny brown, her smile an enchantment. She stepped into his embrace and winced. 'Why do you have to wear so many knives?' she asked, moving back from him and tapping the brown leather baldric from which hung four diamond-shaped throwing-blades.

'Affectation, my love. I'll not wear them tonight. And as for your necklace – I'll have it with me.' Taking her hand he kissed it. 'However, at the moment, duty calls.'

'Duty, my poet? What would you know of duty?'

He chuckled. 'Very little – but I always pay my debts; it is my last fingerhold on the cliff of respectability. I will see you later.' He bowed, then walked across the street.

The tavern was an old, three-storeyed building with a high gallery on the second floor overlooking a long room with open fires at both ends. There was a score of bench tables and seats and a sixty-foot brass-inlaid bar behind which six tavern maids were serving ale, mead and mulled wine. The tavern was crowded, unusually so, but this was market day and farmers and cattle-breeders from all over the region had gathered for the auctions. Sieben stepped to the long bar, where a young tavern maid with honey-blonde hair smiled and approached him. 'At last you visit me,' she said.

'Who could stay away from you for long, dear heart?' he said with a smile, straining to remember her name.

'I will be finished here by second watch,' she told him.

'Where's my ale?' shouted a burly farmer, some way to the left.

'I was before you, goat-face!' came another voice. The girl gave a shy smile to Sieben, then moved down the bar to quell the threat-ened row.

'Here I am now, sirs, and I've only one pair of hands. Give me a moment, won't you?'

Sieben strolled through the crowds, seeking out the axeman, and found him sitting alone by a narrow, open window. Sieben eased on to the bench alongside him. 'Might be a good idea to start again,' said the poet. 'Let me buy you a jug of ale.'

'I buy my own ale,' grunted the axeman. 'And don't sit so close.'

Sieben stood and moved to the far side of the table, seating himself opposite the young man. 'Is that more to your liking?' he asked, with heavy sarcasm.

'Aye, it is. Are you wearing perfume?'

'Scented oil on the hair. You like it?'

The axeman shook his head, but refrained from comment. He cleared his throat. 'My wife has been taken by slavers. She is in Mashrapur.'

59

Sieben sat back and gazed at the young man. 'I take it you weren't home at the time,' he said.

'No. They took all the women. I freed them. But Rowena wasn't with them; she was with someone called Collan. He left before I got to the other raiders.'

'Before you got to the other raiders?' repeated Sieben. 'Isn't there a little more to it?'

'To what?'

'How did you free the other women?'

'What in Hell's name does that matter? I killed a few of them and the rest ran away. But that's not the point. Rowena wasn't there – she's in Mashrapur.'

Sieben raised a slender hand. 'Slow down, there's a good fellow. Firstly, how does Shadak come into this? And secondly, are you saying that you single-handedly attacked Harib Ka and his killers?'

'Not single-handedly. Shadak was there; they were going to torture him. Also I had two girls with me; good archers. Anyway, all that is past. Shadak said you could help me to find Rowena and come up with a plan to rescue her.'

'From Collan?'

'Yes, from Collan,' stormed the axeman. 'Are you deaf or stupid?'

Sieben's dark eyes narrowed and he leaned forward. 'You have an appealing way of asking for help, my large and ugly friend. Good luck with your quest!' He rose and moved back through the throng, emerging into the late afternoon sunlight. Two men were lounging close to the entrance, a third was whittling a length of wood with a razor-sharp hunting-knife.

The first of the men moved in front of the poet; it was the warrior who had first lost money at the barrel head. 'Get your emerald back, did you?'

'No,' answered Sieben, still angry. 'What a bumptious, ill-bred boor!'

'Not a friend, then?'

'Hardly. I don't even know his name. More to the point, I don't want to.'

60

'It's said you're crafty with those knives,' said the warrior, pointing to the throwing-blades. 'Is it true?'

'Why do you ask?'

'Could be you'll get the emerald back if you are.'

'You plan to attack him? Why? As far as I could see he carries no wealth.'

'It's not his wealth!' snapped the second warrior. Sieben stepped back as the man's body odour reached him. 'He's a madman. He attacked our camp two days ago, stampeded our horses. Never did find my grey. And he killed Harib. Asta's tits! He must have downed a dozen men with that cursed axe.'

'If he killed a dozen, what makes you think that three of you can deal with him?'

The noxious warrior tapped his nose. 'Surprise. When he steps out, Rafin will ask him a question. As he turns, Zhak and I will move in and gut him. But you could help. A knife through the eye would slow him up some, eh?'

'Probably,' agreed Sieben, and he moved away several paces to seat himself on a hitching rail. He drew a knife from its sheath and began to clean his nails.

'You with us?' hissed the first man.

'We'll see,' said Sieben.

Druss sat at the table and gazed down at the shining blades of the axe. He could see his reflection there, cold-eyed and grim. The features were flat and sullen, the mouth a tight, angry line. He removed the black helm and laid it on the blades, covering the face in the axe.

'*Whenever you speak someone gets angry.*' The words of his father drifted up from the halls of memory. And it was true. Some men had a knack for friendship, for easy chatter and simple jests. Druss envied them. Until Rowena had walked into his life he had believed such qualities were entirely lacking in him. But with her he felt at ease, he could laugh and joke – and see himself for a moment as others saw him, huge and bear-like, short-tempered and frightening. 'It was your childhood, Druss,' Rowena told him one morning, as they sat on the hillside overlooking the village. 'Your father moved from place to place, always frightened he would be recognised, never allowing himself to become close to people. It was easier for him, for he was a man. But it must have been hard for a boy who never learned how to make friends.'

'I don't need friends,' he said.

'I need you.'

The memory of those three softly spoken words made his heart lurch. A tavern maid passed the table and Druss reached out and caught her arm. 'Do you have Lentrian Red?' he asked.

'I'll bring you a goblet, sir.'

'Make it a jug.'

He drank until his senses swam and his thoughts became jumbled and confused. He remembered Alarin, and the punch which broke the man's jaw, and then, after the raid, hauling Alarin's body into the meeting hall. He had been stabbed through the back by a lance which had snapped in half in his body. The dead man's eyes had been open. So many of the dead had open eyes . . . all accusing.

'Why are you alive and we dead?' they asked him. 'We had families, lives, dreams, hopes. Why should you outlive us?'

'More wine!' he bellowed and a young girl with honey-blonde hair leaned over the table.

'I think you've had enough, sir. You've drunk a quart already.'

'All the eyes were open,' he said. 'Old women, children. The children were the worst. What kind of a man kills a child?'

'I think you should go home, sir. Have a little sleep.'

'Home?' He laughed, the sound harsh and bitter. 'Home to the dead? And what would I tell them? The forge is cold. There is no smell of fresh-baked bread; no laughter among the children. Just eyes. No, not even eyes. Just ashes.'

'We heard there was a raid to the north,' she said. 'Was that your home?'

'Bring me more wine, girl. It helps me.'

'It is a false friend, sir,' she whispered.

'It is the only one I have.'

A burly, bearded man in a leather apron moved in close. 'What does he want?' he asked the girl.

62

'More wine, sir.'

'Then fetch it for him – if he can pay.'

Druss reached into the pouch at his side, drawing out one of the six silver pieces Shadak had given him. He flipped it to the innkeeper. 'Well, serve him!' the man ordered the maid.

The second jug went the way of the first and, when it was finished, Druss pushed himself ponderously to his feet. He tried to don the helm, but it slipped from his fingers and rolled to the floor. As he bent down, he rammed his brow against the edge of the table. The serving maid appeared alongside him. 'Let me help you, sir,' she said, scooping up the helm and gently placing it on his head.

'Thank you,' he said, slowly. He fumbled in his pouch and gave her a silver piece. 'For . . . your . . . kindness,' he told her, enunciating the words with care.

'I have a small room at the back, sir. Two doors down from the stable. It is unlocked; you may sleep there if you wish.'

He picked up the axe, but it too fell to the floor, the prongs of the blades embedding in a wooden plank. 'Go back and sleep, sir. I'll bring your . . . weapon with me later.'

He nodded and weaved his way towards the door.

Pulling open the door, he stepped out into the fading sunlight, his stomach lurching. Someone spoke from his left, asking him a question. Druss tried to turn, but stumbled into the man and they both fell against the wall. He tried to right himself, grabbing the man's shoulder and heaving himself upright. Through the fog in his mind he heard other men running in. One of them screamed. Druss lurched back and saw a long-bladed dagger clatter to the ground. The former wielder was standing alongside him, his right arm raised unnaturally. Druss blinked. The man's wrist was pinned to the inn door by a throwing knife.

He heard the rasp of swords being drawn. 'Defend yourself, you fool!' came a voice.

A swordsman ran at him and Druss stepped in to meet him, parrying the lunging blade with his forearm and slamming a right cross to the warrior's chin. The swordsman went down as if poleaxed.

Swinging to meet the second attacker, Druss lost his balance and fell heavily. But in mid-swing the swordsman also stumbled and Druss lashed out with his foot, catching his assailant on the heel and catapulting him to the ground. Rolling to his knees, Druss grabbed the fallen man by the hair and hauled him close, delivering a bone-crunching head-butt to the warrior's nose. The man slumped forward, unconscious. Druss released him.

Another man moved alongside him and Druss recognised the handsome young poet. 'Gods, you reek of cheap wine,' said Sieben.

'Who ... are you?' mumbled Druss, trying to focus on the man with his arm pinned to the door.

'Miscreants,' Sieben told him, moving alongside the stricken warrior and levering his knife clear. The man screamed in pain but Sieben ignored him and returned to the street. 'I think you'd better come with me, old horse.'

Druss remembered little of the walk through the town, only that he stopped twice to vomit, and his head began to ache abominably.

He awoke at midnight and found himself lying on a porch under the stars. Beside him was a bucket. He sat up ... and groaned as the terrible pounding began in his head. It felt as if an iron band had been riveted to his brow. Hearing sounds from within the house, he stood and moved to the door. Then he halted. The sounds were unmistakable.

'Oh, Sieben ... Oh ... Oh ... !'

Druss swore and returned to the edge of the porch. A breath of wind touched his face, bringing with it an unpleasant smell, and he gazed down at himself. His jerkin was soiled with vomit, and he stank of stale sweat and travel. To his left was a well. Forcing himself upright, he walked to it, and slowly raised the bucket. Somewhere deep within his head a demon began to strike at his skull with a red-hot hammer. Ignoring the pain, Druss stripped to the waist and washed himself with the cold water.

He heard the door open and turned to see a dark-haired young woman emerge from the house. She looked at him, smiled, then ran off through the narrow streets. Lifting the bucket, Druss tipped the last of the contents over his head.

'At the risk of being offensive,' said Sieben from the doorway, 'I think you need a little soap. Come inside. There's a fire burning in the hearth and I've heated some water. Gods, it's freezing out here.'

Gathering his clothes, Druss followed the poet inside. The house was small, only three rooms, all on the ground floor – a cook-room with an iron stove, a bedroom and a square dining room with a stone-built hearth in which a fire was blazing. There was a table with four wooden chairs and on either side of the hearth were comfort seats of padded leather stuffed with horsehair.

Sieben led him to the cloakroom where he filled a bowl with hot water. Handing Druss a slab of white soap and a towel, he opened a cupboard door and removed a plate of sliced beef and a loaf of bread. 'Come in and eat when you're ready,' said the poet, as he walked back to the dining room.

Druss scrubbed himself with the soap, which smelled of lavender, then cleaned his jerkin and dressed. He found the poet sitting by the fire with his long legs stretched out, a goblet of wine in one hand. The other slender hand swept through the shoulder-length blond hair, sweeping it back over his head. Holding it in place, he settled a black leather headband over his brow; at the centre of the band was a glittering opal. The poet lifted a small oval mirror and studied himself. 'Ah, what a curse it is to be so good-looking,' he said, laying aside the mirror. 'Care for a drink?' Druss felt his stomach heave and shook his head. 'Eat, my large friend. You may feel as if your stomach will revolt, but it is the best thing for you. Trust me.'

Druss tore off a hunk of bread and sat down, slowly chewing it. It tasted of ashes and bile, but he finished it manfully. The poet was right. His stomach settled. The salted beef was harder to take but, washed down with cool water, he soon began to feel his strength returning. 'I drank too much,' he said.

'No, really? Two quarts, I understand.'

'I don't remember how much. Was there a fight?'

'Not much of one, by your standards.'

'Who were they?'

'Some of the raiders you attacked.'

'I should have killed them.'

'Perhaps – but in the state you were in you should consider yourself lucky to be alive.'

Druss filled a clay cup with water and drained it. 'You helped me, I remember that. Why?'

'A passing whim. Don't let it concern you. Now, tell me again about your wife and the raid.'

'To what purpose? It's done. All I care about is finding Rowena.'

'But you will need my help – otherwise Shadak wouldn't have sent you to me. And I like to know the kind of man I'm expected to travel with. You understand? So tell me.'

'There isn't a great deal to tell. The raiders ...'

'How many?'

'Forty or so. They attacked our village, killed all the men, the old women, the children. They took the younger women prisoner. I was in the woods, felling timber. Some killers came to the woods and I dealt with them. Then I met Shadak, who was also following them; they raided a town and killed his son. We freed the women. Shadak was captured. I stampeded their horses and attacked the camp. That's it.'

Sieben shook his head and smiled. 'I think you could tell the entire history of the Drenai in less time than it takes to boil an egg. A storyteller you are not, my friend – which is just as well, since that is my main source of income and I loathe competition.'

Druss rubbed his eyes and leaned back in the chair, resting his head on the high padded leather cushion. The heat from the fire was soothing and his body was weary beyond anything he had known before. The days of the chase had taken their toll. He felt himself drifting on a warm sea. The poet was speaking to him, but his words failed to penetrate.

He awoke with the dawn to find the fire was burned down to a few glowing coals and the house empty. Druss yawned and stretched, then walked to the kitchen, helping himself to stale bread and a hunk of cheese. He drank some more water, then heard the main door creak open. Wandering out, he saw Sieben and a young, blonde woman. The poet was carrying his axe and his gauntlets.

'Someone to see you, old horse,' said Sieben, laying the axe in the doorway and tossing the gauntlets to a chair. The poet smiled and walked back out into the sunlight.

The blonde woman approached Druss, smiling shyly. 'I didn't know where you were. I kept your axe for you.'

'Thank you. You are from the inn.' She was dressed now in a woollen dress of poor quality, that once had been blue but was now a pale grey. Her figure was shapely, her face gentle and pretty, her eyes warm and brown.

'Yes. We spoke yesterday,' she said, moving to a chair and sitting down with her hands on her knees. 'You seemed . . . very sad.'

'I am . . . myself now,' he told her gently.

'Sieben told me your wife was taken by slavers.'

'I will find her.'

'When I was sixteen raiders attacked our village. They killed my father and wounded my husband. I was taken, with seven other girls, and we were sold in Mashrapur. I was there two years. I escaped one night, with another girl, and we fled into the wilderness. She died there, killed by a bear, but I was found by a company of pilgrims on their way to Lentria. I was almost dead from starvation. They helped me, and I made my way home.'

'Why are you telling me all this?' asked Druss softly, seeing the sadness in her eyes.

'My husband had married someone else. And my brother, Loric, who had lost an arm in the raid, told me I was no longer welcome. He said I was a *fallen* woman, and if I had any pride I would have taken my own life. So I left.'

Druss reached out and took her hand. 'Your husband was a worthless piece of dung, and your brother likewise. But I ask again, why are you telling me this?'

'When Sieben told me you were hunting for your wife . . . it made me remember. I used to dream Karsk was coming for me. But a slave has no rights, you know, in Mashrapur. Anything the Lord wishes, he can have. You cannot refuse. When you find your . . . lady . . . she may well have been roughly used.' She fell silent and sat staring at her hands. 'I don't know how to say what I mean . . . When I was a

67

slave I was beaten, I was humiliated. I was raped and abused. But nothing was as bad as the look on my husband's face when he saw me, or the disgust in my brother's voice when he cast me out.'

Still holding to her hand, Druss leaned in towards her. 'What is your name?'

'Sashan.'

'If I had been your husband, Sashan, I would have followed you. I would have found you. And when I did I would have taken you in my arms and brought you home. As I will bring Rowena home.'

'You will not judge her?'

He smiled. 'No more than I judge you, save to say that you are a brave woman and any man – any true man – would be proud to have you walk beside him.'

She reddened and rose. 'If wishes were horses, then beggars would ride,' she said, then turned away and walked to the doorway. She looked back once, but said nothing; then she stepped from the house.

Sieben entered. 'That was well said, old horse. Very well said. You know, despite your awful manners and your lack of conversation, I think I like you. Let's go to Mashrapur and find your lady.'

Druss looked hard at the slim young man. He was perhaps an inch taller than the axeman and his clothes were of fine cloth, his long hair barber-trimmed, not hacked by a knife nor cut with shears using a basin for a guide. Druss glanced down at the man's hands; the skin was soft, like that of a child. Only the baldric and the knives gave any evidence Sieben was a fighter.

'Well? Do I pass inspection, old horse?'

'My father once said that fortune makes for strange bedfellows,' said Druss.

'You should see the problem from where I'm standing,' answered Sieben. 'You will travel with a man versed in literature and poetry, a storyteller without equal. While I, on the other hand, get to ride beside a peasant in a vomit-flecked jerkin.'

Amazingly Druss found no rising anger, no surging desire to strike out. Instead he laughed, tension flowing from him.

'I like you, little man,' he said.

* * *

Within the first day they had left the mountains behind them, and rode now through valleys and vales, and sweeping grassland dotted with hills and ribbon streams. There were many hamlets and villages beside the road, the buildings of whitewashed stone with roofs of timber or slate.

Sieben rode gracefully, straight of back and easy in the saddle, sunlight gleaming from his riding tunic of pale blue silk and the silver edging on his knee-length riding boots. His long blond hair was tied back in a ponytail, and he also sported a silver headband. 'How many headbands do you have?' asked Druss as they set off.

'Pitifully few. Pretty though, isn't it? I picked it up in Drenan last year. I've always liked silver.'

'You look like a fop.'

'Just what I needed this morning,' said Sieben, smiling, 'hints on sartorial elegance from a man whose hair has apparently been cut with a rusty saw, and whose only shirt carries wine stains, and . . . no, don't tell me what the other marks are.'

Druss glanced down. 'Dried blood. But it's not mine.'

'Well, what a relief. I shall sleep more soundly tonight for knowing that.'

For the first hour of the journey the poet tried to give helpful advice to the young axeman. 'Don't grip the horse with your calves, just your thighs. And straighten your back.' Finally he gave up. 'You know, Druss, my dear, some men are born to ride. You on the other hand have no feel for it. I've seen sacks of carrots with more grace than you.'

The axeman's reply was short and brutally obscene. Sieben chuckled and gazed up at the sky which was cloudless and gloriously blue. 'What a day to set off in search of a kidnapped princess,' he said.

'She's not a princess.'

'All kidnapped women are princesses,' Sieben told him. 'Have you never listened to the stories? Heroes are tall, golden-haired and wondrously handsome. Princesses are demure and beautiful, spending their lives waiting for the handsome prince who will free them. By the gods, Druss, no one would want to hear tales of the truth. Can you imagine? The young hero unable to ride in search of his sweetheart because the large boil on his buttocks prevents him from sitting on a horse?' Sieben's laughter rippled out.

Even normally grim Druss smiled and Sieben continued. 'It's the romance, you see. A woman in stories is either a goddess or a whore. The princess, being a beautiful virgin, falls into the former category. The hero must also be pure, waiting for the moment of his destiny in the arms of the virginal princess. It's wonderfully quaint – and quite ridiculous of course. Lovemaking, like playing the lyre, requires enormous practice. Thankfully the stories always end before we see the young couple fumbling their way through their first coupling.'

'You talk like a man who has never been in love,' said Druss.

'Nonsense. I have been in love scores of times,' snapped the poet.

Druss shook his head. 'If that were true, then you would know just how . . . how fine the *fumbling* can be. How far is it to Mashrapur?'

'Two days. But the slave markets are always held on Missael or Manien, so we've time. Tell me about her.'

'No.'

'No? You don't like talking about your wife?'

'Not to strangers. Have you ever been wed?'

'No – nor ever desired to be. Look around you, Druss. See all those flowers on the hillsides? Why would a man want to restrict himself to just one bloom? Just one scent? I had a horse once, Shadira, a beautiful beast, faster than the north wind. She could clear a four-bar fence with room to spare. I was ten when my father gave her to me, and Shadira was fifteen. But by the time I was twenty Shadira could no longer run as fast, and she jumped not at all. So I got a new horse. You understand what I am saying?'

'Not a word of it,' grunted Druss. 'Women aren't horses.'

'That's true,' agreed Sieben. 'Most horses you want to ride more than once.'

Druss shook his head. 'I don't know what it is that you call love. And I don't want to know.'

The trail wound to the south, the hills growing more gentle as the mountain range receded behind them. Ahead on the road they saw an old man shuffling towards them. He wore robes of faded blue and he leaned heavily on a long staff. As they neared, Sieben saw that the man was blind.

The old man halted as they rode closer. 'Can we help you, old one?' asked Sieben.

'I need no help,' answered the man, his voice surprisingly strong and resonant. 'I am on my way to Drenan.'

'It is a long walk,' said Sieben.

'I am in no hurry. But if you have food, and are willing to entertain a guest at your midday meal, I would be glad to join you.'

'Why not?' said Sieben. 'There is a stream some little way to your right; we will see you there.' Swinging his mount Sieben cantered the beast across the grass, leaping lightly from the saddle and looping the reins over the horse's head as Druss rode up and dismounted.

'Why did you invite him to join us?'

Sieben glanced back. The old man was out of earshot and moving slowly towards them. 'He is a seeker, Druss. A mystic. Have you not heard of them?'

'No.'

'Source Priests who blind themselves in order to increase their powers of prophecy. Some of them are quite extraordinary. It's worth a few oats.'

Swiftly the poet prepared a fire over which he placed a copper pot half-filled with water. He added oats and a little salt. The old man sat cross-legged nearby. Druss removed his helm and jerkin and stretched out in the sunshine. After the porridge had cooked, Sieben filled a bowl and passed it to the priest.

'Do you have sugar?' asked the Seeker.

'No. We have a little honey. I will fetch it.'

After the meal was concluded the old man shuffled to the stream and cleaned his bowl, returning it to Sieben. 'And now you wish to know the future?' asked the priest, with a crooked smile.

'That would be pleasant,' said Sieben.

'Not necessarily. Would you like to know the day of your death?'

'I take your point, old man. Tell me of the next beautiful woman who will share my bed.'

71

The old man chuckled. 'A talent so large, yet men only require such infinitesimal examples of it. I could tell you of your sons, and of moments of peril. But no, you wish to hear of matters inconsequential. Very well. Give me your hand.'

Sieben sat opposite him and extended his right hand. The old man took it, and sat silently for several minutes. Finally he sighed. 'I have walked the paths of your future, Sieben the Poet, Sieben the Sagamaster. The road is long. The next woman? A whore in Mashrapur, who will ask for seven silver pennies. You will pay it.'

He released Sieben's hand and turned his blind eyes towards Druss. 'Do you wish your future told?'

'I will make my own future,' answered Druss.

'Ah, a man of strength and independent will. Come. Let me at least see, for my own interest, what tomorrow holds for you.'

'Come on, lad,' pleaded Sieben. 'Give him your hand.'

Druss rose and walked to where the old man sat. He squatted down before him and thrust out his hand. The priest's fingers closed around his own. 'A large hand,' he said. 'Strong ... very strong.' Suddenly he winced, his body stiffening. 'Are you yet young, Druss the Legend? Have you stood at the pass?'

'What pass?'

'How old are you?'

'Seventeen.'

'Of course. Seventeen. And searching for Rowena. Yes... Mashrapur. I see it now. Not yet the *Deathwalker*, the Silver Slayer, the Captain of the Axe. But still mighty.' He released his hold and sighed. 'You are quite right, Druss, you will make your own future; you will need no words from me.' The old man rose and took up his staff. 'I thank you for your hospitality.'

Sieben stood also. 'At least tell us what awaits in Mashrapur,' he said.

'A whore and seven silver pennies,' answered the priest with a dry smile. He turned his blind eyes towards Druss. 'Be strong, axeman. The road is long and there are legends to be made. But Death awaits, and he is patient. You will see him as you stand beneath the gates in the fourth Year of the Leopard.'

He walked slowly away. 'Incredible,' whispered Sieben.

'Why?' responded Druss. 'I could have foretold that the next woman you meet would be a whore.'

'He knew our names, Druss; he knew everything. Now, when is the fourth Year of the Leopard?'

'He told us nothing. Let's move on.'

'How can you say that it was nothing? He called you Druss the Legend. What legend? How will you build it?'

Ignoring him, Druss walked to his horse and climbed into the saddle. 'I don't like horses,' he said. 'Once we reach Mashrapur I'll sell it. Rowena and I will walk back.'

Sieben looked up at the pale-eyed young man. 'It meant nothing to you, did it? His prophecy, I mean.'

'They were just words, poet. Noises on the air. Let's ride.'

After a while Sieben spoke. 'The Year of the Leopard is forty-three years away. Gods, Druss, you'll live to be an old man. I wonder where the gates are.'

Druss ignored him and rode on.

5

Bodasen threaded his way through the crowds milling on the dock, past the gaudily dressed women with their painted faces and insincere smiles, past the stallholders bellowing their bargains, past the beggars with their deformed limbs and their pleading eyes. Bodasen hated Mashrapur, loathed the smell of the teeming multitudes who gathered here seeking instant wealth. The streets were narrow and choked with the detritus of humanity, the houses built high – three-, four- and five-storey – all linked by alleyways and tunnels and shadowed pathways where robbers could plunge their blades into unsuspecting victims and flee through the labyrinthine backstreets before the undermanned city guards could apprehend them.

What a city, thought Bodasen. A place of filth and painted women, a haven for thieves, smugglers, slavers and renegades.

A woman approached him. 'You look lonely, my love,' she said, flashing a gold-toothed smile. He gazed down at her and her smile faded. She backed away swiftly and Bodasen rode on.

He came to a narrow alleyway and paused to push his black cloak above his left shoulder. The hilt of his sabre shone in the fading sunlight. As Bodasen walked on, three men stood in the shadows. He felt their eyes upon him and turned his face towards them, his stare challenging; they looked away, and he continued along the alley until it broadened out to a small square with a fountain at the centre, constructed around a bronze statue of a boy riding a dolphin. Several whores were sitting beside the fountain, chatting to one another. They saw him, and instantly their postures changed. Leaning back to thrust out their breasts, they assumed their customary smiles. As he passed he heard their chatter begin again.

74

The inn was almost empty. An old man sat at the bar, nursing a jug of ale, and two maids were cleaning tables, while a third prepared the night's fire in the stone hearth. Bodasen moved to a window table and sat, facing the door. A maid approached him.

'Good evening, my lord. Are you ready for your usual supper?'

'No. Bring me a goblet of good red wine and a flagon of fresh water.'

'Yes, my lord.' She curtsied prettily and walked away. Her greeting eased his irritation. Some, even in this disgusting city, could recognise nobility. The wine was of an average quality, no more than four years old and harsh on the tongue, and Bodasen drank sparingly.

The inn door opened and two men entered. Bodasen leaned back in his chair and watched them approach. The first was a handsome man, tall and wide-shouldered; he wore a crimson cloak over a red tunic, and a sabre was scabbarded at his hip. The second was a huge, bald warrior, heavily muscled and grim of feature.

The first man sat opposite Bodasen, the second standing alongside the table. 'Where is Harib Ka?' Bodasen asked.

'Your countryman will not be joining us,' replied Collan.

'He said he would be here; that is the reason I agreed to this meeting.'

Collan shrugged. 'He had an urgent appointment elsewhere.'

'He said nothing of it to me.'

'I think it was unexpected. You wish to do business, or not?'

'I do not *do business*, Collan. I seek to negotiate a treaty with the ... free traders of the Ventrian Sea. My understanding is that you have ... shall we say, contacts, among them?'

Collan chuckled. 'Interesting. You can't bring yourself to say *pirates*, can you? No, that would be too much for a Ventrian nobleman. Well, let us think the situation through. The Ventrian fleet has been scattered or sunk. On land your armies are crushed, and the Emperor slain. Now you pin your hopes on the pirate fleet; only they can ensure that the armies of Naashan do not march all the way to the capital. Am I in error on any of these points?'

Bodasen cleared his throat. 'The Empire is seeking friends. The Free Traders are in a position to aid us in our struggle against the forces of evil. We always treat our friends with great generosity.'

'I see,' said Collan, his eyes mocking. 'We are fighting the forces of *evil* now? And there I was believing that Naashan and Ventria were merely two warring empires. How naïve of me. However, you speak of generosity. How generous is the Prince?'

'The *Emperor* is noted for his largess.'

Collan smiled. 'Emperor at nineteen – a rapid rise to power. But he has lost eleven cities to the invader, and his treasury is severely depleted. Can he find two hundred thousand gold raq?'

'Two . . . surely you are not serious?'

'The Free Traders have fifty warships. With them we could protect the coastline and prevent invasion from the sea; we could also shepherd the convoys that carry Ventrian silk to the Drenai and the Lentrians and countless others. Without us you are doomed, Bodasen. Two hundred thousand is a small price to pay.'

'I am authorised to offer fifty. No more.'

'The Naashanites have offered one hundred.'

Bodasen fell silent, his mouth dry. 'Perhaps we could pay the difference in silks and trade goods?' he offered at last.

'Gold,' said Collan. 'That is all that interests us. We are not merchants.'

No, thought Bodasen bitterly, you are thieves and killers, and it burns my soul to sit in the same room with such as you. 'I will need to seek counsel of the ambassador,' he said. 'He can communicate your request to the Emperor. I will need five days.'

'That is agreeable,' said Collan, rising. 'You know where to find me?'

Under a flat rock, thought Bodasen, with the other slugs and lice. 'Yes,' he said, softly, 'I know where to find you. Tell me, when will Harib be back in Mashrapur?'

'He won't.'

'Where is this appointment then?'

'In Hell,' answered Collan.

'You must have patience,' said Sieben, as Druss stalked around the small room on the upper floor of the Tree of Bone Inn. The poet

76

had stretched out his long, lean frame on the first of the two narrow beds, while Druss strode to the window and stood staring out over the dock and the sea beyond the harbour.

'Patience?' stormed the axeman. 'She's here somewhere, maybe close.'

'And we'll find her,' promised Sieben, 'but it will take a little time. First there are the established slave traders. This evening I will ask around, and find out where Collan has placed her. Then we can plan her rescue.'

Druss swung round. 'Why not go to the White Bear Inn and find Collan? He knows.'

'I expect he does, old horse.' Sieben swung his legs from the bed and stood. 'And he'll have any number of rascals ready to plunge knives in our backs. Foremost among them will be Borcha. I want you to picture a man who looks as if he was carved from granite, with muscles that dwarf even yours. Borcha is a killer. He has beaten men to death in fist-fights, snapped necks in wrestling bouts; he doesn't need a weapon. I have seen him crush a pewter goblet in one hand, and watched him lift a barrel of ale above his head. And he is just one of Collan's men.'

'Frightened, are you, poet?'

'Of course I'm frightened, you young fool! Fear is sensible. Never make the mistake of equating it with cowardice. But it is senseless to go after Collan; he is known here and has friends in very high places. Attack him and you will be arrested, tried and sentenced. Then there will be no one to rescue Rowena.'

Druss slumped down, his elbows resting on the warped table. 'I hate sitting here doing nothing,' he said.

'Then let's walk around the city for a while,' offered Sieben. 'We can gather some information. How much did you get for your horse?'

'Twenty in silver.'

'Almost fair. You did well. Come on, I'll show you the sights.' Druss stood and gathered his axe. 'I don't think you'll need that,' Sieben told him. 'It's one thing to wear a sword or carry a knife, but the City Watch will not take kindly to that monstrosity. In a crowded street you're likely to cut off someone's arm by mistake. Here, I'll loan you one of my knives.'

'I won't need it,' said Druss, leaving the axe on the table and striding out of the room.

Together they walked down into the main room of the inn, then out into the narrow street beyond.

Druss sniffed loudly. 'This city stinks,' he said.

'Most cities do – at least in the poorest areas. No sewers. Refuse is thrown from windows. So walk warily.'

They moved towards the docks where several ships were being unloaded, bales of silk from Ventria and Naashan and other eastern nations, herbs and spices, dried fruit and barrels of wine. The dock was alive with activity.

'I've never seen so many people in one place,' said Druss.

'It's not even busy yet,' Sieben pointed out. They strolled around the harbour wall, past temples and large municipal buildings, through a small park with a statue-lined walkway and a central fountain. Young couples were walking hand in hand and to the left an orator was addressing a small crowd. He was speaking of the essential selfishness of the pursuit of altruism. Sieben stopped to listen for a few minutes, then walked on.

'Interesting, don't you think?' he asked his companion. 'He was suggesting that good works are ultimately selfish because they make the man who undertakes them feel good. Therefore he has not been unselfish at all, but has merely acted for his own pleasure.'

Druss shook his head and glowered at the poet. 'His mother should have told him the mouth is not for breaking wind with.'

'I take it this is your subtle way of saying you disagree with his comments?' snapped Sieben.

'The man's a fool.'

'How would you set about proving that?'

'I don't need to prove it. If a man serves up a plate of cow dung, I don't need to taste it to know it's not steak.'

'Explain it,' Sieben urged him. 'Share some of that vaunted frontier philosophy.'

'No,' said Druss, walking on.

'Why not?' asked Sieben, moving alongside him.

'I am a woodsman. I know about trees. Once I worked in an orchard. Did you know you can take cuttings from any variety and graft them to another apple tree? One tree can have twenty varieties. It's the same with pears. My father always said men were like that with knowledge. So much can be grafted on, but it must match what the heart feels. You can't graft apple to pear. It's a waste of time – and I don't like wasting my time.'

'You think I could not understand your arguments?' asked Sieben with a sneering smile.

'Some things you either know or you don't. And I can't graft that knowledge on to you. Back in the mountains I watched farmers plant tree lines across the fields; they did it because the winds can blow away the topsoil. But the trees would take a hundred years to form a real windbreak, so those farmers were building for the future, for others they will never know. They did it because it was right to do it – and not one of them would be able to debate with that pompous windbag back there. Or with you. Nor is it necessary that they should.'

'That *pompous windbag* is the first minister of Mashrapur, a brilliant politician and a poet of some repute. I'm sure he would be mortally humiliated to know that a young uneducated peasant from the frontier disagrees with his philosophy.'

'Then we won't tell him,' said Druss. 'We'll just leave him here serving up his cowpats to people who *will* believe they're steaks. Now I'm thirsty, poet. Do you know of a decent tavern?'

'It depends what you're looking for. The taverns on the docks are rough, and usually filled with thieves and whores. If we walk on for another half-mile we'll come to a more civilised area. There we can have a quiet drink.'

'What about those places over there?' asked Druss, pointing to a row of buildings alongside the wharf.

'Your judgement is unerring, Druss. That is East Wharf, better known to the residents here as Thieves Row. Every night there are a score of fights – and murders. Almost no one of quality would go there – which makes it perfect for you. You go on. I'll visit some old friends who might have news of recent slave movements.'

'I'll come with you,' said Druss.

'No, you won't. You'd be out of place. Most of my friends, you see, are pompous windbags. I'll meet you back at the Tree of Bone by midnight.' Druss chuckled, which only increased Sieben's annoyance as the poet swung away and strode through the park.

The room was furnished with a large bed with satin sheets, two comfort chairs padded with horsehair and covered with velvet, and a table upon which sat a jug of wine and two silver goblets. There were rugs upon the floor, woven with great skill and soft beneath her bare feet. Rowena sat upon the edge of the bed, her right hand clasping the brooch Druss had fashioned for her. She could see him walking beside Sieben. Sadness overwhelmed her and her hand dropped to her lap. Harib Ka was dead – as she had known he would be – and Druss was now closer to his dread destiny.

She felt powerless and alone in Collan's house. There were no locks upon the door, but there were guards in the corridor beyond. Yet there was no escape.

On the first night, when Collan had taken her from the camp, he had raped her twice. On the second occasion she had tried to empty her mind, losing herself in dreams of the past. In doing so she had unlocked the doors to her Talent. Rowena had floated free of her abused body and hurtled through darkness and Time. She saw great cities, huge armies, mountains that breached the clouds. Lost, she sought for Druss and could not find him.

Then a voice came to her, a gentle voice, warm and reassuring. 'Be calm, sister. I will help you.'

She paused in her flight, floating above a night-dark ocean. A man appeared alongside her; he was slim of build and young, perhaps twenty. His eyes were dark, his smile friendly. 'Who are you?' she asked him.

'I am Vintar of the Thirty.'

'I am lost,' she said.

'Give me your hand.'

Reaching out she felt his spirit fingers, then his thoughts washed over hers. On the verge of panic Rowena felt herself swamped by his memories, seeing a temple of grey stone, a dwelling-place of white-clad monks. He withdrew from her as swiftly as he had entered her thoughts. 'Your ordeal is over,' he said. 'He has left you and now sleeps beside you. I shall take you home.'

'I cannot bear it. He is a vile man.'

'You will survive, Rowena.'

'Why should I wish to?' she asked him. 'My husband is changing, becoming day by day as vicious as the men who took me. What kind of life will I face?'

'I will not answer that, though probably I could,' he told her. 'You are very young, and you have experienced great pain. But you are alive, and while living can achieve great good. You have the Talent, not only to Soar but also to Heal, to Know. Few are blessed with this gift. Do not concern yourself with Collan; he raped you only because Harib Ka said that he should not and he will not touch you again.'

'He has defiled me.'

'No,' said Vintar sternly, 'he has defiled himself. It is important to understand that.'

'Druss would be ashamed of me, for I did not fight.'

'You fought, Rowena, in your own way. You gave him no pleasure. To have tried to resist would have increased his lust, and his satisfaction. As it was – and you know this to be true – he felt deflated and full of melancholy. And you know his fate.'

'I don't want any more deaths!'

'We all die. You ... me ... Druss. The measure of us all is established by how we live.'

He had returned her to her body, taking care to instruct her in the ways of Spirit travel, and the routes by which she could return by herself in the future. 'Will I see you again?' she asked him.

'It is possible,' he answered.

Now, as she sat on the satin-covered bed, she wished she could speak with him again.

The door opened and a huge warrior entered. He was bald and heavily muscled. There were scars around his eyes and his nose was flattened against his face. He moved towards the bed but there was

81

no threat, she knew. Silently he laid a gown of white silk upon the bed. 'Collan has asked that you wear this for Kabuchek.'

'Who is Kabuchek?' she enquired.

'A Ventrian merchant. If you do well he will buy you. It won't be a bad life, girl. He has many palaces and treats his slaves with care.'

'Why do you serve Collan?' she asked.

His eyes narrowed. 'I serve no one. Collan is a friend. I help him sometimes.'

'You are a better man than he.'

'That is as may be. But several years ago, when I was first champion, I was waylaid in an alley by supporters of the vanquished champion. They had swords and knives. Collan ran to my aid. We survived. I always pay my debts. Now put on the gown, and prepare your skill. You need to impress the Ventrian.'

'And if I refuse?'

'Collan will not be pleased and I don't think you would like that. Trust me on this, lady. Do your best and you will be clear of this house.'

'My husband is coming for me,' she said softly. 'When he does, he will kill any who have harmed me.'

'Why tell me?'

'Do not be here when he comes, Borcha.'

The giant shrugged. 'The Fates will decide,' he said.

Druss strolled across to the wharf buildings. They were old, a series of taverns created from derelict warehouses and there were recesses and alley entrances everywhere. Garishly dressed women lounged against the walls and ragged men sat close by, playing knucklebones or talking in small groups.

A woman approached him. 'All the delights your mind can conjure for just a silver penny,' she said wearily.

'Thank you, but no,' he told her.

'I can get you opiates, if you desire them?'

'No,' he said, more sternly, and moved on. Three bearded men pushed themselves to their feet and walked in front of him. 'A gift for the poor, my lord?' asked the first.

Druss was about to reply when he glimpsed the man to his left edge his hand into the folds of a filthy shirt. He chuckled. 'If that hand comes out with a knife in it – I'll make you eat it, little man.' The beggar froze.

'You shouldn't be coming here with threats,' said the first man. 'Not unarmed as you are. It's not wise, *my lord*.' Reaching behind his back, he drew a long-bladed dagger.

As the blade appeared Druss stepped forward and casually backhanded the man across the mouth. The robber cartwheeled to the left, scattering a group of watching whores and colliding with a wall of brick. He moaned once, then lay still. Ignoring the other two beggars, Druss strode to the nearest tavern and stepped inside.

The interior was windowless and high-ceilinged, lit by lanterns which hung from the beams. The tavern smelt of burning oil and stale sweat. It was crowded, and Druss eased his way to a long tres-tle table on which several barrels of ale were set. An old man in a greasy apron approached him. 'You don't want to be drinking before the bouts begin; it'll fill you with wind,' he warned.

'What bouts?'

The man looked at him appraisingly, and his glittering eyes held no hint of warmth. 'You wouldn't be trying to fool Old Thom, would you?'

'I'm a stranger here,' said Druss. 'Now, what bouts?'

'Follow me, lad,' said Thom, and he pushed his way through the crowd towards the back of the tavern and on through a narrow doorway. Druss followed him and found himself standing in a rectangular warehouse where a wide circle of sand had been roped off at the centre. By the far walls were a group of athletes, moving through a series of exercises to loosen the muscles of shoulders and back.

'You ever fought?'

'Not for money.'

Thom nodded, then reached out and lifted Druss's hand. 'A good size, and flat knuckles. But are you fast, boy?'

'What is the prize?' countered the young man.

'It won't work that way – not for you. This is a standard contest and all the entrants are nominated well in advance so that sporting gentlemen can have opportunities to judge the quality of the fighter. But just before the start of the competition there'll be offers to men in the crowd to earn a few pennies by taking on various champions. A golden raq, for example, to the man who can stay on his feet for one turn of the sandglass. They do it to allow the fighters to warm up against low-quality opposition.'

'How long is one turn?' asked Druss.

'About as long as it's been since you first walked into the Blind Corsair.'

'And what if a man won?'

'It doesn't happen, lad. But if it did, then he'd take the loser's place in the main event. No, the main money is made on wagers among the crowd. How much coin are you carrying?'

'You ask a lot of questions, old man.'

'Pah! I'm not a robber, lad. Used to be, but then I got old and slow. Now I live on my wits. You look like a man who could stand up for himself. At first I mistook you for Grassin the Lentrian – that's him over there, by the far door.' Druss followed the old man's pointing finger and saw a powerfully built young man with short-cropped black hair. He was talking to another heavily muscled man, a blond warrior with a dangling moustache. 'The other one is Skatha, he is a Naashanite sailor. And the big fellow at the back is Borcha. He'll win tonight. No question. Deadly, he is. Most likely someone will be crippled by him before the evening is out.'

Druss gazed at the man and felt the hackles on his neck rise. Borcha was enormous, standing some seven inches above six feet tall. He was bald, his head vaguely pointed as if his skin was stretched over a Vagrian helm. His shoulders were massively muscled, his neck huge with muscles swollen and bulging.

'No good looking at him like that, boy. He's too good for you. Trust me on that. He's skilled and very fast. He won't even step up for the warming bouts. No one would face him – not even for twenty golden raq. But that Grassin now, I think you could stand against him for a turn of the glass. And if you've some coin to wager, I'll find takers.'

'What do you get, old man?'

'Half of what we make.'

'What odds could you bargain for?'

'Two to one. Maybe three.'

'And if I went against Borcha?'

'Put it from your mind, boy. We want to make money – not coffin fuel.'

'How much?' persisted Druss.

'Ten to one – twenty to one. The gods alone know!'

Druss opened the pouch at his side, removing ten silver pieces. Casually he dropped them into the old man's outstretched hand. 'Let it be known that I wish to stand against Borcha for a turn of the glass.'

'Asta's tits, he'll kill you.'

'If he doesn't, you could make a hundred pieces of silver. Maybe more.'

'There is that, of course,' said Old Thom, with a crooked grin.

Crowds slowly began to fill the warehouse arena. Rich nobles clad in silks and fine leathers, their ladies beside them in lace and satin, were seated on high tiers overlooking the sand circle. On the lower levels were the merchants and traders in their conical caps and long capes. Druss felt uncomfortable, hemmed in by the mass. The air was growing foul, the temperature rising as more and more people filed in.

Rowena would hate this place, with its noise and its pressing throng. His mood darkened as he thought of her – a prisoner somewhere, a slave to the whims and desires of Collan. He forced such thoughts from his mind, and concentrated instead on his conversation with the poet. He had enjoyed irritating the man; it had eased his own anger, an anger generated by the unwilling acceptance that much of what the speaker in the park had said was true. He loved Rowena, heart and soul. But he needed her also, and he often wondered which was the stronger, love or need. And was he trying to rescue her because he loved her, or because he was lost without her? The question tormented him.

Rowena calmed his turbulent spirit in a way no other living soul ever could. She helped him to see the world through gentle eyes. It was a rare and beautiful experience. If she had been with him now, he thought, he too would have been filled with distaste at the sweating multitude waiting for blood and pain. Instead the young man stood amidst the crowd and felt his heartbeat quicken, his excitement rise at the prospect of combat.

His pale eyes scanned the crowd, picking out the fat figure of Old Thom talking to a tall man in a red velvet cloak. The man was smiling. He turned from Thom and approached the colossal figure of Borcha. Druss saw the fighter's eyes widen, then the man laughed. Druss could not hear the sound above the chatter and noise about him, but he felt his anger grow. This was Borcha, one of Collan's men – perhaps one of those who had taken Rowena.

Old Thom returned through the crowd and led Druss to a fairly quiet corner. 'I've set events in motion,' he said. 'Now listen to me – don't try for the head. Men have broken their hands on that skull. He has a habit of dipping into punches so that the other man's knuckles strike bone. Go for the lower body. And watch his feet – he's a skilled kicker, lad ... what's your name, by the way?'

'Druss.'

'Well, Druss, you've grabbed a bear by the balls this time. If he hurts you, don't try to hold on; he'll use that head on you, and cave in the bones of your face. Try backing away and covering up.'

'Let him try backing away,' snarled Druss.

'Ah, you're a cocky lad, for sure. But you've never faced a man like Borcha. He's like a living hammer.'

Druss chuckled. 'You really know how to lift a man's spirits. What odds did you find?'

'Fifteen to one. If you hold to your feet, you'll have seventy-five pieces of silver – plus your original ten.'

'Is that enough to buy a slave?'

'What would you want with a slave?'

'Is it enough?'

'Depends on the slave. Some girls fetch upwards of a hundred. You have someone in mind?'

86

Druss dipped into his pouch, removing the last four silver pieces. 'Wager these also.'

The old man took the money. 'I take it this is your entire wealth?'

'It is.'

'She must be a very special slave?'

'She's my wife. Collan's men took her.'

'Collan takes lots of women. Your wife's not a witch, is she?'

'What?' snarled Druss.

'No offence, lad. But Collan sold a witch woman to Kabuchek the Ventrian today. Five thousand silver pieces she brought.'

'No, she is not a witch. Just a mountain girl, sweet and gentle.'

'Ah well, a hundred should be enough,' said Thom. 'But first you have to win it. Have you ever been hit?'

'No. But a tree fell on me once.'

'Knock you out?'

'No. I was dazed for a while.'

'Well, Borcha will feel like a mountain fell on you. I hope you've the strength to withstand it.'

'We'll see, old man.'

'If you go down, roll under the ropes. Otherwise he'll stomp you.'

Druss smiled. 'I like you, old man. You don't honey the medicine, do you?'

'Does you no good unless it tastes bad,' replied Thom, with a crooked grin.

Borcha enjoyed the admiring glances from the crowd – fear and respect from the men and healthy lust from the women. He felt he had earned such silent accolades during the past five years. His blue eyes scanned the tiers and he picked out Mapek, the First Minister of Mashrapur, Bodasen the Ventrian envoy, and a dozen more notables from the Emir's government. He kept his face impassive as he gazed around the converted warehouse. It was well known that he never smiled, save in the sand circle when his opponent began to weaken under his iron fists.

He glanced at Grassin, watching the man move through a series of loosening exercises. He had to hold back his smile then. Others

87

might believe Grassin was merely stretching tight muscles, but Borcha could read fear in the man's movements. He focused on the other fighters, staring at them. Few looked his way, and those who did cast fleeting glances, avoiding his eyes.

Losers, all of them, he thought.

He took a deep breath, filling his massive lungs. The air was hot and damp. Signalling to one of his aides, Borcha told the man to open the wide windows at either end of the warehouse. A second aide approached him. 'There is a yokel who wants to try a turn of the glass with you, Borcha.' The fighter was irritated and he surreptitiously studied the crowd. All eyes were on him. So the word was already out! He threw back his head and forced a laugh.

'Who is this man?'

'A stranger from the mountains. Youngster – around twenty, I'd say.'

'That explains his stupidity,' hissed Borcha. No man who had ever seen him fight would relish the prospect of four minutes in the sand circle with the champion of Mashrapur. But still he was annoyed.

Winning involved far more skills than with fists and feet, he knew. It was a complex mix of courage and heart, allied to the planting of the seeds of doubt in the minds of opponents. A man who believed his enemy was invincible had already lost, and Borcha had spent years building such a reputation.

No one in two years had dared to risk a turn of the glass with the champion.

Until now. Which threw up a second problem. Arena fights were without rules: a fighter could legitimately gouge out an opponent's eyes or, after downing him, stamp upon his neck. Deaths were rare, but not unknown, and many fighters were crippled for life. But Borcha would not be able to use his more deadly array of skills against an unknown youngster. It would suggest he feared the boy.

'They're offering fifteen to one against him surviving,' whispered the aide.

'Who is negotiating for him?'

'Old Thom.'

'How much has he wagered?'

88

'I'll find out.' The man moved away into the crowd.

The tournament organiser, a huge, obese merchant named Bilse, stepped into the sand circle. 'My friends,' he bellowed, his fat chins wobbling, 'welcome to the Blind Corsair. Tonight you will be privileged to witness the finest fist-fighters in Mashrapur.'

Borcha closed his mind to the man's droning voice. He had heard it all before. Five years ago his mood had been different. His wife and son sick from dysentery, the young Borcha had finished his work on the docks and had run all the way to the Corsair to win ten silver pieces in a warm-up contest. To his surprise he had beaten his opponent, and had taken his place in the tournament. That night, after hammering six fighters to defeat, he had taken home sixty golden raq. He had arrived at their rooms triumphant, only to find his son dead and his wife comatose. The best doctor in Mashrapur was summoned. He had insisted Caria be removed to a hospital in the rich northern district – but only after Borcha had parted with all his hard-won gold. There Caria rallied for a while, only to be struck down with consumption.

The treatment over the next two years cost three hundred raq.

And still she died, her body ravaged by sickness.

Borcha's bitterness was colossal, and he unleashed it in every fight, focusing his hatred and his fury on the men who faced him.

He heard his name called and raised his right arm. The crowd cheered and clapped.

Now he had a house in the northern quarter, built of marble and the finest timber, with terracotta tiles on the roof. Twenty slaves were on hand to do his bidding, and his investments in slaves and silks brought him an income to rival any of the senior merchants. Yet still he fought, the demons of the past driving him on.

Bilse announced that the warm-up contest would begin and Borcha watched as Grassin stepped into the circle to take on a burly dock-worker. The bout lasted barely a few seconds, Grassin lifting the man from his feet with an uppercut. Borcha's aide approached him. 'They have wagered around nine silver pieces. Is it important?'

Borcha shook his head. Had there been large sums involved it would have indicated trickery of some kind, perhaps a foreign fighter drafted in, a tough man from another city, a bruiser unknown in Mashrapur. But no. This was merely stupidity and arrogance combined.

Bilse called his name and Borcha stepped into the circle. He tested the sand beneath his feet. Too thick and it made for clumsy movement, too thin and a fighter could slide and lose balance. It was well raked. Satisfied, Borcha turned his gaze on the young man who had entered the circle from the other side.

He was young and some inches shorter than Borcha, though his shoulders were enormous. His chest was thick, the pectoral muscles well developed, and his biceps were huge. Watching him move, Borcha saw that he was well balanced and lithe. His waist was thick, but carried little fat, and his neck was large and well protected by the powerful, swollen muscles of the trapezius. Borcha transferred his gaze to his opponent's face. Strong cheekbones and a good chin. The nose was wide and flat, the brows heavy. The champion looked into the challenger's eyes; they were pale, and they showed no fear. Indeed, thought Borcha, he looks as if he hates me.

Bilse introduced the young man as 'Druss from the lands of the Drenai'. The two fighters approached one another. Borcha towered over Druss. The champion held out his hands but Druss merely smiled and walked back to the ropes, turning to wait for the signal to begin.

The casual insult did not concern the champion. Lifting his hands into the orthodox fighting position, left arm extended and right fist held close to the cheek, he advanced on the young man. Druss surged forward, almost taking Borcha by surprise. But the champion was fast and sent a thudding left jab into the young man's face, following it with a stinging right cross that thundered against Druss's jaw. Borcha stepped back, allowing room for Druss to fall, but something exploded against the side of the champion. For a moment he thought a large rock had been hurled from the crowd, then he realised it was the fist of his opponent. Far from falling, the young man had taken the two punches and hit back with one of his own. Borcha reeled from the blow, then counter-attacked with a series of combination strikes that snapped Druss's head back. Yet still he came on. Borcha feinted a jab to the head, then swept an uppercut into the young man's belly, whereupon Druss snarled and threw a wild right. Borcha ducked under it, dipping just in time to meet a rising left uppercut. He managed to roll his head, the blow striking his cheek. Surging upright, he crashed an overhand right into Druss's face, splitting the skin above the man's left eye; then he hit him with a left.

Druss staggered back, thrown off-balance, and Borcha moved in for the kill, but a hammer-blow hit him just under the heart and he felt a rib snap. Anger roared through him and he began to smash punches into the youngster's face and body – brutal, powerful blows that forced his opponent back towards the ropes. Another cut appeared, this time over Druss's right eye. The young man ducked and weaved, but more and more blows hammered home. Sensing victory, Borcha increased the ferocity of his attack and the pace of his punches. But Druss refused to go down and, ducking his head, he charged at Borcha. The champion side-stepped and threw a left that glanced from Druss's shoulder. The young man recovered his balance and Borcha stepped in. Druss wiped the blood from his eyes and advanced to meet him. The champion feinted with a left, but Druss ignored it and sent a right that swept under Borcha's guard and smashed into his injured ribs. The champion winced as pain lanced his side. A huge fist crashed against his chin and he felt a tooth snap; he responded with a left uppercut that lifted Druss to his toes and a right hook that almost felled the youngster. Druss hit him with another right to the ribs and Borcha was forced back. The two men began to circle one another, and only now did Borcha hear the baying of the crowd. They were cheering for Druss, just as five years before they had cheered for Borcha.

Druss attacked. Borcha threw a left that missed and a right that didn't. Druss rocked back on his heels, but advanced again. Borcha hit him three times, further opening the cuts that saw blood streaming into the young man's face. Almost blinded, Druss lashed out, one punch catching Borcha on the right bicep, numbing his arm, a second cracking against his brow. Blood seeped from the champion's face now, and a tremendous roar went up from the crowd.

Oblivious to the noise Borcha counter-attacked, driving Druss back across the circle, hitting him time and again with brutal hooks and jabs.

Then the horn sounded. The sandglass had run out. Borcha stepped back, but Druss attacked. Borcha grabbed him around the waist, pinning his arms and hauling him in close. 'It is over, boy,' he hissed. 'You won your wager.'

Druss jerked himself loose and shook his head, spraying blood to the sand. Then he lifted his hand and pointed at Borcha. 'You go to Collan,' he snarled, 'and you tell him that if anyone has harmed my wife I'll tear his head from his neck.'

Then the young man swung away and stalked from the circle.

Borcha turned and saw the other fighters watching him.

They were all willing to meet his eyes now . . . and Grassin was smiling.

Sieben entered the Tree of Bone just after midnight. There were still some hardened drinkers present, and the serving maids moved wearily among them. Sieben mounted the stairs to the gallery above and made his way to the room he shared with Druss. Just as he was about to open the door, he heard voices from within. Drawing his dagger, he threw open the door and leapt inside. Druss was sitting on one of the beds, his face bruised and swollen, the marks of rough stitches over both eyes. A dirt-streaked fat man was sitting on Sieben's bed and a slim, black-cloaked nobleman with a trident beard was standing by the window. As the poet entered the nobleman swung, a shining sabre hissing from its scabbard. The fat man screamed and dived from the bed, landing with a dull thud behind the seated Druss.

'You took your time, poet,' said the axeman.

Sieben gazed down at the point of the sabre which was motionless in the air some two inches from his throat. 'It didn't take you long to make new friends,' he said, with a forced smile. With great care he slipped the knife back into its sheath, and was relieved to see the nobleman return his sabre to its scabbard.

'This is Bodasen; he's a Ventrian,' said Druss. 'And the man on his knees behind me is Thom.'

The fat man rose, grinning sheepishly. 'Good to meet you, my lord,' he said, bowing.

'Who the Devil gave you those black eyes?' asked Sieben, moving forward to examine Druss's wounds.

'Nobody gave them to me. I had to fight for them.'

'He fought Borcha,' said Bodasen, with the faintest trace of an eastern accent. 'And a fine bout it was. Lasted a full turn of the glass.'

'Aye, it was something to see,' added Thom. 'Borcha didn't look none too pleased – especially when Druss cracked his rib! We all heard it. Wonderful, it was.'

'You fought Borcha?' whispered Sieben.

'To a standstill,' said the Ventrian. 'There were no surgeons present, so I assisted with the stitching. You are the poet Sieben, are you not?'

'Yes. Do I know you, my friend?'

'I saw you perform once in Drenan, and in Ventria I read your saga of Waylander. Wonderfully inventive.'

'Thank you. Much needed to be invention since little is known of him. I did not know that the book had travelled so far. Only fifty copies were made.'

'My Emperor acquired one on his travels, bound in leather and embossed with gold leaf. The script is very fine.'

'There were five of those,' said Sieben. 'Twenty raq each. Beautiful works.'

Bodasen chuckled. 'My Emperor paid six hundred for it.'

Sieben sighed and sat down on the bed. 'Ah well, better the fame than gold, eh? So tell me, Druss, what made you fight Borcha?'

'I earned a hundred silver pieces. Now I shall buy Rowena. Did you find out where she is held?'

'No, my friend. Collan has sold only one woman recently. A Seer. He must be keeping Rowena for himself.'

'Then I shall kill him and take her – and to Hell with the law of Mashrapur.'

'If I may,' said Bodasen, 'I think I can help. I am acquainted with this Collan. It may be that I can secure the release of your lady – without bloodshed.'

Sieben said nothing, but he noted the concern in the Ventrian's dark eyes.

'I'll not wait much longer,' said Druss. 'Can you see him tomorrow?'

'Of course. You will be here?'

'I'll wait for your word,' promised Druss.

'Very well. I bid you all good night,' said Bodasen, with a short bow.

After he had left Old Thom also made for the door. 'Well, lad, it were quite a night. If you decide to fight again I'd be honoured to make the arrangements.'

'No more for me,' said Druss. 'I'd sooner have trees fall on me than that man again.'

Thom shook his head. 'I wish that I'd had more faith,' he said. 'I only bet one silver piece of my share.' He chuckled and spread his hands. 'Ah well, that is life, I suppose.' His smile faded. 'A word of warning, Druss. Collan has many friends here. And there are those who will slit a man's throat for the price of a jug of ale. Walk with care.' He turned and left the room.

There was a jug of wine on the small table and Sieben filled a clay goblet and sat. 'You are a curious fellow, to be sure,' he said, grinning. 'But at least Borcha has improved your looks. I think your nose is broken.'

'I think you are right,' said Druss. 'So tell me of your day.'

'I visited four well-known slave traders. Collan brought no women with him to the slave markets. The story of your attack on Harib Ka is known everywhere. Some of the men who survived have now joined Collan, and they speak of you as a demon. But it is a mystery, Druss. I don't know where she could be – unless at his home.'

The wound above Druss's right eye began to seep blood. Sieben found a cloth and offered it to the axeman. Druss waved it away. 'It will seal. Forget about it.'

'By the gods, Druss, you must be in agony. Your face is swollen, your eyes black.'

'Pain lets you know you're alive,' said Druss. 'Did you spend your silver pennies on the whore?'

Sieben chuckled. 'Yes. She was very good – told me I was the best lovemaker she had ever known.'

'There's a surprise,' said Druss and Sieben laughed.

'Yes – but it's nice to hear.' He sipped his wine, then stood and gathered his belongings.

'Where are you going?' asked Druss.

'Not I . . . we. We'll move rooms.'

'I like it here.'

'Yes, it is quaint. But we need to sleep and – convivial as they both were – I see no reason to trust men I do not know. Collan will send killers after you, Druss. Bodasen may be in his employ, and as for the walking lice-sack who just left I think he'd sell his mother for a copper farthing. So trust me, and let's move.'

'I liked them both – but you are right. I do need sleep.'

Sieben stepped outside and called to a tavern maid, slipping her a silver piece and asking for their move to be kept secret – even from the landlord. She slipped the coin into the pocket of her leather apron and took the two men to the far end of the gallery. The new room was larger than the first, boasting three beds and two lanterns. A fire had been laid in the hearth, but it was unlit and the room was cold.

When the maid had departed Sieben lit the fire and sat beside it, watching the flames lick at the tinder. Druss pulled off his boots and jerkin and stretched out on the widest of the beds. Within moments he was asleep, his axe on the floor beside the bed.

Sieben lifted the baldric of knives from his shoulder and hooked it over the back of the chair. The fire blazed more brightly and he added several thick chunks of wood from the log basket beside the hearth. As the hours passed, all sounds from the inn below faded, and only the crackling of burning wood disturbed the silence. Sieben was tired, but he did not sleep.

Then he heard the sounds of men upon the stairs, stealthy footfalls. Drawing one of his knives he moved to the door, opening it a fraction and peering out. At the other end of the gallery some seven men were crowding around the door of their previous quarters; the landlord was with them. The door was wrenched open and the men surged inside, but moments later they returned. One of the newcomers took hold of the landlord by his shirt and pushed him against the wall. The frightened man's voice rose, and Sieben could just make out some of his words: 'They were ... honestly ... lives of my children ... they ... without paying ...' Sieben watched as the man was hurled to the floor. The would-be assassins then trooped down the gallery stairs and out into the night.

Pushing shut the door, Sieben returned to the fire.

And slept.

Borcha sat quietly while Collan berated the men he had sent in search of Druss. They stood shamefaced before him, heads down. 'How long have you been with me, Kotis?' he asked one of them, his voice low and thick with menace.

'Six years,' answered the man at the centre of the group, a tall, wide-shouldered bearded fist-fighter. Borcha remembered his destruction of this man; it had taken no more than a minute.

'Six years,' echoed Collan. 'And in that time have you seen other men fall foul of me?'

'Aye, I have. But we got the information from Old Thom. He swore they were staying in the Tree of Bone – and so they were. But they went into hiding after the fight with Borcha. We've men still looking; they won't be hard to find tomorrow.'

'You're right,' said Collan. 'They won't be hard to find; they'll be coming here!'

'You could give his wife back,' offered Bodasen, who was lounging on a couch on the far side of the room.

'I don't *give women back*. I take them! Anyway, I don't know which farm wench he's talking about. Most of those we took were freed when the madman attacked the camp. I expect his wife took a welcome opportunity to escape from his clutches.'

'He's not a man I'd want hunting me,' said Borcha. 'I've never hit anyone so hard – and seen them stay on their feet.'

'Get back out on the streets, all of you. Scour the inns and taverns near the docks. They won't be far. And understand this, Kotis, if he does walk into my home tomorrow I'll kill you!'

The men shuffled out and Borcha leaned back on the couch,

suppressing a groan as his injured rib lanced pain into his side. He had been forced to withdraw from the tournament, and that hurt his pride. Yet he felt a grudging admiration for the young fighter; he, too, would have taken on an army for Caria. 'You know what I think?' he offered.

'What?' snapped Collan.

'I think she's the witch you sold to Kabuchek. What was her name?'

'Rowena.'

'Did you rape her?'

'I didn't touch her,' lied Collan. 'And anyway, I've sold her to Kabuchek. He gave me five thousand in silver – just like that. I should have asked for ten.'

'I think you should see the Old Woman,' advised Borcha.

'I don't need a prophet to tell me how to deal with one country bumpkin and an axe. Now to business.' He turned to Bodasen. 'It is too early to have received word on our demands, so why are you here tonight?'

The Ventrian smiled, his teeth startlingly white against the black trident beard. 'I came because I told the young fighter that we were acquainted. I said I might be able to secure the release of his wife. But if you have already sold her, then I have wasted my time.'

'What concern is it of yours?'

Bodasen rose and flung his black cloak around his shoulders. 'I am a soldier, Collan – as you once were. And I know men. You should have seen his fight with Borcha. It wasn't pretty, it was brutal and almost terrifying. You are not dealing with a country bumpkin, you are facing a terrible killer. I don't believe you have the men to stop him.'

'Why should you care?'

'Ventria needs the Free Traders and you are my link to them. I don't want to see you dead just yet.'

'I am a fighter too, Bodasen,' said Collan.

'Indeed you are, Drenai. But let us review what we know. Harib Ka, according to those of his men who survived the raid, sent six men into the woods. They did not return. I spoke to Druss tonight and he

98

told me he killed them. I believe him. Then he attacked a camp where forty armed men were based. The men ran away. Now he has fought Borcha, whom most men, including myself, believed to be invincible. The rabble you just sent out will have no chance against him.'

'True,' admitted Collan, 'but as soon as he kills them the City Watch will take him. And I have only four more days to spend here; then I sail for the Free Trading ports. However, I take it you have some advice to offer?'

'Indeed I do. Get the woman back from Kabuchek and deliver her to Druss. Buy her or steal her – but do it, Collan.'

With a short, perfunctory bow the Ventrian officer left the room.

'I'd listen to him if I were you,' advised Borcha.

'Not you as well!' stormed Collan. 'By the gods, did he scramble your brains tonight? You and I both know what keeps us at the top of this filthy pile. Fear. Awe. Sometimes sheer terror. Where would my reputation be if I gave back a stolen woman?'

'You are quite right,' said Borcha, rising, 'but a reputation can be rebuilt. A life is something else. He said he'd tear off your head and he's a man who could do just that.'

'I never thought to see you running scared, my friend. I thought you were impervious to fear.'

Borcha smiled. 'I am strong, Collan. I use my reputation because it makes it easier to win but I don't *live* it. If I were to be in the path of a charging bull, then I would step aside, or turn and run, or climb a tree. A strong man should always know his limitations.'

'Well, he's helped you know yours, my friend,' said Collan, with a sneer.

Borcha smiled and shook his head. He left Collan's house and wandered through the northern streets. They were wider here, and lined with trees. Officers of the Watch marched by him, the captain saluting as he recognised the champion.

Former champion, thought Borcha. Now it was Grassin who would win the accolades.

Until next year. 'I'll be back,' whispered Borcha. 'I have to. It is all I have.'

*   *   *

Sieben floated to consciousness through layers of dreams. He was drifting on a blue lake, yet his body was dry; he was standing on an island of flowers, but could not feel the earth beneath his feet; he was lying on a satin bed, beside a statue of marble. At his touch she became flesh, but remained cold.

He opened his eyes and the dreams whispered away from his memory. Druss was still asleep. Sieben rose from the chair and stretched his back, then he gazed down on the sleeping warrior. The stitches on Druss's brows were tight and puckered, dried blood had stained both eyelids and his nose was swollen and discoloured. Yet despite the wounds his face radiated strength and Sieben felt chilled by the almost inhuman power of the youth.

Druss groaned and opened his eyes.

'How are you feeling this morning?' asked the poet.

'Like a horse galloped over my face,' answered Druss, rolling from the bed and pouring himself a goblet of water. Someone tapped at the door.

Sieben rose from his chair and drew a knife from its sheath. 'Who is it?'

'It is me, sir,' came the voice of the tavern-maid. 'There is a man to see you; he is downstairs.'

Sieben opened the door and the maid curtsied. 'Do you know him?' asked Sieben.

'He is the Ventrian gentleman who was here last night, sir.'

'Is he alone?'

'Yes, sir.'

'Send him up,' ordered Sieben. While they were waiting he told Druss about the men who had come searching for them the night before.

'You should have woken me,' said Druss.

'I thought we could do without a scene of carnage,' Sieben replied.

Bodasen entered and immediately crossed to where Druss stood by the window. He leaned in and examined the stitches on the axeman's eyebrows. 'They've held well,' said Bodasen, with a smile.

'What news?' asked Druss.

The Ventrian removed his black cloak and draped it over a chair. 'Last night Collan had men scouring the city for you. Assassins. But today he has come to his senses. This morning he sent a man to me with a message for you. He has decided to return your wife to you.'

'Good. When and where?'

'There is a quay about a half-mile west of here. He will meet you there tonight, one hour after dusk, and he will have Rowena with him. But he is a worried man, Druss; he doesn't want to die.'

'I'll not kill him,' promised Druss.

'He wants you to come alone – and unarmed.'

'Madness!' stormed Sieben. 'Does he think he is dealing with fools?'

'Whatever else he may be,' said Bodasen, 'he is still a Drenai noble. His word must be accepted.'

'Not by me,' hissed Sieben. 'He is a murdering renegade who has become rich by dealing in the misery of others. Drenai noble indeed!'

'I'll go,' said Druss. 'What other choices are there?'

'It is a trap, Druss. There is no honour in men like Collan. He'll be there, right enough – with a dozen or so killers.'

'They won't stop me,' insisted the axeman, his pale eyes gleaming. 'A knife through the throat can stop anyone.'

Bodasen stepped forward and laid his hand on Druss's shoulder. 'Collan assured me this was an honest trade. I would not have brought this message had I believed it to be false.'

Druss nodded and smiled. 'I believe you,' he said.

'How did you find us?' enquired Sieben.

'This is where you said you would be,' answered Bodasen.

'Exactly where will this meeting take place?' asked Druss. Bodasen gave directions and then bade them farewell.

When he had left Sieben turned on the young axeman. 'You truly believe him?'

'Of course. He is a Ventrian gentleman. My father told me they are the world's worst traders because they have a hatred of lies and deceit. They are reared that way.'

'Collan isn't a Ventrian,' Sieben pointed out.

101

'No,' agreed Druss, his expression grim. 'No, he is not. He is everything you described. And you are quite right, poet. It will be a trap.'

'And yet you will still go?'

'As I have already said, there are no other choices. But you don't have to be there. You owe Shadak – not me.'

Sieben smiled. 'You are quite right, old horse. So how shall we play this little game?'

An hour before dusk Collan sat in an upper room overlooking the quay. The bearded Kotis stood beside him. 'Is everyone in place?' asked the Drenai swordsman.

'Aye. Two crossbowmen, and six knife-fighters. Is Borcha coming?'

Collan's handsome face darkened. 'No.'

'He would make a difference,' observed Kotis.

'Why?' snapped Collan. 'He's already taken one beating from the peasant!'

'You really think he will come alone and unarmed?'

'Bodasen believes he will.'

'Gods, what a fool!'

Collan laughed. 'The world is full of fools, Kotis. That is how we grow rich.' He leaned out of the window and gazed down on the quayside. Several whores were lounging in doorways, and two beggars were accosting passers-by. A drunken dock-worker staggered from a tavern, collided with a wall and slid to the ground by a mooring post. He tried to rise, but as he lifted his work-sack he fell back, and then curled up on the stone and went to sleep. What a city, thought Collan! What a wonderful city. A whore moved to the sleeping man and dipped her fingers expertly into his money-pouch.

Collan stepped back from the window and drew his sabre. Taking a whetstone, he sharpened the edge. He had no intention of facing the peasant, but a man could never be too careful.

Kotis poured a goblet of cheap wine. 'Don't drink too much of that,' warned Collan. 'Even unarmed, the man can fight.'

'He won't fight so well with a crossbow bolt through the heart.'

Collan sat down in a padded leather chair and stretched out his long legs. 'In a few days we'll be rich, Kotis. Ventrian gold – enough to fill this squalid room. Then we'll sail to Naashan and buy a palace. Maybe more than one.'

'You think the pirates will aid Ventria?' asked Kotis.

'No, they've already taken Naashanite gold. Ventria is finished.'

'Then we keep Bodasen's money?'

'Of course. As I said, the world is full of fools. You know, I used to be one of them. I had dreams, I wasted half my life on them. Chivalry, gallantry. My father fed me the concepts until my mind was awash with dreams of knighthood and I truly believed it all.' Collan chuckled. 'Incredible! But I learnt the error of my ways. I became wise to the way of the world.'

'You are in good humour today,' observed Kotis. 'You'll have to kill Bodasen too. He won't be pleased when he learns he's been tricked.'

'Him I'll fight,' said Collan. 'Ventrians! A pox on them! They think they're better than everyone else. Bodasen more than most; he thinks he's a swordsman. We'll see. I'll cut him a piece at a time, a nick here and a slash there. He'll suffer well enough. I'll break his pride before I kill him.'

'He may be better than you,' ventured Kotis.

'No one is better than me, with sabre or short blade.'

'They say Shadak is one of the best who ever lived.'

'Shadak is an old man!' stormed Collan, surging to his feet, 'and even at his best he could not have faced me.'

Kotis paled and began to stammer out an apology. 'Be silent!' snapped Collan. 'Get outside and check that the men are in position.'

As Kotis backed from the room, Collan poured himself a goblet of wine and sat down by the window. Shadak! Always Shadak. What was it about the man that inspired men to revere him? What had he ever done? Shema's balls, I've killed twice as many swordsmen as the old man! But do they sing songs about Collan? No.

One day I'll hunt him out, he promised himself. Somewhere in public view, where men can see the great Shadak humbled. He glanced out of the window. The sun was setting, turning the sea to fire.

Soon the peasant would arrive. Soon the enjoyment would begin.

* * *

Druss approached the quayside. There was a ship moored at the far end; dock-workers were untying the mooring ropes and hurling them to the decks, while aloft sailors were unfurling the great square of the main-mast. Gulls swooped above the vessel, their wings silver in the moonlight.

The young warrior glanced along the quayside, which was almost deserted save for two whores and a sleeping man. He scanned the buildings, but all the windows were closed. He could taste fear in his mouth, not for his own safety but for Rowena's should Collan kill him. A life of slavery beckoned for her, and Druss could not bear that.

The wounds above his eyes were stinging, and a dull, thudding headache reminded him of the bout with Borcha. He hawked and spat, then made for the quay. From the shadows to his right a man moved.

'Druss!' came a low voice. He stopped and turned his head to see Old Thom standing just inside the mouth of a dark alleyway.

'What do you want?' asked Druss.

'They're waiting for you, lad. There's nine of them. Go back!'

'I cannot. They have my wife.'

'Damn you, boy, you're going to die.'

'We'll see.'

'Listen to me. Two have crossbows. Keep close to the wall on the right. The bowmen are in upper rooms; they'll not be able to sight their weapons if you keep to the wall.'

'I'll do that,' said Druss. 'Thank you, old man.'

Thom faded back into the shadows and was gone. Drawing in a deep breath, Druss moved on to the quay. Above and ahead of him he saw a window open. Altering his line, he moved in towards the walls of the moonlit buildings.

'Where are you, Collan?' he shouted.

Armed men moved out of the shadows and he saw the tall, handsome figure of Collan among them. Druss walked forward. 'Where is my wife?' he called.

'That's the beauty of it,' answered Collan, pointing at the ship. 'She's on board – sold to the merchant Kapuchek, who is even now sailing for his home in Ventria. Maybe she will even see you die!'

'In your dreams!' snarled Druss as he charged the waiting men. Behind them the drunken dock-worker suddenly rose, two knives in his hands. One blade flashed by Collan's head, burying itself to the hilt in Kotis's neck.

A dagger swept towards Druss's belly, but he brushed the attacker's arm aside and delivered a bone-crunching blow to the man's chin, spinning him into the path of the warriors behind him. A knife plunged into Druss's back. Twisting, he grabbed the wielder by the throat and groin and hurled him into the remaining men.

Sieben pulled Snaga from the work-sack and threw it through the air. Druss caught the weapon smoothly. Moonlight glittered from the terrible blades and the attackers scattered and ran.

Druss ran towards the ship, which was gliding slowly away from the quayside.

'Rowena!' he yelled. Something struck him in the back and he staggered, then fell to his knees. He saw Sieben run forward. The poet's arm went back, then swept down. Druss half turned to see a crossbowman outlined against a window-frame; the man dropped his bow, then tumbled from the window with a knife embedded in his eye.

Sieben knelt alongside Druss. 'Lie still,' he said. 'You've a bolt in your back!'

'Get away from me!' shouted Druss, levering himself to his feet. 'Rowena!'

He stumbled forward but the ship was moving away from the quay more swiftly now, the wind catching the sail. Druss could feel blood from his wounds streaming down his back and pooling above his belt. A terrible lethargy swept over him and he fell again.

Sieben came alongside. 'We must get you to a surgeon,' he heard Sieben say. Then the poet's voice receded away from him, and a great roaring filled his ears. Straining his eyes, he saw the ship angle towards the east, the great sail filling.

'Rowena!' he shouted. 'Rowena!' The stone of the quay was cold against his face, and the distant cries of the gulls mocked his anguish. Pain flowed through him as he struggled to rise . . .

And fell from the edge of the world.

*   *   *

Collan raced along the quay, then glanced back. He saw the giant warrior down, his companion kneeling beside him. Halting his flight, he sat down on a mooring-post to recover his breath. It was unbelievable! Unarmed, the giant had attacked armed men, scattering them. Borcha was right. The charging bull analogy had been very perceptive. Tomorrow Collan would move to a hiding place in the south of the city and then, as Borcha had advised, seek out the old woman. That was the answer. Pay her to cast a spell, or send a demon, or supply poison. Anything.

Collan rose – and saw a dark figure standing in the moon shadows by the wall. The man was watching him. 'What are you staring at?' he said.

The shadowy figure moved towards him, moonlight bathing his face. He wore a tunic shirt of soft black leather, and two short swords were scabbarded at his hips. His hair was black and long, and tied in a ponytail. 'Do I know you?' asked Collan.

'You will, renegade,' said the man, drawing his right-hand sword.

'You've chosen the wrong man to rob,' Collan told him. His sabre came up and he slashed the air to left and right, loosening his wrist.

'I'm not here to rob you, Collan,' said the man, advancing. 'I'm here to kill you.'

Collan waited until his opponent was within a few paces and then he leapt forward, lunging his sabre towards the man's chest. There was a clash of steel as their blades met. Collan's sabre was parried and a lightning riposte swept at the swordsman's throat. Collan jumped back, the point of the sword missing his eye by less than an inch. 'You are swift, my friend. I underestimated you.'

'It happens,' said the man.

Collan attacked again, this time with a series of sweeps and thrusts aiming for neck and belly. Their blades glittered in the moonlight and all around them windows were opened as the discordant clashing of steel echoed along the quay. Whores leaned out over the window-sills, yelling encouragement; beggars appeared from alleyways; a nearby tavern emptied and a crowd gathered in a large circle around the duelling men. Collan was enjoying himself. His attacks were forcing his opponent back, and he had now taken the measure of the man. The stranger was fast and lithe, cool under pressure; but he was no longer young and Collan could sense he was tiring. At first he had made several counter-attacks, but these were fewer now as he desperately fended off the younger man's blade. Collan feinted a cut, then rolled, his wrist lunging forward on to his right foot. The stranger blocked too late, the point of the sabre piercing the man's left shoulder. Collan leapt back, his blade sliding clear. 'Almost time to die, old man,' said Collan.

'Yes. How does it feel?' countered his opponent.

Collan laughed. 'You have nerve, I'll say that for you. Before I kill you, will you tell me why you are hunting me? A wronged wife, perhaps? A despoiled daughter? Or are you a hired assassin?'

'I am Shadak,' said the man.

Collan grinned. 'So the night is not a total waste.' He glanced at the crowd. 'The great Shadak!' he said, his voice rising. 'This is the famed hunter, the mighty swordsman. See him bleed? Well, my friends, you can tell your children how you saw him die! How Collan slew the man of legend.'

He advanced on the waiting Shadak, then raised his sabre in a mock salute. 'I have enjoyed this duel, old man,' he said, 'but now it is time to end it.' Even as he spoke he leapt, sending a fast reverse cut towards Shadak's right side. As his opponent parried Collan rolled his wrist, the sabre rolling over the blocking blade and sweeping up towards Shadak's unprotected neck. It was the classic killing stroke, and one Collan had employed many times, but Shadak swayed to his left, the sabre cutting into his right shoulder. Collan felt a searing pain in his belly and glanced down. Horrified, he saw Shadak's sword jutting there.

'Burn in Hell!' hissed Shadak, wrenching the blade clear. Collan screamed and fell to his knees, his sabre clattering against the stones of the quay. He could feel his heart hammering and agony, red-hot acid pain, scorched through him. He cried out: 'Help me!'

The crowd was silent now. Collan fell face down on the stones. I can't be dying, he thought. Not me. Not Collan.

The pain receded, replaced by a soothing warmth that stole across his tortured mind. He opened his eyes and could see his sabre glinting on the stones just ahead. He reached out for it, his fingers touching the hilt.

'I can still win!' he told himself. 'I can . . .'

Shadak sheathed his sword and stared down at the dead man. Already the beggars were around him, pulling at his boots and ripping at his belt. Shadak turned away and pushed through the crowd.

He saw Sieben kneeling beside the still figure of Druss, and his heart sank. Moving more swiftly, he came alongside the body and knelt down.

'He's dead,' said Sieben.

'In your . . . dreams,' hissed Druss. 'Get me to my feet.'

Shadak chuckled. 'Some men take a sight of killing,' he told the poet. The two men hauled Druss upright.

'She's out there,' said Druss, staring at the ship that was slowly shrinking against the distant horizon.

'I know, my friend,' said Shadak softly. 'But we'll find her. Now let's get you to a surgeon.'

Book Two

The Demon in the Axe

Prologue

The ship glided from the harbour, the early evening swell rippling against the hull. Rowena stood on the aft deck, the tiny figure of Pudri beside her. Above them, unnoticed on the raised tiller deck, stood the Ventrian merchant Kabuchek. Tall and cadaverously thin, he stared at the dock. He had seen Collan cut down by an unknown swordsman, and had watched the giant Drenai warrior battle his way through Collan's men. Interesting, he thought, what men will do for love.

His thoughts flew back to his youth in Varsipis and his desire for the young maiden Harenini. Did I love her then, he wondered? Or has time added colours to the otherwise grey days of youth?

The ship lifted on the swell as the vessel approached the harbour mouth and the surging tides beyond. Kabuchek glanced down at the girl; Collan had sold her cheaply. Five thousand pieces of silver for a talent such as hers? Ludicrous. He had been prepared for a charlatan, or a clever trickster. But she had taken his hand, looked into his eyes and said a single word: 'Harenini'. Kabuchek had kept the shock from his face. He had not heard her name in twenty-five years, and certainly there was no way that the pirate Collan could have known of his juvenile infatuation. Though already convinced of her talents, Kabuchek asked many questions until finally he turned to Collan. 'It appears she has a modicum of talent,' he said. 'What price are you asking?'

'Five thousand.'

Kabuchek swung to his servant, the eunuch Pudri. 'Pay him,' he said, concealing the smile of triumph and contenting himself with the tormented look which appeared on Collan's face. 'I will take her to the ship myself.'

Now, judging by how close the axeman had come, he congratulated himself upon his shrewdness. He heard Pudri's gentle voice speaking to the girl.

'I pray your husband is not dead,' said Pudri. Kabuchek glanced back at the dock and saw two Drenai warriors were kneeling beside the still figure of the axeman.

'He will live,' said Rowena, tears filling her eyes. 'And he will follow me.'

If he does, thought Kabuchek, I will have him slain.

'He has a great love for you, *Pahtai*,' said Pudri soothingly. 'So it should be between husband and wife. It rarely happens that way, however. I myself have had three wives – and none of them loved me. But then a eunuch is not the ideal mate.'

The girl watched the tiny figures on the dock until the ship had slipped out of the harbour and the lights of Mashrapur became distant twinkling candles. She sighed and sank down on the rail seat, her head bowed, tears spilling from her eyes.

Pudri sat beside her, his slender arm on her shoulders. 'Yes,' he whispered, 'tears are good. Very good.' Patting her back as if she were a small child, he sat beside her and whispered meaningless platitudes.

Kabuchek climbed down the deck steps and approached them. 'Bring her to my cabin,' he ordered Pudri.

Rowena glanced up at the harsh face of her new master. His nose was long and hooked, like the beak of an eagle, and his skin was darker than any she had seen, almost black. His eyes, however, were a bright blue beneath thick brows. Beside her Pudri stood, helping her to her feet, and together they followed the Ventrian merchant down the steps to the aft cabin. Lanterns were lit here, hanging on bronze hooks from low oak beams.

Kabuchek sat down behind a desk of polished mahogany. 'Cast the runes for the voyage,' he ordered Rowena.

'I do not cast runes,' she said. 'I would not know how.'

He waved his hand dismissively. 'Do whatever it is you do, woman. The sea is a treacherous mistress and I need to know how the voyage will be.'

Rowena sat opposite him. 'Give me your hand,' she said. Leaning forward, he struck her face with his open palm. It was not a heavy blow, but it stung the skin.

'You will address me always as *master*,' he said, without any display of anger. His bright blue eyes scrutinised her face for any sign of anger or defiance, but found himself gazing into calm hazel eyes which appeared to be appraising him. Curiously he felt like apologising for the blow, which was a ridiculous thought. It was not intended to hurt, being merely a swift method of establishing authority – ownership. He cleared his throat. 'I expect you to learn swiftly the ways of Ventrian households. You will be well cared for and well fed; your quarters will be comfortable and warm in winter, cool in summer. But you are a slave: understand that. I own you. You are property. Do you understand this?'

'I understand . . . *master*,' said the girl. The title was said with just a touch of emphasis, but without insolence.

'Very well. Then let us move on to more important matters.' He extended his hand.

Rowena reached out and touched his open palm. At first she could see only the details of his recent past, his agreement with the traitors who had slain the Ventrian Emperor, one of them a hawk-faced man. Kabuchek was kneeling before him and there was blood on the man's sleeve. A name whispered into her mind – Shabag.

'What's that you say?' hissed Kabuchek.

Rowena blinked, then realised she must have spoken the name. 'I see a tall man with blood on his sleeve. You are kneeling before him . . .'

'The future, girl! Not the past.' From the decks above came a great flapping as if some giant flying beast was descending from the sky. Rowena was startled. 'It is just the mainsail,' said Kabuchek. 'Concentrate, girl!'

Closing her eyes, Rowena allowed her mind to drift. She could see the ship now from above, floating on a clear sea beneath a sky of brilliant blue. Then another ship hove into sight, a trireme, its three banks of oars sending up a white spray as it sheared through the waves towards them. Rowena floated closer . . . closer. Armed men filled the trireme's deck.

Silver-grey forms swam around the trireme – great fish, twenty feet long, with fins like spear points cutting through the water. Rowena watched as the two ships crashed together, saw men falling into the water and the sleek grey fish rising up towards them. Blood billowed into the sea, and she saw the jagged teeth in the mouths of the fish, saw them rend and tear and dismember the helpless sailors thrashing in the water.

The battle on the ship's deck was short and brutal. She saw herself and Pudri, and the tall form of Kabuchek clambering over the aft rail and leaping out into the waves.

The killer fish circled them – then moved in.

Rowena could watch no more and, jerking her mind to the present, she opened her eyes.

'Well, what did you see?' asked Kabuchek.

'A black-sailed trireme, master.'

'Earin Shad,' whispered Pudri, his face pale, his eyes fearful.

'Do we escape him?' asked Kabuchek.

'Yes,' said Rowena, her voice dull, her thoughts full of despair, 'we escape Earin Shad.'

'Good. I am well satisfied,' announced Kabuchek. He glanced at Pudri. 'Take her to her cabin and give her some food. She is looking pale.'

Pudri led Rowena back along the narrow corridor to a small door. Pushing it open, he stepped inside. 'The bed is very small, but you are not large. I think it will suffice, *Pahtai*.' Rowena nodded dumbly and sat.

'You saw more than you told the master,' he said.

'Yes. There were fish, huge fish, dark with terrible teeth.'

'Sharks,' said Pudri, sitting beside her.

'This ship will be sunk,' she told him. 'And you and I, and Kabuchek, will leap into the sea, where the sharks will be waiting.'

114

1

Sieben sat in an outer room, sunlight slanting through the shuttered window at his back. He could hear low voices from the room beyond – a man's deep, pleading tones, and the harsh responses from the Old Woman. Muffled by the thick walls of stone and the oak door, the words were lost – which was just as well, since Sieben had no wish to hear the conversation. The Old Woman had many clients, most seeking the murder of rivals – at least, according to the whispered gossip he had heard.

He closed his ears to the voices and concentrated instead on the shafts of light and the gleaming dust motes dancing within them. The room was bare of ornament save for the three seats of plain, unfinished wood. They were not even well made and Sieben guessed they had been bought in the southern quarter, where the poor spent what little money they had.

Idly he swept his hand through a shaft of light. The dust scattered and swirled.

The oak door opened and a middle-aged man emerged. Seeing Sieben, he swiftly turned his face away and hurried from the house. The poet rose and moved towards the open door. The room beyond was scarcely better furnished than the waiting area. There was a broad table with ill-fitting joints, two hard wood chairs and a single shutter window. No light shone through the slats and Sieben saw that old cloths had been wedged between them.

'A curtain would have been sufficient to block the light,' he said, forcing a lightness of tone he did not feel.

The Old Woman did not smile, her face impassive in the light of the red-glassed lantern on the table before her.

'Sit,' she said.

He did so, and tried to stop himself from considering her awesome ugliness. Her teeth were multi-coloured – green, grey and the brown of rotting vegetation. Her eyes were rheumy, and a cataract had formed in the left. She was wearing a loose-fitting gown of faded red, and a gold talisman was partially hidden in the wrinkled folds of her neck.

'Put the gold upon the table,' she said. He lifted a single gold raq from the pouch at his side and slid it towards her. Making no move to pick up the coin, she looked into his face. 'What do you require of me?' she asked him.

'I have a friend who is dying.'

'The young axeman.'

'Yes. The surgeons have done all they can, but there is poison within his lungs, and the knife wound in his lower back will not heal.'

'You have something of his with you?'

Sieben nodded and pulled the silver-knuckled gauntlet from his belt. She took it from his hand and sat in silence, running the calloused skin of her thumb across the leather and metal. 'The surgeon is Calvar Syn,' she said. 'What does he say?'

'Only that Druss should already be dead. The poison in his system is spreading; they are forcing liquids into him, but his weight is falling away and he has not opened his eyes in four days.'

'What would you have me do?'

Sieben shrugged. 'It is said you are very skilled in herbs. I thought you might save him.'

She laughed suddenly, the sound dry and harsh. 'My herbs do not usually prolong life, Sieben.' Laying the gauntlet upon the table, she leaned back in her chair. 'He suffers,' she said. 'He has lost his lady, and his will to live is fading. Without the will, there is no hope.'

'There is nothing you can do?'

'About his will? No. But his lady is on board a ship bound for Ventria and she is safe – for the moment. But the war sweeps on and who can say what will become of a slave-girl if she reaches that battle-torn continent? Go back to the hospital. Take your friend to the house Shadak is preparing for you.'

'He will die, then?'

She smiled, and Sieben tore his eyes from the sudden show of rotting teeth. 'Perhaps ... Place him in a room where the sunlight enters in the morning, and lay his axe upon his bed, his fingers upon the hilt.' Her hand snaked across the table, and the gold raq vanished into her palm.

'That is all you can tell me for an ounce of gold?'

'It is all you need to know. Place his hand upon the hilt.'

Sieben rose. 'I had expected more.'

'Life is full of disappointments, Sieben.'

He moved to the door, but her voice stopped him. 'Do not touch the blades,' she warned.

'What?'

'Carry the weapon with care.'

Shaking his head, he left the house. The sun was hidden now behind dark clouds, and rain began to fall.

Druss was sitting alone and exhausted upon a grim mountainside, the sky above him grey and forlorn, the earth around him arid and dry. He gazed up at the towering peaks so far above him and levered himself to his feet. His legs were unsteady, and he had been climbing for so long that all sense of time had vanished. All he knew was that Rowena waited on the topmost peak, and he must find her. Some twenty paces ahead was a jutting finger of rock and Druss set off towards it, forcing his aching limbs to push his weary body on and up. Blood was gushing from the wounds in his back, making the ground treacherous around his feet. He fell. Then he crawled.

It seemed that hours had passed.

He looked up. The jutting finger of rock was now forty paces from him.

Despair came fleetingly, but was washed away on a tidal wave of rage. He crawled on. Ever on.

'I won't give up,' he hissed. 'Ever.'

117

Something cold touched his hand, his fingers closing around an object of steel. And he heard a voice. 'I am back, my brother.'

Something in the words chilled him. He gazed down at the silver axe – and felt his wounds heal, his strength flooding back into his frame.

Rising smoothly, he looked up at the mountain.

It was merely a hill.

Swiftly he strode to the top. And woke.

Calvar Syn patted Druss's back. 'Put on your shirt, young man,' he said. 'The wounds have finally healed. There is a little pus, but the blood is fresh and the scab contains no corruption. I congratulate you on your strength.'

Druss nodded, but did not reply. Slowly and with care he pulled on his shirt of grey wool, then leaned back exhausted on the bed. Calvar Syn reached out, gently pressing his index finger to the pulse point on the young man's throat. The beat was erratic and fast, but this was to be expected after such a long infection. 'Take a deep breath,' ordered the surgeon and Druss obeyed. 'The right lung is still not operating at full efficiency; but it will. I want you to move out into the garden. Enjoy the sunshine and the sea air.'

The surgeon rose and left the room, walking down the long hallways and out into the gardens beyond. He saw the poet, Sieben, sitting beneath a spreading elm and tossing pebbles into a manmade pond. Calvar Syn wandered to the poolside.

'Your friend is improving, but not as swiftly as I had hoped,' he said.

'Did you bleed him?'

'No. There is no longer a fever. He is very silent ... withdrawn.'

Sieben nodded. 'His wife was taken from him.'

'Very sad, I'm sure. But there are other women in the world,' observed the surgeon.

'Not for him. He loves her, he's going after her.'

'He'll waste his life,' said Calvar. 'Has he any idea of the size of the Ventrian continent? There are thousands upon thousands of small towns and villages, and more than three hundred major cities. Then there is the war. All shipping has ceased. How will he get there?'

'Of course he understands. But he's Druss – he's not like you or me, surgeon.' The poet chuckled and threw another pebble. 'He's an old-fashioned hero. You don't see many these days. He'll find a way.'

Calvar cleared his throat. 'Hmmm. Well, your old-fashioned hero is currently as strong as a three-day lamb. He is deep in a melancholic state, and until he recovers from it I cannot see him improving. Feed him red meat and dark green vegetables. He needs food for the blood.' He cleared his throat again, and stood silently.

'Was there something else?' asked the poet.

Calvar cursed inwardly. People were always the same. As soon as they were sick, they sent at speed for the doctor. But when it came to the time for settling accounts . . . No one expected a baker to part with bread without coin. Not so a surgeon. 'There is the question of my fee,' he said coldly.

'Ah, yes. How much is it?'

'Thirty raq.'

'Shema's balls! No wonder you surgeons live in palaces.'

Calvar sighed, but kept his temper. 'I do not live in a palace; I have a small house to the north. And the reason why surgeons must charge such fees is that a great number of patients renege. Your friend has been ill now for two months. During this time I have made more than thirty visits to this house, and I have had to purchase many expensive herbs. Three times now you have promised to settle the account. On each occasion you ask me how much is it. So you have the money?'

'No,' admitted Sieben.

'How much do you have?'

'Five raq.'

Calvar held out his hand and Sieben handed him the coins. 'You have until this time next week to find the rest of the money. After that I shall inform the Watch. In Mashrapur the law is simple: if you do not honour your debts your property will be sequestered. Since this house does not belong to you and, as far as I know, you have no source of income, you are likely to be imprisoned until sold as a slave. Until next week then.'

Calvar turned away and strode through the garden, his anger mounting.

Another bad debt.

One day I really will go to the Watch, he promised himself. He strolled on through the narrow streets, his medicine bag swinging from his narrow shoulders.

'Doctor! Doctor!' came a woman's voice and he swung to see a young woman running towards him. Sighing he waited. 'Could you come with me? It's my son, he has a fever.' Calvar looked down at the woman. Her dress was of poor quality, and old. She wore no shoes.

'And how will you pay me?' he asked, the question springing from the residue of his anger.

She stood silent for a moment. 'You can take everything I have,' she said simply.

He shook his head, his anger finally disappearing. 'That will not be necessary,' he told her, with a professional smile.

He arrived home a little after midnight. His servant had left him a cold meal of meat and cheese. Calvar stretched out on a leather-covered couch and sipped a goblet of wine.

Untying his money-pouch, he tipped the contents to the table. Three raq tumbled to the wooden surface. 'You will never be rich, Calvar,' he said, with a wry smile.

He had sat with the boy while the mother was out buying food. She had returned with eggs, and meat, and milk, and bread, her face glowing. It was worth two raq just to see her expression, he thought.

Druss made his way slowly out into the garden. The moon was high, the stars bright. He remembered a poem of Sieben's: *Glitter dust in the lair of night*. Yes, that's how the stars looked. He was breathing heavily by the time he reached the circular seat constructed around the bole of the elm. Take a deep breath, the surgeon had ordered. Deep? It felt as if a huge lump of stone had been wedged into his lungs, blocking all air.

The crossbow bolt had pierced cleanly, but it had also driven a tiny portion of his shirt into the wound, and this had caused the poison that drained his strength.

The wind was cool, and bats circled above the trees. *Strength*. Druss realised now just how much he had undervalued the awesome power of his body. One small bolt and a hastily thrust knife had reduced him to this shambling, weak shell. How, in this state, could he rescue Rowena?

Despair struck him like a fist under the heart. Rescue her? He did not even know where she was, save that thousands of miles now separated them. No Ventrian ships sailed, and even if they did he had no gold with which to purchase passage.

He gazed back at the house where golden light gleamed from Sieben's window. It was a fine house, better than any Druss had ever visited. Shadak had arranged for them to rent the property, the owner being trapped in Ventria. But the rent was due.

The surgeon had told him it would be two months before his strength began to return.

We'll starve before then, thought Druss. Levering himself to his feet, he walked on to the high wall at the rear of the garden. By the time he reached it his legs felt boneless, his breath coming in ragged gasps. The house seemed an infinite distance away. Druss struck out for it, but had to stop by the pond and sit at the water's edge. Splashing his face, he waited until his feeble strength returned, then rose and stumbled to the rear doors. The iron gate at the far end of the garden was lost in shadow now. He wanted to walk there once more, but his will was gone.

As he was about to enter the building he saw movement from the corner of his eye. He swung, ponderously, and a man moved from the shadows.

'Good to see you alive, lad,' said Old Thom.

Druss smiled. 'There is an ornate door-knocker at the front of the house,' he said.

'Didn't know as I'd be welcome,' the old man replied.

Druss led the way into the house, turning left into the large meeting room with its four couches and six padded chairs. Thom moved to the hearth, lighting a taper from the dying flames of the fire, then touching it to the wick of a lantern set on the wall. 'Help yourself to a drink,' offered Druss. Old Thom poured a goblet of red wine, then a second which he passed to the young man.

'You've lost a lot of weight, lad, and you look like an old man,' said Thom cheerfully.

'I've felt better.'

'I see Shadak spoke up for you with the magistrates. No action to be taken over the fight at the quay. Good to have friends, eh? And don't worry about Calvar Syn.'

'Why should I worry about him?'

'Unpaid debt. He could have you sold into slavery – but he won't. Soft, he is.'

'I thought Sieben had paid him. I'll not be beholden to any man.'

'Good words, lad. For good words and a copper farthing you can buy a loaf of bread.'

'I'll get the money to pay him,' promised Druss.

'Of course you will, lad. The best way – in the sand circle. But we've got to get your strength up first. You need to work – though my tongue should turn black for saying it.'

'I need time,' said Druss.

'You've little time, lad. Borcha is looking for you. You took away his reputation and he says he'll beat you to death when he finds you.'

'Does he indeed?' hissed Druss, his pale eyes gleaming.

'That's more like it, my bonny lad! Anger, that's what you need! Right, well I'll leave you now. By the way, they're felling trees to the west of the city, clearing the ground for some new buildings. They're looking for workers. Two silver pennies a day. It ain't much, but it's work.'

'I'll think on it.'

'I'll leave you to your rest, lad. You look like you need it.'

Druss watched the old man leave, then walked out into the garden once more. His muscles ached, and his heart was beating to a ragged drum. But Borcha's face was fixed before his mind's eye and he forced himself to walk to the gate and back.

Three times . . .

Vintar rose from his bed, moving quietly so as not to wake the four priests who shared the small room in the southern wing. Dressing himself in a long white habit of rough wool, he padded barefoot

122

along the cold stone of the corridor and up the winding steps to the ancient battlements.

From here he could see the mountain range that separated Lentria from the lands of the Drenai. The moon was high, half full, the sky cloudless. Beyond the temple the trees of the forest shimmered in the spectral light.

'The night is a good time for meditation, my son,' said the Abbot, stepping from the shadows. 'But you will need your strength for the day. You are falling behind in your sword work.' The Abbot was a broad-shouldered, powerful man who had once been a mercenary. His face bore a jagged scar from his right cheekbone down to his rugged jaw.

'I am not meditating, Father. I cannot stop thinking about the woman.'

'The one taken by slavers?'

'Yes. She haunts me.'

'You are here because your parents gave you into my custody, but you remain of your own free will. Should you desire to leave and find this girl you may do so. The Thirty will survive, Vintar.'

The young man sighed. 'I do not wish to leave, Father. And it is not that I desire her.' He smiled wistfully. 'I have never desired a woman. But there was something about her that I cannot shake from my thoughts.'

'Come with me, my boy. It is cold here, and I have a fire. We will talk.'

Vintar followed the burly Abbot into the western wing and the two men sat in the Abbot's study as the sky paled towards dawn. 'Sometimes,' said the Abbot, as he hung a copper kettle over the flames, 'it is hard to define the will of the Source. I have known men who wished to travel to far lands. They prayed for guidance. Amazingly they found that the Source was guiding them to do just what they wished for. I say *amazingly* because, in my experience, the Source rarely sends a man where he wants to go. That is part of the sacrifice we make when we serve Him. I do not say it never happens, you understand, for that would be arrogance. No, but when one prays for guidance it should be with an open mind, all thoughts of one's own desires put aside.'

The kettle began to hiss, clouds of vapour puffing from the curved spout. Shielding his hands with a cloth, the Abbot poured the water into a second pot, in which he had spooned dried herbs. Placing the kettle in the hearth, he sat back in an old leather chair.

'Now the Source very rarely speaks to us directly, and the question is: How do we know what is required? These matters are very complex. You chose to absent yourself from study, and soar across the Heavens. In doing so you rescued the spirit of a young girl and led her home to her abused body. Coincidence? I distrust coincidence. Therefore it is my belief, though I may be wrong, that the Source led you to her. And that is why she now haunts your mind. Your dealings with her are not yet concluded.'

'You think I should seek her out?'

'I do. Take yourself to the south wing library. There is a small cell beyond it. I will excuse you from all studies tomorrow.'

'But how shall I find her again, Lord Abbot? She was a slave. She could be anywhere.'

'Start with the man who was abusing her. You know his name – Collan. You know where he was planning to take her – Mashrapur. Let your spirit search begin there.'

The Abbot poured tea into two clay cups. The aroma was sweet and heady. 'I am the least talented of all the priests,' said Vintar sorrowfully. 'Surely it would be better to pray for the Source to send someone stronger?'

The Abbot chuckled. 'It is so strange, my boy. Many people say they wish to serve the Lord of All Peace. But in an advisory capacity: "Ah, my God, you are most wondrous, having created all the planets and the stars. However, you are quite wrong to choose me. I know this, for I am Vintar, and I am weak." '

'You mock me, Father.'

'Of course I mock you. But I do so with at least a modicum of love in my heart. I was a soldier, a killer, a drunkard, a womaniser. How do you think I felt when He chose me to become a member of the Thirty? And when my brother priests stood facing death, can you imagine my despair at being told I was the one who must survive? I was to be the new Abbot. I was to gather the new Thirty. Oh, Vintar, you have much to learn. Find this girl. I rather believe that in doing so you will find something for yourself.'

The young priest finished his tea and stood. 'Thank you, Father, for your kindness.'

'You told me she has a husband who was searching for her,' said the Abbot.

'Yes. A man named Druss.'

'Perhaps he will still be in Mashrapur.'

An hour later, in the bright sky above the city, the spirit of the young priest hovered. From here, despite the distance that made the buildings and palaces seem tiny, like the building bricks of an infant, he could feel the pulsing heart of Mashrapur, like a beast upon wakening; ravenous, filled with greed and lust. Dark emotions radiated from the city, filling his thoughts and swamping the purity he fought so hard to maintain. He dropped closer, closer still.

Now he could see the dock-workers strolling to work, and the whores plying the early-morning trade and the merchants opening their shops and stalls.

Where to begin? He had no idea.

For hours he flew aimlessly, touching a mind here, a thought there, seeking knowledge of Collan, Rowena or Druss. He found nothing save greed, or want, hunger or dissipation, lust or, so rarely, love.

Tired and defeated, he was ready to return to the Temple when he felt a sudden pull on his spirit, as if a rope had attached itself to him. In panic he tried to pull away, but though he used all his strength he was drawn inexorably down into a room where all the windows had been barred. An elderly woman was sitting before a red lantern. She gazed up at him as he floated just below the ceiling.

'Ah, but you are a treat to these old eyes, my pretty,' she said. Suddenly shocked, Vintar realised that his form was naked and he clothed himself in an instant in robes of white. She gave a dry laugh. 'And modest too.' The smile faded, and with it her good humour. 'What are you doing here? Hmmm? This is my city, child.'

'I am a priest, lady,' he said. 'I am seeking knowledge of a woman called Rowena, the wife of Druss, the slave of Collan.'

'Why?'

'My Abbot instructed me to find her. He believes the Source may want her protected.'

'By you?' Her good humour returned. 'Boy, you can't even protect yourself from an old witch. Were I to desire it, I could send your soul flaming into Hell.'

'Why would you desire such a terrible thing?'

She paused for a moment. 'It might be a whim, or a fancy. What will you give me for your life?'

'I don't have anything to give.'

'Of course you do,' she said. Her old eyes closed and he watched her spirit rise from her body. She took the form of a beautiful woman, young and shapely, with golden hair and large blue eyes. 'Does this form please you?'

'Of course. It is flawless. Is that how you looked when younger?'

'No, I was always ugly. But this is how I choose for you to see me.' She glided in close to him and stroked his face. Her touch was warm, and he felt a ripple of arousal.

'Please do not continue,' he said.

'Why? Is it not pleasurable?' Her hand touched his robes and they disappeared.

'Yes, it is. Very. But my vows ... do not allow for the pleasures of the flesh.'

'Silly boy,' she whispered into his ear. 'We are not flesh. We are spirit.'

'No,' he said sternly. Instantly he transformed himself into the image of the old woman sitting at the table.

'Clever boy,' said the beautiful vision. 'Yes, very clever. And virtuous too. I don't know if I like that, but it does have the charm of being novel. Very well. I will help you.'

He felt the invisible chains holding him disappear, as did the vision. The old woman opened her eyes.

'She was at sea, heading for Ventria when the ship came under attack. She leapt into the water, and the sharks took her.'

Vintar reeled back and cried out, 'It's my fault! I should have sought her sooner.'

'Go back to your Temple, boy. My time is precious, and I have clients waiting.'

Her laughter rang out and she waved her hand dismissively. Once more he felt the pull on his spirit. It dragged him out, hurling him high into the sky over Mashrapur.

Vintar returned to the tiny cell at the Temple, merging once more with his body. As always he felt nauseous and dizzy and lay still for a few moments, experiencing the weight of his flesh, feeling the rough blanket beneath his skin. A great sadness fell upon him. His talents were far beyond those of normal men, yet they had brought him no pleasure. His parents had treated him with cold reverence, frightened by his uncanny skills. They had been both delighted and relieved when the Abbot came to them one autumn evening, offering to take the boy into his custody. It mattered nothing to them that the Abbot represented a Temple of the Thirty, where men with awesome talents trained and studied with one purpose only – to die in some battle, some distant war, and thus become one with the Source. The prospect of his death could not grieve his parents, for they had never treated him as a human being, flesh of their flesh, blood of their blood. They saw him as a changeling, a demonic presence.

He had no friends. Who wants to be around a boy who can read minds, who can peek into the darkest corners of your soul and know all your secrets? Even in the Temple he was alone, unable to share in the simple camaraderie of others with talents the equal of his.

And now he had missed an opportunity to help a young woman, indeed to save her life.

He sat up and sighed. The old woman had been a witch, and he had felt the malevolence of her personality. Even so the vision she created had aroused him. He could not even withstand such a petty evil.

And then the thought struck him, like a blow between the eyes. Evil! Malice and deceit walked hand in hand beneath the darkness of evil. Perhaps she lied!

He lay back and forced his mind to relax, loosening the spirit once more. Soaring from the Temple, he sped across the ocean, seeking the ship and praying that he was not too late.

127

Clouds were gathering in the east, promising a storm. Vintar swooped low over the water, spirit eyes scanning the horizon. Forty miles from the coast of Ventria he saw the ships, a trireme with a huge black sail and a slender merchant vessel seeking to avoid capture.

The merchant ship swung away, but the trireme ploughed on, its bronze-covered ram striking the prey amidships, smashing the timbers and ripping into the heart of the vessel. Armed men swarmed over the trireme's prow. On the rear deck Vintar saw a young woman dressed in white, with two men – one tall and dark-skinned, the other small and slightly built. The trio leapt into the waves. Sharks glided through the water towards them.

Vintar flew to Rowena, his spirit hand touching her shoulder as she bobbed in the water, clinging to a length of timber, the two men on either side of her. 'Stay calm, Rowena,' he pulsed.

A shark lunged up at the struggling trio and Vintar entered its mind, tasting the bleakness of its non-thoughts, the coldness of its emotions, the hunger that consumed it. He felt himself becoming the shark, seeing the world through black, unblinking eyes, tasting the environment through a sense of smell a hundred, perhaps a thousand times more powerful than Man's. Another shark glided below the three people, its jaws opening as it swept up towards them.

With a flick of his tail Vintar rammed the beast, which turned and snapped at his side, barely missing his dorsal fin.

Then came a scent in the water, sweet and beguiling, promising infinite pleasure and a cessation of hunger. Almost without thinking Vintar swam for it, sensing and seeing the other sharks racing towards it.

And then he knew, and his soaring lust was quelled as swiftly as it had risen.

Blood. The victims of the pirates were being thrown to the sharks.

Releasing control of the sea beast, he flew back to where Rowena and the others were clinging to the beam. 'Get your friends to kick out. You must swim away from here,' he told her. He heard her tell the others, and slowly the three of them began to move away from the carnage.

Vintar soared high into the sky and scanned the horizon. Another ship was just in sight, a merchant vessel, and the young priest sped towards it. Dropping to where the captain stood by the tiller Vintar entered the man's mind, screening out his thoughts of wife, family, pirates and bad winds. The ship was manned by two hundred rowers and thirty seamen; it was carrying wine from Lentria to the Naashanite port of Virinis.

Vintar flowed through the captain's body, seeking control. In the lungs he found a small, malignant cancer. Swiftly Vintar neutralised it, accelerating the body's healing mechanism to carry away the corrupt cell. Moving up once more into the brain, he made the captain swing the ship towards the north-west.

The captain was a kindly man, his thoughts mellow. He had seven children, and one of them – the youngest daughter – had been sick with yellow fever when he set sail. He was praying for her recovery.

Vintar imprinted the new course on the man's unsuspecting mind and flew back to Rowena, telling her of the ship that would soon arrive. Then he moved to the pirate trireme. Already they had sacked the merchant vessel and were backing oars, pulling clear the ram and allowing the looted ship to sink.

Vintar entered the captain's mind – and reeled with the horror of his thoughts. Swiftly he made the man see the distant merchant ship and filled his mind with nameless fears. The approaching ship, he made the captain believe, was filled with soldiers. It was an ill omen, it would be the death of him. Then Vintar left him, and listened with satisfaction as Earin Shad bellowed orders to his men to turn about and make for the north-west.

Vintar floated above Rowena and the two men until the merchant ship arrived and hauled them aboard. Then he departed for the Lentrian port of Chupianin, where he healed the captain's daughter.

Only then did he return to the Temple, where he found the Abbot sitting beside his bed.

'How are you feeling, my boy?' he asked.

'Better than I have in years, Father. The girl is safe now. And I have enhanced two lives.'

'Three,' said the Abbot. 'You have enhanced your own.'

'That is true,' admitted Vintar, 'and it is good to be home.'

Druss could hardly believe the chaos at the clearing site. Hundreds of men scurried here and there without apparent direction, felling trees, digging out roots, hacking at the dense, overgrown vegetation. There was no order to the destruction. Trees were hacked down, falling across paths used by men with wheelbarrows who were trying to clear the debris. Even while he waited to see the Overseer he watched a tall pine topple on to a group of men digging out tree roots. No one was killed, but one worker suffered a broken arm and several others showed bloody gashes to face or arm.

The Overseer, a slender yet pot-bellied man, called him over. 'Well, what are your skills?' he asked.

'Woodsman,' answered Druss.

'Everyone here claims to be a woodsman,' said the man wearily. 'I'm looking for men with skill.'

'You certainly need them,' observed Druss.

'I have twenty days to clear this area, then another twenty to prepare footings for the new buildings. The pay is two silver pennies a day.' The man pointed to a burly, bearded man sitting on a tree-stump. 'That's Togrin, the charge-hand. He organises the workforce and hires the men.'

'He's a fool,' said Druss, 'and he'll get someone killed.'

'Fool he may be,' admitted the Overseer, 'but he's also a very tough man. No one shirks when he's around.'

Druss gazed at the site. 'That may be true; but you'll never finish on time. And I'll not work for any man who doesn't know what he's doing.'

'You're a little young to be making such sweeping comments,' observed the Overseer. 'So tell me, how would you reorganise the work?'

'I'd move the axemen further west and allow the rest of the men to clear behind them. If it carries on like this, all movement will cease. Look there,' said Druss, pointing to the right. Trees had been felled in a rough circle, at the centre of which were men digging out huge roots. 'Where will they take the roots?' asked the axeman. 'There is no longer a path. They will have to wait while the trees are hauled away. Yet how will you move horses and trace chains through to them?'

The Overseer smiled. 'You have a point, young man. Very well. The charge-hand earns four pennies a day. Take his place and show me what you can do.'

Druss took a deep breath. His muscles were already tired from the long walk to the site, and the wounds in his back were aching. He was in no condition to fight, and had been hoping to ease himself in to the work. 'How do you signal a break in the work?' he asked.

'We ring the bell for the noon break. But that's three hours away.'

'Have it rung now,' said Druss.

The Overseer chuckled. 'This should break the monotony,' he said. 'Do you want me to tell Togrin he has lost his job?'

Druss looked into the man's brown eyes. 'No. I'll tell him myself,' he said.

'Good. Then I'll see to the bell.'

The Overseer strolled away and Druss picked his way through the chaos until he was standing close to the seated Togrin. The man glanced up. He was large and round-shouldered, heavy of arm and sturdy of chin. His eyes were dark, almost black under heavy brows. 'Looking for work?' he asked.

'No.'

'Then get off my site. I don't like idlers.'

The clanging of a bell sounded through the wood. Togrin swore and rose as everywhere men stopped working. 'What the . . . ?' He swung around. 'Who rang that bell?' he bellowed.

Men began to gather around the charge-hand and Druss approached the man. 'I ordered the bell rung,' he said.

Togrin's eyes narrowed. 'And who might you be?' he asked.

'The new charge-hand,' replied Druss.

'Well, well,' said Togrin, with a wide grin. 'Now there are two charge-hands. I think that's one too many.'

'I agree,' Druss told him. Stepping in swiftly, he delivered a thundering blow to the man's belly. The air left Togrin's lungs with a

131

great whoosh and he doubled up, his head dropping. Druss's left fist chopped down the man's jaw and Togrin hit the ground face first. The charge-hand twitched, then lay still.

Druss sucked in a great gulp of air. He felt unsteady and white lights danced before his eyes as he looked around at the waiting men. 'Now we are going to make some changes,' he said.

Day by day Druss's strength grew, the muscles of his arms and shoulders swelling with each sweeping blow of the axe, each shovelful of hard clay, each wrenching lift that tore a stubborn tree root clear of the earth. For the first five days Druss slept at the site in a small canvas tent supplied by the Overseer. He had not the energy to walk the three miles back to the rented house. And each lonely night two faces hovered in his mind as he drifted to sleep: Rowena, whom he loved more than life, and Borcha, the fist-fighter he knew he had to face.

In the quiet of the tent his thoughts were many. He saw his father differently now and wished he had known him better. It took courage to live down a father like Bardan the Slayer, and to raise a child and build a life on the frontier. He remembered the day when the wandering mercenary had stopped at the village. Druss had been impressed by the man's weapons, knife, short sword and hand-axe, and by his battered breastplate and helm. 'He lives a life of real courage,' he had observed to his father, putting emphasis on the word *real*. Bress had merely nodded. Several days later, as they were walking across the high meadow, Bress had pointed towards the house of Egan the farmer. 'You want to see courage, boy,' he said. 'Look at him working in that field. Ten years ago he had a farm on the Sentran Plain, but Sathuli raiders came in the night, burning him out. Then he moved to the Ventrian border, where locusts destroyed his crops for three years. He had borrowed money to finance his farm and he lost everything. Now he is back on the land, working from first light to last. That's *real* courage. It doesn't take much for a man to abandon a life of toil for a sword. The real heroes are those who battle on.'

The boy had known better. You couldn't be a hero and a farmer. 'If he was so brave, why didn't he fight off the Sathuli?'

'He had a wife and three children to protect.'

'So he ran away?'

'He ran away,' agreed Bress.

'I'll never run from a fight,' said Druss.

'Then you'll die young,' Bress told him.

Druss sat up and thought back to the raid. What would he have done if the choice had been to fight the slavers – or run with Rowena? His sleep that night was troubled.

On the sixth night as he walked from the site a tall, burly figure stepped into his path. It was Togrin, the former charge-hand. Druss had not seen him since the fight. The young axeman scanned the darkness, seeking other assailants, but there were none.

'Can we talk?' asked Togrin.

'Why not?' countered Druss.

The man took a deep breath. 'I need work,' he said. 'My wife's sick. The children have not eaten in two days.'

Druss looked hard into the man's face, seeing the hurt pride and instantly sensing what it had cost him to ask for help. 'Be on site at dawn,' he said, and strolled on. He felt uncomfortable as he made his way home, telling himself he would never have allowed his own dignity to be lost in such a way. But even as he thought the words, a seed of doubt came to him. Mashrapur was a harsh, unforgiving city. A man was valued only so long as he contributed to the general wellbeing of the community. And how dreadful it must be, he thought, to watch your children starve.

It was dusk when he arrived at the house. He was tired, but the bone-weariness he had experienced for so long had faded. Sieben was not home. Druss lit a lantern and opened the rear door to the garden allowing the cool sea breeze to penetrate the house.

Removing his money-pouch, he counted out the twenty-four silver pennies he had earned thus far. Twenty was the equivalent of a single raq, and that was one month's rent on the property. At this rate he would never earn enough to settle his debts. Old Thom was right: he could make far more in the sand circle.

He recalled the bout with Borcha, the terrible pounding he had received. The memory of the punches he had taken was strong within him – but so too was the memory of those he had thundered into his opponent.

He heard the iron gate creak at the far end of the garden and saw a shadowy figure making his way towards the house. Moonlight glinted from the man's bald pate, and he seemed colossal as he strode through the shadowed trees. Druss rose from his seat, his pale eyes narrowing.

Borcha halted just before the door. 'Well,' he asked, 'are you going to invite me in?'

Druss stepped into the garden. 'You can take your beating out here,' he hissed. 'I've not the money to pay for broken furniture.'

'You're a cocky lad,' said Borcha amiably, stepping into the house and draping his green cloak across the back of a couch. Nonplussed, Druss followed him inside. The big man stretched out in a padded chair, crossing his legs and leaning his head back against the high back. 'A good chair,' he said. 'Now how about a drink?'

'What do you want here?' demanded Druss, fighting to control his rising temper.

'A little hospitality, farm boy. I don't know about you, but where I come from we normally offer a guest a goblet of wine when he takes the trouble to call.'

'Where I'm from,' responded Druss, 'uninvited guests are rarely welcome.'

'Why such hostility? You won your wager and you fought well. Collan did not take my advice – which was to return your wife – and now he is dead. I had no part in the raid.'

'And I suppose you haven't been looking for me, seeking your revenge?'

Borcha laughed. 'Revenge? For what? You stole nothing from me. You certainly did not beat me – nor could you. You have the strength but not the skill. If that had been a genuine bout I would have broken you, boy – eventually. However, you are quite right – I have been looking for you.'

Druss sat opposite the giant. 'So Old Thom told me. He said you were seeking to destroy me.'

Borcha shook his head and grinned. 'The drunken fool misunderstood, boy. Now tell me, how old do you think I am?'

'What? How in the name of Hell should I know?' stormed Druss.

'I'm thirty-eight, thirty-nine in two months. And yes, I could still beat Grassin, and probably all the others. But you showed me the mirror of time, Druss. No one lasts for ever – not in the sand circle. My day is over; my few minutes with you taught me that. Your day is beginning. But it won't last long unless you learn how to fight.'

'I need no instruction in that,' said Druss.

'You think not? Every time you throw a right-hand blow, you drop your left shoulder. All of your punches travel in a curve. And your strongest defence is your chin which, though it may appear to be made of granite, is in fact merely bone. Your footwork is adequate, though it could be improved, but your weaknesses are many. Grassin will exploit them; he will wear you down.'

'That's one opinion,' argued Druss.

'Don't misunderstand me, lad. You are good. You have heart and great strength. But you also know how you felt after four minutes with me. Most bouts last ten times that long.'

'Mine won't.'

Borcha chuckled. 'It will with Grassin. Do not let arrogance blind you to the obvious, Druss. They say you were a woodsman. When you first picked up an axe, did it strike with every blow?'

'No,' admitted the younger man.

'It is the same with combat. I can teach you many styles of punch, and even more defences. I can show you how to feint, and lure an opponent in to your blows.'

'Perhaps you can – but why would you?'

'Pride,' said Borcha.

'I don't understand.'

'I'll explain it – after you beat Grassin.'

'I won't be here long enough,' said Druss. 'As soon as a ship bound for Ventria docks in Mashrapur, I shall sail on her.'

'Before the war such a journey would cost ten raq. Now...? Who knows? But in one month there is a small tournament at Visha, with a first prize of one hundred raq. The rich have palaces in Visha, and a great deal of money can be made on side wagers. Grassin will be taking part, and several of the other notable figures. Agree to let me train you and I will enter your name in my place.'

Druss stood and poured a goblet of wine, which he passed to the bald fighter. 'I have taken employment, and I promised the Overseer I would see the work done. It will take a full month.'

'Then I will train you in the evenings.'

'On one condition,' said Druss.

'Name it!'

'The same one I gave the Overseer. If a ship bound for Ventria docks and I can get passage, then I will up and go.'

'Agreed.' Borcha thrust out his hand. Druss clasped it and Borcha stood. 'I'll leave you to your rest. By the way, warn your poet friend that he is taking fruit from the wrong tree.'

'He is his own man,' said Druss.

Borcha shrugged. 'Warn him anyway. I'll see you tomorrow.'

2

Sieben lay awake, staring at the ornate ceiling. Beside him the woman slept, and he could feel the warmth of her skin against his side and legs. There was a painting on the ceiling, a hunting scene showing men armed with spears and bows pursuing a red-maned lion. What kind of man would have such a composition above the marital bed, he thought? Sieben smiled. The First Minister of Mashrapur must have an enormous ego since, whenever he and his wife made love, she would be gazing up at a group of men more handsome than her husband.

Rolling to his side, he looked down at the sleeping woman. Her back was turned towards him, her arm thrust under the pillow, her legs drawn up. Her hair was dark, almost black against the creamy-white of the pillow. He could not see her face, but he pictured again the full lips and the long, beautiful neck. When first he had seen her she was standing beside Mapek in the market-place. The minister was surrounded by underlings and sycophants, Evejorda looking bored and out of place.

Sieben had stood very still, waiting for her eyes to glance in his direction. When they did, he sent her a smile. One of his best – a swift, flashing grin that said, 'I am bored too. I understand you. I am a linked soul.' She raised an eyebrow at him, signifying her distaste for his impertinence, and then turned away. He waited, knowing she would look again. She moved to a nearby stall and began to examine a set of ceramic bowls. He angled himself through the crowd and she looked up, startled to see him so close.

'Good morning, my lady,' he said. She ignored him. 'You are very beautiful.'

'And you are presumptuous, sir.' Her voice had a northern burr, which he normally found irritating. Not so now.

'Beauty demands presumption. Just as it demands adoration.'

'You are very sure of yourself,' she said, moving in close to disconcert him.

She was wearing a simple gown of radiant blue and a Lentrian shawl of white silk. But it was her perfume that filled his senses – a rich, scented musk he recognised as *Moserche*, a Ventrian import costing five gold raq an ounce.

'Are you happy?' he asked her.

'What a ridiculous question! Who could answer it?'

'Someone who is happy,' he told her.

She smiled. 'And you, sir, are you happy?'

'I am now.'

'I think you are an accomplished womaniser, and there is no truth to your words.'

'Then judge me by my deeds, my lady. My name is Sieben.' He whispered the address of the house he shared with Druss and then, taking her hand, he kissed it.

Her messenger arrived at the house two days later.

She moved in her sleep. Sieben's hand slid under the satin sheet, cupping her breast. At first she did not stir, but he gently continued to caress her skin, squeezing her nipple until it swelled erect. She moaned and stretched. 'Do you never sleep?' she asked him.

He did not reply.

Later, as Evejorda slept again, he lay silently beside her, his passion gone, his thoughts sorrowful. She was without doubt the most beautiful woman he had ever enjoyed. She was bright, intelligent, dynamic and full of passion.

And he was bored ...

As a poet he had sung of love, but never known it, and he envied the lovers of legend who looked into each other's eyes and saw eternity beckoning. He sighed and slipped from the bed, dressing swiftly and leaving the room, padding softly down the back stairs to the garden before pulling on his boots. The servants were not yet awake, and dawn was only just breaking in the eastern sky. A cockerel crowed in the distance.

Sieben walked through the garden and out on to the avenue beyond. As he walked he could smell the fresh bread baking, and he stopped at a bakery to buy some cheese bread which he ate as he strolled home.

Druss was not there, and he remembered the labouring work the young man had undertaken. God, how could a man spend his days digging in the dirt, he wondered? Moving through to the kitchen, he stoked up the iron stove and set a copper pan filled with water atop it.

Making a tisane of mint and herbs, he stirred the brew and carried it to the main sitting room where he found Shadak asleep on a couch. The hunter's black jerkin and trews were travel-stained, his boots encrusted with mud. He awoke as Sieben entered, and swung his long legs from the couch.

'I was wondering where you were,' said Shadak, yawning. 'I arrived last night.'

'I stayed with a friend,' said Sieben, sitting opposite the hunter and sipping his tisane.

Shadak nodded. 'Mapek is due in Mashrapur later today. He cut short his visit to Vagria.'

'Why would that concern me?'

'I'm sure that it does not. But now you know it anyway.'

'Did you come to give me a sermon, Shadak?'

'Do I look like a priest? I came to see Druss. But when I got here he was in the garden, sparring with a bald giant. From the way he moved I concluded his wounds are healed.'

'Only the physical wounds,' said Sieben.

'I know,' responded the hunter. 'I spoke to him. He still intends to sail for Ventria. Will you go with him?'

Sieben laughed. 'Why should I? I don't know his wife. Gods, I hardly know him.'

'It might be good for you, poet.'

'The sea air, you mean?'

'You know what I mean,' said Shadak gravely. 'You have chosen to make an enemy of one of the most powerful men in Mashrapur. His enemies die, Sieben. Poison, or the blade, or a knotted rope around your throat as you sleep.'

139

'Is my business known all over the city?'

'Of course. There are thirty servants in that house. You think to keep secrets from them when her ecstatic cries reverberate around the building in the middle of the afternoon, or the morning, or in the dead of night?'

'Or indeed all three,' said Sieben, smiling.

'I see no humour in this,' snapped Shadak. 'You are no more than a rutting dog and you will undoubtedly ruin her life as you have ruined others. Yet I would sooner you lived than died – only the gods know why!'

'I gave her a little pleasure, that's all. Which is more than that dry stick of a husband could do. But I will think on your advice.'

'Do not think too long. When Mapek returns he will soon find out about his wife's . . . *little pleasure*. Do not be surprised if he has her killed also.'

Sieben paled. 'He wouldn't . . .'

'He is a proud man, poet. And you have made a profound error.'

'If he touches her I'll kill him.'

'Ah, how noble. The dog bares its fangs. You should never have wooed her. You do not even have the defence of being in love; you merely wanted to rut.'

'Is that not what love is?' countered Sieben.

'For you, yes.' Shadak shook his head. 'I don't believe you'll ever understand it, Sieben. To love means giving, not receiving. Sharing your soul. But this argument is wasted on you, like teaching algebra to a chicken.'

'Oh, please, don't try to spare my feelings with pretty words. Just come right out with it!'

Shadak rose. 'Bodasen is hiring warriors, mercenaries to fight in the Ventrian war. He has chartered a ship which will sail in twelve days. Lie low until then, and do not seek to see Evejorda again – not if you want *her* to live.'

The hunter moved towards the door, but Sieben called out, 'You don't think very highly of me, do you?'

Shadak half turned. 'I think more of you than you think of yourself.'

'I am too tired for riddles.'

'You can't forget Gulgothir.'

Sieben jerked as if struck, then lunged to his feet. 'That is all past. It means nothing to me. You understand? Nothing!'

'If you say so. I'll see you in twelve days. The ship is called *The Thunderchild*. She will sail from Quay 12.'

'I may be on it. I may not.'

'A man always has two choices, my friend.'

'No! No! No!' roared Borcha. 'You are still thrusting out that chin, and leading with your head.' Stepping back from his opponent, Borcha swept up a towel and wiped the sweat from his face and head. 'Try to understand, Druss, that if Grassin gets the opportunity he will take out one – or both – of your eyes. He will step in close, and as you charge he will strike with a sudden thrust, his thumb like a dagger.'

'Let's go again,' said Druss.

'No. You are too angry and it swamps your thoughts. Come and sit for a while.'

'The light is fading,' Druss pointed out.

'Then let it fade. You are four days from the competition. *Four days*, Druss. In that time you must learn to control your temper. Winning is everything. It means nothing if an opponent sneers at you, or mocks you, or claims your mother sold herself to sailors. You understand? These insults are merely weapons in a fighter's armoury. You will be goaded – because every fighter knows that his enemy's rage is his greatest weakness.'

'I can control it,' snapped Druss.

'A few moments ago you were fighting well – your balance was good, the punches crisp. Then I slapped you with a straight left . . . then another. The blows were too fast for your defences and they began to irritate you. Then the curve came back to your punches and you exposed your chin, your face.'

Druss sat beside the fighter and nodded. 'You are right. But I do not like this sparring, this holding back. It does not feel real.'

'It isn't real, my friend, but it prepares the body for genuine combat.' He slapped the younger man on the shoulder. 'Do not

141

despair; you are almost ready. I think your digging in the dirt has brought back your strength. How goes it at the clearing site?'

'We finished today,' said Druss. 'Tomorrow the stonemasons and builders move in.'

'On time. The Overseer must have been pleased – I know I am.'

'Why should it please you?'

'I own a third of the land. The value will rise sharply when the houses are completed.' The bald fighter chuckled. 'Were you happy with your bonus?'

'Was that your doing?' asked Druss suspiciously.

'It is standard practice, Druss. The Overseer received fifty raq for completing within the time allocated. The charge-hand is usually offered one tenth of this sum.'

'He gave me ten raq – in gold.'

'Well, well, you must have impressed him.'

'He asked me to stay on and supervise the digging of the footings.'

'But you declined?'

'Yes. There is a ship bound for Ventria. I told him my assistant, Togrin, could take my place. He agreed.'

Borcha was silent for a moment. He knew of Druss's fight with Togrin on the first day, and how he had welcomed the defeated charge-hand back on the site, training him and giving him responsibility. And the Overseer had told him at their progress meetings how well the men responded to Druss.

'He is a natural leader who inspires by example. No work is too menial, nor too hard. He's a real find, Borcha; I intend to promote him. There is a new site planned to the north, with difficult terrain. I shall make him Overseer.'

'He won't take it.'

'Of course he will. He could become rich.'

Borcha pulled his thoughts back to the present. 'You know you may never find her,' he said softly.

Druss shook his head. 'I'll find her, Borcha – if I have to walk across Ventria and search every house.'

'You are a woodman, Druss, so answer me this: If I marked a single fallen leaf in a forest, how would you begin to search for it?'

'I hear you – but it is not that difficult. I know who bought her: Kabuchek. He is a rich man, an important man; I will find him.' Reaching behind the bench seat, Druss drew forth Snaga. 'This was my grandfather's axe,' he said. 'He was an evil man, they say. But when he was young a great army came out of the north, led by a Gothir King named Pasia. Everywhere there was panic. How could the Drenai stand against such an army? Towns emptied, people piled their possessions on to carts, wagons, coaches, the backs of horses, ponies. Bardan – my grandfather – led a small raiding party deep into the mountains, to where the enemy was camped. He and twenty men walked into the camp, found the King's tent and slew him in the night. In the morning they found Pasia's head stuck atop a lance. The army went home.'

'An interesting story, and one I have heard before,' said Borcha. 'What do you think we learn from it?'

'There is nothing a man cannot achieve if he has the will, the strength and the courage to attempt it,' answered Druss.

Borcha rose and stretched the massive muscles of his shoulders and back. 'Then let's see if it is true,' he said, with a smile. 'Let's see if you have the will, the strength and the courage to keep your chin tucked in.'

Druss chuckled and placed the axe beside the seat as he stood. 'I like you, Borcha. How in the name of Chaos did you ever come to serve a man like Collan?'

'He had a good side, Druss.'

'He *did*?'

'Aye, he paid well.' As he spoke his hand snaked out, the open palm lashing across Druss's cheek. The younger man snarled and leapt at him but Borcha swayed left, his fist glancing from Druss's cheek. 'The chin, you ox! Keep it in!' he bellowed.

'I was hoping for men with more quality,' said Bodasen, as he scanned the crowds milling in the Celebration Field.

Borcha chuckled. 'Do not be misled by appearances. Some of these men *are* quality. It really depends on what you are seeking.'

Bodasen stared moodily at the rabble – some in rags, most filthy. More than two hundred had assembled so far, and a quick glance

143

to the gate showed others moving along the access road. 'I think we have different views on what constitutes quality,' he said gloomily.

'Look over there,' said Borcha, pointing to a man sitting on a fence rail. 'That is Eskodas the Bowman. He can hit a mark no larger than your thumbnail from fifty paces. A man to walk the mountains with, as they say in my home country. And there, the swordsman Kelva – fearless and highly skilled. A natural killer.'

'But do they understand the concept of honour?'

Borcha's laughter rang out. 'You have listened to too many tales of glory and wonder, my friend. These men are fighters; they fight for pay.'

Bodasen sighed. 'I am trapped in this . . . this blemish of a city. My emperor is beset on all sides by a terrible enemy, and I cannot join him. No ship will sail unless it is manned by seasoned troops, and I must choose them from among the gutter scum of Mashrapur. I had hoped for more.'

'Choose wisely, and they may yet surprise you,' advised Borcha.

'Let us see the archers first,' Bodasen ordered.

For more than an hour Bodasen watched the bowmen sending their shafts at targets stuffed with straw. When they had finished he selected five men, the youthful Eskodas among them. Each man was given a single gold raq, and told to report to *The Thunderchild* at dawn on the day of departure.

The swordsmen were more difficult to judge. At first he ordered them to fence with one another, but the warriors set about their task with mindless ferocity and soon several men were down with cuts, gashes, and one with a smashed collar-bone. Bodasen called a halt to the proceedings and, with Borcha's help, chose ten. The injured men were each given five silver pieces.

The day wore on, and by noon Bodasen had chosen thirty of the fifty men he required to man *The Thunderchild*. Dismissing the remainder of the would-be mercenaries, he strode from the field with Borcha beside him.

'Will you leave a place for Druss?' asked the fighter.

'No. I will have room only for men who will fight for Ventria. His quest is a personal one.'

144

'According to Shadak he is the best fighting man in the city.'

'I am not best disposed towards Shadak. Were it not for him the pirates would not be fighting Ventria's cause.'

'Sweet Heaven!' snorted Borcha. 'How can you believe that? Collan would merely have taken your money and given nothing in return.'

'He gave me his word,' said Bodasen.

'How on earth did you Ventrians ever build an empire?' enquired Borcha. 'Collan was a liar, a thief, a raider. Why would you believe him? Did he not tell you he was going to give back Druss's wife? Did he not lie to you in order for you to lure Druss into a trap? What kind of man did you believe you were dealing with?'

'A nobleman,' snapped Bodasen. 'Obviously I was wrong.'

'Indeed you were. You have just paid a gold raq to Eskodas, the son of a goat-breeder and a Lentrian whore. His father was hanged for stealing two horses and his mother abandoned him. He was raised in an orphanage run by two Source priests.'

'Is there some point to this sordid tale?' asked the Ventrian.

'Aye, there is. Eskodas will fight to the death for you; he'll not run. Ask him his opinion, and he'll give an honest answer. Hand him a bag of diamonds and tell him to deliver it to a man a thousand leagues distant, and he will do so – and never once will he consider stealing a single gem.'

'So I should hope,' observed Bodasen. 'I would expect no less from any Ventrian servant I employed. Why do you make honesty sound like a grand virtue?'

'I have known rocks with more common sense than you,' said Borcha, struggling to hold his temper.

Bodasen chuckled. 'Ah, the ways of you barbarians are mystifying. But you are quite right about Druss – I was instrumental in causing him grievous wounds. Therefore I shall leave a place for him on *The Thunderchild*. Now let us find somewhere that serves good food and passable wine.'

Shadak, Sieben and Borcha stood with Druss on the quayside as dock-workers moved by them, climbing the gangplank, carrying the last of the ship's stores to the single deck. *The Thunderchild* was riding low in the water, her deck crammed with mercenaries who leaned on the rail, waving goodbyes to the women who thronged the quay. Most were whores, but there were a few wives with small children, and many were the tears.

Shadak gripped Druss's hand. 'I wish you fair sailing, laddie,' the hunter told him. 'And I hope the Source leads you to Rowena.'

'He will,' said Druss. The axeman's eyes were swollen, the lids discoloured – a mixture of dull yellow and faded purple – and there was a lump under his left eye, where the skin was split and badly stitched.

Shadak grinned at him. 'It was a good fight. Grassin will long remember it.'

'And me,' grunted Druss.

Shadak nodded, and his smile faded. 'You are a rare man, Druss. Try not to change. Remember the code.'

'I will,' promised Druss. The two men shook hands again, and Shadak strolled away.

'What code?' Sieben asked.

Druss watched as the black-garbed hunter vanished into the crowd. 'He once told me that all true warriors live by a code: *Never violate a woman, nor harm a child. Do not lie, cheat or steal. These things are for lesser men. Protect the weak against the evil strong. And never allow thoughts of gain to lead you into the pursuit of evil.*'

'Very true, I'm sure,' said Sieben with a dry, mocking laugh. 'Ah well, Druss, I can hear the call of the fleshpots and the taverns. And with the money I won on you, I can live like a lord for several months.' He thrust out his slender hand and Druss clasped it.

'Spend your money wisely,' he advised.

'I shall . . . on women and wine and gambling.' Laughing, he swung away.

Druss turned to Borcha. 'I thank you for your training, and your kindness.'

'The time was well spent, and it was gratifying to see Grassin humbled. But he still almost took out your eye. I don't think you'll ever learn to keep that chin protected.'

'Hey, Druss! Are you coming aboard?' yelled Bodasen from the deck and Druss waved.

'I'm on my way,' he shouted. The two men clasped hands in the warrior's grip, wrist to wrist. 'I hope we meet again,' said Druss.

'Who can say what the fates will decree?'

Druss hefted his axe and turned for the gangplank. 'Tell me now why you helped me?' he asked suddenly.

Borcha shrugged. 'You frightened me, Druss. I wanted to see just how good you could be. Now I know. You could be the best. It makes what you did to me more palatable. Tell me, how does it feel to leave as champion?'

Druss chuckled. 'It hurts,' he said, rubbing his swollen jaw.

'Move yourself, dog-face!' yelled a warrior, leaning over the rail.

The axeman glanced up at the speaker, then turned back to Borcha. 'Be lucky, my friend,' he said, then strode up the gangplank.

With the ropes loosed, *The Thunderchild* eased away from the quayside.

Warriors were lounging on the deck, or leaning over the rail waving goodbye to friends and loved ones. Druss found a space by the port rail and sat, laying his axe on the deck beside him. Bodasen was standing beside the mate at the tiller; he waved and smiled at the axeman.

Druss leaned back, feeling curiously at peace. The months trapped in Mashrapur had been hard on the young man. He pictured Rowena.

'I'm coming for you,' he whispered.

Sieben strolled away from the quay, and off into the maze of alleys leading to the park. Ignoring the whores who pressed close around him, his thoughts were many. There was sadness at the departure of Druss. He had come to like the young axeman; there were no hidden sides to him, no cunning, no guile. And much as he laughed at the axeman's rigid morality, he secretly admired the strength that gave birth to it. Druss had even sought out the surgeon Calvar Syn and settled his debt. Sieben had gone with him and would long remember the surprise that registered on the young doctor's face.

But Ventria? Sieben had no wish to visit a land torn by war.

He thought of Evejorda and regret washed over him. He'd like to have seen her just one more time, to have felt those slim thighs sliding up over his hips. But Shadak was right; it was too dangerous for both of them.

Sieben turned left and started to climb the Hundred Steps to the park gateway. Shadak was wrong about Gulgothir. He remembered the filth-strewn streets, the limbless beggars and the cries of the dispossessed. But he remembered them without bitterness. And was it his fault that his father had made such a fool of himself with the Duchess? Anger flared briefly. Stupid fool, he thought. Stupid, stupid man! She had stripped him first of his wealth, then his dignity, and finally his manhood. They called her the Vampire Queen and it was a good description, save that she didn't drink blood. No, she drank the very life force from a man, sucked him dry and left him thanking her for doing it, begging her to do it again.

Sieben's father had been thrown aside – a useless husk, an empty, discarded shell of a man. While Sieben and his mother had almost starved, his father was sitting like a beggar outside the home of the Duchess. He sat there for a month, and finally cut his own throat with a rusty blade.

Stupid, stupid man!

But I am not stupid, thought Sieben as he climbed the steps. I am not like my father.

He glanced up to see two men walking down the steps towards him. They wore long cloaks that were drawn tightly across their bodies. Sieben paused in his climb. It was a hot morning, so why would they be dressed in such a manner? Hearing a sound, he turned to see another man climbing behind him. He also wore a long cloak.

Fear flared suddenly in the poet's heart and, spinning on his heel, he descended towards the single man. As he neared the climber the cloak flashed back, a long knife appearing in the man's hand. Sieben leapt feet first, his right boot cracking into the man's chin and sending him tumbling down the steps. Sieben landed heavily but rose swiftly and began to run, taking the steps three at a time. He could hear the men behind him also running.

Reaching the bottom, he set off through the alleyways. A hunting horn sounded and a tall warrior leapt into his path with a sword in hand. Sieben, at full run, turned his shoulder into the man, barging him aside. He swerved right, then left. A knife sliced past his head to clatter against a wall.

Increasing his speed, he raced across a small square and into a side street. He could see the docks ahead. It was more crowded here and he pushed his way through. Several men shouted abuse, and a young woman fell behind him. He glanced back – there were at least half a dozen pursuers.

Close to panic now, he emerged on to the quay. To his left he saw a group of men emerge from a side street; they were all carrying weapons and Sieben swore.

The Thunderchild was slipping away from the quayside as Sieben ran across the cobbles and launched himself through the air, reaching out to grab at a trailing rope. His fingers curled around it, and his body cracked against the ship's timbers. Almost losing his grip, he clung to the rope as a knife thudded into the wood beside his head. Fear gave him strength and he began to climb.

A familiar face loomed above him and Druss leaned over, grabbing him by the shirt and hauling him on to the deck.

'Changed your mind, I see,' said the axeman. Sieben gave a weak smile and glanced back at the quay. There were at least a dozen armed men there now.

'I thought the sea air would be good for me,' said Sieben.

The captain, a bearded man in his fifties, pushed his way through to them. 'What's going on?' he said. 'I can only carry fifty men. That's the limit.'

'He doesn't weigh much,' said Druss goodnaturedly.

Another man stepped forward. He was tall and broad-shouldered, and wore a dented breastplate, two short swords and a baldric boasting four knives. 'First you keep us waiting, dog-face, and now you bring your boyfriend aboard. Well, Kelva the Swordsman won't sail with the likes of you.'

'Then don't!' Druss's left hand snaked out, his fingers locking to the man's throat, his right slamming home into the warrior's groin.

With one surging heave Druss lifted the struggling man into the air and tossed him over the side. He hit with a great splash and came up struggling under the weight of his armour.

The Thunderchild pulled away and Druss turned to the captain. 'Now we are fifty again,' he said, with a smile.

'Can't argue with that,' the captain agreed. He swung to the sailors standing by the mast. 'Let loose the mainsail!' he bellowed.

Sieben walked to the rail and saw that people on the quayside had thrown a rope to the struggling warrior in the water. 'He might have friends aboard the ship,' observed the poet.

'They're welcome to join him,' answered Druss.

3

Each morning Eskodas paced the deck, moving along the port rail all the way to the prow and then back along the starboard rail, rising the six steps to the tiller deck at the stern, where either the captain or the first mate would be standing alongside the curved oak tiller.

The bowman feared the sea, gazing with undisguised dread at the rolling waves and feeling the awesome power that lifted the ship like a piece of driftwood. On the first morning of the voyage Eskodas had climbed to the tiller deck and approached the captain, Milus Bar.

'No passengers up here,' said the captain sternly.

'I have questions, sir,' Eskodas told him politely.

Milus Bar looped a hemp rope over the tiller arm, securing it. 'About what?' he asked.

'The boat.'

'Ship,' snapped Milus.

'Yes, the ship. Forgive me, I am not versed in nautical terms.'

'She's seaworthy,' said Milus. 'Three hundred and fifty feet of seasoned timber. She leaks no more than a man can sweat, and she'll ride any storm the gods can throw our way. She's sleek. She's fast. What else do you need to know?'

'You talk of the ... ship ... as a woman.'

'Better than any woman I ever knew,' said Milus, grinning. 'She's never let me down.'

'She seems so small against the immensity of the ocean,' observed Eskodas.

'We are all small against the ocean, lad. But there are few storms at this time of year. Our danger is pirates, and that's why you are

151

here.' He stared at the young bowman, his grey eyes narrowing under heavy brows. 'If you don't mind me saying so, lad, you seem a little out of place among these killers and villains.'

'I don't object to you saying it, sir,' Eskodas told him. 'They might object to hearing it, however. Thank you for your time and your courtesy.'

The bowman climbed down to the main deck. Men were lounging everywhere, some dicing, others talking. By the port rail several others were engaged in an arm-wrestling tourney. Eskodas moved through them towards the prow.

The sun was bright in a blue sky, and there was a good following breeze. Gulls circled high above the ship, and to the north he could just make out the coast of Lentria. At this distance the land seemed misty and unreal, a place of ghosts and legends.

There were two men sitting by the prow. One was the slim young man who had boarded the ship so spectacularly. Blond and handsome, long hair held in place by a silver headband, his clothes were expensive – a pale blue shirt of fine silk, dark blue leggings of lambswool seamed with soft leather. The other man was huge; he had lifted Kelva as if the warrior weighed no more than a few ounces, and hurled him into the sea like a spear. Eskodas approached them. The giant was younger than he had first thought, but the beginnings of a dark beard gave him the look of someone older. Eskodas met his gaze. Cold blue eyes, flint-hard and unwelcoming. The bowman smiled. 'Good morning,' he said. The giant grunted something, but the blond dandy rose and extended his hand.

'Hello, there. My name is Sieben. This is Druss.'

'Ay, yes. He defeated Grassin at the tournament – broke his jaw, I believe.'

'In several places,' said Sieben.

'I am Eskodas.' The bowman sat down on a coiled rope and leaned his back against a cloth-bound bale. Closing his eyes, he felt the sun warm on his face. The silence lasted for several moments, then the two men resumed their conversation.

Eskodas didn't listen too intently . . . something about a woman and assassins.

He thought of the journey ahead. He had never seen Ventria, which according to the story books was a land of fabled wealth, dragons, centaurs and many wild beasts. He tended to disbelieve the part about the dragons; he was widely travelled, and in every country there were stories of them, but never had Eskodas seen one. In Chiatze there was a museum where the bones of a dragon had been reassembled. The skeleton was colossal, but it had no wings, and a neck that was at least eight feet long. No fire could have issued from such a throat, he thought.

But dragons or not, Eskodas looked forward with real pleasure to seeing Ventria.

'You don't say much, do you?' observed Sieben.

Eskodas opened his eyes and smiled. 'When I have something to say, I will speak,' he said.

'You'll never get the chance,' grunted Druss. 'Sieben talks enough for ten men.'

Eskodas smiled politely. 'You are the saga-master,' he said.

'Yes. How gratifying to be recognised.'

'I saw you in Corteswain. You gave a performance of *The Song of Karnak*. It was very good; I particularly enjoyed the tale of Dros Purdol and the siege, though I was less impressed by the arrival of the gods of war, and the mysterious princess with the power to hurl lightning.'

'Dramatic licence,' said Sieben, with a tight smile.

'The courage of men needs no such licence,' said Eskodas. 'It lessens the heroism of the defenders to suggest that they had divine help.'

'It was not a history lesson,' Sieben pointed out, his smile fading. 'It was a poem – a song. The arrival of the gods was merely an artistic device to highlight that courage will sometimes bring about good fortune.'

'Hmmm,' said Eskodas, leaning back and closing his eyes.

'What does that mean?' demanded Sieben. 'Are you disagreeing?'

Eskodas sighed. 'It is not my wish to provoke an argument, sir poet, but I think the device was a poor one. You maintain it was inserted to supply dramatic effect. There is no point in further discussion; I have no desire to increase your anger.'

'I am not angry, damn you!' stormed Sieben.

'He doesn't take well to criticism,' said Druss.

'That's very droll,' snapped Sieben, 'coming as it does from the man who tosses shipmates over the side at the first angry word. Now why was it a poor device?'

Eskodas leaned forward. 'I have been in many sieges. The point of greatest courage comes at the end, when all seems lost; that is when weak men break and run, or beg for their lives. You had the gods arrive just before that moment, and offer divine assistance to thwart the Vagrians. Therefore the truly climactic moment was lost, for as soon as the gods appeared we knew victory was assured.'

'I would have lost some of my best lines. Especially the end, where the warriors wonder if they will ever see the gods again.'

'Yes, I remember . . . *the eldritch rhymes, the wizard spells, the ringing of sweet Elven bells*. That one.'

'Precisely.'

'I prefer the grit and the reality of your earlier pieces:

> But came the day, when youth was worn away,
> and locks once thought of steel and fire,
> proved both ephemeral and unreal
> against the onslaught of the years.
> How wrong are the young to believe in secrets
> or enchanted woods.'

He lapsed into silence.

'Do you know all my work?' asked Sieben, clearly astonished.

Eskodas smiled. 'After you performed at Corteswain I sought out your books of poetry. There were five, I think. I have two still – the earliest works.'

'I am at a loss for words.'

'That'll be the day,' grunted Druss.

'Oh, be quiet. At last we meet a man of discernment on a ship full of rascals. Perhaps this voyage will not be so dreadful. So, tell me, Eskodas, what made you sign on for Ventria?'

'I like killing people,' answered Eskodas.

Druss's laughter bellowed out.

For the first few days the novelty of being at sea kept most of the mercenaries amused. They sat up on the deck during daylight hours, playing dice or telling stories. At night they slept under a tarpaulin that was looped and tied to the port and starboard rails.

Druss was fascinated by the sea and the seemingly endless horizons. Berthed at Mashrapur *The Thunderchild* had looked colossal, unsinkable. But here on the open sea she seemed fragile as a flower stem in a river torrent. Sieben had grown bored with the voyage very swiftly. Not so Druss. The sighing of the wind, the plunging and the rising of the ship, the call of the gulls high above – all these fired the young axeman's blood.

One morning he climbed the rigging to the giant crossbeam that held the mainsail. Sitting astride it he could see no sign of land, only the endless blue of the sea. A sailor walked along the beam towards him, barefooted, and using no handholds. He stood in delicate balance with hands on hips and looked down at Druss.

'No passengers should be up here,' he said.

Druss grinned at the young man. 'How can you just stand there, as if you were on a wide road? A puff of breeze could blow you away.'

'Like this?' asked the sailor, stepping from the beam. He twisted in mid-air, his hands fastening to a sail rope. For a moment he hung there, then lithely pulled himself up alongside the axeman.

'Very good,' said Druss. His eye was caught by a silver-blue flash in the water below and the sailor chuckled.

'The gods of the sea,' he told the passenger. 'Dolphins. If they are in the mood, you should see some wonderful sights.' A gleaming shape rose out of the water, spinning into the air before entering the sea again with scarcely a splash. Druss clambered down the rigging, determined to get a closer look at the sleek and beautiful animals performing in the water. High-pitched cries echoed around the ship as the creatures bobbed their heads above the surface.

Suddenly an arrow sped from the ship, plunging into one of the dolphins as it soared out of the water.

Within an instant the creatures had disappeared.

Druss glared at the archer while other men shouted at him, their anger sudden, their mood ugly.

'It was just a fish!' said the archer.

Milus Bar pushed his way through the crowd. 'You fool!' he said, his face almost grey beneath his tan. 'They are the gods of the sea; they come for us to pay homage. Sometimes they will even lead us through treacherous waters. Why did you have to shoot?'

'It was a good target,' said the man. 'And why not? It was my choice.'

'Aye, it was, lad,' Milus told him, 'but if our luck turns bad now it will be my choice to cut out your innards and feed them to the sharks.' The burly skipper stalked back to the tiller deck. The earlier good mood had evaporated now and the men drifted back to their pursuits with little pleasure.

Sieben approached Druss. 'By the gods, they were wondrous,' said the poet. 'According to legend, Asta's chariot is drawn by six white dolphins.'

Druss sighed. 'Who would have thought that anyone would consider killing one of them? Do they make good food, do you know?'

'No,' said Sieben. 'In the north they sometimes become entangled in the nets and drown. I have known men who cooked the meat; they say it tastes foul, and is impossible to digest.'

'Even worse then,' Druss grunted.

'It is no different from any other kind of hunting for sport, Druss. Is not a doe as beautiful as a dolphin?'

'You can eat a doe. Venison is fine meat.'

'But most of them don't hunt for food, do they? Not the nobles. They hunt for *pleasure*. They enjoy the chase, the terror of the prey, the final moment of the kill. Do not blame this man alone for his stupidity. He comes, as do we all, from a cruel world.'

Eskodas joined them. 'Not very inspiring, was he?' said the bowman.

'Who?'

'The man who shot the fish.'

'We were just talking about it.'

'I didn't know you understood the skills of archery,' said Eskodas, surprised.

'Archery? What are you talking about?'

'The bowman. He drew and loosed in a single movement. No hesitation. It is vital to pause and sight your target; he was over-anxious for the kill.'

'Be that as it may,' said Sieben, his irritation rising, 'we were talking about the morality of hunting.'

'Man is a killer by nature,' said Eskodas amiably. 'A natural hunter. Like him there!' Sieben and Druss both turned to see a silver-white fin cutting through the water. 'That's a shark. He scented the blood from the wounded dolphin. Now he'll hunt him down, following the trail as well as a Sathuli scout.'

Druss leaned over the side and watched the shimmering form slide by. 'Big fellow,' he said.

'They come bigger than that,' said Eskodas. 'I was on a ship once that sank in a storm off the Lentrian coast. Forty of us survived the wreck, and struck out for shore. Then the sharks arrived. Only three of us made it – and one of those had his right leg ripped away. He died three days later.'

'A storm, you say?' ventured Druss.

'Aye.'

'Like that one?' asked Druss, pointing to the east, where massive dark clouds were bunching. A flash of lightning speared across the sky, followed by a tremendous roll of thunder.

'Yes, like that. Let's hope it is not blowing our way.'

Within minutes the sky darkened, the sea surging and rising. *The Thunderchild* rolled and rose on the crests of giant waves, sliding into ever larger valleys of water. Then the rain began, faster and faster, icy needles that came from the sky like arrows.

Crouching by the port rail Sieben glanced to where the unfortunate archer was huddled. The man who had shot the dolphin was alone, and holding fast to a rope. Lightning flashed above the ship.

'I would say our luck has changed,' observed Sieben.

But neither Druss nor Eskodas could hear him above the screaming of the wind.

Eskodas hooked his arms around the port rail and clung on as the storm raged. A huge wave crashed over the side of the ship, dislodging several men from their precarious holds on ropes and bales, sweeping them across the deck to crash into the dipping starboard rail. A post cracked, but no one heard it above the ominous roll of thunder booming from the night-dark sky. *The Thunderchild* rode high on the crest of an enormous wave, then slid down into a valley of raging water. A sailor carrying a coiled rope ran along the deck trying to reach the warriors at the starboard rail. A second wave crashed over him, hurling him into the struggling men. The port rail gave way, and within the space of a heartbeat some twenty men were swept from the deck. The ship reared like a frightened horse. Eskodas felt his grip on the rail post weaken. He tried to readjust his hold, but the ship lurched again. Torn from his position of relative safety, he slid headlong towards the yawning gap in the starboard rail.

A huge hand clamped down around his ankle, then he was hauled back. The axeman grinned at him, then handed him a length of rope. Swiftly Eskodas slipped it around his waist, fastening the other end to the mast. He glanced at Druss. The big man was *enjoying* the storm. Secure now, Eskodas scanned the deck. The poet was clinging to a section of the starboard rail that seemed none too secure, and high on the tiller deck the bowman could see Milus Bar wrestling with the tiller, trying to keep *The Thunderchild* ahead of the storm.

Another massive wave swept over the deck. The starboard rail cracked and Sieben slid over the edge of the deck. Druss untied his rope and rose. Eskodas shouted at him, but the axeman either did not hear, or ignored him. Druss ran across the heaving deck, fell once, then righted himself until he came alongside the shattered rail. Dropping to his knees Druss leaned over, dragging Sieben back to the deck.

Just behind them the man who had shot the dolphin was reaching for a rope with which to tie himself to a hauling ring set in the deck.

The ship reared once more. The man tumbled to the deck, then slid on his back, cannoning into Druss who fell heavily. Still holding Seiben with one hand, the axeman tried to reach the doomed archer, but the man vanished into the raging sea.

Almost at that instant the sun appeared through broken clouds and the rain lessened, the sea settling. Druss rose and gazed into the water. Eskodas untied the rope that held him to the mast and stood, his legs unsteady. He walked to where Druss stood with Sieben.

The poet's face was white with shock. 'I'll never sail again,' he said. 'Never!'

Eskodas thrust out his hand. 'Thank you, Druss. You saved my life.'

The axeman chuckled. 'Had to, laddie. You're the only one on this boat who can leave our saga-master speechless.'

Bodasen appeared from the tiller deck. 'That was a reckless move, my friend,' he told Druss, 'but it was well done. I like to see bravery in the men who fight alongside me.'

As the Ventrian moved on, counting the men who were left, Eskodas shivered. 'I think we lost nearly thirty men,' he said.

'Twenty-seven,' said Druss.

Sieben crawled back to the edge of the deck and vomited into the sea. 'Make that twenty-seven and a half,' Eskodas added.

4

The young Emperor climbed down from the battlement walls and strode along the quayside, his staff officers following; his aide, Nebuchad, beside him. 'We can hold for months, Lord,' said Nebuchad, squinting his eyes against the glare from the Emperor's gilded breastplate. 'The walls are thick and high, and the catapults will prevent any attempt to storm the harbour mouth from the sea.'

Gorben shook his head. 'The walls will not protect us,' he told the young man. 'We have fewer than three thousand men here. The Naashanites have twenty times that number. Have you ever seen tiger ants attack a scorpion?'

'Yes, Lord.'

'They swarm all over it – that is how the enemy will storm Capalis.'

'We will fight to the death,' promised an officer.

Gorben halted and turned. 'I know that,' he said, his dark eyes angry now. 'But dying will not bring us victory, will it, Jasua?'

'No, Lord.'

Gorben strode on, along near-empty streets, past boarded, deserted shops and empty taverns. At last he reached the entrance to the Magisters' Hall. The City Elders had long since departed and the ancient building had become the headquarters of the Capalis militia. Gorben entered the hallway and stalked to his chambers, waving away his officers and the two servants who ran towards him – one bearing wine in a golden goblet, the second carrying a towel soaked with warm, scented water.

Once inside, the young Emperor kicked off his boots and hurled his white cloak across a nearby chair. There was one large window facing east, and before it was a desk of oak upon which were laid many maps, and reports from scouts and spies. Gorben sat down and stared at the largest map; it was of the Ventrian Empire and had been commissioned by his father six years ago.

He smoothed out the hide and gazed with undisguised fury at the map. Two-thirds of the Empire had been overrun. Leaning back in his chair, he remembered the palace at Nusa where he had been born and raised. Built on a hill overlooking a verdant valley, and a glistening city of white marble, the palace had taken twelve years to construct, and at one time more than eight thousand workers had laboured on the task, bringing in blocks of granite and marble and towering trunks of cedar, oak and elm to be fashioned by the Royal masons and carpenters.

Nusa – the first of the cities to fall. 'By all the gods of Hell, Father, I curse thee!' hissed Gorben. His father had reduced the size of the national army, relying on the wealth and power of his Satraps to protect the borders. But four of the nine Satraps had betrayed him, opening a path for the Naashanites to invade. His father had gathered an army to confront them, but his military skills were non-existent. He had fought bravely, so Gorben had been informed – but then they would say that to the new Emperor.

The new Emperor! Gorben rose now and walked to the silvered mirror on the far wall. What he saw was a young, handsome man, with black hair that gleamed with scented oils, and deep-set dark eyes. It was a strong face – but was it the face of an Emperor? Can you overcome the enemy, he asked himself silently, aware that any spoken word could be heard by servants and repeated? The gilded breastplate had been worn by warrior Emperors for two hundred years, and the cloak of purple was the mark of ultimate royalty. But these were merely adornments. What mattered was the man who wore them. Are you man enough? He gazed hard at his reflection, taking in the broad shoulders and the narrow waist, the muscular legs and powerful arms. But these too were merely adornments, he knew. The cloak of the soul.

Are you man enough?

The thought haunted him and he returned to his studies. Leaning forward with his elbows on the table, Gorben stared down at the map once more. Scrawled across it in charcoal was the new line of defence: Capalis to the west, Larian and Ectanis to the east. Gorben hurled the map aside. Beneath it lay a second map of the port city of Capalis. Four gates, sixteen towers and a single wall which stretched from the sea in the south in a curving half-circle to the cliffs of the north. Two miles of wall, forty feet high, guarded by three thousand men, many of them raw recruits with no shields nor breastplates.

Rising, Gorben moved to the window and the balcony beyond. The harbour and the open sea met his gaze. 'Ah, Bodasen, my brother, where are you?' he whispered. The sea seemed so peaceful under the clear blue sky and the young Emperor sank into a padded seat and lifted his feet to rest on the balcony rail.

On this warm, tranquil day it seemed inconceivable that so much death and destruction had been visited upon the Empire in so short a time. He closed his eyes and recalled the Summer Banquet at Nusa last year. His father had been celebrating his forty-fourth birthday, and the seventeenth anniversary of his accession to the throne. The banquet had lasted eight days and there had been circuses, plays, knightly combat, displays of archery, running, wrestling and riding. The nine Satraps were all present, smiling and offering toasts to the Emperor. Shabag, tall and slim, hawk-eyed, and cruel of mouth. Gorben pictured him. He always wore black gloves, even in the hottest weather, and tunics of silk buttoned to the neck. Berish, fat and greedy, but a wonderful raconteur with his tales of orgies and humorous calamities. Darishan, the Fox of the North, the cavalry-man, the Lancer, with his long silver hair braided like a woman. And Ashac, the Peacock, the lizard-eyed lover of boys. They had been given pride of place on either side of the Emperor, while his eldest son was forced to sit on the lower table, gazing up at these men of power!

Shabag, Berish, Darishan, and Ashac! Names and faces that burned Gorben's heart and soul. Traitors! Men who swore allegiance to his father, then saw him done to death, his lands overrun and his people slaughtered.

Gorben opened his eyes and took a deep breath. 'I will seek you out – each one of you,' he promised, 'and I will pay you back for your treachery.'

162

The threat was as empty as the treasury coffers, and Gorben knew it.

A soft tapping came at the outer door. 'Enter!' he called.

Nebuchad stepped inside and bowed low. 'The scouts are in, Lord. The enemy is less than two days' march from the walls.'

'What news from the east?'

'None, Lord. Perhaps our riders did not get through.'

'What of the supplies?'

Nebuchad reached inside his tunic and produced a parchment scroll which he unrolled. 'We have sixteen thousand loaves of unleavened bread, a thousand barrels of flour, eight hundred beef cattle, one hundred and forty goats. The sheep have not been counted yet. There is little cheese left, but a great quantity of oats and dried fruit.'

'What about salt?'

'Salt, Lord?'

'When we kill the cattle, how will we keep the meat fresh?'

'We could kill them only when we need them,' offered Nebuchad, reddening.

'To keep the cattle we must feed them, but there is no food to spare. Therefore they must be slaughtered, and the meat salted. Scour the city. And Nebuchad?'

'Lord?'

'You did not mention water?'

'But, Lord, the river flows through the city.'

'Indeed it does. But what will we drink when the enemy dam it, or fill it with poisons?'

'There are artesian wells, I believe.'

'Locate them.'

The young man's head dropped. 'I fear, Lord, that I am not serving you well. I should have anticipated these requirements.'

Gorben smiled. 'You have much to think of and I am well pleased with you. But you do need help. Take Jasua.'

'As you wish, Lord,' said Nebuchad doubtfully.

'You do not like him?'

Nebuchad swallowed hard. 'It is not a question of "like", Lord. But he treats me with . . . contempt.'

Gorben's eyes narrowed, but he held the anger from his voice. 'Tell him it is my wish that he assist you. Now go.'

As the door closed, Gorben slumped down on to a satin-covered couch. 'Sweet Lords of Heaven,' he whispered, 'does my future depend on men of such little substance?' He sighed, then gazed once more out to sea. 'I need you, Bodasen,' he said. 'By all that is sacred, I need you!'

Bodasen stood on the tiller deck, his right hand shading his eyes, his vision focusing on the far horizon. On the main deck sailors were busy repairing the rail, while others were aloft in the rigging, or refastening bales that had slipped during the storm.

'You'll see pirates soon enough if they are near,' said Milus Bar.

Bodasen nodded and swung back to the skipper. 'With a mere twenty-four warriors, I am hoping not to see them at all,' he said softly.

The captain chuckled. 'In life we do not always get what we want, my Ventrian friend. I did not want a storm. I did not want my first wife to leave me – nor my second wife to stay.' He shrugged. 'Such is life, eh?'

'You do not seem unduly concerned.'

'I am a fatalist, Bodasen. What will be will be.'

'Could we outrun them?'

Milus Bar shrugged once more. 'It depends on which direction they are coming from.' He waved his hand in the air. 'The wind. Behind us? Yes. There is not a swifter ship on the ocean than my *Thunderchild*. Ahead and to the west – probably. Ahead and to the east – no. They would ram us. They have a great advantage, for many of their vessels are triremes with three banks of oars. You would be amazed, my friend, at the speed with which they can turn and ram.'

'How long now to Capalis?'

'Two days – maybe three if the wind drops.'

Bodasen moved across the tiller deck, climbing down the six steps to the main deck. He saw Druss, Sieben and Eskodas by the prow and walked towards them. Druss saw him and glanced up.

'Just the man we need,' said the axeman. 'We are talking about Ventria. Sieben maintains there are mountains there which brush the moon. Is it so?'

'I have not seen all of the Empire,' Bodasen told him, 'but according to our astronomers the moon is more than a quarter of a million miles from the surface of the earth. Therefore I would doubt it.'

'Such eastern nonsense,' mocked Sieben. 'There was a Drenai archer once, who fired a shaft into the moon. He had a great bow called Akansin, twelve feet long and woven with spells. He fired a black arrow, which he named Paka. Attached to the arrow was a thread of silver, which he used to climb to the moon. He sat upon it as it sailed around the great plate of the earth.'

'Mere fable,' insisted Bodasen.

'It is recorded in the library at Drenan – in the *Historic* section.'

'All that tells me is how limited is your understanding of the universe,' said Bodasen. 'Do you still believe the sun is a golden chariot drawn by six white, winged horses?' He sat down upon a coiled rope. 'Or perhaps that the earth sits upon the shoulders of an elephant, or some such beast?'

Sieben smiled. 'No, we do not. But would it not be better if we did? Is there not a certain beauty in the tale? One day I shall craft a bow and shoot at the moon.'

'Never mind the moon,' said Druss. 'I want to know about Ventria.'

'According to the census ordered by the Emperor fifteen years ago, and concluded only last year, the Greater Ventrian empire is 214,969 square miles. It has an estimated population of fifteen and a half million people. On a succession of fast horses, a rider galloping along the borders would return to where he started in just under four years.'

Druss looked crestfallen. He swallowed hard. 'So large?'

'So large,' agreed Bodasen.

Druss's eyes narrowed. 'I will find her,' he said at last.

'Of course you will,' said Bodasen. 'She left with Kabuchek and he will have headed for his home in Ectanis, which means he will have docked at Capalis. Kabuchek is a famous man, senior advisor to the Satrap, Shabag. He will not be hard to find. Unless ...'

'Unless what?' queried Druss.

'Unless Ectanis has already fallen.'

'Sail! Sail!' came a cry from the rigging. Bodasen leapt up, eyes scanning the glittering water. Then he saw the ship in the east with sails furled, three banks of oars glistening like wings. Swinging back towards the main deck, he drew his sabre.

'Gather your weapons,' he shouted.

Druss donned his jerkin and helm and stood at the prow, watching the trireme glide towards them. Even at this distance he could see the fighting men thronging the decks.

'A magnificent ship,' he said.

Beside him Sieben nodded. 'The very best. Two hundred and forty oars. See there! At the prow!'

Druss focused on the oncoming ship, and saw a glint of gold at the waterline. 'I see it.'

'That is the ram. It is an extension of the keel, and it is covered with reinforced bronze. With three banks of oars at full stretch, that ram could punch through the hull of the strongest vessel!'

'Will that be their plan?' Druss asked.

Sieben shook his head. 'I doubt it. This is a merchant vessel, ripe for plunder. They will come in close, the oars will be withdrawn, and they'll try to drag us in with grappling-hooks.'

Druss hefted Snaga and glanced back along the deck. The remaining Drenai warriors were armoured now, their faces grim. Bowmen, Eskodas among them, were climbing the rigging to hook themselves into place high above the deck, ready to shoot down into the enemy. Bodasen was standing on the tiller deck with a black breastplate buckled to his torso.

The Thunderchild swung away towards the west, then veered back. In the distance two more sails could be seen and Sieben swore. 'We can't fight them all,' he said. Druss glanced at the billowing sail, and then back at the newly sighted vessel.

'They don't look the same,' he observed. 'They're bulkier. No oars. And they're tacking against the wind. If we can deal with the trireme, they'll not catch us.'

Sieben chuckled. 'Aye, aye, captain. I bow to your superior knowledge of the sea.'

'I'm a swift learner. That's because I listen.'

'You never listen to me. I've lost count of the number of times you've fallen asleep during our conversations on this voyage.'

The Thunderchild swung again, veering away from the trireme. Druss swore and ran back along the deck, climbing swiftly to where Bodasen stood with Milus Bar at the tiller.

'What are you doing?' he yelled at the skipper.

'Get off my deck!' roared Milus.

'If you keep this course, we'll have three ships to fight,' Druss snarled.

'What other choices are there?' queried Bodasen. 'We cannot defeat a trireme.'

'Why?' asked Druss. 'They are only men.'

'They have close to one hundred fighting men – plus the oarsmen. We have twenty-four, and a few sailors. The odds speak for themselves.'

Druss glanced back at the sailing-ships to the west. 'How many men do they have?'

Bodasen spread his hands and looked to Milus Bar. The captain thought for a moment. 'More than two hundred on each ship,' he admitted.

'Can we outrun them?'

'If we get a mist, or if we can keep them off until dusk.'

'What chance of either?' enquired the axeman.

'Precious little,' said Milus.

'Then let's at least take the fight to them.'

'How do you suggest we do that, young man?' the captain asked.

Druss smiled. 'I'm no sailor, but it seems to me their biggest advantage lies in the oars. Can we not try to smash them?'

'We could,' admitted Milus, 'but that would bring us in close enough for their grappling-hooks. We'd be finished then; they'd board us.'

'Or we board them!' snapped Druss.

Milus laughed aloud. 'You are insane!'

'Insane and quite correct,' said Bodasen. 'They are hunting us down like wolves around a stag. Let's do it, Milus!'

For a moment the captain stood and stared at the two warriors, then he swore and leaned in to the tiller. *The Thunderchild* swung towards the oncoming trireme.

His name was Earin Shad, though none of his crew used it. They addressed him to his face as Sea Lord, or Great One, while behind his back they used the Naashanite slang – *Bojeeba*, The Shark.

Earin Shad was a tall man, slim and round-shouldered, long of neck, with protruding eyes that glimmered pearl-grey and a lipless mouth that never smiled. No one aboard the *Darkwind* knew from whence he came, only that he had been a pirate leader for more than two decades. One of the Lords of the Corsairs, mighty men who ruled the seas, he was said to own palaces on several of the Thousand Islands, and to be as rich as one of the eastern kings. This did not show in his appearance. He wore a simple breastplate of shaped bronze, and a winged helm looted from a merchant ship twelve years before. At his hip hung a sabre with a simple hilt of polished wood and a fist-guard of plain brass. Earin Shad was not a man who liked extravagance.

He stood at the stern as the steady, rhythmic pound of the drums urged the rowers to greater efforts, and the occasional crack of the whip sounded against the bare skin of a slacker's back. His pale eyes narrowed as the merchant vessel swung towards the *Darkwind*.

'What is he doing?' asked the giant Patek.

Earin Shad glanced up at the man. 'He has seen Reda's ship and he is trying to cut by us. He won't succeed.' Swinging to the steersman, a short toothless old man named Luba, Earin Shad saw that the man was already altering course. 'Steady now,' he said. 'We don't want her rammed.'

'Aye, Sea Lord!'

'Make ready with the hooks!' bellowed Patek. The giant watched as the men gathered coiled ropes, attaching them to the three-clawed grappling hooks. Then he transferred his gaze to the oncoming ship. 'Look at that, Sea Lord!' he said, pointing at *The Thunderchild*'s prow. There was a man there, dressed in black; he had raised a double-headed axe above his head in a gesture of defiance.

'They'll never cut all the ropes,' said Patek. Earin Shad did not reply – he was scanning the decks of the enemy ship, seeking any sign of female passengers. He saw none, and his mood darkened. To compensate for his disappointment he found himself remembering the last ship they had taken three weeks ago, and the Satrap's daughter she had carried. He licked his lips at the memory. Proud, defiant, and comely – the whip alone had not tamed her, nor the stinging slaps. And even after he had raped her repeatedly, still her eyes shone with murderous intent. Ah, she was lively, no doubt about that. But he had found her weakness; he always did. And when he had he experienced, as always, both triumph and disappointment. The moment of conquest, when she had begged him to take her – had promised to serve him always, in any way that he chose – had been exquisite. But then sadness had flowed within him, followed by anger. He had killed her quickly, which disappointed the men. But then she had earned that, he thought. She had held her nerve for five days in the darkness of the hold, in the company of the black rats.

Earin Shad sniffed, then cleared his throat. This was no time to be considering pleasures.

A cabin door opened behind him and he heard the soft footfalls of the young sorcerer.

'Good day, Sea Lord,' said Gamara. Patek moved away, avoiding the sorcerer's gaze.

Earin Shad nodded to the slender Chiatze. 'The omens are good, I take it?' he asked.

Gamara spread his hands in an elegant gesture. 'It would be a waste of power to cast the stones, Sea Lord. During the storm they lost half their men.'

'And you are sure they are carrying gold?'

The Chiatze grinned, showing a perfect line of small, white teeth. Like a child's, thought Earin Shad. He looked into the man's dark, slanted eyes. 'How much are they carrying?'

'Two hundred and sixty thousand gold pieces. Bodasen gathered it from Ventrian merchants in Mashrapur.'

'You should have cast the stones,' said Earin Shad.

'We will see much blood,' answered Gamara. 'Aha! See, my good Lord, the sharks, as ever, follow in your wake. They are like pets, are they not?'

Earin Shad did not glance at the grey forms slipping effortlessly through the water, fins like raised sword-blades. 'They are the vultures of the sea,' he said, 'and I like them not at all.'

The wind shifted and *The Thunderchild* swung like a dancer on the white-flecked waves. On the decks of the *Darkwind* scores of warriors crouched by the starboard rail as the two ships moved ever closer. It will be close, thought Earin Shad; they will veer again and try to pull away. Anticipating the move he bellowed an order to Patek, who now stood on the main deck among the men. The giant leaned over the side and repeated the instruction to the oars chief. Immediately the starboard oars lifted from the water, the one hundred and twenty rowers on the port side continuing to row. *Darkwind* spun to starboard.

The Thunderchild sped on, then veered towards the oncoming vessel. On the prow the dark-bearded warrior was still waving the gleaming axe – and in that instant Earin Shad knew he had miscalculated. 'Bring in the oars!' he shouted.

Patek glanced up, astonished. 'What, Lord?'

'The oars, man! They're attacking *us*!'

It was too late. Even as Patek leaned over the side to shout the order *The Thunderchild* leapt to the attack, swinging violently towards *Darkwind*, the prow striking the first ranks of oars. Wood snapped violently with explosive cracks, mingled with the screams of the slave rowers as the heavy oars smashed into arms and skulls, shoulders and ribs.

Grappling lines were hurled out, iron claws biting into wood or hooking into *The Thunderchild*'s rigging. An arrow slashed into the chest of a corsair; the man pitched back, struggled to rise, then fell again. The corsairs hauled on the grappling-lines and the two ships edged together.

Earin Shad was furious. Half the oars on the starboard side had been smashed, and the gods alone knew how many slaves were crippled. Now he would be forced to limp to port. 'Ready to board!' he yelled.

The two ships crashed together. The corsairs rose and clambered to the rails.

In that moment the black-bearded warrior on the enemy ship stepped up to the prow and leaped into the massed ranks of waiting corsairs. Earin Shad could hardly believe what he was seeing. The black-garbed axeman sent several men spinning to the deck, almost fell himself, then swung his axe. A man screamed as blood sprayed from a terrible wound in his chest. The axe rose and fell – and the corsairs scattered back from the apparently deranged warrior.

He charged them, the axe cleaving into their ranks. Further along the deck other corsairs were still trying to board the merchant ship and meeting ferocious resistance from the Drenai warriors, but at the centre of the main deck all was chaos. A man ran in behind the axeman, a curved knife raised to stab him in the back. But an arrow slashed into the assailant's throat and he stumbled and fell.

Several Drenai warriors leapt to join the axeman. Earin Shad swore and drew his sabre, vaulting the rail and landing smoothly on the deck below. When a swordsman ran at him he parried the lunge and sent a riposte that missed the neck but opened the man's face from cheekbone to chin. As the warrior fell back Earin Shad plunged his blade into the man's mouth and up into the brain.

A lithe warrior in black breastplate and helm despatched a corsair and moved in on Earin Shad. The Corsair captain blocked a fierce thrust and attempted a riposte, only to leap back as his opponent's blade slashed by his face. The man was dark-skinned and dark-eyed, and a master swordsman.

Earin Shad stepped back and drew a dagger. 'Ventrian?' he enquired.

The man smiled. 'Indeed I am.' A Corsair leapt from behind the swordsman. He spun and disembowelled the man, then swung back in time to block a thrust from Earin Shad. 'I am Bodasen.'

The Corsairs were tough, hardy men, long used to battles and the risk of death. But they had never had to face a phenomenon like the man

171

with the axe. Watching from the tiller deck of *The Thunderchild*, Sieben saw them fall back, again and again, from Druss's frenzied, tireless assaults. Though the day was warm Sieben felt a chill in his blood as he watched the axe cleaving into the hapless pirates. Druss was unstoppable – and Sieben knew why. When swordsmen fought the outcome rested on skill, but armed with the terrible double-headed axe there was no skill needed, just power and an eagerness for combat – a battle lust that seemed unquenchable. No one could stand against him, for the only way to win was to run within the reach of those deadly blades. Death was not a risk; it was a certainty. And Druss himself seemed to possess a sixth sense. Corsairs circled behind him, but even as they rushed in he swung to face them, the axe-blades slashing through skin, flesh and bone. Several of the corsairs threw down their weapons, backing away from the huge, blood-smeared warrior. These Druss ignored.

Sieben flicked his gaze to where Bodasen fought with the enemy captain. Their swords, shimmering in the sunlight, seemed fragile and insubstantial against the raw power of Druss and his axe.

A giant figure bearing an iron warhammer leapt at Druss – just as Snaga became embedded in the ribs of a charging corsair. Druss ducked under the swinging weapon and sent a left hook that exploded against the man's jaw. Even as the giant fell, Druss snatched up his axe and near beheaded a daring attacker. Other Drenai warriors ran to join him and the corsairs backed away, dismayed and demoralised.

'Throw your weapons down!' bellowed Druss, 'And live!'

There was little hesitation and swords, sabres, cutlasses and knives clattered to the deck. Druss turned to see Bodasen block a thrust and send a lightning counter that ripped across the enemy captain's throat. Blood sprayed from the wound. The captain half fell, and tried for one last stab. But his strength fled from him and he pitched face first to the deck.

A man in flowing green robes appeared at the tiller deck rail. Slender and tall, his hair waxed to his skull, he lifted his hands. Sieben blinked. He seemed to be holding two spheres of glowing brass – no, the poet realised, not brass – but fire!

'Look out, Druss!' he shouted.

The sorcerer threw out his hands and a sheet of flame seared towards the axeman. Snaga flashed up; the flames struck the silver heads.

Time stopped for the poet. In a fraction of a heartbeat he saw a scene he would never forget. At the moment when the flames struck the axe, a demonic figure appeared above Druss, its skin iron-grey and scaled, its long, powerful arms ending in taloned fingers. The flames rebounded from the creature and slashed back into the sorcerer. His robes blazed and his chest imploded – a gaping hole appearing in his torso, through which Sieben could see the sky. The sorcerer toppled from the deck and the demon disappeared.

'Sweet mother of Cires!' whispered Sieben. He turned to Milus Bar. 'Did you see it?'

'Aye! The axe saved him right enough.'

'Axe? Did you not see the creature?'

'What are you talking about, man?'

Sieben felt his heart hammering. He saw Eskodas climbing down from the rigging and ran to him. 'What did you see when the flames came at Druss?' he asked, grabbing the bowman's arm.

'I saw him deflect them with his axe. What is wrong with you?'

'Nothing. Nothing at all.'

'We'd better cut free these ropes,' said Eskodas. 'The other ships are closing in.'

The Drenai warriors on the *Darkwind* also saw the two battle vessels approaching. With the defeated corsair standing by, they hacked at the ropes and then leapt back to *The Thunderchild*. Druss and Bodasen came last. None tried to stop them.

The giant Druss had felled rose unsteadily, then ran to the rail and leapt after the axeman, landing amidst a group of Drenai warriors and scattering them.

'It's not over!' he yelled. 'Face me!'

The Thunderchild eased away from the corsair ship, the wind gathering once more in her sails as Druss dropped Snaga to the deck and advanced on the giant. The corsair – almost a foot taller than the blood-drenched Drenai – landed the first blow, a juddering right that split the skin above Druss's left eye. Druss pushed through the blow and sent an uppercut that thundered against the man's rib-cage. The corsair grunted and smashed a left hook into Druss's jaw, making him stumble, then hit him again with lefts and rights. Druss rode them and hammered an overhand right that spun his opponent in a half-circle. Following up he hit him again, clubbing the man to his knees. Stepping back, Druss sent a vicious kick that almost lifted the giant from the deck. He slumped down, tried to rise, then lay still.

'Druss! Druss! Druss!' yelled the surviving Drenai warriors as *The Thunderchild* slipped away from the pursuing vessels.

Sieben sat down and stared at his friend.

No wonder you are so deadly, he thought. Sweet Heaven, Druss, you are possessed!

Druss moved wearily to the starboard rail, not even looking at the pursuing ships which were even now falling further behind *The Thunderchild*. Blood was clotting on his face, and he rubbed his left eye where the lashes were matted and sticky. Dropping Snaga to the deck Druss peeled off his jerkin, allowing the breeze to cool his skin.

Eskodas appeared alongside him, carrying a bucket of water. 'Is any of that blood yours?' the bowman asked.

Druss shrugged, uncaring. Removing his gauntlets, he dipped his hands into the bucket, splashing water to his face and beard. Then he lifted the bucket and tipped the contents over his head.

Eskodas scanned his body. 'You have minor wounds,' he said, probing at a narrow cut on Druss's shoulder and a gash in the side. 'Neither are deep. I'll get needle and thread.'

Druss said nothing. He felt a great weariness settle on him, a dullness of the spirit that left him leached of energy. He thought of Rowena, her gentleness and tranquillity, and of the peace he had known when beside her. Lifting his head, he leaned his huge hands on the rail. Behind him he heard laughter, and turned to see some of the warriors baiting the giant corsair. They had tied his hands behind his back and were jabbing at him with knives, forcing him to leap and dance.

Bodasen climbed down from the tiller deck. 'Enough of that!' he shouted.

'It's just a little sport before we throw him to the sharks,' replied a wiry warrior with a black and silver beard.

'No one will be thrown to the sharks,' snapped Bodasen. 'Now untie him.'

The men grumbled, but obeyed the order, and the giant stood rubbing his chafed wrists. His eyes met Druss's gaze, but the corsair's expression was unreadable. Bodasen led the man to the small cabin door below the tiller deck and they disappeared from view.

Eskodas returned and stitched the wounds in the axeman's shoulder and side. He worked swiftly and expertly. 'You must have had the gods with you,' he said. 'They granted you good luck.'

'A man makes his own luck,' said Druss.

Eskodas chuckled. 'Aye. Trust in the Source – but keep a spare bowstring handy. That's what my old teacher used to tell me.'

Druss thought back to the action on the trireme. 'You helped me,' he said, remembering the arrow that had killed the man coming in behind him.

'It was a good shot,' agreed Eskodas. 'How are you feeling?'

Druss shrugged. 'Like I could sleep for a week.'

'It is very natural, my friend. Battle lust roars through the blood, but the aftermath is unbearably depressing. Not many poets sing songs about that.' Eskodas took up a cloth and sponged the blood from Druss's jerkin, handing it back to the axeman. 'You are a great fighter, Druss – perhaps the best I've seen.'

Druss slipped on his jerkin, gathered Snaga and walked to the prow where he stretched out between two bales. He slept for just under an hour, but was woken by Bodasen; he opened his eyes and saw the Ventrian bending over him as the sun was setting.

'We need to talk, my friend,' said Bodasen and Druss sat up. The stitches in his side pulled tight as he stretched. He swore softly. 'I'm tired,' said the axeman. 'So let's make this brief.'

'I have spoken with the corsair. His name is Patek ...'

'I don't care what his name is.'

Bodasen sighed. 'In return for information about the numbers of corsair vessels, I have promised him his liberty when we reach Capalis. I have given him my word.'

'What has this to do with me?'

'I would like your word also that you will not kill him.'

'I don't want to kill him. He means nothing to me.'

'Then say the words, my friend.'

Druss looked into the Ventrian's dark eyes. 'There is something else,' he said, 'something you are not telling me.'

'Indeed there is,' agreed Bodasen. 'Tell me that you will allow my promise to Patek to be honoured, and I shall explain all.'

'Very well. I will not kill him. Now say what you have to say – and then let me get some sleep.'

Bodasen drew in a long, deep breath. 'The trireme was the *Darkwind*. The captain was Earin Shad, one of the leading Corsair . . . kings, if you like. They have been patrolling these waters for some months. One of the ships they . . . plundered . . .' Bodasen fell silent. He licked his lips. 'Druss, I'm sorry. Kabuchek's ship was taken and sunk, the passengers and crew thrown to the sharks. No one survived.'

Druss sat very still. All anger vanished from him.

'I wish there was something I could say or do to lessen your pain,' said Bodasen. 'I know that you loved her.'

'Leave me be,' whispered Druss. 'Just leave me be.'

176

5

Word soon spread among the warriors and crew of the tragedy that had befallen the huge axeman. Many of the men could not understand the depth of his grief, knowing nothing of love, but all could see the change in him. He sat at the prow, staring out over the sea, the massive axe in his hands. Sieben alone could approach him, but even the poet did not remain with him for long.

There was little laughter for the remaining three days of the voyage, for Druss's brooding presence seemed to fill the deck. The corsair giant, Patek, remained as far from the axeman as space would allow, spending his time on the tiller deck.

On the morning of the fourth day the distant towers of Capalis could be seen, white marble glinting in the sun.

Sieben approached Druss. 'Milus Bar intends to pick up a cargo of spices and attempt the return journey. Shall we stay on board?'

'I'm not going back,' said Druss.

'There is nothing here for us now,' pointed out the poet.

'There is the enemy,' the axeman grunted.

'What enemy?'

'The Naashanites.'

Sieben shook his head. 'I don't understand you. We don't even know a Naashanite!'

'They killed my Rowena. I'll make them pay.'

Sieben was about to debate the point, but he stopped himself. The Naashanites had bought the services of the corsairs and in Druss's mind this made them guilty. Sieben wanted to argue, to hammer home to Druss that the real villain was Earin Shad, and that he was

177

now dead. But what was the use? In the midst of his grief Druss would not listen. His eyes were cold, almost lifeless, and he clung to the axe as if it were his only friend.

'She must have been a very special woman,' observed Eskodas when he and Sieben stood by the port rail as *The Thunderchild* eased her way into the harbour.

'I never met her. But he speaks of her with reverence.'

Eskodas nodded, then pointed to the quayside. 'There are no dock-workers,' he said, 'only soldiers. The city must be under siege.'

Sieben saw movement at the far end of the quay, a column of soldiers wearing black breastplates adorned with silver marching behind a tall, wide-shouldered nobleman. 'That must be Gorben,' he said. 'He walks as if he owns the world.'

Eskodas chuckled. 'Not any more – but I'll agree he is a remarkably handsome fellow.'

The Emperor wore a simple black cloak above an unadorned breastplate, yet he still – like a hero of legend – commanded attention. Men ceased in their work as he approached, and Bodasen leapt from the ship even before the mooring ropes were fastened, landing lightly and stepping into the other man's embrace. The Emperor clapped him on the back, and kissed Bodasen on both cheeks.

'I'd say they were friends,' observed Eskodas dryly.

'Strange customs they have in foreign lands,' said Sieben, with a grin.

The gangplank was lowered and a squad of soldiers moved on board, vanishing below decks and reappearing bearing heavy chests of brass-bound oak.

'Gold, I'd say,' whispered Eskodas and Sieben nodded. Twenty chests in all were removed before the Drenai warriors were allowed to disembark. Sieben clambered down the gangplank just behind the bowman. As he stepped ashore he felt the ground move beneath him and he almost stumbled, then righted himself.

'Is it an earthquake?' he asked Eskodas.

'No, my friend, it is merely that you are so used to the pitching and rolling of the ship that your legs are unaccustomed to solid stone. It will pass very swiftly.'

Druss strode down to join them as Bodasen stepped forward, the Emperor beside him.

'And this, my Lord, is the warrior I spoke of – Druss the Axeman. Almost single-handedly he destroyed the corsairs.'

'I would like to have seen it,' said Gorben. 'But there is time yet to admire your prowess. The enemy are camped around our city and the attacks have begun.'

Druss said nothing, but the Emperor seemed unconcerned. 'May I see your axe?' he asked. Druss nodded and passed the weapon to the monarch. Gorben accepted it and lifted the blades to his face. 'Remarkable workmanship. Not a nick or a rust mark – the surface is entirely unblemished. A rare kind of steel.' He examined the black haft and the silver runes. 'This is an ancient weapon, and has seen much death.'

'It will see more,' said Druss, his voice low and rumbling. At the sound Sieben shivered.

Gorben smiled and handed back the axe, then turned to Bodasen. 'When you have settled your men into their quarters you will find me at the Magisters' Hall.' He strode away without another word.

Bodasen's face was white with anger. 'When you are in the presence of the Emperor you should bow deeply. He is a man to respect.'

'We Drenai are not well versed in subservient behaviour,' Sieben pointed out.

'In Ventria such disrespect is punishable by disembowelling,' said Bodasen.

'But I think we can learn,' Sieben told him cheerfully.

Bodasen smiled. 'See that you do, my friends. These are not Drenai lands, and there are other customs here. The Emperor is a good man, a fine man. Even so he must maintain discipline, and he will not tolerate such bad manners again.'

The Drenai warriors were billeted in the town centre, all save Druss and Sieben who had not signed on to fight for the Ventrians. Bodasen took the two of them to a deserted inn and told them to choose their

179

own rooms. Food, he said, could be found at either of the two main barracks, although there were still some shops and stalls in the town centre.

'Do you want to look at the city?' asked Sieben, after the Ventrian general had left. Druss sat on a narrow bed staring at his hands; he did not seem to hear the question. The poet sat alongside him. 'How are you feeling?' he asked softly.

'Empty.'

'Everyone dies, Druss. Even you and I. It is not your fault.'

'I don't care about *fault*. I just keep thinking about our time in the mountains together. I can still feel . . . the touch of her hand. I can still hear . . .' He stumbled to silence, his face reddened and his jaw set in a tight line. 'What was that about the city?' he growled.

'I thought we could take a look around.'

'Good. Let's go.' Druss rose, gathered his axe and strode through the door. The inn was situated on Vine Street. Bodasen had given them directions through the city and these were easy to follow, the roads being wide, the signs in several languages including the western tongue. The buildings were of white and grey stone, some more than four levels high. There were gleaming towers, domed palaces, gardens and tree-lined avenues. The scent of flowers, jasmine and rose, was everywhere.

'It is very beautiful,' observed Sieben. They passed a near-deserted barracks and headed on towards the eastern wall. From the distance they could hear the clash of blades and the thin cries of wounded men. 'I think I've seen enough,' announced Sieben, halting.

Druss gave a cold smile. 'As you wish,' he said.

'There's a temple back there I'd like to see more of. You know, the one with the white horses?'

'I saw it,' said Druss. The two men retraced their steps until they came to a large square. The temple was domed, and around it were twelve exquisitely sculpted statues of rearing horses, three times larger than life. A huge arched gateway, with open gates of polished brass and silver between beckoned the two men into the temple. The domed roof had seven windows, all of coloured glass, and beams

180

of light criss-crossed the high altar. There were benches that could seat almost a thousand people, Sieben calculated, and upon the altar was a table on which was set a hunting horn of gold encrusted with gems. The poet walked down the aisle and climbed to the altar. 'It's worth a fortune,' he said.

'On the contrary,' came a low voice, 'it is priceless.' Sieben turned to see a priest in robes of grey wool, embroidered with silver thread. The man was tall, his shaven head and long nose giving him a birdlike appearance. 'Welcome to the shrine of Pashtar Sen.'

'The citizens here must be worthy of great trust,' said Sieben. 'Such a prize as this would gain a man enormous wealth.'

The priest gave a thin smile. 'Not really. Lift it!'

Sieben reached out his hand, but his fingers closed on air. The golden horn, so substantial to the eye, was merely an image. 'Incredible!' whispered the poet. 'How is it done?'

The priest shrugged and spread his thin arms. 'Pashtar Sen worked the miracle a thousand years ago. He was a poet and a scholar, but also a man of war. According to myth he met the goddess, Ciris, and she gave him the hunting horn as a reward for his valour. He placed it here. And the moment it left his grasp it became as you see it.'

'What is its purpose?' Sieben asked.

'It has healing properties. Barren women are said to become fertile if they lie upon the altar and cover the horn. There is some evidence that this is true. And once every ten years the horn is said to become solid once more and then, so we are told, it can bring a man back from the halls of death, or carry his spirit to the stars.'

'Have you ever seen it become solid?'

'No. And I have been a servant here for thirty-seven years.'

'Fascinating. What happened to Pashtar Sen?'

'He refused to fight for the Emperor and was impaled on a spike of iron.'

'Not a good ending.'

'Indeed not, but he was a man of principle and believed the Emperor to be in the wrong. Are you here to fight for Ventria?'

'No. We are visitors.'

The priest nodded and turned to Druss. 'Your mind is far away, my son,' he said. 'Are you troubled?'

'He has suffered a great loss,' said Sieben swiftly.

'A loved one? Ah, I see. Would you wish to commune with her, my son?'

'What do you mean?' growled Druss.

'I could summon her spirit. It might bring you peace.'

Druss stepped forward. 'You could do that?'

'I could try. Follow me.' The priest led them into the shadowed recesses at the rear of the temple, then along a narrow corridor to a small, windowless room. 'You must leave your weapons outside,' said the priest. Druss leaned Snaga against the wall, and Sieben hung his baldric of knives to the haft. Inside the room there were two chairs facing one another; the priest sat in the first, beckoning Druss to take the second. 'This room,' said the priest, 'is a place of harmony. No profane language has ever been heard here. It is a room of prayer and kind thoughts. It has been so for a thousand years. Whatever happens, please remember that. Now give me your hand.'

Druss stretched out his arm and the priest took hold of his hand, asking who it was that he wished to call. Druss told him. 'And your name, my son?'

'Druss.'

The man licked his lips and sat, eyes closed, for several minutes. Then he spoke. 'I call to thee, Rowena, child of the mountains. I call to thee on behalf of Druss. I call to thee across the plains of Heaven, I speak to thee across the vales of Earth. I reach out to thee, even unto the dark places below the oceans of the world, and the arid deserts of Hell.' For a moment nothing happened. Then the priest stiffened and cried out. He slumped down in the chair, head dropping to his chest.

His mouth opened and a single word issued forth: 'Druss!' It was a woman's voice. Sieben was startled. He glanced at the axeman; all colour faded from Druss's face.

'Rowena!'

182

'I love you, Druss. Where are you?'

'In Ventria. I came for you.'

'I am here waiting. Druss! Oh no, everything is fading. Druss, can you hear ...?'

'Rowena!' shouted Druss, storming to his feet. The priest jerked and awoke. 'I am sorry,' he said. 'I did not find her.'

'I spoke to her,' said Druss, hauling the man to his feet. 'Get her again!'

'I cannot. There was no one. Nothing happened!'

'Druss! Let him go!' shouted Sieben, grabbing Druss's arm. The axeman released his hold on the priest's robes and walked from the room.

'I don't understand,' whispered the man. 'There was nothing!'

'You spoke with the voice of a woman,' Sieben told him. 'Druss recognised it.'

'It is most peculiar, my son. Whenever I commune with the dead I know their words. But it was as if I slept.'

'Do not concern yourself,' said Sieben, fishing in his money-pouch for a silver coin.

'I take no money,' said the man, with a shy smile. 'But I am perplexed and I will think on what just happened.'

'I'm sure he will too,' said Sieben.

He found Druss standing by the altar, reaching out to the shimmering golden horn, his huge fingers trying to close around it. The axeman's face was set in concentration, the muscles of his jaw showing through the dark beard.

'What are you doing?' asked Sieben, his voice gentle.

'He said it could bring back the dead.'

'No, my friend. He said that was the *legend*. There is a difference. Come away. We'll find a tavern somewhere in this city, and we'll drink.'

Druss slammed his hand down on to the altar, the golden horn apparently growing through the skin of his fist. 'I don't need to drink! Gods, I need to fight!' Snatching up the axe, the big man strode from the temple.

The priest appeared alongside Sieben. 'I fear that, despite my good intentions, the result of my labour was not as I had hoped,' he said.

'He'll survive, Father.' Sieben turned to the priest. 'Tell me, what do you know of demon possession?'

'Too much – and too little. You think you are possessed?'

'No, not I. Druss.'

The priest shook his head. 'Had he been so ... afflicted ... I would have sensed it when I touched his hand. No, your friend is his own man.'

Sieben sat down on a bench seat and told the priest what he had seen on the deck of the corsair trireme. The priest listened in silence. 'How did he come by the axe?' he asked.

'Family heirloom, I understand.'

'If there is a demonic presence, my son, I believe you will find it hidden within the weapon. Many of the ancient blades were crafted with spells, in order to give the wielder greater strength or cunning. Some even had the power to heal wounds, so it is said. Look to the axe.'

'What if it is just the axe? Surely that will only help him in times of combat?'

'Would that were true,' said the priest, shaking his head. 'But evil does not exist in order to serve, but to rule. If the axe is possessed it will have a history – a dark history. Ask him of its past. And when you hear it, and of the men who wielded it, you will understand my words.'

Sieben thanked the man and left the temple. There was no sign of Druss, and the poet had no wish to venture near the walls. He strolled through the near-deserted city until he heard the sound of music coming from a courtyard nearby. He approached a wrought-iron gate and saw three women sitting in a garden. One of them was playing a lyre, the others were singing a gentle love song as Sieben stepped into the gateway.

'Good afternoon, ladies,' he said, offering them his most dazzling smile. The music ceased and the three all gazed at him. They were young and pretty – the oldest, he calculated, around seventeen. She was dark-haired and dark-eyed, full-lipped and slender. The other two were smaller, their hair blonde, their eyes blue. They were dressed in shimmering gowns of satin, the dark-haired beauty in blue and the others in white.

'Have you come to see our brother, sir?' asked the dark-haired girl, rising from her seat and placing the lyre upon it.

'No, I was drawn here by the beauty of your playing and the sweet voices which accompanied it. I am a stranger here, and a lover of all things beautiful, and I can only thank the fates for the vision I find here.' The younger girls laughed, but the older sister merely smiled.

'Pretty words, sir, well phrased, and I don't doubt well rehearsed. They have the smooth edges of weapons that have seen great use.'

Sieben bowed. 'Indeed, my lady, it has been my pleasure and my privilege to observe beauty wherever I can find it; to pay homage to it; to bend the knee before it. But it makes my words no less sincere.'

She gave a full smile, then laughed aloud. 'I think you are a rascal, sir, and a libertine, and in more interesting times I would summon a servant to see you from the premises. However, since we are at war and that makes for the dullest entertainment, I shall welcome you – but only for so long as you are entertaining.'

'Sweet lady, I think I can promise you entertainment enough, both in word and deed.' He was delighted that she did not blush at his words, though the younger sisters reddened.

'Such fine promises, sir. But then perhaps you would feel less secure in your boasting were you aware of the quality of entertainment I have enjoyed in the past.'

Now it was Sieben's turn to laugh. 'Should you tell me that Azhral, the Prince of Heaven, came to your chambers and transported you to the Palace of Infinite Variety, then truly I might be mildly concerned.'

'Such a book should not be mentioned in polite company,' she chided.

He stepped closer and took her hand, raising it to his lips and turning it to kiss her palm. 'Not so,' he said softly, 'the book has great merit, for it shines like a lantern in the hidden places. It parts the veils and leads us to the paths of pleasure. I recommend the sixteenth chapter for all new lovers.'

'My name is Asha,' she said, 'and your deeds will need to be as fine as your words, for I react badly to disappointment.'

'You were dreaming, *Pahtai*,' said Pudri as Rowena opened her eyes and found herself sitting in the sunshine beside the lake.

'I don't know what happened,' she told the little eunuch. 'It was as if my soul was dragged from my body. There was a room, and Druss was sitting opposite me.'

'Sadness gives birth to many visions of hope,' quoted Pudri.

'No, it was real, but the hold loosened and I came back before I could tell him where I was.'

He patted her hand. 'Perhaps it will happen again,' he said reassuringly, 'but for now you must compose yourself. The master is entertaining the great Satrap, Shabag. He is being sent to command the forces around Capalis and it is very important that you give him good omens.'

'I can offer only the truth.'

'There are many truths, *Pahtai*. A man may have only days to live, yet in that time will find great love. The seeress who tells him he is about to die will cause him great sorrow – but it will be the truth. The prophet who says that love is only a few hours away will also be telling the truth, but will create great joy in the doomed man.'

Rowena smiled. 'You are very wise, Pudri.'

He shrugged and smiled. 'I am old, Rowena.'

'That is the first time you have used my name.'

He chuckled. 'It is a good name, but so is *Pahtai*; it means *gentle dove*. Now we must go to the shrine. Shall I tell you something of Shabag? Would it help your talent?'

She sighed. 'No. Tell me nothing. I will see what there is to see – and I will remember your advice.'

Arm in arm they strolled into the palace, along the richly carpeted corridors, past the beautifully carved staircase that led to the upper apartments. Statues and busts of marble were set into recesses every ten feet on both sides of the corridor, and the ceiling above them was embellished with scenes from Ventrian literature, the architraves covered with gold leaf.

As they approached the shrine room a tall warrior stepped out from a side door. Rowena gasped, for at first she took the man to be Druss. He had the same breadth of shoulder and jutting jaw, and his eyes beneath thick brows were startlingly blue. Seeing her, he smiled and bowed.

'This is Michanek, *Pahtai*. He is the champion of the Naashanite Emperor – a great swordsman and a respected officer.' Pudri bowed to the warrior. 'This is the Lady Rowena, a guest of the Lord Kabuchek.'

'I have heard of you, lady,' said Michanek, taking her hand and drawing it to his lips. His voice was low and vibrant. 'You saved the merchant from the sharks, no mean feat. But now I have seen you I can understand how even a shark would wish to do nothing to mar your beauty.' Keeping hold of her hand he smiled and moved in close. 'Can you tell me my fortune, lady?'

Her throat was dry, but she met his gaze. 'You will . . . you will achieve your greatest ambition, and realise your greatest hope.'

His eyes showed his cynicism. 'Is that it, lady? Surely any street charlatan could say the same. How will I die?'

'Not fifty feet from where we stand,' she said. 'Out in the court-yard. I see soldiers with black cloaks and helms, storming the walls. You will gather your men for a last stand outside these walls. Beside you will be . . . your strongest brother and a second cousin.'

'And when will this be?'

'One year after you are wed. To the day.'

'And what is the name of the lady I shall marry?'

'I will not say,' she told him.

'We must go, Lord,' said Pudri swiftly. 'The Lords Kabuchek and Shabag await.'

'Of course. It was a pleasure meeting you, Rowena. I hope we will meet again.'

Rowena did not reply, but followed Pudri into the shrine room.

At dusk the enemy drew back, and Druss was surprised to see the Ventrian warriors leaving the walls and strolling back through the city streets. 'Where is everyone going?' he asked the warrior beside him. The man had removed his helm and was wiping his sweat-streaked face with a cloth.

'To eat and rest,' the warrior answered.

Druss scanned the walls. Only a handful of men remained, and these were sitting with their backs to the ramparts. 'What if there is another attack?' asked the axeman.

'There won't be. That was the fourth.'

'Fourth?' queried Druss, surprised.

The warrior, a middle-aged man with a round face and keen blue eyes, grinned at the Drenai. 'I take it that you are no student of strategy. Your first siege, is it?' Druss nodded. 'Well, the rules of engagement are precise. There will be a maximum of four attacks during any twenty-four-hour period.'

'Why only four?'

The man shrugged. 'It's a long time since I studied the manual, but, as I recall, it is a question of morale. When Zhan Tsu wrote *The Art of War* he explained that after four attacks the spirit of the attackers can give way to despair.'

'There won't be very much despair among them if they attack now – or after night falls,' Druss pointed out.

'They won't attack,' said his comrade slowly, as if speaking to a child. 'If a night attack was planned there would have only been three assaults during the day.'

Druss was nonplussed. 'And these rules were written in a book?'

'Yes, a fine work by a Chiatze general.'

'And you will leave these walls virtually unmanned during the night because of a book?'

The man laughed. 'Not the *book*, the rules of engagement. Come with me to the barracks and I'll explain a little more.'

As they strolled the warrior, Oliquar, told Druss that he had served in the Ventrian army for more than twenty years. 'I was even an officer once, during the Opal Campaign. Damn near wiped out we were, so I got to command a troop of forty men. It didn't last. The General offered me a commission, but I couldn't afford the armour, so that was it. Back to the rankers. But it's not a bad life. Comradeship, two good meals a day.'

'Why couldn't you afford the armour? Don't they pay officers?'

'Of course, but only a *disha* a day. That's half of what I earn now.'

'The officers receive less than the rankers? That's stupid.'

Oliquar shook his head. 'Of course it isn't. That way only the rich can afford to be officers, which means that only noblemen – or the sons of merchants, who desire to be noblemen – can command. In this way the noble families retain power. Where are you from, young man?'

'I am Drenai.'

'Ah, yes. I have never been there of course, but I understand the mountains of Skeln are exceptionally beautiful. Green and lush, like the Saurab. I miss the mountains.'

Druss sat with Oliquar in the Western Barracks and ate a meal of beef and wild onions before setting off back to the empty tavern. It was a calm night, with no clouds, and the moon turned the white, ghostly buildings to a muted silver.

Sieben was not in their room and Druss sat by the window, staring out over the harbour, watching the moonlit waves and the water which looked like molten iron. He had fought in three of the four attacks – the enemy, red-cloaked, with helms boasting white horsehair plumes, running forward carrying ladders which they leaned against the walls. Rocks had been hurled down upon them, arrows peppered them. Yet on they came. The first to reach the walls were speared, or struck with swords, but a few doughty fighters made their way to the battlements, where they were cut down by the defenders. Halfway through the second attack a dull, booming sound, like controlled thunder, was heard on the walls.

'Battering ram,' said the soldier beside him. 'They won't have much luck, those gates are reinforced with iron and brass.'

Druss leaned back in his chair and stared down at Snaga. In the main, he had used the axe to push back ladders, sliding them along the wall, sending attackers tumbling to the rocky ground below. Only twice had the weapon drawn blood. Reaching out Druss stroked the black haft, remembering the victims – a tall, beardless warrior and a swarthy, pot-bellied man in an iron helm. The first had died when Snaga crunched through his wooden breastplate, the second when the silver blades had sheared his iron helm in two. Druss ran his thumb along the blades. Not a mark, or a nick.

Sieben arrived at the room just before midnight. His eyes were red-rimmed and he yawned constantly. 'What happened to you?' asked Druss.

The poet smiled. 'I made new friends.' Pulling off his boots he settled back on one of the narrow beds.

Druss sniffed the air. 'Smells like you were rolling in a flowerbed.'

'A bed of flowers,' said Sieben with a smile. 'Yes, almost exactly how I would describe it.'

Druss frowned. 'Well, never mind that, do you know anything about rules of engagement?'

'I know everything about *my* rules of engagement, but I take it you are talking about Ventrian warfare?' Swinging his legs from the bed, he sat up. 'I'm tired, Druss, so let's make this conversation brief. I have a meeting in the morning and I need to build up my strength.'

Druss ignored the exaggerated yawn with which Sieben accompanied his words. 'I saw hundreds of men wounded today, and scores killed. Yet now, with only a few men on the walls, the enemy sits back and waits for sunrise. Why? Does no one want to win?'

'Someone will win,' answered Sieben. 'But this is a *civilised* land. They have practised warfare for thousands of years. The siege will go on for a few weeks, or a few months, and every day the combatants will count their losses. At some point, if there is no breakthrough, either one or the other will offer terms to the enemy.'

'What do you mean, terms?'

'If the besiegers decide they cannot win, they will withdraw. If the men here decide all is lost, they will desert to the enemy.'

'What about Gorben?'

Sieben shrugged. 'His own troops might kill him, or hand him over to the Naashanites.'

'Gods, is there no honour among these Ventrians?'

'Of course there is, but most of the men here are mercenaries from many eastern tribes. They are loyal to whoever pays them the most.'

'If the rules of war here are so civilised,' said Druss, 'why have the inhabitants of the city fled? Why not just wait until the fighting is over, and serve whoever wins?'

'They would, at best, be enslaved; at worst, slaughtered. It may be a civilised land, Druss, but it is also a harsh one.'

'Can Gorben win?'

'Not as matters stand, but he may be lucky. Often Ventrian sieges are settled by single combat between champions, though such an event would take place only if both factions were of equal strength, and both had champions they believed were invincible. That won't happen here, because Gorben is heavily outnumbered. However, now that he has the gold Bodasen brought he will send spies in to the enemy camp to bribe the soldiers to desert to his cause. It's unlikely to work, but it might. Who knows?'

'Where did you learn all this?' asked Druss.

'I have just spent an informative afternoon with the Princess Asha – Gorben's sister.'

'What?' stormed Druss. 'What is it with you? Did you learn nothing from what happened in Mashrapur? One day! And already you are rutting!'

'I do not *rut*,' snapped Sieben. 'I make love. And what I do is none of your concern.'

'That's true,' admitted Druss, 'and when they take you for disembowelling, or impaling, I shall remind you of that.'

'Ah, Druss!' said Sieben, settling back on the bed. 'There are some things worth dying for. And she is very beautiful. By the gods, a man could do worse than marry her.'

Druss stood and turned away to the window. Sieben was instantly contrite. 'I am sorry, my friend. I wasn't thinking.' He approached Druss and laid his hand on his shoulder. 'I am sorry about what happened with the priest.'

'It was her voice,' said Druss, swallowing hard and fighting to keep his emotions in check. 'She said she was waiting for me. I thought that if I went to the wall I might be killed, and then I'd be with her again. But no one came with the skill or the heart. No one ever will . . . and I don't have the courage to do the deed myself.'

191

'That would not be courage, Druss. And Rowena would not want it. She'd want you to be happy, to marry again.'

'Never!'

'You are not yet twenty, my friend. There are other women.'

'None like her. But she's gone, and I'll speak no more of her. I'll carry her here,' he said, touching his chest, 'and I'll not forget her. Now go back to what you were saying about Eastern warfare.'

Sieben lifted a clay goblet from a shelf by the window, blew the dust from it, and filled it with water which he drained at a single swallow. 'Gods, that tastes foul! All right . . . Eastern warfare. What is it you wish to know now?'

'Well,' said Druss, slowly, 'I know that the enemy can attack four times in a day. But why did they only attack one wall? They have the numbers to surround the city and attack in many places at once.'

'They will, Druss, but not in the first month. This is the testing time. Untried new soldiers are judged on their courage during the first few weeks; then they will bring up the siege-engines. That should be the second month. After that perhaps ballistae, hurling huge rocks over the walls. If at the end of the month there has been no success, they will call in the engineers and they will burrow under the walls, seeking to bring them down.'

'And what rules over the besieged?' asked the axeman.

'I don't understand you?'

'Well, suppose we were to attack them. Could we only do it four times? Can we attack at night? What are the rules?'

'It is not a question of rules, Druss, it's more a matter for common sense. Gorben is outnumbered by around twenty to one; if he attacked, he'd be wiped out.'

Druss nodded, and lapsed into silence. Finally he spoke. 'I'll ask Oliquar for his book. You can read it to me, then I'll understand.'

'Can we sleep now?' asked Sieben.

Druss nodded and took up his axe. He did not remove his boots or jerkin and stretched out on the second bed with Snaga beside him.

'You don't need an axe in bed in order to sleep.'

'It comforts me,' answered Druss, closing his eyes.

'Where did you get it?'

'It belonged to my grandfather.'

'Was he a great hero?' asked Sieben, hopefully.

'No, he was a madman, and a terrible killer.'

'That's nice,' said Sieben, settling down on his own bed. 'It's good to know you have a family trade to fall back on if times get hard.'

6

Gorben leaned back in his chair as his servant, Mushran, carefully shaved the stubble from his chin. He glanced up at the old man. 'Why do you stare so?' he asked.

'You are tired, my boy. Your eyes are red-rimmed and there are purple patches beneath them.'

Gorben smiled. 'One day you will call me, "great Lord" or "my Emperor". I live for that day, Mushran.'

The old man chuckled. 'Other men can bestow upon you these titles. They can fall to the ground before you and bounce their brows from the stone. But when I look upon you, *my boy*, I see the child that was before the man, and the babe who was before the child. I prepared your food and I wiped your arse. And I am too old to crash my poor head to the stones every time you walk into a room. Besides, you are changing the subject. You need more rest.'

'Has it escaped your notice that we have been under siege for a month? I must show myself to the men; they must see me fight, or they will lose heart. And there are supplies to be organised, rations set – a hundred different duties. Find me some more hours in a day and I will rest, I promise you.'

'You don't need more hours,' snapped the old man, lifting the razor and wiping oil and stubble from the blade. 'You need better men. Nebuchad is a good boy – but he's slow-witted. And Jasua . . .' Mushran raised his eyes to the ceiling. 'A wonderful killer, but his brain is lodged just above his . . .'

'Enough of that!' said Gorben amiably. 'If my officers knew how you spoke of them, they'd have you waylaid in an alley and beaten to death. Anyway, what about Bodasen?'

'The best of them – but let's be fair, that isn't saying much.'

Gorben's reply was cut off as the razor descended to his throat and he felt the keen blade gliding up over his jawline and across to the edge of his mouth. 'There!' said Mushran proudly. 'At least you look like an Emperor now.'

Gorben stood and wandered to the window. The fourth attack was under way; it would be repulsed, he knew, but even from here he could see the huge siege-towers being dragged into place for tomorrow. He pictured the hundreds of men pulling them into position, saw in his mind's eye the massive attack ramps crashing down on to the battlements, and heard the war cries of the Naashanite warriors as they clambered up the steps, along the ramp, and hurled themselves on to the defenders. Naashanites? He laughed bitterly. Two-thirds of the *enemy* soldiers were Ventrians, followers of Shabag, one of the renegade Satraps. Ventrians killing Ventrians! It was obscene. And for what? How much richer could Shabag become? How many palaces could a man occupy at one time? Gorben's father had been a weak man, and a poor judge of character, but for all that he had been an Emperor who cared for his people. Every city boasted a university, built from funds supplied by the Royal treasury. There were colleges where the brightest students could learn the arts of medicine, listen to lectures from Ventria's finest herbalists. There were schools, hospitals, and a road system second to none on the continent. But his greatest achievement had been the forming of the Royal Riders, who could carry a message from one end of the Empire to another in less than twelve weeks. Such swift communication meant that if any satrapy suffered a natural disaster – plague, famine, flood – then help could be sent almost immediately.

Now the cities were either conquered or besieged, the death toll was climbing towards a mountainous total, the universities were closed, and the chaos of war was destroying everything his father had built. With great effort he forced down the heat of anger, and concentrated coolly on the problem facing him at Capalis.

Tomorrow would be a pivotal day in the siege. If his warriors held, then dismay would spread among the enemy. If not ... He smiled grimly. If not we are finished, he thought. Shabag would have him dragged before the Naashanite Emperor. Gorben sighed.

'Never let despair enter your mind,' said Mushran. 'There is no profit in it.'

'You read minds better than any seer.'

'Not minds, faces. So wipe that expression clear and I'll fetch Bodasen.'

'When did he arrive?'

'An hour ago. I told him to wait. You needed the shave – and the rest.'

'In a past life you must have been a wonderful mother,' said Gorben. Mushran laughed, and left the room. Returning, he ushered Bodasen inside and bowed. 'The general Bodasen, great Lord, my Emperor,' he said, then backed out, pulling shut the door behind him.

'I don't know why you tolerate that man, Lord!' snapped Bodasen. 'He is always insolent.'

'You wished to see me, general?'

Bodasen snapped to attention. 'Yes, sir. Druss the Axeman came to see me last night. He has a plan concerning the siege-towers.'

'Go on.'

Bodasen cleared his throat. 'He wants to attack them.'

Gorben stared hard at the general, observing the deep blush that was appearing on the warrior's cheeks. 'Attack them?'

'Yes, Lord. Tonight, under cover of darkness – attack the enemy camp and set fire to the towers.'

'You feel this is feasible?'

'No, Lord . . . well . . . perhaps. I watched this man attack a corsair trireme and force fifty men to throw down their weapons. I don't know whether he can succeed this time, but . . .'

'I'm still listening.'

'We have no choice. They have thirty siege-towers, Lord. They'll take the wall and we'll not hold them.'

Gorben moved to a couch and sat. 'How does he intend to set these fires? And what does he think the enemy will be doing while he does so? The timbers are huge, old, weathered. It will take a great flame to bring one of them down.'

'I appreciate that, Lord. But Druss says the Naashanites will be too busy to think of towers.' He cleared his throat. 'He intends to attack the centre of the camp, kill Shabag and the other generals, and generally cause enough mayhem to allow a group of men to sneak out from Capalis and set fires beneath the towers.'

'How many men has he asked for?'

'Two hundred. He says he's already chosen them.'

'*He* has chosen them?'

Bodasen glanced down at the floor. 'He is a very . . . popular man, Lord. He has fought every day and he knows many of the men well. They respect him.'

'Has he chosen any officers?'

'Only one . . . Lord.'

'Let me guess. You?'

'Yes, Lord.'

'And you are willing to lead this . . . insane venture?'

'I am, Lord.'

'I forbid it. But you can tell Druss that I agree, and that I will choose an officer to accompany him.'

Bodasen seemed about to protest, but he held his tongue, and bowed deeply. He backed to the door.

'General,' called Gorben.

'Yes, Lord?'

'I am well pleased with you,' said Gorben, not looking at the man. He walked out to the balcony and breathed the evening air. It was cool and flowing from the sea.

Shabag watched the setting sun turn the mountains to fire, the sky burning like the vaults of Hades, deep crimson, flaring orange. He shuddered. He had never liked sunsets. They spoke of endings, inconstancy – the death of a day.

The siege-towers stood in a grim line facing Capalis, monstrous giants promising victory. He gazed up at the first. Tomorrow they would be dragged to the walls, then the mouths of the giants would open, the attack ramps would drop to the ramparts like stiff tongues. He paused. How would one continue the analogy? He pictured the warriors climbing from the belly of the beast and hurling themselves on to the enemy. Then he chuckled. Like the breath of death, like a dragon's fire? No, more like a demon disgorging acid. Yes, I like that, he thought.

The towers had been assembled from sections brought on huge wagons from Resha in the north. They had cost twenty thousand gold pieces, and Shabag was still angry that he alone had been expected to finance them. The Naashanite Emperor was a parsimonious man.

'We will have him tomorrow, sir?' said one of his aides. Shabag jerked his mind to the present and turned to his staff officers. The *him* was Gorben. Shabag licked his thin lips.

'I want him alive,' he said, keeping the hatred from his voice. How he loathed Gorben! How he despised both the man and his appalling conceit. A trick of fate had left him with a throne that was rightly Shabag's. They shared the same ancestors, the kings of glory who had built an empire unrivalled in history. And Shabag's grandfather had sat upon the throne. But he died in battle leaving only daughters surviving him. Thus had Gorben's father ascended the golden steps and raised the ruby crown to his head.

And what happened then to the Empire? Stagnation. Instead of armies, conquest and glory, there were schools, fine roads and hospitals. And to what purpose? The weak were kept alive in order to breed more weaklings, peasants learned their letters and became obsessed with thoughts of betterment. Questions that should never have been voiced were debated openly in city squares: *By what right do the noble families rule our lives? Are we not free men?* By what right? By the right of blood, thought Shabag. By the right of steel and fire!

He thought back with relish to the day when he had surrounded the university at Resha with armed troops, after the students there had voiced their protests at the war. He had called out their leader, who came armed not with a sword, but with a scroll. It was an ancient work, written by Pashtar Sen, and the boy had read it aloud. What a fine voice he had. It was a well-written piece, full of thoughts of honour, and patriotism, and brotherhood. But then when Pashtar

Sen had written it the serfs knew their places, the peasants lived in awe of their betters. The sentiments were outworn now.

He had allowed the boy to finish the work, for anything less would have been ill-mannered, and ill befitting a nobleman. Then he had gutted him like a fish. Oh, how the brave students ran then! Save that there was nowhere to run, and they had died in their hundreds, like maggots washed from a pus-filled sore. The Ventrian Empire was decaying under the old emperor, and the only chance to resurrect her greatness was by war. Yes, thought Shabag, the Naashanites will think they have won, and I will indeed be a vassal king. But not for long.

Not for long . . .

'Excuse me, sir,' said an officer and Shabag turned to the man.

'Yes?'

'A ship has left Capalis. It is heading north along the coast. There are quite a number of men aboard.'

Shabag swore. 'Gorben has fled,' he announced. 'He saw our *giants* and realised he could not win.' He felt a sick sense of disappointment, for he had been anticipating tomorrow with great expectation. He turned his eyes towards the distant walls, half expecting to see the Herald of Surrender. 'I shall be in my tent. When they send for terms wake me.'

'Yes, sir.'

He strode through the camp, his anger mounting. Now some whore-born corsair would capture Gorben, maybe even kill him. Shabag glanced up at the darkening sky. 'I'd give my soul to have Gorben before me!' he said.

But sleep would not come and Shabag wished he had brought the Datian slave girl with him. Young, innocent, and exquisitely compliant, she would have brought him sleep and sweet dreams.

He rose from his bed and lit two lanterns. Gorben's escape – if he managed to avoid the corsairs – would prolong the war. But only by a few months, reasoned Shabag. Capalis would be his by tomorrow, and after that Ectanis would fall. Gorben would be forced to fall back into the mountains, throwing himself upon the mercy of the wild tribes who inhabited them. It would take time to hunt him down, but not too much. And the hunt might afford amusement during the bleak winter months.

He thought of his palace in Resha, deciding that after organising the surrender of Capalis he would return home for a rest. Shabag pictured the comforts of Resha, the theatres, the arena and the gardens. By now the flowering cherry trees would be in bloom by the lake, dropping their petals to the crystal waters, the sweet scent filling the air.

Was it only a month since he had sat by the lake with Darishan beside him, sunlight gleaming upon his braided silver hair?

'Why do you wear those gloves, cousin?' Darishan had asked, tossing a pebble into the water. A large golden fish flicked its tail at the sudden disturbance, then vanished into the depths.

'I like the feel of them,' answered Shabag irritated. 'But I did not come here to discuss matters sartorial.'

Darishan chuckled. 'Always so serious? We are on the verge of victory.'

'You said that half a year ago,' Shabag pointed out.

'And I was correct then. It is like a lion hunt, cousin. While he is in the dense undergrowth he has a chance, but once you have him on open ground, heading into the mountains, it is only a matter of time before he runs out of strength. Gorben is running out of strength *and* gold.'

'He still has three armies.'

'He began with seven. Two of them are now under my command. One is under yours, and one has been destroyed. Come, cousin, why the gloom?'

Shabag shrugged. 'I want to see an end to the war, so I can begin to rebuild.'

'I? Surely you mean *we*?'

'A slip of the tongue, cousin,' said Shabag swiftly, forcing a smile. Darishan leaned back on the marble seat and idly twisted one of his braids. Though not yet forty his hair was startlingly pale, silver and white, and braided with wires of gold and copper.

'Do not betray me, Shabag,' he warned. 'You will not be able to defeat the Naashanites alone.'

'A ridiculous thought, Darishan. We are of the same blood – and we are friends.'

Darishan's cold eyes held to Shabag's gaze, then he too smiled. 'Yes,' he whispered, 'friends and cousins. I wonder where our cousin – and former friend – Gorben is hiding today.'

Shabag reddened. 'He was never my friend. I do not betray my friends. Such thoughts are unworthy of you.'

'Indeed, you are right,' agreed Darishan, rising. 'I must leave for Ectanis. Shall we have a small wager as to which of us conquers first?'

'Why not? A thousand in gold that Capalis falls before Ectanis.'

'A thousand – plus the Datian slave girl?'

'Agreed,' said Shabag, masking his irritation. 'Take care, cousin.' The men shook hands.

'I shall.' The silver-haired Darishan swung away, then glanced back over his shoulder. 'By the way, did you see the wench?'

'Yes, but she told me little of use. I think Kabuchek was swindled.'

'That may be true, but she saved him from the sharks and predicted a ship would come. She also told me where to find the opal brooch I lost three years ago. What did she tell you?'

Shabag shrugged. 'She talked of my past, which was interesting, but then she could easily have been schooled by Kabuchek. When I asked her about the coming campaign she closed her eyes and took hold of my hand. She held it for maybe three heartbeats, then pulled away and said she could tell me nothing.'

'Nothing at all?'

'Nothing that made any sense. She said . . . "*He is coming!*" She seemed both elated and yet, moments later, terrified. Then she told me not to go to Capalis. That was it.'

Darishan nodded and seemed about to speak. Instead he merely smiled and walked away.

Putting thoughts of Darishan from his mind, Shabag moved to the tent entrance. The camp was quiet. Slowly he removed the glove from his left hand. The skin itched, red open sores covering the surface as they had done since adolescence. There were herbal ointments and emollients that could ease them, but nothing had

201

ever healed the diseased skin, nor fully removed the other sores that stretched across his back and chest, thighs and calves.

Slowly he peeled back the right-hand glove. The skin here was clean and smooth. This was the hand she had held.

He had offered Kabuchek sixty thousand gold pieces for her, but the merchant had politely refused. When the battle is over, thought Shabag, I shall have her taken from him.

Just as he was about to turn into the tent Shabag saw a line of soldiers marching slowly down towards the camp, their armour gleaming in the moonlight. They were moving in columns of twos, with an officer at the head; the man looked familiar, but he was wearing a plumed helm with a thick nasal guard that bisected his face. Shabag rubbed at his tired eyes to focus more clearly on the man; it was not the face but the walk that aroused his interest. One of Darishan's officers, he wondered? Where have I seen him before?

Pah, what difference does it make, he thought suddenly, pulling shut the tent-flap. He had just blown out the first of the two lanterns when a scream rent the air. Then another. Shabag ran to the entrance, tearing aside the flap.

Warriors were running through his camp, cutting and killing. Someone had picked up a burning brand and had thrown it against a line of tents. Flames rippled across the bone-dry cloth, the wind carrying the fire to other tents.

At the centre of the fighting Shabag saw a huge warrior dressed in black, brandishing a double-headed axe. Three men ran at him, and he killed them in moments. Then Shabag saw the officer – and remembrance rose like a lightning blast from the halls of his memory.

Gorben's soldiers surrounded Shabag's tent. It had been set at the centre of the camp, with thirty paces of clear ground around it to allow the Satrap a degree of privacy. Now it was ringed by armed men.

Shabag was bewildered by the speed at which the enemy had struck, but surely, he reasoned, it would avail them nothing. Twenty-five thousand men were camped around the besieged harbour city. How many of the enemy were here? Two hundred? Three hundred?

What could they possibly hope to achieve, save to slay Shabag himself? And how would that serve them, for they would die in the act?

Nonplussed, he stood – a still, silent spectator as the battle raged and the fires spread. He could not tear his eyes from the grim, blood-smeared axeman, who killed with such deadly efficiency, such a minimum of effort. When a horn sounded, a high shrill series of notes that flowed above the sounds of combat, Shabag was startled. The trumpeter was sounding the truce signal and the soldiers fell back, momentarily bewildered. Shabag wanted to shout at his men: 'Fight on! Fight on!' But he could not speak. Fear paralysed him. The silent circle of soldiers around him stood ready, their blades shining in the moonlight. He felt that were he to even move they would fall upon him like hounds upon a stag. His mouth was dry, his hands trembling.

Two men rolled a barrel into view, upending it and testing the top. Then the enemy officer stepped forward and climbed on to the barrel, facing out towards the massed ranks of Shabag's men. The Satrap felt bile rise in his throat.

The officer threw back his cloak. Armour of gold shone upon his breast and he removed his helm.

'You know me,' he bellowed, his voice rich and resonant, compelling. 'I am Gorben, the son of the God King, the heir of the God King. In my veins runs the blood of Pashtar Sen, and Cyrios the Lord of Battles, and Meshan Sen, who walked the Bridge of Death. I am Gorben!' The name boomed out, and the men stood silently, spellbound. Even Shabag felt the goose-flesh rising on his diseased skin.

Druss eased back into the circle and stared out at the massed ranks of the enemy. There was a kind of divine madness about the scene which he found himself enjoying immensely. He had been angry when Gorben himself had appeared at the harbour to take command of the troops, and doubly so when the Emperor casually informed him there would be a change of plan.

'What's wrong with the plan we have?' asked Druss.

Gorben chuckled, and, taking Druss's arm, led him out of earshot of the waiting men. 'Nothing is wrong with it, axeman – save for

203

the objective. You seek to destroy the towers. Admirable. But it is not the towers that will determine success or failure in this siege; it is the men. So tonight we do not seek to hamper them, we seek to defeat them.'

Druss chuckled. 'Two hundred against twenty-five thousand?'

'No. One against one.' He had outlined his strategy and Druss had listened in awed silence. The plan was audacious and fraught with peril. Druss loved it.

The first phase had been completed. Shabag was surrounded and the enemy were listening to Gorben speak. But now came the testing time. Success and glory or failure and death? Druss did not know, but he sensed that the strategy was now teetering on a razor's edge. One wrong word from Gorben and the horde would descend upon them.

'I am Gorben!' roared the Emperor again. 'And every man of you has been led into treachery by this ... this miserable wretch here behind me.' He waved his hand contemptuously in the direction of Shabag. 'Look at him! Standing like a frightened rabbit. Is this the man you would set upon the throne? It will not be easy for him, you know. He will have to ascend the Royal steps. How will he accomplish this with his lips fastened to a Naashanite arse?'

Nervous laughter rose from the massed ranks. 'Aye, it is an amusing thought,' agreed Gorben, 'or it would be were it not so tragic. Look at him! How can warriors follow such a creature? He was lifted to high position by my father; he was trusted; and he betrayed the man who had helped him, who loved him like a son. Not content with causing the death of my father, he has also done everything within his power to wreak havoc upon Ventria. Our cities burn. Our people are enslaved. And for why? So that this quivering rodent can pretend to be a king. So that he can creep on all fours to lie at the feet of a Naashanite goat-breeder.'

Gorben gazed out over the ranks. 'Where are the Naashanites?' he called. A roar went up from the rear. 'Ah yes,' he said, 'ever at the back!' The Naashanties began to shout, but their calls were submerged beneath the laughter of Shabag's Ventrians. Gorben raised his hands for silence. 'No!' he bellowed. 'Let them have their say. It is rude to laugh, to mock others because they do not have your skills, your understanding of honour, your sense of history. I had a Naashanite slave once – ran off with one of my father's goats. I'll say this for him, though – he picked a pretty one!' Laughter rose in a wall of sound and Gorben waited until it subsided. 'Ah, my lads,' he said at last. 'What are we doing with this land we love? How did we allow the Naashanites to rape our sisters and daughters?' An eerie silence settled over the camp. 'I'll tell you how. Men like Shabag opened the doors to them. "Come in," he shouted, "and do as you will. I will be your dog. But please, please, let me have the crumbs that fall from your table. Let me lick the scrapings from your plates!"' Gorben drew his sword and raised it high as his voice thundered out. 'Well, I'll have none of it! I am the Emperor, anointed by the gods. And I'll fight to the death to save my people!'

'And we'll stand by you!' came a voice from the right. Druss recognised the caller. It was Bodasen; and with him were the five thousand defenders of Capalis. They had marched silently past the siege-towers while the skirmish raged and had crept up to the enemy lines while the soldiers listened to the voice of Gorben.

As Shabag's Ventrians began to shift nervously, Gorben spoke again. 'Every man here – save the Naashanites – is forgiven for following Shabag. More than this, I will allow you to serve me, to purge your crimes by freeing Ventria. And more than this, I shall give you each the pay that is owed you – and ten gold pieces for every man who pledges to fight for his land, his people and his Emperor.' At the rear the nervous Naashanites eased away from the packed ranks, forming a fighting square a little way distant.

'See them cower!' shouted Gorben. 'Now is the time to earn your gold! Bring me the heads of the enemy!'

Bodasen forced his way through the throng. 'Follow me!' he shouted. 'Death to the Naashanites!' The cry was taken up, and almost thirty thousand men hurled themselves upon the few hundred Naashanite troops.

Gorben leapt down from the barrel and strode to where Shabag waited. 'Well, cousin,' he said, his voice soft yet tinged with acid, 'how did you enjoy my speech?'

'You always could talk well,' replied Shabag, with a bitter laugh.

'Aye, and I can sing and play the harp, and read the works of our finest scholars. These things are dear to me – as I am sure they are to you, cousin. Ah, what an awful fate it must be to be born blind, or to lose the use of speech, the sense of touch.'

'I am noble born,' said Shabag, sweat gleaming on his face. 'You cannot maim me.'

'I am the Emperor,' hissed Gorben. 'My will is the law!'

Shabag fell to his knees. 'Kill me cleanly, I beg of you . . . cousin!'

Gorben drew a dagger from the jewel-encrusted scabbard at his hip, tossing the weapon to the ground before Shabag. The Satrap swallowed hard as he lifted the dagger and stared with grim malevolence at his tormentor. 'You may choose the manner of your passing,' said Gorben.

Shabag licked his lips, then held the point of the blade to his chest. 'I curse you, Gorben,' he screamed. Then taking the hilt with both hands, he rammed the blade home. He groaned and fell back. His body twitched, and his bowels opened.

'Remove . . . it,' Gorben ordered the soldiers close by. 'Find a ditch and bury it.' He swung to Druss and laughed merrily. 'Well, axeman, the deed is done.'

'Indeed it is, my Lord,' answered Druss.

'*My Lord?* Truly this is a night of wonders!'

At the edge of the camp the last of the Naashanites died begging for mercy, and a grim quiet descended. Bodasen approached the Emperor and bowed deeply. 'Your orders have been obeyed, Majesty.'

Gorben nodded. 'Aye, you have done well, Bodasen. Now take Jasua and Nebuchad and gather Shabag's officers. Promise them anything, but take them into the city, away from their men. Interrogate them. Kill those who do not inspire your confidence.'

'As you order it, so shall it be,' said Bodasen.

Michanek lifted Rowena from the carriage. Her head lolled against his shoulder, and he smelt the sweetness of her breath. Tying the reins to the brake bar, Pudri scrambled down and gazed apprehensively at the sleeping woman.

'She is all right,' said Michanek. 'I will take her to her room. You fetch the servants to unload the chests.' The tall warrior carried Rowena towards the house. A slave girl held open the door and he moved inside, climbing the stairs to a sunlit room in the eastern wing. Gently he laid her down, covering her frail body with a satin sheet and a thin blanket of lamb's wool. Sitting beside her, he lifted her hand. The skin was hot and feverish; she moaned, but did not stir.

Another slave girl appeared and curtsied to the warrior. He rose. 'Stay by her,' he ordered.

He found Pudri standing in the main doorway of the house. The little man looked disconsolate and lost, his dark eyes fearful. Michanek summoned him to the huge oval library, and bade him sit on a couch. Pudri slumped down, wringing his hands.

'Now, from the beginning,' said Michanek. 'Everything.'

The eunuch looked up at the powerful soldier. 'I don't know, Lord. At first she seemed merely withdrawn, but the more the Lord Kabuchek made her tell fortunes the more strange she became. I sat with her and she told me the Talent was growing within her. At first she needed to concentrate her mind upon the subject, and then visions would follow – short, disjointed images. Though after a while no concentration was needed. But the visions did not stop when she released the hands of Lord Kabuchek's . . . guests. Then the dreams began. She would talk as if she was old, and then in different voices. She stopped eating, and moved as if in a trance. Then, three days ago, she collapsed. Surgeons were called and she was bled, but to no avail.' His lip trembled and tears flowed to his thin cheeks. 'Is she dying, Lord?'

Michanek sighed. 'I don't know, Pudri. There is a doctor here whose opinions I value. He is said to be a mystic healer; he will be here within the hour.' He sat down opposite the little man. He thought he could read the fear in the eunuch's eyes. 'No matter what happens, Pudri, you will have a place here in my household. I did not purchase you from Kabuchek merely because you are close to Rowena. If she . . . does not recover I will not discard you.'

Pudri nodded, but his expression did not change. Michanek was surprised. 'Ah,' he said softly, 'you love her, even as I do.'

'Not as you, Lord. She is like a daughter to me. She is sweet, without a feather's weight of malice in her whole body. But such Talent as she has should not have been used so carelessly. She was not ready, not prepared.' He stood. 'May I sit with her, Lord?'

'Of course.'

The eunuch hurried from the room and Michanek rose and opened the doors to the gardens, stepping through into the sunlight. Flowering trees lined the paths and the air was full of the scent of jasmine, lavender and rose. Three gardeners were working, watering the earth and clearing the flowerbeds of weeds. As he appeared they stopped their work and fell to their knees, their foreheads pressed into the earth. 'Carry on,' he said, walking past them and entering the maze, moving swiftly through it to the marble bench at the centre where the statue of the Goddess was set in the circular pool. Of white marble, it showed a beautiful young woman, naked, her arms held aloft, her head tilted back to stare at the sky. In her hands was an eagle with wings spread, about to fly.

Michanek sat and stretched out his long legs. Soon the story would spread all over the city. The Emperor's champion had paid two thousand silver pieces for a dying seeress. Such folly! Yet, since the day he had first seen her, he had not been able to push her from his mind. Even on the campaign, while fighting against Gorben's troops, she had been with him. He had known more beautiful women, but at twenty-five had found none with whom he wished to share his life.

Until now. At the thought that she might be dying, he found himself trembling. Recalling the first meeting, he remembered her prophecy that he would die in this city, in a last stand against black-cloaked troops.

Gorben's Immortals. The Ventrian Emperor had re-formed the famous regiment, manning it with the finest of his fighters. Seven cities had been retaken by them, two of them after single combat between Gorben's new champion, a Drenai axeman they called *Deathwalker*, and two Naashanite warriors, both known to

208

Michanek. Good men, strong and brave, skilful beyond the dreams of most soldiers. Yet they had died.

Michanek had asked for the right to join the army and challenge this axeman. But his Emperor had refused. 'I value you too highly,' said the Emperor.

'But, Lord, is this not my role? Am I not your champion?'

'My seers tell me that the man cannot be slain by you, Michanek. They say his axe is demon-blessed. There will be no more single-combat settlements; we will crush Gorben by the might of our armies.'

But the man was not being crushed. The last battle had been no more than a bloody draw, with thousands slain on both sides. Michanek had led the charge which almost turned the tide, but Gorben had withdrawn into the mountains, two of his general officers having been slain by Michanek.

Nebuchad and Jasua. The first had little skill; he had charged his white horse at the Naashanite champion, and had died with Michanek's lance in his throat. The second was a canny fighter, fast and fearless – but not fast enough, and too fearless to accept that he had met a better swordsman. He had died with a curse on his lips.

'The war is not being won,' Michanek told the marble goddess. 'It is being lost – slowly, day by day.' Three of the renegade Ventrian Satraps had been slain by Gorben: Shabag at Capalis; Berish, the fat and greedy sycophant, hanged at Ectanis; and Ashac, Satrap of the south-west, impaled after the defeat at Gurunur. Only Darishan, the silver-haired fox of the north, survived. Michanek liked the man. The others he had treated with barely concealed contempt, but Darishan was a warrior born. Unprincipled, amoral, but gifted with courage.

His thoughts were interrupted by the sound of a man moving through the maze. 'Where in Hades are you, lad?' came a deep voice.

'I thought you were a mystic, Shalatar,' he called.

The response was both an obscenity and an instruction. 'If I could do that,' replied Michanek, chuckling, 'I could make a fortune with public performances.'

A bald, portly man in a long white tunic appeared and sat beside Michanek. His face was round and red and his ears protruded like those of a bat. 'I hate mazes,' he said. 'What on earth is the point of them? A man walks three times as far to reach a destination, and when he arrives there's nothing there. Futile!'

'Have you seen her?' asked Michanek.

Shalatar's expression changed, and he turned his eyes from the warrior's gaze. 'Yes. Interesting. Why ever did you buy her?'

'That is beside the point. What is your prognosis?'

'She is the most talented seer I have ever known – but that Talent overwhelmed her. Can you imagine what it must be like to *know* everything about everyone you meet? Their pasts and their futures. Every hand you touch flashes an entire life and death into your mind. The influx of such knowledge – at such speed – has had a catastrophic effect on her. She doesn't just see the lives, she experiences them, lives them. She became not Rowena but a hundred different people – including you, I might add.'

'Me?'

'Yes. I only touched her mind fleetingly, but your image was there.'

'Will she live?'

Shalatar shook his head. 'I am a mystic, my friend, but not a prophet. I would say she has only one chance: we must close the doors of her talent.'

'Can you do this?'

'Not alone, but I will gather those of my colleagues with experience of such matters. It is not unlike the casting-out of demons. We must close off the corridors of her mind that lead to the source of her power. It will be expensive, Michanek.'

'I am a rich man.'

'You will need to be. One of the men I need is a former Source priest and he will ask for at least ten thousand in silver for his services.'

'He will have it.'

Shalatar laid his hand on his friend's shoulder. 'You love her so dearly?'

'More than life.'

'Did she share your feelings?'

'No.'

210

'Then you will have a chance to start anew. For after we have finished she will have no memory. What will you tell her?'

'I don't know. But I will give her love.'

'You intend to marry her?'

Michanek thought back to her prophecy. 'No, my friend. I have decided never to marry.'

Druss wandered along the dark streets of the newly captured city, his head aching, his mood restless. The battle had been bloody and all too brief, and he was filled with a curious sense of anticlimax. He sensed a change in himself, unwelcome and yet demanding; a need for combat, to feel the axe crushing bone and flesh, to watch the light of life disappear from an enemy's eyes.

The mountains of his homeland seemed an eternity from him, lost in some other time.

How many men had he slain since setting off in search of Rowena? He no longer knew, nor cared. The axe felt light in his hand, warm and companionable. His mouth was dry and he longed for a cool drink of water. Glancing up, he saw a sign proclaiming 'Spice Street'. Here in more peaceful times traders had delivered their herbs and spices to be packed into bales for export to the west. Even now there was a scent of pepper in the air. At the far end of the street, where it intersected with the market square, was a fountain and beside it a brass pump with a long curved handle and a copper cup attached by a slender chain to an iron ring. Druss filled the cup, then resting the axe against the side of the fountain wall he sat quietly drinking. Every so often, though, his hand would drop to touch Snaga's black haft.

When Gorben had ordered the last attack on the doomed Naashanites, Druss had longed to hurl himself into the fray, had felt the call of blood and the need to kill. It had taken all of his strength to resist the demands of his turbulent spirit. For the enemy in the keep had begged to surrender and Druss had known with certainty that such a slaughter was wrong. The words of Shadak came back to him:

'The true warrior lives by a code. He has to. For each man there are different perspectives, but at the core they are the same. Never *violate a woman, nor harm a child. Do not lie, cheat or steal. These things are for lesser men. Protect the weak against the evil strong. And never allow thoughts of gain to lead you into pursuit of evil.'*

Numbering only a few hundred, the Naashanites had had no chance. But Druss still felt somehow cheated, especially when, as now, he recalled the warm, satisfying, triumphant surging of spirit during the fight in the camp of Harib Ka, or the blood-letting following his leap to the deck of the corsair trireme. Pulling clear his helm, he dipped his head into the water of the fountain pool and then stood, removed his jerkin and washed his upper body. Movement from his left caught his eye as a tall, bald man in robes of grey wool came into sight.

'Good evening, my son,' said the priest from the temple back in Capalis. Druss nodded curtly, then donned his jerkin and sat down. The priest made no move to walk on but stood gazing down at the axeman. 'I have been looking for you these past months.'

'You have found me,' said Druss, his voice even.

'May I join you for a few moments?'

'Why not?' responded Druss, making room on the seat where the priest sat alongside the black-garbed warrior.

'Our last meeting troubled me, my son. I have spent many an evening in prayer and meditation since then; finally I walked the Paths of Mist to seek out the soul of your loved one, Rowena. This proved fruitless. I journeyed through the Void on roads too dark to speak of. But she was not there, nor did I find any souls who knew of her death. Then I met a spirit, a grossly evil creature, who in this life bore the name Earin Shad. A corsair captain also called *Bojeeba*, the Shark, he knew of your wife, for this was the ship that plundered the vessel on which she was sailing. He told me that when his corsairs boarded the ship a merchant named Kabuchek, another man and a young woman leapt over the side. There were sharks everywhere, and much blood in the water once the slaughter started on the deck.'

'I don't need to know how she died!' snapped Druss.

'Ah, but that is my point,' said the priest. 'Earin Shad believes that she and Kabuchek were slain. But they were not.'

'What?'

'Kabuchek is in Resha, building more fortunes. He has a seeress with him whom they call *Pahtai*, the little dove. I have seen her, in spirit. I read her thoughts; she is Rowena, your Rowena.'

'She is alive?'

'Yes,' said the priest softly.

'Sweet Heaven!' Druss laughed and threw his arms around the priest's scrawny shoulders. 'By the gods, you have done me a great service. I'll not forget it. If ever there is anything you need from me, you have only to ask.'

'Thank you, my son. I wish you well in your quest. But there is one more matter to discuss: the axe.'

'What about it?' asked Druss, suddenly wary, his hands reaching down to curl around the haft.

'It is an ancient weapon, and I believe that spells were cast upon the blades. Someone of great power, in the distant past, used sorcery to enhance the weapon.'

'So?'

'There were many methods. Sometimes the spell would merely involve the armourer's blood being splashed upon the blades. At other times a binding spell would be used. This served to keep the edge keen, giving it greater cutting power. Small spells, Druss. Occasionally a master of the arcane arts would bring his skills to bear on a weapon, usually one borne by a king or lord. Some blades could heal wounds, others could cut through the finest armour.'

'As indeed can Snaga,' said Druss, hefting the axe. The blades glittered in the moonlight and the priest drew back. 'Do not be frightened,' said Druss. 'I'll not harm you, man.'

'I do not fear you, my son,' the priest told him. 'I fear what lives within those blades.'

Druss laughed. 'So someone cast a spell a thousand years ago? It is still an axe.'

'Yes, an axe. But the greatest of spells was woven around these blades, Druss. An enchantment of colossal skill was used. Your friend Sieben told me that when you were attacking the corsairs a sorcerer cast a spell at you, a spell of fire. When you lifted your

213

axe Sieben saw a demon appear, scaled and horned; he it was who turned back the fire.'

'Nonsense,' said Druss, 'it bounced from the blades. You know, Father, you shouldn't take a great deal of notice when Sieben speaks. The man is a poet. He builds his tales well, but he embroiders them, adds little touches. A demon indeed!'

'He needed to add no touches, Druss. I know of Snaga the Sender. For in finding your wife I also learned something of you, and the weapon you bear: Bardan's weapon. Bardan the Slayer, the butcher of babes, the rapist, the slaughterer. Once he was a hero, yes? But he was corrupted. Evil wormed into his soul, and the evil came from that!' he said, pointing to the axe.

'I don't believe it. I am not evil, and I have carried this axe for almost a year now.'

'And you have noticed no change in yourself? No lusting after blood and death? You do not feel a need to hold the axe, even when battle is not near? Do you sleep with it beside you?'

'It is not possessed!' roared Druss. 'It is a fine weapon. It is my. . . .' he stumbled to silence.

'My *friend*? Is that what you were going to say?'

'What if I was? I am a warrior, and in war only this axe will keep me alive. Better than any friend, eh?' As he spoke he lifted the axe . . . and it slipped from his grip. The priest threw up his hands as Snaga plunged down towards his throat, but in that instant Druss's left hand slammed into the haft, just as the priest pushed at the shining blades. The axe crashed to the stones, sending up a shower of sparks from the flints embedded in the paving slabs.

'God, I'm sorry. It just slipped!' said Druss. 'Are you hurt?'

The priest rose. 'No, it did not cut me. And you are wrong, young man. It did not slip; it wanted me dead, and had it not been for your swift response, so would I have been.'

'It was an accident, Father, I assure you.'

The priest gave a sad smile. 'You saw me push away the blades with my hand?'

'Aye?' responded Druss, mystified.

'Then look,' said the priest, lifting his hand with the palm outward. The flesh was seared and blackened, the skin burned black, blood and water streaming from the wound. 'Beware, Druss, the beast within will seek to kill any who threaten it.'

Druss gathered the axe and backed from the priest. 'Look after that wound,' he said. Then he turned and strode away.

He was shocked by what he had seen. He knew little of demons and spells, save what the storytellers sang of when they had visited the village. But he did know the value of a weapon like Snaga – especially in an alien, war-torn land. Druss came to a halt and, lifting the axe, he gazed into his own reflection in the blades.

'I need you,' he said softly. 'If I am to find Rowena and get her home.' The haft was warm, the weapon light in his hand. He sighed. 'I'll not give you up. I can't. And anyway, damn it all, you are mine!'

You are mine! came an echo deep inside his mind. *You are mine!*

Book Three

The Chaos Warrior

1

Varsava was enjoying the first sip of his second goblet of wine when the body hit the table. It arrived head first, splintering the central board of the trestle table, striking a platter of meat and sliding towards Varsava. With great presence of mind the bladesman lifted his goblet high and leaned back as the body hurtled past to slam head first into the wall. Such was the impact that a jagged crack appeared in the white plaster, but there was no sound from the man who caused it as he toppled from the table and hit the floor with a dull thud.

Glancing to his right, Varsava saw that the inn was crowded, but the revellers had moved back to form a circle around a small group struggling to overcome a black-bearded giant. One fighter – a petty thief and pickpocket Varsava recognised – hung from the giant's shoulders, his arms encircling the man's throat. Another was slamming punches into the giant's midriff, while a third pulled a dagger and ran in. Varsava sipped his wine. It was a good vintage – at least ten years old, dry and yet full-bodied.

The giant hooked one hand over his shoulder, grabbing the jerkin of the fighter hanging there. Spinning, he threw the man into the path of the oncoming knifeman, who stumbled and fell into the giant's rising boot. There followed a sickening crack and the knifeman slumped to the floor, either his neck or his jaw broken.

The giant's last opponent threw a despairing punch at the black-bearded chin and the fist landed – to no effect. The giant reached forward and pulled the fighter into a head-butt. The sound made even Varsava wince. The fighter took two faltering steps backwards, then keeled over in perfect imitation of a felled tree.

'Anyone else?' asked the giant, his voice deep and cold. The crowd melted away and the warrior strode through the inn, coming to Varsava's table. 'Is this seat taken?' he asked, slumping down to sit opposite the bladesman.

'It is now,' said Varsava. Lifting his hand he waved to a tavern maid and, once he had her attention, pointed to his goblet. She smiled and brought a fresh flagon of wine. The bench table was split down the centre, and the flagon sat drunkenly between the two men. 'May I offer you some wine?' Varsava asked.

'Why not?' countered the giant, filling a clay goblet. A low moan came from behind the table.

'He must have a hard head,' said Varsava. 'I thought he was dead.'

'If he comes near me again, he will be,' promised the man. 'What is this place?'

'It's called the All but One,' Varsava told him.

'An odd name for an inn?'

Varsava looked into the man's pale eyes. 'Not really. It comes from a Ventrian toast: *may all your dreams – save one – come true.*'

'What does it mean?'

'Quite simply that a man must always have a dream unfulfilled. What could be worse than to achieve everything one has ever dreamed of? What would one do then?'

'Find another dream,' said the giant.

'Spoken like a man who understands nothing about dreams.'

The giant's eyes narrowed. 'Is that an insult?'

'No, it is an observation. What brings you to Lania?'

'I am passing through,' said the man. Behind him two of the injured men had regained their feet; both drew daggers and advanced towards them, but Varsava's hand came up from beneath the table with a huge hunting-knife glittering in his fist. He rammed the point into the table and left the weapon quivering there.

'Enough,' he told the would-be attackers, the words softly spoken, a smile upon his face. 'Pick up your friend here and find another place to drink.'

'We can't let him get away with this!' said one of the men, whose eye was blackened and swollen almost shut.

'He did get away with it, my friends. And if you persist in this foolishness, I think he will kill you. Now go away, I am trying to hold a conversation.' Grumbling, the men sheathed their blades and moved back into the crowd. 'Passing through to where?' he asked the giant. The fellow seemed amused.

'You handled that well. Friends of yours?'

'They know me,' answered the bladesman, offering his hand across the table. 'I am Varsava.'

'Druss.'

'I've heard that name. There was an axeman at the siege of Capalis. There's a song about him, I believe.'

'Song!' snorted Druss. 'Aye, there is, but I had no part in the making of it. Damn fool of a poet I was travelling with – he made it up. Nonsense, all of it.'

Varsava smiled. '*They speak in hushed whispers of Druss and his axe, even demons will scatter when this man attacks.*'

Druss reddened. 'Asta's tits! You know there's a hundred more lines of it?' He shook his head. 'Unbelievable!'

'There are worse fates in life than to be immortalised in song. Isn't there some part of it about a lost wife? Is that also an invention?'

'No, that's true enough,' admitted Druss, his expression changing as he drained his wine and poured a second goblet. In the silence that followed, Varsava leaned back and studied his drinking companion. The man's shoulders were truly immense and he had a neck like a bull. But it was not the size that gave him the appearance of a giant, Varsava realised, it was more a power that emanated from him. During the fight he had seemed seven feet tall, the other warriors puny by comparison. Yet here, sitting quietly drinking, Druss seemed no more than a large, heavily muscled young man. Intriguing, thought Varsava.

'If I remember aright, you were also at the relief of Ectanis, and four other southern cities?' he probed. The man nodded, but said nothing. Varsava called for a third flagon of wine and tried to recall all he had heard of the young axeman. At Ectanis, it was said, he had fought the Naashanite champion, Cuerl, and been one of the first to scale the walls. And two years later he had held, with fifty other men, the pass of Kishtay, denying the road to a full legion of Naashanite troops until Gorben could arrive with reinforcements.

'What happened to the poet?' asked Varsava, searching for a safe route to satisfy his curiosity.

Druss chuckled. 'He met a woman . . . several women, in fact. Last I heard he was living in Pusha with the widow of a young officer.' He laughed again and shook his head. 'I miss him; he was merry company.' The smile faded from Druss's face. 'You ask a lot of questions?'

Varsava shrugged. 'You are an interesting man, and there is not much of interest these days in Lania. The war has made it dull. Did you ever find your wife?'

'No. But I will. What of you? Why are you here?'

'I am paid to be here,' said Varsava. 'Another flagon?'

'Aye, and I'll pay for it,' promised Druss. Reaching out, he took hold of the huge knife embedded in the table and pulled it clear. 'Nice weapon, heavy but well balanced. Good steel.'

'Lentrian. I had it made ten years ago. Best money I ever spent. You have an axe, do you not?'

Druss shook his head. 'I had one once. It was lost.'

'How does one lose an axe?'

Druss smiled. '*One* falls from a cliff into a raging torrent.'

'Yes, I would imagine that would do it,' responded Varsava. 'What do you carry now?'

'Nothing.'

'Nothing at all? How did you cross the mountains to Lania without a weapon?'

'I walked.'

'And suffered no attacks from robbers? Did you travel with a large group?'

'I have answered enough questions. Now it is your turn. Who pays you to sit and drink in Lania?'

'A nobleman from Resha who has estates near here. While he was away fighting alongside Gorben, raiders came down from the mountains and plundered his palace. His wife and son were taken, his

222

servants murdered – or fled. He has hired me to locate the where-abouts – if still alive – of his son.'

'Just the son?'

'Well, he wouldn't want the wife back, would he?'

Druss's face darkened. 'He would – if he loved her.'

Varsava nodded. 'Of course, you are a Drenai,' he said. 'The rich here do not marry for love, Druss; they wed for alliances or wealth, or to continue family lines. It is not rare for a man to find that he does love the woman he has been told to marry, but neither is it common. And a Ventrian nobleman would find himself a laughing stock if he took back a wife who had been – shall we say – abused. No, he has already divorced her; it is the son who matters to him. If I can locate him, I receive one hundred gold pieces. If I can rescue him, the price goes up to one thousand.'

Another flagon of wine arrived. Druss filled his goblet and offered the wine to Varsava, who declined. 'My head is already beginning to spin, my friend. You must have hollow legs.'

'How many men do you have?' asked Druss.

'None. I work alone.'

'And you know where the boy is?'

'Yes. Deep in the mountains there is a fortress called Valia, a place for thieves, murderers, outlaws and renegades. It is ruled by Cajivak – you have heard of him?' Druss shook his head. 'The man is a monster in every respect. Bigger than you, and terrifying in battle. He is also an axeman. And he is insane.'

Druss drank the wine, belched and leaned forward. 'Many fine warriors are considered mad.'

'I know that – but Cajivak is different. During the last year he has led raids which have seen mindless slaughter that you would not believe. He has his victims impaled on spikes, or skinned alive. I met a man who served him for almost five years; that's how I found out where the boy was. He said Cajivak sometimes speaks with a different voice, low and chilling, and that when he does so his eyes gleam with a strange light. And always – when such madness is upon him – he kills. It could be a servant or a tavern wench, or a man who looks up just as Cajivak's eyes meet his. No, Druss, we are dealing with madness ... or possession.'

'How do you intend to rescue the boy?'

Varsava spread his hands. 'I was contemplating that when you arrived. As yet, I have no answers.'

'I will help you,' said Druss.

Varsava's eyes narrowed. 'For how much?'

'You can keep the money.'

'Then why?' asked the bladesman, mystified.

But Druss merely smiled and refilled his goblet.

Druss found Varsava an agreeable companion. The tall bladesman said little as they journeyed through the mountains and up into the high valleys far above the plain on which Lania sat. Both men carried packs, and Varsava wore a wide-brimmed brown leather hat with an eagle feather tucked into the brim. The hat was old and battered, the feather ragged and without sheen. Druss had laughed when first he saw it, for Varsava was a handsome man – his clothes immaculately styled from fine green wool, his boots of soft lambskin. 'Did you lose a wager?' asked Druss.

'A wager?' queried Varsava.

'Aye. Why else would a man wear such a hat?'

'Ah!' said the bladesman. 'I imagine that is what passes as humour among you barbarians. I'll have you know that this hat belonged to my father.' He grinned. 'It is a magic hat and it has saved my life more than once.'

'I thought Ventrians never lied,' said Druss.

'Only noblemen,' Varsava pointed out. 'However, on this occasion I am telling the truth. The hat helped me escape from a dungeon.' He removed it and tossed it to Druss. 'Take a look under the inside band.'

Druss did so and saw that a thin-saw blade nestled on the right side, while on the left was a curved steel pin. At the front he felt three coins and slipped one clear; it was gold. 'I take it all back,' said Druss. 'It is a fine hat!'

The air was fresh and cool here and Druss felt free. It had been almost four years since he had left Sieben in Ectanis and journeyed alone to the occupied city of Resha, searching for the merchant

Kabuchek and, through him, Rowena. He had found the house, only to discover that Kabuchek had left a month before to visit friends in the lands of Naashan. He had followed to the Naashanite city of Pieropolis, and there lost all traces of the merchant.

Back once more in Resha, he discovered that Kabuchek had sold his palace and his whereabouts were unknown. Out of money and supplies, Druss took employment with a builder in the capital who had been commissioned to rebuild the shattered walls of the city. For four months he laboured every day until he had enough gold to head back to the south.

In the five years since the victories at Capalis and Ectanis the Ventrian Emperor, Gorben, had fought eight major battles against the Naashanites and their Ventrian allies. The first two had been won decisively, the last also. But the others had been fought to stalemate, with both sides suffering huge losses. Five years of bloody warfare and neither side, as yet, could claim they were close to victory.

'Come this way,' said Varsava. 'There is something I want you to see.'

The bladesman left the path and climbed a short slope to where a rusted iron cage had been set into the earth. Within the domed cage was a pile of mouldering bones, and a skull that still had vestiges of skin and hair clinging to it.

Varsava knelt down by the cage. 'This was Vashad – the peacemaker,' he said. 'He was blinded and his tongue cut out. Then he was chained here to starve to death.'

'What was his crime?' asked Druss.

'I have already told you: he was a peacemaker. This world of war and savagery has no place for men like Vashad.' Varsava sat down and removed his wide-brimmed leather hat.

Druss eased his pack from his shoulders and sat beside the bladesman. 'But why would they kill him in such a fashion?' he asked.

Varsava smiled, but there was no humour in his eyes. 'Do you see so much and know so little, Druss? The warrior lives for glory and battle, testing himself against his fellows, dealing death. He likes to see himself as noble, and we allow him such vanities because we admire him. We make songs about him; we tell stories of his greatness. Think of all the Drenai legends. How many concern peacemakers or poets? They are stories of *heroes* – men of blood and carnage. Vashad was a philosopher, a believer in something he called the *nobility of man*. He was a mirror, and when warmakers looked into his eyes they saw themselves – their true selves – reflected there. They saw the darkness, the savagery, the lust and the enormous stupidity of their lives. They could not resist killing him, they had to smash the mirror: so, they put out his eyes and they ripped out his tongue. Then they left him here . . . and here he lies.'

'You want to bury him? I'll help with the grave.'

'No,' said Varsava sadly, 'I don't want to bury him. Let others see him, and know the folly of trying to change the world.'

'Did the Naashanites kill him?' asked Druss.

'No, he was killed long before the war.'

'Was he your father?'

Varsava shook his head, his expression hardening. 'I only knew him long enough to put out his eyes.' He stared hard at Druss's face, trying to read his reaction, then he spoke again. 'I was a soldier then. Such eyes, Druss – large and shining, blue as a summer sky. And the last sight they had was of my face, and the burning iron that melted them.'

'And now he haunts you?'

Varsava stood. 'Aye, he haunts me. It was an evil deed, Druss. But those were my orders and I carried them out as a Ventrian should. Immediately afterwards, I resigned my commission and left the army.' He glanced at Druss. 'What would you have done in my place?'

'I would not be in your place,' said Druss, hoisting his pack to his shoulder.

'Imagine that you were. Tell me!'

'I would have refused.'

'I wish I had,' Varsava admitted, and the two men returned to the trail. They walked on in silence for a mile, then Varsava sat down beside the path. The mountains loomed around them, huge and towering, and a shrill wind was whistling through the peaks. High overhead two eagles were circling. 'Do you despise me, Druss?' asked Varsava.

'Yes,' admitted Druss, 'but I also like you.'

Varsava shrugged. 'I do so admire a plain speaker. I despise myself sometimes. Have you ever done anything which shamed you?'

'Not yet, but I came close in Ectanis.'

'What happened?' asked Varsava.

'The city had fallen several weeks before, and when the army arrived the walls were already breached. I went in with the first assault and I killed many. And then, with the bloodlust on me, I forced my way into the main barracks. A child ran at me. He was carrying a spear and before I could think about what I was doing I cut at him with my axe. He slipped, and only the flat of the blade caught him; he was knocked out. But I had tried to kill him. Had I succeeded it would not have sat well with me.'

'And that is all?'

'It is enough,' said Druss.

'You have never raped a woman? Or killed an unarmed man? Or stolen?'

'No. And I never shall.'

Varsava rose. 'You are an unusual man, Druss. I think this world will either come to hate you or revere you.'

'I don't much care which,' said Druss. 'How far to this mountain city?'

'Another two days. We'll camp in the high pines, where it will be cold but the air is wonderfully fresh. By the way, you haven't told me yet why you offered to help me.'

'That's true,' said Druss, with a grin. 'Now let us find a campsite.'

They walked on, through a long pass which opened out on to a stand of pine trees and a wide pear-shaped valley beyond. Houses dotted the valley, clustered in the main along both banks of a narrow river. Druss scanned the valley. 'There must be fifty homes here,' he said.

'Yes,' agreed Varsava. 'Farmers mostly. Cajivak leaves them alone, for they supply him with meat and grain during the winter months. But it will be best if we make a cold camp in the trees, for Cajivak will have spies in the village, and I don't want our presence announced.'

227

The two men moved out from the pass and into the shelter of the trees. The wind was less powerful here and they walked on, seeking a campsite. The landscape was similar to the mountains of home and Druss found himself once more thinking of days of happiness with Rowena. When he had set out with Shadak to find her, he had been convinced that only a matter of days separated them. Even on board ship he had believed his quest was almost over. But the months, and years, of pursuit had gnawed at his confidence. He knew he would never give up the hunt, but to what purpose? What if she were wed, or had children? What if she had found happiness without him? What then, as he walked back into her life?

His thoughts were broken by the sounds of laughter echoing through the trees. Varsava stopped and moved silently from the trail and Druss followed him. Ahead and to the left was a hollow through which ran a ribbon stream, and at the centre of the hollow a group of men were throwing knives at a tree-trunk. An old man was tied to the trunk, his arms spread. A blade had nicked the skin of his face, there were wounds to both arms and a knife jutted from his thigh. It was obvious to Druss that the men were playing a game with the old man, seeing how close they could come with their knives. To the left of the scene three other men were struggling with a young girl, who screamed as they tore her dress and pushed her to the earth. As Druss loosed his pack and started down the slope, Varsava grabbed him. 'What are you doing? There are ten of them!'

But Druss shrugged him off and strode through the trees to come up behind the seven knife-throwers. Intent as they were on their victim, they did not notice his approach. Reaching out, he grabbed the heads of the two nearest knifemen and rammed them together; there followed a sickening crack and both men dropped without a murmur. A third man swung at the sound, but had no time to regis-ter surprise as a silver-skinned gauntlet slammed into his mouth, splintering teeth. Unconscious, the knifeman flew backwards to cannon into a comrade. A warrior leapt at Druss, thrusting his blade towards his belly, but Druss slapped the blade aside and hammered a straight left into the man's chin. The remaining warriors ran at him, and a knife-blade slashed through his jerkin, ripping a narrow gash across his hip. Druss grabbed the nearest warrior, dragging him into a ferocious head-butt, then swung and backhanded another attacker. The man cartwheeled across the hollow, struggled to rise, then sat back against a tree having lost all interest in the fight.

Grappling with two men, Druss heard a bloodcurdling scream. His attackers froze. Druss dragged an arm free and struck the first of the men a terrible blow to the neck. The second released his hold on the axeman and sprinted from the hollow. Druss's pale eyes scanned the area, seeking new opponents. But only Varsava was standing there, his huge hunting-knife dripping blood. Two corpses lay beside him. Three other men Druss had struck lay where they had fallen, and the warrior he had backhanded was still sitting by the tree. Druss walked to where he sat, then hauled him to his feet. 'Time to go, laddie!' said Druss.

'Don't kill me!' pleaded the man.

'Who said anything about killing? Be off with you!'

The man tottered away on boneless legs as Druss moved to the old man tied to the tree. Only one of his wounds was deep. Druss untied him and eased him to the ground. Swiftly he dragged the knife clear of the man's thigh as Varsava came alongside. 'That will need stitching,' he said. 'I'll get my pack.'

The old man forced a smile. 'I thank you, my friends. I fear they would have killed me. Where is Dulina?'

Druss glanced round, but the girl was nowhere in sight. 'She was not harmed,' he said. 'I think she ran when the fight started.' Druss applied a tourniquet to the thigh wound, then stood and moved back to check the bodies. The two men who had attacked Varsava were dead, as was one other, his neck broken. The remaining two were unconscious. Rolling them to their backs, Druss shook them awake and then pulled them upright. One of the men immediately sagged back to the ground.

'Who are you?' asked the warrior still standing.

'I am Druss.'

'Cajivak will kill you for this. Were I you, I would leave the mountains.'

'You are not me, laddie. I go where I please. Now pick up your comrade and take him home.'

229

Druss dragged the fallen warrior to his feet and watched as the two men left the hollow. When Varsava returned with his pack, a young girl was walking beside him. She was holding her ruined dress in place. 'Look what I found,' said Varsava. 'She was hiding under a bush.' Ignoring the girl, Druss grunted and moved to the stream where he knelt and drank.

Had Snaga been with him, the hollow would now be awash in blood and bodies. He sat back and stared at the rippling water.

When the axe was lost Druss had felt as if a burden had been lifted from his heart. The priest back in Capalis had been right: it was a demon blade. He had felt its power growing as the battles raged, had enjoyed the soaring, surging bloodlust that swept over him like a tidal wave. But after the battles came the sense of emptiness and disenchantment. Even the spiciest food was tasteless; summer days seemed grey and colourless.

Then came the day in the mountains when the Naashanites had come upon him alone. He had killed five, but more than fifty men had pursued him through the trees. He had tried to traverse the cliff, but holding to the axe made his movements slow and clumsy. Then the ledge had given way and he had fallen, twisting and turning through the air. Even as he fell he hurled the axe from him, and tried to turn the fall into a dive; but his timing was faulty and he had landed on his back, sending up a huge splash, the air exploding from his lungs. The river was in flood and the currents swept him on for more than two miles before he managed to grab a root jutting from the river-bank. Hauling himself clear he had sat, as now, staring at the water.

Snaga was gone.

And Druss felt free. 'Thank you for helping my grandfather,' said a sweet voice and he turned and smiled.

'Did they hurt you?'

'Only a little,' said Dulina. 'They hit me in the face.'

'How old are you?'

'Twelve – almost thirteen.' She was a pretty child with large hazel eyes and light brown hair.

'Well, they've gone now. Are you from the village?'

'No. Grandfather is a tinker. We go from town to town; he sharpens knives and mends things. He's very clever.'

'Where are your parents?'

The girl shrugged. 'I never had any; only grandfather. You are very strong – but you are bleeding!'

Druss chuckled. 'I heal fast, little one.' Removing his jerkin, he examined the wound on his hip. The surface skin had been sliced, but the cut was not deep.

Varsava joined them. 'That should also be stitched, *great hero*,' he said, irritation in his voice.

Blood was still flowing freely from the wound. Druss stretched out and lay still while Varsava, with little gentleness, drew the flaps of skin together and pierced them with a curved needle. When he had finished the bladesman stood. 'I suggest we leave this place and head back for Lania. I think our friends will return before too long.'

Druss donned his jerkin. 'What about the city and your thousand gold pieces?'

Varsava shook his head in disbelief. 'This ... escapade ... of yours has put paid to any plan of mine. I shall return to Lania and claim my hundred gold pieces for locating the boy. As to you, well, you can go where you like.'

'You give up very easily, bladesman. So we cracked a few heads! What difference does that make? Cajivak has hundreds of men; he won't interest himself in every brawl.'

'It is not Cajivak who concerns me, Druss. It is you. I am not here to rescue maidens or kill dragons, or whatever else it is that makes heroes of myth. What happens when we walk into the city and you see some ... some hapless victim? Can you walk by? Can you hold fast to a plan of action that will see us succeed in our mission?'

Druss thought for a moment. 'No,' he said at last. 'No, I will never walk by.'

'I thought not, damn you! What are you trying to prove, Druss? You want more songs about you? Or do you just want to die young?'

'No, I have nothing to prove, Varsava. And I may die young, but I'll never look in a mirror and be ashamed because I let an old man suffer or a child be raped. Nor will I ever be haunted by a

231

peacemaker who died unjustly. Go where you will, Varsava. Take these people back to Lania. I shall go to the city.'

'They'll kill you there.'

Druss shrugged. 'All men die. I am not immortal.'

'No, just stupid,' snapped Varsava and spinning on his heel, the bladesman strode away.

Michanek laid his bloody sword on the battlements and untied the chin-straps of his bronze helm, lifting it clear and enjoying the sudden rush of cool air to his sweat-drenched head. The Ventrian army was falling back in some disarray, having discarded the huge battering-ram which lay outside the gate, surrounded by corpses. Michanek walked to the rear of the ramparts and yelled orders to a squad of men below.

'Open the gate and drag that damned ram inside,' he shouted. Pulling a rag from his belt, he wiped his sword clean of blood and sheathed it.

The fourth attack of the day had been repulsed; there would be no further fighting today. However, few of the men seemed anxious to leave the wall. Back in the city the plague was decimating the civilian population. No, he thought, it is worse than decimation. Far more than one in ten were now suffering the effects.

Gorben had not dammed the river. Instead he had filled it with every kind of corruption – dead animals, bloated and maggot-ridden, rotting food, and the human waste from an army of eleven thousand men. Small wonder that sickness had ripped into the population.

Water was now being supplied by artesian wells, but no one knew how deep they were or how long the fresh water would last. Michanek gazed up at the clear blue sky: not a cloud in sight, and rain had not fallen for almost a month.

A young officer approached him. 'Two hundred with superficial wounds, sixty dead, and another thirty-three who will not fight again,' he said.

Michanek nodded, his mind elsewhere. 'What news from the inner city, brother?' he asked.

'The plague is abating. Only seventy dead yesterday, most of them either children or old people.'

Michanek stood and smiled at the young man. 'Your section fought well today,' he said, clapping his hand on his brother's shoulder. 'I shall see that a report is placed before the Emperor when we return to Naashan.' The man said nothing and their eyes met, the unspoken thought passing between them: *If* we return to Naashan. 'Get some rest, Narin. You look exhausted.'

'So do you, Michi. And I was only here for the last two attacks – you've been here since before dawn.'

'Yes, I am tired. *Pahtai* will revive me; she always does.'

Narin chuckled. 'I never expected love to last so long for you. Why don't you marry the girl? You'll never find a better wife. She's revered in the city. Yesterday she toured the poorest quarter, healing the sick. It's amazing; she has more skill than any of the doctors. It seems that all she needs to do is lay her hands upon the dying and their sores disappear.'

'You sound as if you're in love with her yourself,' said Michanek.

'I think I am – a little,' admitted Narin, reddening. 'Is she still having those dreams?'

'No,' lied Michanek. 'I'll see you this evening.' He moved down the battlement steps and strode through the streets towards his home. Every other house, it seemed, boasted the white chalked cross denoting plague. The market was deserted, the stalls standing empty. Everything was rationed now, the food – four ounces of flour, and a pound of dried fruit – doled out daily from storehouses in the west and east.

Why don't you marry her?

For two reasons he could never share. One: she was already wed to another, though she did not know it. And secondly, it would be like signing his death warrant. Rowena had predicted that he would die here, with Narin beside him, one year to the day after he was wed.

She no longer remembered this prediction either, for the sorcerers had done their work well. Her Talent was lost to her, and all the memories of her youth in the lands of the Drenai. Michanek felt no guilt over this. Her Talent had been tearing her apart and now, at

233

least, she smiled and was happy. Only Pudri knew the whole truth, and he was wise enough to stay silent.

Michanek turned up the Avenue of Laurels and pushed open the gates of his house. There were no gardeners now, and the flower-beds were choked with weeds. The fountain was no longer in operation, the fish-pool dry and cracked. As he strode to the house, Pudri came running out to him.

'Master, come quickly, it is the *Pahtai*!'

'What has happened?' cried Michanek, grabbing the little man by his tunic.

'The plague, master,' he whispered, tears in his dark eyes. 'It is the plague.'

Varsava found a cave nestling against the rock-face to the north; it was deep and narrow, and curled like a figure six. He built a small fire near the back wall, below a split in the rock that created a natural chimney. The old man, whom Druss had carried to the cave, had fallen into a deep, healing sleep with the child, Dulina, alongside him. Having walked from the cave to check whether the glare of the fire could be seen from outside, Varsava was now sitting in the cave-mouth staring out over the night-dark woods.

Druss joined him. 'Why so angry, bladesman?' he asked. 'Do you not feel some satisfaction at having rescued them?'

'None at all,' replied Varsava. 'But then no one ever made a song about me. I look after myself.'

'That does not explain your anger.'

'Nor could I explain it in any way that would be understood by your simple mind. Borza's Blood!' He rounded on Druss. 'The world is such a mind-numbingly uncomplicated place for you, Druss. There is good, and there is evil. Does it ever occur to you that there may be a vast area in between that is neither pure nor malevolent? Of course it doesn't! Take today as an example. The old man could have been a vicious sorcerer who drank the blood of innocent babes; the men punishing him could have been the fathers of those babes. You didn't know, you just roared in and downed them.' Varsava shook his head and took a deep breath.

'You are wrong,' said Druss softly. 'I have heard the arguments before, from Sieben and Bodasen – and others. I will agree that I am a simple man. I can scarcely read more than my name, and I do not understand complicated arguments. But I am not blind. The man tied to the tree wore homespun clothes, old clothes; the child was dressed in like manner. These were not rich, as a sorcerer would be. And did you listen to the laughter of the knife-throwers? It was harsh, cruel. These were not farmers; their clothes were bought, their boots and shoes of good leather. They were scoundrels.'

'Maybe they were,' agreed Varsava, 'but what business was it of yours? Will you criss-cross the world seeking to right wrongs and protect the innocent? Is this your ambition in life?'

'No,' said Druss, 'though it would not be a bad ambition.' He fell silent for several minutes, lost in thought. Shadak had given him a code, and impressed upon him that without such an iron discipline he would soon become as evil as any other reaver. Added to this there was Bress, his father, who had lived his whole life bearing the terrible burden of being the son of Bardan. And lastly there was Bardan himself, driven by a demon to become one of the most hated and vilified villains in history. The lives, the words and deeds of these three men had created the warrior who now sat beside Varsava. But Druss had no words to explain, and it surprised him that he desired them; he had never felt the need to explain to Sieben or Bodasen. 'I had no choice,' he said at last.

'No choice?' echoed Varsava. 'Why?'

'Because I was there. There wasn't anyone else.'

Feeling Varsava's eyes upon him, and seeing the look of blank incomprehension, Druss turned away and stared at the night sky. It made no sense, he knew that, but he also knew that he felt good for having rescued the girl and the old man. It might make no sense, but it was *right*.

Varsava rose and moved back to the rear of the cave, leaving Druss alone. A cold wind whispered across the mountainside, and Druss could smell the coming of rain. He remembered another cold night, many years before, when he and Bress had been camped in the mountains of Lentria. Druss was very young, seven or eight, and he was unhappy. Some men had shouted at his father, and gathered outside the workshop that Bress had set up in a small village. He had expected his father to rush out and thrash them but instead, as night fell, he had gathered a few belongings and led the boy out into the mountains.

'Why are we running away?' he had asked Bress.

'Because they will talk a lot, and then come back to burn us out.'

'You should have killed them,' said the boy.

'That would have been no answer,' snapped Bress. 'Mostly they are good men, but they are frightened. We will find somewhere where no one knows of Bardan.'

'I won't run away, not ever,' declared the boy and Bress had sighed. Just then a man approached the campfire. He was old and bald, his clothes ragged, but his eyes were bright and shrewd.

'May I share your fire?' he asked and Bress had welcomed him, offering some dried meat and a herb tisane which the man accepted gratefully. Druss had fallen asleep as the two men talked, but had woken several hours later. Bress was asleep, but the old man was sitting by the fire feeding the flames with twigs. Druss rose from his blankets and walked to sit alongside him.

'Frightened of the dark, boy?'

'I am frightened of nothing,' Druss told him.

'That's good,' said the old man, 'but I am. Frightened of the dark, frightened of starvation, frightened of dying. All my life I've been frightened of something or other.'

'Why?' asked the boy, intrigued.

The old man laughed. 'Now there's a question! Wish I could answer it.' As he picked up a handful of twigs and reached out, dropping them to the dying flames, Druss saw his right arm was criss-crossed with scars.

'How did you get them?' asked the boy.

'Been a soldier most of my life, son. Fought against the Nadir, the Vagrians, the Sathuli, corsairs, brigands. You name the enemy, and I've crossed swords with them.'

'But you said you were a coward.'

'I said no such thing, lad. I said I was *frightened*. There's a difference. A coward is a man who knows what's right, but is afraid to do

236

it; there're plenty of them around. But the worst of them are easy to spot: they talk loud, they brag big, and given a chance they're as cruel as sin.'

'My father is a coward,' said the boy sadly.

The old man shrugged. 'If he is, boy, then he's the first in a long, long while to fool me. And if you are talking about him running away from the village, there's times when to run away is the bravest thing a man can do. I knew a soldier once. He drank like a fish, rutted like an alley-cat and would fight anything that walked, crawled or swam. But he got religion; he became a Source priest. When a man he once knew, and had beaten in a fist-fight, saw him walking down the street in Drenan, he walked up and punched the priest full in the face, knocking him flat. I was there. The priest surged to his feet and stopped. He wanted to fight – everything in him wanted to fight. But then he remembered what he was, and he held back. Such was the turmoil within him that he burst into tears. And he walked away. By the gods, boy, that took some courage.'

'I don't think that was courage,' said Druss.

'Neither did anyone else who was watching. But then that's something you'll learn, I hope. If a million people believe a foolish thing, it is still a foolish thing.'

Druss's mind jerked back to the present. He didn't know why he had remembered that meeting, but the recollection left him feeling sad and low in spirit.

2

A storm broke over the mountains, great rolls of thunder that made the walls of the cave vibrate, and Druss moved back as the rain lashed into the cave-mouth. The land below was lit by jagged spears of lightning which seemed to change the very nature of the valley – the gentle woods of pine and elm becoming shadow-haunted lairs, the friendly homes looking like tombstones across the vault of Hell.

Fierce winds buffeted the trees and Druss saw a herd of deer running from the woods, their movements seeming disjointed and ungainly against the flaring lightning bolts. A tree was struck and seemed to explode from within, splitting into two halves. Fire blazed briefly from the ruined trunk, but died within seconds in the sheeting rain.

Dulina crept alongside him, pushing herself against him. He felt the stitches in his side pull as she snuggled in, but he lifted his arm around her shoulders. 'Is is only a storm, child,' he said. 'It cannot harm us.' She said nothing and he drew her to his lap, holding her close. She was warm, almost feverish, he thought.

Sighing, Druss felt again the weight of loss, and wondered where Rowena was on this dark and ferocious night. Was there a storm where she lay? Or was the night calm? Did she feel the loss, or was Druss just a dim memory of another life in the mountains? He glanced down to see that the child was asleep, her head in the crook of his arm.

Holding her firmly but gently, Druss rose and carried her back to the fireside, laying her down on her blanket and adding the last of the fuel to the fire.

238

'You are a good man,' came a soft voice. Druss looked up and saw that the old tinker was awake.

'How is the leg?'

'It hurts, but it will heal. You are sad, my friend.'

Druss shrugged. 'These are sad times.'

'I heard your talk with your friend. I am sorry that in helping me you have lost the chance to help others.' He smiled. 'Not that I would change anything, you understand?'

Druss chuckled. 'Nor I.'

'I am Ruwaq the Tinker,' said the old man, extending a bony hand.

Druss shook it and sat beside him. 'Where are you from?'

'Originally? The lands of Matapesh, far to the east of Naashan and north of the Opal Jungles. But I have always been a man who needed to see new mountains. People think they are all the same, but it is not so. Some are lush and green, others crowned with shining ice and snow. Some are sharp, like sword-blades, others old and rounded, comfortable within eternity. I love mountains.'

'What happened to your children?'

'Children? Oh, I never had children. Never married.'

'I thought the child was your granddaughter?'

'No, I found her outside Resha. She had been abandoned and was starving to death. She is a good girl. I love her dearly. I can never repay the debt to you for saving her.'

'There is no debt,' said Druss.

The old man lifted his hand and wagged his finger. 'I don't accept that, my friend. You gave her – and me – the gift of life. I do not like storms, but I was viewing this one with the greatest pleasure. Because until you entered the hollow I was a dead man, and Dulina would have been raped and probably murdered. Now the storm is a vision of beauty. No one ever gave me a greater gift.' The old man had tears in his eyes and Druss's discomfort grew. Instead of feeling elated by his gratitude he experienced a sense of shame. A true hero, he believed, would have gone to the man's aid from a sense of justice, of compassion. Druss knew that was not why he had helped them.

239

Not even close. The right deed . . . for the wrong reason. He patted the old man's shoulder and returned to the cave-mouth where he saw that the storm was moving on towards the east, the rain lessening. Druss's spirits sank. He wished Sieben were with him. Irritating as the poet could be, he still had a talent for lifting the axeman's mood.

But Sieben had refused to accompany him, preferring the pleasures of city life to an arduous journey across the mountains to Resha. No, thought Druss, not the journey; that was just an excuse.

'I'll make a bargain with you though, old horse,' said Sieben on that last day. 'Leave the axe and I'll change my mind. Bury it. Throw it in the sea. I don't care which.'

'Don't tell me you believe that nonsense?'

'I saw it, Druss. Truly. It will be the death of you – or at least the death of the man I know.'

Now he had no axe, no friend, and no Rowena. Unused to despair Druss felt lost, his strength useless.

Dawn brightened the sky, the land glistening and fresh from the rain as Dulina came alongside him. 'I had a wonderful dream,' she said brightly. 'There was a great knight on a white horse. And he rode up to where grandfather and I were waiting, and he leaned from his saddle and lifted me to sit beside him. Then he took off his golden helmet and he said, "I am your father." And he took me to live in a castle. I never had a dream like it. Do you think it will come true?'

Druss did not answer. He was staring down at the woods at the armed men making their way towards the cave.

The world had shrunk now to a place of agony and darkness. All Druss could feel was pain as he lay in the windowless dungeon, listening to the skittering of unseen rats that clambered over him. There was no light, save when at the end of the day the jailer strode down the dungeon corridor and a tiny, flickering beam momentarily lit the narrow grille of the door-stone. Only in those seconds could Druss see his surroundings. The ceiling was a mere four feet from the floor, the airless room six feet square. Water dripped from the walls, and it was cold.

Druss brushed a rat from his leg, the movement causing him a fresh wave of pain from his wounds. He could hardly move his neck, and his right shoulder was swollen and hot to the touch. Wondering if the bones were broken, he began to shiver.

How many days? He had counted to sixty-three, but then lost track for a while. Guessing at seventy, he had begun to count again. But his mind wandered. Sometimes he dreamt of the mountains of home, under a blue sky, with a fresh northerly wind cooling his brow. At other times he tried to remember events in his life.

'I will break you, and then I will watch you beg for death,' said Cajivak on the day they had hauled Druss into the castle Hall.

'In your dreams, you ugly whoreson.'

Cajivak had beaten him then, pounding his face and body with brutal blows. His hands tied behind him, a tight rope around his neck, Druss could do nothing but accept the hammering.

For the first two weeks he was kept in a larger cell. Every time he slept men would appear alongside his narrow bed to beat him with clubs and sticks. At first he had fought them, grabbing one man by the throat and cracking his skull against the cell wall. But deprived of food and water for days on end, his strength had given out and he could only curl himself into a tight ball against the merciless beatings.

Then they had thrown him into this tiny dungeon, and he had watched with horror as they slid the door-stone into place. Once every two days a guard would push stale bread and a cup of water through the narrow grille. Twice he caught rats and ate them raw, cutting his lips on the tiny bones.

Now he lived for those few seconds of light as the guard walked back to the outside world.

'We caught the others,' the jailer said one day, as he pushed the bread through the grille. But Druss did not believe him. Such was Cajivak's cruelty that he would have dragged Druss out to see them slain.

241

He pictured Varsava pushing the child up into the chimney crack in the cave, urging her to climb, and remembered lifting Ruwaq up to where Varsava could haul the old man out of sight. Druss himself was about to climb when he heard the warriors approaching the cave. He had turned.

And charged them . . .

But there were too many, and most bore clubs which finally smashed him from his feet. Boots and fists thundered into him and he awoke to find a rope around his neck, his hands bound. Forced to walk behind a horseman, he was many times dragged from his feet, the rope tearing the flesh of his neck.

Varsava had described Cajivak as a monster, which could not be more true. The man was close to seven feet tall, with an enormous breadth of shoulder and biceps as thick as most men's thighs. His eyes were dark, almost black, and no hair grew on the right side of his head where the skin was white and scaly, covered in scar tissue that only a severe burn could create. Madness shone in his eyes, and Druss had glanced to the man's left and the weapon that was placed there, resting against the high-backed throne.

Snaga!

Druss shook himself free of the memory now and stretched. His joints creaked and his hands trembled in the cold that seeped from the wet walls. Don't think of it, he urged himself. Concentrate on something else. He tried to picture Rowena, but instead found himself remembering the day when the priest of Pashtar Sen had found him in a small village, four days east of Lania. Druss had been sitting in the garden of an inn, enjoying a meal of roast meat and onions and a jug of ale. The priest bowed and sat opposite the axeman. His bald head was pink and peeling, burned by the sun.

'I am glad to find you in good health, Druss. I have searched for you for the last six months.'

'You found me,' said Druss.

'It is about the axe.'

'Do not concern yourself, Father. It is gone. You were right, it was an evil weapon. I am glad to be rid of it.'

The priest shook his head. 'It is back,' he said. 'It is now in the possession of a robber named Cajivak. Always a killer, he succumbed far more swiftly than a strong man like yourself and now he is terrorising the lands around Lania, torturing, killing and maiming. With the war keeping our troops from the area, there is little that can be done to stop him.'

'Why tell me?'

The priest said nothing for a moment, averting his eyes from Druss's direct gaze. 'I have watched you,' he said at last. 'Not just in the present, but through the past, from your birth through your childhood, to your marriage to Rowena and your quest to find her. You are a rare man, Druss. You have iron control over those areas of your soul which have a capacity for evil. And you have a dread of becoming like Bardan. Well, Cajivak is Bardan reborn. Who else can stop him?'

'I don't have time to waste, priest. My wife is somewhere in these lands.'

The priest reddened and hung his head. His voice was a whisper, and there was shame in the words. 'Recover the axe and I will tell you where she is,' he said.

Druss leaned back and stared long and hard at the slender man before him. 'This is unworthy of you,' he observed.

The priest looked up. 'I know.' He spread his hands. 'I have no other . . . payment . . . to offer.'

'I could take hold of your scrawny neck and wring the truth from you,' Druss pointed out.

'But you will not. I know you, Druss.'

The warrior stood. 'I'll find the axe,' he promised. 'Where shall we meet?'

'You find the axe – and I'll find you,' the priest told him.

Alone in the dark, Druss remembered with bitterness the confidence he had felt. Find Cajivak, recover the axe, then find Rowena. So simple!

What a fool you are, he thought. His face itched and he scratched at the skin of his cheek, his grimy finger breaking a scab upon his cheek. A rat ran across his leg and Druss lunged for it, but missed.

Struggling to his knees, he felt his head touch the cold stone of the ceiling.

Torchlight flickered as the guard moved down the corridor. Druss scrambled to the grille, the light burning his eyes. The jailer, whose face Druss could not see, bent and thrust a clay cup into the door-stone cavity. There was no bread. Druss lifted the cup and drained the water. 'Still alive, I see,' said the jailer, his voice deep and cold. 'I think the Lord Cajivak has forgotten about you. By the gods, that makes you a lucky man – you'll be able to live down here with the rats for the rest of your life.' Druss said nothing and the voice went on, 'The last man who lived in that cell was there for five years. When we dragged him out his hair was white and all his teeth were rotten. He was blind, and bent like a crippled old man. You'll be the same.'

Druss focused on the light, watching the shadows on the dark wall. The jailer stood, and the light receded. Druss sank back.

No bread . . .

You'll be able to live down here with the rats for the rest of your life.

Despair struck him like a hammer blow.

Pahtai felt the pain recede as she floated clear of her plague-wracked body. I am dying, she thought, but there was no fear, no surging panic, merely a peaceful sense of harmony as she rose into the air.

It was night, and the lanterns were lit. Hovering just below the ceiling, she gazed down on Michanek as he sat beside the frail woman in the bed, holding to her hand, stroking the fever-dry skin and whispering words of love. That is me, thought *Pahtai*, staring down at the woman.

'I love you, I love you,' whispered Michanek. 'Please don't die!'

He looked so tired, and *Pahtai* wanted to reach out to him. He was all the security and love she had ever known, and she recalled the first morning when she had woken in his home in Resha. She remembered the bright sunshine and the smell of jasmine from the gardens, and she knew that the bearded man sitting beside her should have been known to her. But when she reached into her mind she could find no trace of him. It was so embarrassing. 'How are you feeling?' he had asked, the voice familiar but doing nothing to unlock her memory. She tried to think of where she might have met him. That was when the second shock struck, with infinitely more power than the first.

She had no memory! Nothing! Her face must have reacted to the shock, for he leaned in close and took her hand. 'Do not concern yourself, *Pahtai*. You have been ill, very ill. But you are getting better now. I know that you do not remember me, but as time passes you will.' He turned his head and called to another man, tiny, slender and dark-skinned. 'Look, here is Pudri,' said Michanek. 'He has been worried about you.'

She had sat up then, and seen the tears in the little man's eyes. 'Are you my father?' she asked.

He shook his head. 'I am your servant and your friend, *Pahtai*.'

'And you, sir,' she said, turning her gaze on Michanek. 'Are you my . . . brother?'

He had smiled. 'If that is what you wish, that is what I will be. But no, I am not your brother. Nor am I your master. You are a free woman, *Pahtai*.' Taking her hand, he kissed the palm, his beard soft as fur against her skin.

'You are my husband, then?'

'No, I am merely a man who loves you. Take my hand and tell me what you feel.'

She did so. 'It is a good hand, strong. And it is warm.'

'You see nothing? No . . . visions?'

'No. Should I?'

He shook his head. 'Of course not. It is only . . . that you were hallucinating when the fever was high. It just shows how much better you are.' He kissed her hand again.

Just as he was doing now. 'I love you,' she thought, suddenly sad that she was about to die. She rose through the ceiling and out into the night, gazing up at the stars. Through spirit eyes they no longer twinkled, but sat perfect and round in the vast bowl of the night. The city was peaceful, and even the campfires of the enemy seemed merely a glowing necklace around Resha.

She had never fully discovered the secrets of her past. It seemed she was a prophet of some kind, and had belonged to a merchant named Kabuchek, but he had fled the city long before the siege began. *Pahtai* remembered walking to his house, hoping that the sight of it would stir her lost memories. Instead she had seen a powerful man, dressed in black and carrying a double-headed axe. He was talking to a servant. Instinctively she had ducked back into an alley, her heart hammering. He looked like Michanek but harder, more deadly. Unable to take her eyes from him, she found the oddest sensations stirring within her.

Swiftly she turned and ran back the way she had come.

And had never since sought to find out her background.

But sometimes as she and Michanek were making love, usually in the garden beneath the flowering trees, she would find herself suddenly thinking of the man with the axe, and then fear would come and with it a sense of betrayal. Michanek loved her, and it seemed disloyal that another man – a man she didn't even know – could intrude into her thoughts at such a time.

Pahtai soared higher, her spirit drawn across the war-torn land, above gutted houses, ruined villages and ghostly, deserted towns. She wondered if this was the route to Paradise? Coming to a range of mountains, she saw an ugly fortress of grey stone. She was thinking of the man with the axe, and found herself drawn into the citadel. There was a hall and within it sat a huge man, his face scarred, his eyes malevolent. Beside him was the axe she had seen carried by the man in black.

Down she journeyed, to a dungeon deep and dark, cold and filthy, the haunt of rats and lice. The axeman lay there, his skin covered in sores. He was asleep and his spirit was gone from the body. Reaching out she tried to touch his face, but her spectral hand flowed beneath the skin. In that moment she saw a slender line of pulsing light radiating around the body. Her hand stroked the light and instantly she found him.

He was alone and in terrible despair. She spoke with him, trying to give him strength, but he reached for her and his words were shocking and filled her with fear. He disappeared then, and she guessed that he had been woken from sleep.

Back in the citadel she floated through the corridors and rooms, the antechambers and halls. An old man was sitting in a deserted kitchen. He too was dreaming, and it was the dream that drew her to him. He was in the same dungeon; he had lived there for years. *Pahtai* entered his mind and spoke with his dream spirit. Then she returned to the night sky. 'I am not dying,' she thought. 'I am merely free.'

In an instant she returned to Resha and her body. Pain flooded through her, and the weight of flesh sank down like a prison around her spirit. She felt the touch of Michanek's hand, and all thoughts of the axeman dispersed like mist under the sun. She was suddenly happy, despite the pain. He had been so good to her, and yet ...

'Are you awake?' he asked, his voice low. She opened her eyes.

'Yes. I love you.'

'And I you. More than life.'

'Why did we never wed?' she said, her throat dry, the words rasping clear. She saw him pale.

'Is that what you wish for? Would it make you well?'

'It would ... make me ... happy,' she told him.

'I will send for a priest,' he promised.

She found him on a grim mountainside where winter winds were howling through the peaks. He was frozen and weak, his limbs trembling, his eyes dull. 'What are you doing?' she asked.

'Waiting to die,' he told her.

'That is no way for you to behave. You are a warrior, and a warrior never gives up.'

'I have no strength left.'

Rowena sat beside him and he felt the warmth of her arms around his shoulders, smelt the sweetness of her breath. 'Be strong,' she said, stroking his hair. 'In despair there is only defeat.'

'I cannot overcome cold stone. I cannot shine a light through the darkness. My limbs are rotting, my teeth shake in their sockets.'

'Is there nothing you would live for?'

247

'Yes,' he said, reaching for her. 'I live for you! I always have. But I can't find you.'

He awoke in the darkness amidst the stench of the dungeon and crawled to the door-stone grille, finding it by touch. Cool air drifted down the corridor and he breathed deeply. Torchlight flickered, burning his eyes. He squinted against it and watched as the jailer tramped down the corridor. Then the darkness returned. Druss's stomach cramped and he groaned. Dizziness swamped him, and nausea rose in his throat.

A faint light showed and, rolling painfully to his knees, he pushed his face against the narrow opening. An old man with a wispy white beard knelt outside the dungeon stone. The light from the tiny clay oil lamp was torturously bright, and Druss's eyes stung.

'Ah, you are alive! Good,' whispered the old man. 'I have brought you this lamp and an old tinderbox. Use it carefully. It will help accustom your eyes to light. Also I have some food.' He thrust a linen package through the door-stone and Druss took it, his mouth too dry for speech. 'I'll come back when I can,' said the old man. 'Remember, only use the light once the jailer has gone.'

Druss listened to the man slowly make his way down the corridor. He thought he heard a door shut, but could not be sure. With unsteady hands he drew the lamp into the dungeon, placing it on the floor beside him. Then he hauled in the package and the small iron tinderbox.

Eyes streaming from the light, he opened the package to find there were two apples, a hunk of cheese and some dried meat. When he bit into one of the apples it was unbearably delicious, the juices stinging his bleeding gums. Swallowing was almost painful, but the minor irritation was swamped by the coolness. He almost vomited, but held it down, and slowly finished the fruit. His shrunken stomach rebelled after the second apple, and he sat holding the cheese and the meat as if they were treasures of gems and gold.

While waiting for his stomach to settle he stared around at his tiny cell, seeing the filth and decay for the first time. Looking at his hands, he saw the skin was split and ugly sores showed on his wrists and arms. His leather jerkin had been taken from him and the woollen shirt was alive with lice. He saw the small hole in the corner of the wall from which the rats emerged.

And despair was replaced by anger.

Unaccustomed to the light, his eyes continued to stream. Removing his shirt, he gazed down at his wasted body. The arms were no longer huge, the wrists and elbows jutting. But I am alive, he told himself. And I will survive.

He finished the cheese and half of the meat. Desperate as he was to consume it all, he did not know if the old man would come back, and he rewrapped the meat and pushed it into his belt.

Examining the working of the tinderbox he saw that it was an old design, a sharp piece of flint that could be struck against the serrated interior, igniting the powdered tinder in the well of the box. Satisfied he could use it in the dark, he reluctantly blew out the lamp.

The old man did return – but not for two days. This time he brought some dried peaches, a hunk of ham and a small sack of tinder. 'It is important that you keep supple,' he told Druss. 'Stretch out on the floor and exercise.'

'Why are you doing this for me?'

'I sat in that cell for years, I know what it is like. You must build your strength. There are two ways to do this, or so I found. Lie on your stomach with your hands beneath your shoulders and then, keeping the legs straight, push yourself up using only your arms. Repeat this as many times as you can manage. Keep count. Each day try for one more. Also you can lie on your back and raise your legs, keeping them straight. This will strengthen the belly.'

'How long have I been here?' asked Druss.

'It is best not to think of that,' the old man advised. 'Concentrate on building your body. I will bring some ointments next time for those sores, and some lice powder.'

'What is your name?'

'Best you don't know – in case they find the lamp.'

'I owe you a debt, my friend. And I always pay my debts.'

'You'll have no chance of that – unless you become strong again.'

'I shall,' promised Druss.

249

When the old man had gone Druss lit the lamp and lay down on his belly. With his hands beneath his shoulders he forced his body up. He managed eight before collapsing to the filthy floor.

A week later it was thirty. And by the end of a month he could manage one hundred.

250

3

The guard at the main gate narrowed his eyes and stared at the three riders. None was known to him, but they rode with casual confidence, chatting to one another and laughing. The guard stepped out to meet them. 'Who are you?' he asked.

The first of the men, a slim blond-haired warrior wearing a baldric from which hung four knives, dismounted from his bay mare. 'We are travellers seeking lodging for the night,' he said. 'Is there a problem? Is there plague in the city?'

'Plague? Of course there's no plague,' answered the guard, hastily making the sign of the Protective Horn. 'Where are you from?'

'We've ridden from Lania, and we're heading for Capalis and the coast. All we seek is an inn.'

'There are no inns here. This is the fortress of Lord Cajivak.'

The other two horsemen remained mounted. The guard looked up at them. One was slim and dark-haired, a bow slung across his shoulder and a quiver hanging from the pommel of his saddle. The third man wore a wide leather hat and sported no weapons save an enormous hunting-knife almost as long as a short sword.

'We can pay for our lodgings,' said the blond man with an easy smile. The guard licked his lips. The man dipped his hand into the pouch by his side and produced a thick silver coin which he dropped into the guard's hand.

'Well . . . it would be churlish to turn you away,' said the guard, pocketing the coin. 'All right. Ride through the main square, bearing left. You'll see a domed building, with a narrow lane running down its eastern side. There is a tavern there. It's a rough place, mind, with much fighting. But the keeper – Ackae – keeps rooms at the back. Tell him that Ratsin sent you.'

'You are most kind,' said the blond man, stepping back into the saddle.

As they rode in to the city the guard shook his head. Be unlikely to see them again, he thought, not with that much silver on them and not a sword between them.

The old man came almost every day, and Druss grew to treasure the moments. He never stayed long, but his conversation was brief, wise and to the point. 'The biggest danger when you get out is to the eyes, boy. They get too used to the dark, and the sun can blind them – permanently. I lost my sight for almost a month after they dragged me out. Stare into the lamp flame, close as you can, force the pupils to contract.'

Druss was now as strong as he would ever be in such a place, and last night he had told the man, 'Do not come tomorrow, or the next day.'

'Why?'

'I'm thinking of leaving,' answered the Drenai. The old man had laughed. 'I'm serious, my friend. Don't come for two days.'

'There's no way out. The door-stone alone requires two men to move it, and there are two bolts holding it in place.'

'If you are correct,' Druss told him, 'then I will see you here in three days.'

Now he sat quietly in the dark. The ointments his friend had supplied had healed most of his sores, and the lice powder – while itching like the devil's touch – had convinced all but the most hardy of the parasites to seek alternative accommodation. The food over the last months had rebuilt Druss's strength, and his teeth no longer rattled in their sockets. Now was the time, he thought. There'll never be a better.

Silently he waited through the long day.

At last he heard the jailer outside. A clay cup was pushed into the opening, with a hunk of stale bread by it. Druss sat in the dark, unmoving.

'Here is it, my black-bearded rat,' the jailer called.

Silence. 'Ah well, suit yourself. You'll change your mind before long.'

The hours drifted by. Torchlight flickered in the corridor and he heard the jailer halt. Then the man walked on. Druss waited for an hour, then he lit his lamp and chewed on the last of the meat the old man had left the night before. Lifting the lamp to his face he stared hard into the tiny flame, passing it back and forth before his eyes. The light didn't sting as once it had. Blowing out the light he turned over on to his stomach, pushing himself through one hundred and fifty press raises.

He slept …

And awoke to the arrival of the jailer. The man knelt down at the narrow opening, but Druss knew he could not see more than a few inches into the dark. The food and water was untouched. The only question now was whether the jailer cared if his prisoner lived or died. Cajivak had threatened to have Druss dragged before him in order to plead for death. Would the Lord be pleased that his jailer had robbed him of such delights?

He heard the jailer curse, then move off back the way he had come. Druss's mouth was dry, and his heart pounded. Minutes passed – long, anxious minutes. Then the jailer returned; he was speaking to someone.

'It's not my fault,' he was saying. 'His rations were set by the Lord himself.'

'So it's *his* fault? Is that what you're saying?'

'No! No! It's nobody's *fault*. Maybe he had a weak heart or something. Maybe he's just sick. That's it, he's probably sick. We'll move him to a bigger cell for a while.'

'I hope you're right,' said a soft voice, 'otherwise you'll be wearing your own entrails for a necklace.'

A grating sound followed, then another, and Druss guessed the bolts were being drawn back. 'All right, together now,' came a voice. 'Heave!' The stone groaned as the men hauled it clear.

'Gods, but it stinks in there!' complained one of the guards as a torch was thrust inside. Druss grabbed the wielder by the

253

throat, hauling him in, then he dived through the opening and rolled. He rose, but dizziness caused him to stagger and a guard laughed.

'There's your dead man,' he said, and Druss heard the rasp of a sword being drawn. It was so hard to see – there were at least three torches, and the light was blinding. A shape moved towards him. 'Back in your hole, rat!' said the guard. Druss leapt forward to smash a punch to the man's face. The guard's iron helm flew from his head as his body shot backwards, his head cannoning into the dungeon wall. A second guard ran in. Druss's vision was clearing now and he saw the man aim a blow at his head. He ducked and stepped inside the blow, thundering his fist in the man's belly. Instantly the guard folded, a great whoosh of air rushing from his lungs. Druss brought his clenched fist down on the man's neck, there was a sickening crack and the guard fell on his face.

The jailer was trying to wriggle clear of the dungeon opening as Druss turned on him. The man squealed in fright and elbowed his way back into the dungeon. Druss hauled the first guard to the entrance, thrusting the unconscious body through into the cell. The second guard was dead; his body followed the first. Breathing heavily Druss looked at the door-stone. Anger rose in him like a sudden fire. Squatting down, he took the stone in both hands and heaved it into place. Then he sat before it and pushed it home with his legs. For several minutes he sat exhausted, then he crawled to the door-stone and pushed the bolts home.

Lights danced before Druss's eyes, and his heart was hammering so fast he could not count the beats. Yet he forced himself upright and moved carefully to the door, which was partly open, and glanced into the corridor beyond. Sunlight was shining through a window, the beam highlighting dust motes in the air. It was indescribably beautiful.

The corridor was deserted. He could see two chairs and a table with two cups upon it. Moving into the corridor, he halted at the table and, seeing the cups contained watered wine, he drained them both. More dungeons lined the walls, but these all had doors of iron bars. He moved on to a second wooden door, beyond which was a stairwell, dark and unlit.

His strength was fading as he slowly climbed the stairs, but anger drove him on.

Sieben gazed down with undisguised horror at the small black insect upon the back of his hand. 'This,' he said, 'is insufferable.'

'What?' asked Varsava from his position at the narrow window.

'The room has fleas,' answered Sieben, taking the insect between thumb and forefinger and crushing it.

'They seem to prefer you, poet,' put in Eskodas with a boyish grin.

'The risk of death is one thing,' said Sieben icily. 'Fleas are quite another. I have not even inspected the bed, but I would imagine it is teeming with wildlife. I think we should make the rescue attempt at once.'

Varsava chuckled. 'After dark would probably be best,' he said. 'I was here three months ago when I took a child back out to his father. That's how I learned that Druss was here. The dungeons are – as you would expect – on the lowest level. Above them are the kitchens, and above them the main Hall. There is no exit from the dungeons save through the Hall, which means we must be inside the Keep by dusk. There is no night jailer; therefore, if we can hide within the Keep until around midnight, we should be able to find Druss and get him out. As to leaving the fortress, that is another matter. As you saw, the two gates are guarded by day and locked by night. There are sentries on the walls, and lookouts in the towers.'

'How many?' asked Eskodas.

'When I was here before, there were five near the main gate.'

'How did you get out with the child?'

'He was a small boy. I hid him in a sack and carried him out just after dawn, draped behind my saddle.'

'I can't see Druss fitting in a sack,' said Sieben.

Varsava moved to sit alongside the poet. 'Do not think of him as you knew him, poet. He has been over a year in a tiny, windowless cell. The food would be barely enough to keep him alive. He will not be the giant we all knew. And he's likely to be blind – or insane. Or both.'

Silence fell upon the room as each man remembered the axeman they had fought alongside. 'I wish I'd known sooner,' muttered Sieben.

'I did not know myself,' said Varsava. 'I thought they'd killed him.'

'It's strange,' put in Eskodas, 'I could never imagine Druss being beaten – even by an army. He was always so – so indomitable.'

Varsava chuckled. 'I know. I watched him walk unarmed into a hollow where a dozen or so warriors were torturing an old man. He went through them like a scythe through wheat. Impressive.'

'So, how shall we proceed?' Sieben asked.

'We will go to the main Hall to pay our respects to the Lord Cajivak. Perhaps he won't kill us outright!'

'Oh, that's a good plan,' said Sieben, his voice dripping with sarcasm.

'You have a better?'

'I believe that I have. One would imagine that a sordid place like this would be short of entertainment. I shall go alone and announce myself by name; I will offer to perform for my supper.'

'At the risk of being considered rude,' said Eskodas, 'I don't think your epic poems will be as well received as you think.'

'My dear boy, I am an entertainer. I can fashion a performance to suit any audience.'

'Well, this audience,' said Varsava, 'will be made up of the dregs of Ventria and Naashan and all points east and west. There will be Drenai renegades, Vagrian mercenaries and Ventrian criminals of all kinds.'

'I shall dazzle them,' promised Sieben. 'Give me half an hour to make my introductions, then make your way into the Hall. I promise you no one will notice your entrance.'

'Where did you acquire such humility?' asked Eskodas.

'It's a gift,' replied Sieben, 'and I'm very proud of it.'

*   *   *

256

Druss reached the second level and paused at the top of the stair-well. He could hear the sounds of many people moving around, the scrape of pans being cleaned and of cutlery being prepared. He could smell fresh bread cooking, mixed with the savoury aroma of roasting beef. Leaning against the wall, he tried to think. There was no way through without being seen. His legs were tired, and he sank down to his haunches.

What to do?

He heard footsteps approaching and pushed himself upright. An old man appeared, his back hideously bent, his legs bowed. He was carrying a bucket of water. His head came up as he approached Druss, his nostrils quivering. The eyes, Druss saw, were rheumy and covered with an opal film. The old man put down the bucket and reached out. 'Is it you?' he whispered.

'You are blind?'

'Almost. I told you I spent five years in that cell. Come, follow me.' Leaving the bucket, the old man retraced his steps, round a winding corridor and down a narrow stair. Pushing open a door, he led Druss inside. The room was small, but there was a slit window that allowed in a shaft of sunshine. 'Wait here,' he said. 'I will bring you some food and drink.'

He returned within minutes with a half-loaf of fresh baked bread, a slab of cheese and a jug of water. Druss devoured the food and drank deeply, then leaned back on the cot-bed.

'I thank you for your kindness,' he said. 'Without it I would be worse than dead; I would have been lost.'

'I owed a debt,' said the cripple. 'Another man fed me, just as I fed you. They killed him for it – Cajivak had him impaled. But I would never have found the courage had the goddess not appeared to me in a dream. Was it she who brought you from the dungeon?'

'Goddess?'

'She told me of you, and your suffering, and she filled me with shame at my cowardice. I swore to her that I would do all in my power to help you. And she touched my hand, and when I awoke all pain had gone from my back. Did she make the stone disappear?'

257

'No, I tricked the jailer.' He told the man of the ruse, and his fight with the guards.

'They will not be discovered until later tonight,' said the cripple. 'Ah, but I would love to hear their screams as the rats come at them in the dark.'

'Why do you say the woman in your dream was a goddess?' asked Druss.

'She told me her name, *Pahtai*, and that is the daughter of the earth mother. And in my dream she walked with me upon the green hillsides of my youth. I shall never forget her.'

'*Pahtai*,' said Druss softly. 'She came to me also in that cell, and gave me strength.' He stood and laid his hand on the old man's back. 'You risked much to help me, and I've no time left in this world in which to repay you.'

'No time?' echoed the old man. 'You can hide here and escape after dark. I can get a rope; you can lower yourself from the wall.'

'No. I must find Cajivak – and kill him.'

'Good,' said the old man. 'The goddess will give you powers, yes? She will pour strength into your body?'

'I fear not,' said Druss. 'In this I shall be alone.'

'You will die! Do not attempt this,' pleaded the old man, tears streaming from the opal eyes. 'I beg you. He will destroy you; he is a monster with the strength of ten men. Look at yourself. I cannot see you clearly, but I know how weak you must be. You have a chance at life, freedom, sunshine on your face. You are young – what will you achieve if you attempt this foolishness? He will crush you, and either kill you or throw you back into that hole in the ground.'

'I was not born to run,' said Druss. 'And, trust me, I am not as weak as you think. You saw to that. Now tell me of the Keep, and where the stairwells lead.'

Eskodas had no fear of death, for he had no love of life – a fact he had known for many years. Ever since his father was dragged from their home and hanged, he had known no depth of joy. He felt the loss, but accepted it in a calm and tranquil manner. On board ship he had told Sieben that he enjoyed killing people, but this was not true. He experienced no sensation whatever when his arrow struck home, save for a momentary satisfaction when his aim was particularly good.

Now, as he strolled with Varsava towards the grey, forbidding Hall, he wondered if he would die. He thought of Druss imprisoned beneath the Keep in a dark, dank dungeon, and found himself wondering what such incarceration would do to his own personality. He took no especial pleasure from the sights of the world, the mountains and lakes, the oceans and valleys. Would he miss them? He doubted it.

Glancing at Varsava, he saw that the bladesman was tense, expectant. Eskodas smiled. No need for fear, he thought.

It is only death.

The two men climbed the stone steps to the Keep gates, which were open and unguarded. Moving inside, Eskodas heard a roar of laughter from the Hall. They walked to the main doors and looked inside. There were some two hundred men seated around three great tables and, at the far end, on a dais raised some six feet from the floor, sat Cajivak. He was seated in a huge, ornately carved chair of ebony, and he was smiling. Before him, standing on the end table, was Sieben.

The poet's voice sang out. He was telling them a tale of such mind-bending raunchiness that Eskodas's jaw dropped. He had heard Sieben tell epic stories, recite ancient poems and discuss philosophy, but never had he heard the poet talk of whores and donkeys. Varsava laughed aloud as Sieben finished the story with an obscene *double entendre*.

Eskodas gazed around the hall. Above them was a gallery, and he located the recessed stairway that led to it. This might be a good place to hide. He nudged Varsava. 'I'll take a look upstairs,' he whispered. The bladesman nodded and Eskodas strolled unnoticed through the throng and climbed the stairs. The gallery was narrow and flowed round the Hall. There were no doors leading from it, and a man seated here would be invisible to those below.

Sieben was now telling the story of a hero captured by a vicious enemy. Eskodas paused to listen:

'He was taken before the leader, and told that he had one opportunity for life: he must survive four trials by ordeal. The first was
to walk barefoot across a trench filled with hot coals. The second
to drink a full quart of the most powerful spirit. Thirdly he had to
enter a cave and, with a small set of tongs, remove a bad tooth from
a mankilling lioness. Lastly, he was told, he had to make love to the
ugliest crone in the village.

'Well, he pulled off his boots and told them to bring on the hot
coals. Manfully he strode through them to the other side of the
trench, where he lifted the quart of spirit and drained it, hurling the
pot aside. Then he stumbled into the cave. There followed the most
terrible sounds of spitting, growling, and banging and shrieking. The
listening men found their blood growing cold. At last the warrior
staggered out into the sunlight. "Right," he said. "Now where's the
woman with the toothache?" '

Laughter echoed around the rafters and Eskodas shook his head
in amazement. He had watched Sieben back in Capalis listening to
warriors swapping jests and jokes. Not once had the poet laughed,
or appeared to find the stories amusing. Yet here he was, performing
the same tales with apparent relish.

Transferring his gaze to Cajivak, the archer saw that the leader was
no longer smiling, but was sitting back in his chair, his fingers drumming on the arm-rest. Eskodas had known many evil men, and knew
well that some could look as fine as angels – handsome, clear-eyed,
golden-haired. But Cajivak looked what he was, dark and malevolent. He was wearing Druss's jerkin of black leather, with the silver
shoulder guards, and Eskodas saw him reach down and stroke the
black haft of an axe that was resting against the chair. It was Snaga.

Suddenly the colossal warrior rose from his chair. 'Enough!' he
bellowed and Sieben stood silently before him. 'I don't like your
performance, bard, so I'm going to have you impaled on an iron
spike.' The Hall was utterly silent now. Eskodas drew a shaft from
his quiver and notched it to his bow. 'Well? Any more jests before
you die?' Cajivak asked.

'Just the one,' answered Sieben, holding to the madman's gaze.
'Last night I had dream, a terrible dream. I dreamt I was beyond the

gates of Hell; it was a place of fire and torture, exquisitely ghastly. I was very frightened and I said to one of the demon guards, "Is there any way out of here?" And he said there was only one, and no one had ever achieved the task set. He led me to a dungeon, and through a narrow grille I saw the most loathsome woman. She was leprous, with weeping sores, toothless and old beyond time. Maggots crawled in what was left of her hair. The guard said, "If you can make love to her all night, you will be allowed to leave." And, you know, I was prepared to have a try. But as I stepped forward I saw a second door, and I glanced through. And you know what I saw, Lord? I saw you. You were making love to one of the most beautiful women I have ever seen. So I said to the guard, "Why is it that I have to bed a crone, when Cajivak gets a beauty?" "Well," he said, " 'tis only fair that the women also have a chance to get out." '

Even from the gallery Eskodas could see Cajivak's face lose its colour. When he spoke, his voice was harsh and trembling. 'I will make your death last an eternity,' he promised.

Eskodas drew back on his bowstring ... and paused. A man had appeared at the back of the dais, his hair and beard matted and filthy, his face blackened with ingrained dirt. He ran forward, throwing his shoulder into the high back of Cajivak's chair, which hurtled forward to catapult the warlord from the dais. He fell head-first on to the table upon which Sieben stood.

The filth-covered warrior swept up the shining axe, and his voice boomed out through the Hall: 'Now do you want me to beg, you miserable whoreson?'

Eskodas chuckled. There were moments in life worth cherishing, he realised.

As he swept up the axe, feeling the cool, black haft in his hand, power surged through him. It felt like fire roaring through his veins to every muscle and sinew. In that moment Druss felt renewed, reborn. Nothing in his life had ever been so exquisite. He felt light-headed and full of life, like a paralysed man who regains the use of his limbs.

His laughter boomed out over the Hall, and he gazed down on Cajivak who was scrambling to his feet amongst the dishes and goblets. The warlord's face was bloody, his mouth contorted.

'It is mine!' shouted Cajivak. 'Give it back!'

The men around him looked surprised at his reaction. Where they had expected fury and violence, they saw instead their dread Lord reaching out, almost begging.

'Come and get it,' invited Druss.

Cajivak hesitated and licked his thin lips. 'Kill him!' he screamed suddenly. The warriors surged to their feet, the nearest man drawing his sword and running towards the dais. An arrow slashed into his throat, pitching him from his feet. All movement ceased then as scores of armed men scanned the Hall, seeking the hidden bowman.

'What a man you chose to follow!' said Druss, his voice booming in the sudden silence. 'He stands with his feet in your stew, too frightened to face a man who has been locked in his dungeon and fed on scraps. You want the axe?' he asked Cajivak. 'I say again, Come and get it.' Twisting the weapon, he slammed it down into the boards of the dais where it stood quivering, the points of the butterfly blades punching deep into the wood. Druss stepped away from the axe and the warriors waited.

Suddenly Cajivak moved, taking two running steps and leaping towards the dais. He was a huge man, with immense shoulders and powerful arms; but he leapt into a straight left from the former champion of Mashrapur which smashed his lips into his teeth, and a right cross that hit his jaw like a thunderbolt. Cajivak fell to the dais and rolled back to the floor, landing on his back. He was up fast, and this time he slowly mounted the steps to the dais.

'I'll break you, little man! I'll rip out your entrails and feed them to you!'

'In your dreams!' mocked Druss. As Cajivak charged, Druss stepped in to meet him, slamming a second straight left into Cajivak's heart. The larger man grunted, but then sent an overhand right that cannoned against Druss's brow, forcing him back. Cajivak's left hand snapped forward with fingers extended to rip out Druss's eyes.

262

Druss dropped his head so that the fingers stabbed into his brow, the long nails gashing the skin. Cajivak grabbed for him, but as his hands closed around Druss's shirt the rotted material gave way. As Cajivak staggered back, Druss stepped in to thunder two blows to his belly. It felt as if he were beating his hands against a wall. The giant warlord laughed and struck out with an uppercut that almost lifted Druss from his feet. His nose was broken and streaming blood, but as Cajivak leapt in for the kill Druss sidestepped, tripping the larger man. Cajivak hit the floor hard, then rolled and came up swiftly.

Druss was tiring now, the sudden surge of power from the axe fading away from his muscles. Cajivak lunged forward, but Druss feinted with a left and Cajivak swayed back from it – straight into the path of a right hook that hammered into his mouth, impaling his lower lip on his teeth. Druss followed this with a left, then another right. A cut opened above Cajivak's right eye, blood spilling to the cheek, and he fell back. Then he pulled the punctured lip from his teeth – and gave a bloody grin. For a moment Druss was nonplussed, then Cajivak leaned over and dragged Snaga from the boards.

The axe shone red in the lantern light. 'Now you die, little man!' Cajivak snarled.

He raised the axe as Druss took one running step and leapt, his right foot coming down hard on Cajivak's knee. The joint gave way with an explosive crack and the giant fell screaming to the ground, losing his hold on the axe. The weapon twisted in the air – then plunged down, the twin points striking the warlord just below the shoulder-blades, lancing through the leather jerkin and the skin beyond. Cajivak twisted and the axe ripped clear of his body. Druss knelt and retrieved the weapon.

Cajivak, his face twisted in pain, pushed himself into a sitting position and stared at the axeman with undisguised hatred. 'Let the blow be a clean one,' he said softly.

Still kneeling Druss nodded, then swept Snaga in a horizontal arc. The blades bit into Cajivak's bull neck, slicing through the muscle, sinew and bone. The body toppled to the right, the head falling left where it bounced once on the dais before rolling to the hall floor below. Druss stood and turned to face the stunned warriors. Suddenly weary, he sat down on Cajivak's throne. 'Someone bring me a goblet of wine!' he ordered.

Sieben grabbed a pitcher and a goblet and moved slowly to where the axeman sat.

'You took your damned time getting here,' said Druss.

4

From the back of the Hall Varsava watched the scene with fascination. Cajivak's body lay on the dais, blood staining the floor around it. In the Hall itself the warriors stood with their eyes locked to the man sitting slumped on Cajivak's throne. Varsava glanced up at the gallery where Eskodas waited, an arrow still strung to his bow.

What now, thought Varsava, scanning the Hall. There must be over a hundred killers here. His mouth was dry. At any moment the unnatural calm would vanish. What then? Would they rush the dais? And what of Druss? Would he take up his axe and attack them all?

I don't want to die here, he thought, wondering what he would do if they did attack Druss. He was close to the rear door – no one would notice if he just slipped away into the night. After all, he owed the man nothing. Varsava had done more than his share, locating Sieben and setting up the rescue attempt. To die now, in a meaningless skirmish, would be nonsense.

Yet he did not move but stood silently, waiting, with all the other men, and watched Druss drain a third goblet of wine. Then the axeman rose and wandered down into the hall, leaving his axe on the dais. Druss moved to the first table and tore a chunk of bread from a fresh-baked loaf. 'None of you hungry?' he asked the men.

A tall, slim warrior wearing a crimson shirt stepped forward. 'What are your plans?' he asked.

'I'm going to eat,' Druss told him. 'Then I'm going to bathe. After that I think I'll sleep for a week.'

'And then?' The Hall was silent, the warriors milling closer to hear the axeman's answer.

265

'One thing at a time, laddie. When you sit in a dungeon, in the dark, with only rats for company, you learn never to make too many plans.'

'Are you seeking to take his place?' persisted the warrior, pointing to the severed head.

Druss laughed. 'By the gods, look at him! Would *you* want to take his place?' Chewing on the bread, Druss returned to the dais and sat. Then he leaned forward and addressed the men. 'I am Druss,' he said. 'Some of you may remember me from the day I was brought here. Others may know of my service with the Emperor. I have no ill-will towards any of you . . . but if any man here wishes to die, then let him take up his weapons and approach me. I'll oblige him.' He stood and hefted the axe. 'Anyone?' he challenged. No one moved and Druss nodded. 'You are all fighting men,' he said, 'but you fight for pay. That is sensible. Your leader is dead – best you finish your meal, and then choose another.'

'Are you putting yourself forward?' asked the man in the crimson shirt.

'Laddie, I've had enough of this fortress. And I have other plans.'

Druss turned back to Sieben, and Varsava could not hear their conversation. The warriors gathered together in small groups, discussing the various merits and vices of Cajivak's under-leaders, and Varsava strolled out of the Hall, confused by what he had seen. Beyond the Hall was a wide antechamber where the bladesman sat on a long couch – his feelings mixed, his heart heavy. Eskodas joined him.

'How did he do it?' asked Varsava. 'A hundred killers, and they just accepted his murder of their leader. Incredible!'

Eskodas shrugged and smiled. 'That's Druss.'

Varsava swore softly. 'You call that an answer?'

'It depends what you are looking for,' responded the bowman. 'Perhaps you should be asking yourself why you are angry. You came here to rescue a friend, and now he is free. What more did you want?'

Varsava laughed, but the sound was dry and harsh. 'You want the truth? I half desired to see Druss broken. I wanted confirmation of his stupidity! The great *hero*! He rescued an old man and child – that's why he's spent a year or more in this cesspit. You understand? It was meaningless. Meaningless!'

'Not for Druss.'

'What is so special about him?' stormed Varsava. 'He's not blessed with a fine mind, he has no intellect to speak of. Any other man who has just done what he did would be ripped to pieces by that mangy crew. But no, not Druss! Why? He could have become their leader – just like that! They would have accepted it.'

'I can give you no definitive answers,' said Eskodas. 'I watched him storm a ship filled with blood-hungry corsairs – they threw down their weapons. It is the nature of the man, I suppose. I had a teacher once, a great bowman, who told me that when we see another man we instinctively judge him as either threat or prey. Because we are hunting, killing animals. Carnivores. We are a deadly breed, Varsava. When we look at Druss we see the ultimate threat – a man who does not understand compromise. He breaks the rules. No, more than that, I think. For him there *are* no rules. Take what happened back there. An ordinary man might well have killed Cajivak – though I doubt it. But he would not have hurled aside the axe and fought the monster hand to hand. And when he'd slain the leader he would have looked out at all those killers and, in his heart, he would have expected death. They would have sensed it . . . and they would have killed him. But Druss didn't sense it; he didn't care. One at a time, or all at once. He'd have fought them all.'

'And died,' put in Varsava.

'Probably. But that's not the point. After he killed Cajivak he sat down and called for a drink. A man doesn't do that if he expects further battles. That left them confused, uncertain – no rules, you see. And when he walked down among them he left the axe behind. *He* knew he wouldn't need it – and they knew too. He played them like a harp. But he didn't do it consciously, it is just the nature of the man.'

'I can't be like him,' said Varsava sadly, remembering the peace-maker and the terrible death he suffered.

'Few can,' agreed Eskodas. 'That's why he is becoming a legend.'

Laughter echoed from the Hall. 'Sieben is entertaining them again,' said Eskodas. 'Come on, let's go and listen. We can get drunk.'

'I don't want to get drunk. I want to be young again. I want to change the past, wipe a wet rag over the filthy slate.'

'It's a fresh day tomorrow,' said Eskodas softly.

'What does that mean?'

'The past is dead, bladesman, the future largely unwritten. I was on a ship once with a rich man when we hit a storm, and the ship went down. The rich man gathered as much gold as he could carry. He drowned. I left behind everything I owned. I survived.'

'You think my guilt weighs more than his gold?'

'I think you should leave it behind,' said Eskodas, rising. 'Now, come and see Druss – and let's get drunk.'

'No,' said Varsava sadly. 'I don't want to see him.' He stood and placed his wide leather hat upon his head. 'Give him my best wishes, and tell him ... tell him ...' His voice faded away.

'Tell him what?'

Varsava shook his head, and smiled ruefully. 'Tell him goodbye,' he said.

Michanek followed the young officer to the base of the wall, then both men knelt with their ears to the stone. At first Michanek could hear nothing, but then came the sound of scraping, like giant rats beneath the earth, and he swore softly.

'You have done well, Cicarin. They are digging beneath the walls. The question is, from where? Follow me.' The young officer followed the powerfully built champion as Michanek scaled the rampart steps and leaned out over the parapet. Ahead was the main camp of the Ventrian army, their tents pitched on the plain before the city. To the left was a line of low hills with the river beyond them. To the right was a higher section of hills, heavily wooded. 'My guess,' said Michanek, 'would be that they began their work on the far side of that hill, about halfway up. They would have taken a bearing and know that if they hold to a level course they would come under the walls by around two feet.'

'How serious is it, sir?' asked Cicarin nervously.

Michanek smiled at the young man. 'Serious enough. Have you ever been down a mine?'

'No, sir.'

Michanek chuckled. Of course he hadn't. The boy was the youngest son of a Naashanite Satrap who until this siege had been surrounded by servants, barbers, valets and huntsmen. His clothes would have been laid out each morning, his breakfast brought to him on a silver tray as he lay in bed with satin sheets. 'There are many aspects to soldiering,' he said. 'They are mining beneath our walls, removing the foundations. As they dig, they are shoring up the walls and ceiling with very dry timber. They will dig along the line of the wall, then burrow on to the hills by the river, emerging somewhere around . . . there.' He pointed to the tallest of the low hills.

'I don't understand,' said Cicarin. 'If they are shoring up the tunnel, what harm can it do?'

'That's an easy question to answer. Once they have two openings there will be a through draught of air; then they will soak the timbers with oil and, when the wind is right, set fire to the tunnel. The wind will drive the flames through, the ceiling will collapse and, if they have done their job well, the walls will come crashing down.'

'Can we do nothing to stop them?'

'Nothing of worth. We could send an armed force to attack the workings, maybe kill a few miners, but they would just bring in more. No. We cannot act, therefore we must react. I want you to assume that this section of wall will fall.' He turned from the parapet and scanned the line of houses behind the wall. There were several alleyways and two major roads leading into the city. 'Take fifty men and block the alleys and roads. Also fill in the ground-floor windows of the houses. We must have a secondary line of defence.'

'Yes, sir,' said the young man, his eyes downcast.

'Keep your spirits up, boy,' advised Michanek. 'We're not dead yet.'

'No, sir. But people are starting to talk openly about the relief army; they say it's not coming – that we've been left behind.'

'Whatever the Emperor's decision, we will abide by it,' said Michanek sternly. The young man reddened, then saluted and strode away. Michanek watched him, then returned to the battlements.

There was no relief force. The Naashanite army had been crushed in two devastating battles and was fleeing now towards the border. Resha was the last of the occupied cities. The intended conquest of Ventria was now a disaster of the first rank.

But Michanek had his orders. He, and the renegade Ventrian Darishan, were to hold Resha as long as possible, tying down Ventrian troops while the Emperor fled back to the safety of the mountains of Naashan.

Michanek dug into the pouch at his side and pulled clear the small piece of parchment on which the message had been sent. He gazed down at the hasty script.

Hold at all costs, until otherwise ordered. No surrender.

The warrior slowly shredded the message. There were no farewells, no tributes, no words of regret. Such is the gratitude of princes, he thought. He had scribbled his own reply, folding it carefully and inserting it into the tiny metal tube which he then tied to the leg of the pigeon. The bird soared into the air and flew east, bearing Michanek's last message to the Emperor he had served since a boy:

As you order, so shall it be.

The stitched wound on his side was itching now, a sure sign of healing. Idly he scratched it. You were lucky, he thought. Bodasen almost had you. By the western gate he saw the first of the food convoys wending its way through the Ventrian ranks, and he strode down to meet the wagons.

The first driver waved as he saw him; it was his cousin, Shurpac. The man leapt down from the plank seat, throwing the reins to the fat man beside him.

'Well met, cousin,' said Shurpac, throwing his arms around Michanek and kissing both bearded cheeks. Michanek felt cold, the thrill of fear coursing through him as he remembered Rowena's warning: *'I see soldiers with black cloaks and helms, storming the walls. You will gather your men for a last stand outside these walls. Beside you will be . . . your youngest brother and a second cousin.'*

'What's wrong, Michi? You look as if a ghost has drifted across your grave.'

Michanek forced a smile. 'I did not expect to see you here. I heard you were with the Emperor.'

'I was. But these are sad times, cousin; he is a broken man. I heard you were here and was trying to find a way through. Then I heard about the duel. Wonderful. The stuff of legends! Why did you not kill him?'

Michanek shrugged. 'He fought well, and bravely. But I pierced his lung and he fell. He was no threat after that, there was no need to make the killing thrust.'

'I'd love to have seen Gorben's face. He is said to have believed Bodasen unbeatable with the blade.'

'No one is unbeatable, cousin. No one.'

'Nonsense,' announced Shurpac. 'You are unbeatable. That's why I wanted to be here, to fight beside you. I think we'll show these Ventrians a thing or three. Where is Narin?'

'At the barracks, waiting for the food. We will test it on Ventrian prisoners.'

'You think Gorben may have poisoned it?'

Michanek shrugged. 'I don't know . . . perhaps. Go on, take them through.'

Shurpac clambered back to his seat, lifted a whip and lightly cracked it over the heads of the four mules. They lurched forward into the traces and the wagon rolled on. Michanek strolled out through the gates and counted the wagons. There were fifty, all filled with flour and dried fruit, oats, cereal, flour and maize. Gorben had promised two hundred. Will you keep your word? wondered Michanek.

As if in answer a lone horseman rode from the enemy camp. The horse was a white stallion of some seventeen hands, a handsome beast built for power and speed. It charged towards Michanek, who held his ground with arms crossed against his chest. At the last moment the rider dragged on the reins. The horse reared, and the rider leapt down. Michanek bowed as he recognised the Ventrian Emperor.

'How is Bodasen?' asked Michanek.

'Alive. I thank you for sparing the last thrust. He means much to me.'

'He's a good man.'

'So are you,' said Gorben. 'Too good to die here for a monarch who has deserted you.'

Michanek laughed. 'When I made my oath of allegiance, I do not recall it having a clause that would allow me to break it. You have such clauses in your own oath of fealty?'

Gorben smiled. 'No. My people pledge to support me to the death.'

Michanek spread his arms. 'Well then, my Lord, what else would you expect this poor Naashanite to do?'

Gorben's smile faded and he stepped in close. 'I had hoped you would surrender, Michanek. I do not seek your death – I owe you a life. You must see now that even with these supplies, you cannot hold out much longer. Why must I send in my Immortals to see you all cut to pieces? Why not merely march out in good order and return home? You may pass unmolested; you have my word.'

'That would be contrary to my orders, my Lord.'

'Might I ask what they are?'

'To hold until ordered otherwise.'

'Your Lord is in full flight. I have captured his baggage train, including his three wives and his daughters. Even now one of his messengers is in my tent, negotiating for their safe return. But he asks nothing for you, his most loyal soldier. Do you not find that galling?'

'Of course,' agreed Michanek, 'but it alters nothing.'

Gorben shook his head and turned to his stallion. Taking hold of rein and pommel, he vaulted to the horse's back. 'You are a fine man, Michanek. I wish you could have served me.'

'And you, sir, are a gifted general. It has been a pleasure to thwart you for so long. Give my regards to Bodasen – and if you wish to stake it all on another duel, I will meet whoever you send.'

'If my champion was here I would hold you to that,' said Gorben, with a wide grin. 'I would like to see how you would fare against Druss and his axe. Farewell, Michanek. May the gods grant you a splendid afterlife.'

The Ventrian Emperor heeled the stallion into a run and galloped back to the camp.

Pahtai was sitting in the garden when the first vision came to her. She was watching a bee negotiate an entry into a purple bloom when suddenly she saw an image of the man with the axe – only he had no axe, and no beard. He was sitting upon a mountainside overlooking a small village with a half-built stockade wall. As quickly as it had come, it disappeared. She was troubled, but with the constant battles upon the walls of Resha, and her fears for Michanek's safety, she brushed her worries away.

But the second vision was more powerful than the first. She saw a ship, and upon it a tall, thin man. A name filtered through the veils of her mind:

Kabuchek.

He had owned her once, long ago in the days when Pudri said she had a rare Talent, a gift for seeing the future and reading the past. The gift was gone now, and she did not regret it. Amid a terrible civil war it was, perhaps, a blessing not to know what perils the future had to offer.

She told Michanek of her visions and watched as the look of sorrow touched his handsome face. He had taken her into his arms, holding her tight, just as he had throughout her sickness. Michanek had risked catching the plague, yet in her fever dreams she drew great strength from his presence and his devotion. And she had survived, though all the surgeons predicted her death. True her heart was now weak, so they said, and any exertion tired her. But her strength was returning month by month.

The sun was bright above the garden, and *Pahtai* moved out to gather flowers with which to decorate the main rooms. In her arms she held a flat wicker basket in which was placed a sharp cutting knife. As the sun touched her face she tilted her head, enjoying

273

the warmth upon her skin. In the distance a high-pitched scream suddenly sounded and her eyes turned towards the direction of the noise. Faintly she could hear the clash of steel on steel, the shouts and cries of warriors in desperate combat.

Will it never end? she thought.

A shadow fell across her and she turned and saw that two men had entered the garden. They were thin, their clothes ragged and filthy.

'Give us food,' demanded one, moving in towards her.

'You must go to the ration centre,' she said, fighting down her fear.

'You don't live on rations, do you, you Naashanite whore!' said the second man, stepping in close. He stank of stale sweat and cheap ale, and she saw his pale eyes glance towards her breasts. She was wearing a thin tunic of blue silk, and her legs were bare. The first man grabbed her arm, dragging her towards him. She thought of grabbing for the cutting knife, but in that instant found herself staring down at a narrow bed in a small room. Upon it lay a woman and a sickly child; their names flashed into her mind.

'What of Katina?' she said suddenly. The man groaned and fell back, releasing his hold, his eyes wide and stricken with guilt. 'Your baby son is dying,' she said softly. 'Dying while you drink and attack women. Go to the kitchen, both of you. Ask for Pudri, and tell him that . . .' she hesitated . . . 'that *Pahtai* said you could have food. There are some eggs and unleavened bread. Go now, both of you.'

The men backed away from her, then turned and ran for the house. *Pahtai*, trembling from the shock, sat down on a marble seat.

Pahtai? Rowena . . . The name rose up from the deepest levels of her memory, and she greeted it like a song of morning after a night of storms.

Rowena. I am Rowena.

A man came walking along the garden path, bowing as he saw her. His hair was silver, and braided, yet his face was young and almost unlined. He bowed again. 'Greetings, *Pahtai*, are you well?'

'I am well, Darishan. But you look tired.'

'Tired of sieges, that's for sure. May I sit beside you?'

'Of course. Michanek is not here, but you are welcome to wait for him.'

He leaned back and sniffed the air. 'I do love roses. Exquisite smell; they remind me of my childhood. You know I used to play with Gorben? We were friends. We used to hide in bushes such as these, and pretend we were being hunted by assassins. Now I am hiding again, but there is not a rose bush large enough to conceal me.'

Rowena said nothing, but she gazed into his handsome face and saw the fear lurking below the surface.

'I saddled the wrong horse, my dear,' he said with a show of brightness. 'I thought the Naashanites would be preferable to watching Gorben's father destroy the Empire. But all I have done is to train a younger lion in the ways of war and conquest. Do you think I could convince Gorben that I have, in fact, done him a service?' He looked into her face. 'No, I suppose I couldn't. I shall just have to face my death like a Ventrian.'

'Don't talk of death,' she scolded. 'The walls still hold and now we have food.'

Darishan smiled. 'Yes. It was a fine duel, but I don't mind admitting that my heart was in my mouth throughout. Michanek might have slipped, and then where would I have been, with the gates open to Gorben?'

'There is no man alive who could defeat Michanek,' she said.

'So far. But Gorben had another champion once . . . Druss, I think his name was. Axeman. He was rather deadly, as I recall.'

Rowena shivered. 'Are you cold?' he asked, suddenly solicitous. 'You're not getting a fever, are you?' Lifting his hand, he laid his palm on her brow. As he touched her she saw him die, fighting upon the battlements, black-cloaked warriors all around him, swords and knives piercing his flesh.

Closing her eyes, she forced the images back. 'You are unwell,' she heard him say, as if from a great distance.

Rowena took a deep breath. 'I am a little weak,' she admitted.

'Well, you must be strong for your celebration. Michanek has found three singers and a lyre player – it should be quite an entertainment. And I have a full barrel of the finest Lentrian Red, which I shall have sent over.'

At the thought of the anniversary Rowena brightened. It was almost a year since she had recovered from the plague ... A year since Michanek had made her happiness complete. She smiled at Darishan. 'You will join us tomorrow? That is good. I know Michanek values your friendship.'

'And I his.' Darishan rose. 'He's a good man, you know, far better than the rest of us. I'm proud to have known him.'

'I'll see you tomorrow,' she said.

'Tomorrow,' he agreed.

'I have to admit, old horse, that life without you was dull,' said Sieben. Druss said nothing, but sat staring into the flames of the small fire, watching them dance and flicker. Snaga was laid beside him, the blades upwards resting against the trunk of a young oak, the haft wedged against a jutting root. On the other side of the fire Eskodas was preparing two rabbits for the spit. 'When we have dined,' continued Sieben, 'I shall regale you with the further adventures of Druss the Legend.'

'No, you damned well won't,' grunted Druss.

Eskodas laughed. 'You really should hear it, Druss. He has you descending into Hell to rescue the soul of a princess.'

Druss shook his head, but a brief smile showed through the black beard and Sieben was heartened. In the month since Druss had killed Cajivak the axeman had said little. For the first two weeks they had rested at Lania, then they had journeyed across the mountains, heading east. Now, two days from Resha, they were camped on a wooded hillside above a small village. Druss had regained much of his lost weight, and his shoulders almost filled the silver-embossed jerkin he had removed from Cajivak's body.

Eskodas placed the spitted rabbits across the fire and sat back, wiping grease and blood from his fingers. 'A man can starve to death eating rabbit,' he observed. 'Not a lot of goodness there. We should have gone down to the village.'

'I like being outside,' said Druss.

'Had I known, I would have come sooner,' said Sieben softly and Druss nodded.

'I know that, poet. But it is in the past now. All that matters is that I find Rowena. She came to me in a dream while I was in that dungeon; she gave me strength. I'll find her.' He sighed. 'Some day.'

'The war is almost over,' said Eskodas. 'Once it is won, I think you'll find her. Gorben will be able to send riders to every city, village and town. Whoever owns her will know that the Emperor wants her returned.'

'That's true,' said Druss, brightening, 'and he did promise to help. I feel better already. The stars are bright, the night is cool. Ah, but it's good to be alive! All right, poet, tell me how I rescued the princess from Hell. And put in a dragon or two!'

'No,' said Sieben with a laugh, 'You are now in altogether too good a mood. It is only amusing when your face is dark as thunder and your knuckles are clenched white.'

'There is truth in that,' muttered Druss. 'I think you only invent these tales to annoy me.'

Eskodas lifted the spit and turned the roasting meat. 'I rather liked the tale, Druss. And it had the ring of truth. If the Chaos Spirit did drag your soul into Hell, I'm sure you'd twist his tail for him.'

Conversation ceased as they heard movement from the woods. Sieben drew one of his knives; Eskodas took up his bow and notched a shaft to the string; Druss merely sat silently, waiting. A man appeared. He was wearing long flowing robes of dusty grey, though they shone like silver in the bright moonlight.

'I was waiting for you in the village,' said the priest of Pashtar Sen, sitting down alongside the axeman.

'I prefer it here,' said Druss, his voice cold and unwelcoming.

'I am sorry, my son, for your suffering, and I feel a weight of shame for asking you to take up the burden of the axe. But Cajivak was laying waste to the countryside, and his power would have grown. What you did . . .'

'I did what I did,' snarled Druss. 'Now live up to your side of the bargain.'

'Rowena is in Resha. She . . . lives . . . with a soldier named Michanek. He is a Naashanite general, and the Emperor's champion.'

'*Lives* with?'

The priest hesitated. 'She is married to him,' he said swiftly.

Druss's eyes narrowed. 'That is a lie. They might force her to do many things, but she would never marry another man.'

'Let me tell this in my own way,' pleaded the priest. 'As you know I searched long and hard for her, but there was nothing. It was as if she had ceased to exist. When I did find her it was by chance – I saw her in Resha just before the siege and I touched her mind. She had no memory of the lands of the Drenai, none whatever. I followed her home and saw Michanek greet her. Then I entered his mind. He had a friend, a mystic, and he employed him to take away Rowena's Talent as a seeress. In doing this they also robbed her of her memories. Michanek is now all she has ever known.'

'They tricked her with sorcery. By the gods, I'll make them pay for that! Resha, eh?' Reaching out Druss curled his hand around the haft of the axe, drawing the weapon to him.

'No, you still don't understand,' said the priest. 'Michanek is a fine man. What he . . .'

'Enough!' thundered Druss. 'Because of you I have spent more than a year in a hole in the ground, with only rats for company. Now get out of my sight – and never, *ever* cross my path again.'

The priest slowly rose and backed away from the axeman. He seemed about to speak, but Druss turned his pale eyes upon the man and the priest stumbled away into the darkness.

Sieben and Eskodas said nothing.

High in the cliffs, far to the east, the Naashanite Emperor sat, his woollen cloak wrapped tightly around him. He was fifty-four years of age and looked seventy, his hair white and wispy, his eyes sunken. Beside him sat his staff officer, Anindais; he was unshaven, and the pain of defeat was etched into his face.

Behind them, down the long pass, the rearguard had halted the advancing Ventrians. They were safe . . . for the moment.

Nazhreen Connitopa, Lord of the Eyries, Prince of the Highlands, Emperor of Naashan, tasted bile in his mouth and his heart was sick with frustration. He had planned the invasion of Ventria for almost eleven years, and the Empire had been his for the taking. Gorben was beaten – everyone knew it, from the lowliest peasant to the highest Satraps in the land. Everyone, that is, except Gorben.

Nazhreen silently cursed the gods for snatching away his prize. The only reason he was still alive was because Michanek was holding Resha and tying down two Ventrian armies. Nazhreen rubbed at his face and saw, in the firelight, that his hands were grubby, the paint on his nails cracked and peeling.

'We must kill Gorben,' said Anindais suddenly, his voice harsh and cold as the winds that hissed through the peaks.

Nazhreen gazed sullenly at his cousin. 'And how do we do that?' he countered. 'His armies have vanquished ours. His Immortals are even now harrying our rearguard.'

'We should do now what I urged two years ago, cousin. Use the Darklight. Send for the Old Woman.'

'No! I will not use sorcery.'

'Ah, you have so many other choices then, cousin?' The tone was derisive, contempt dripping from every word. Nazhreen swallowed hard. Anindais was a dangerous man, and Nazhreen's position as a losing Emperor left him exposed.

'Sorcery has a way of rebounding on those who use it,' he said softly. 'When you summon demons they require payment in blood.'

Anindais leaned forward, his pale eyes glittering in the firelight. 'Once Resha falls, you can expect Gorben to march into Naashan. Then there'll be blood aplenty. Who will defend you, Nazhreen? Our troops have been cut to pieces, and the best of our men are trapped in Resha and will be butchered. Our only hope is for Gorben to die; then the Ventrians can fight amongst themselves to choose a successor and that will give us time to rebuild, to negotiate. Who else can guarantee his death? The Old Woman has never failed, they say.'

'*They say*,' mocked the Emperor. 'Have you used her yourself then? Is that why your brother died in so timely a fashion?' As soon as the words were spoken he regretted them, for Anindais was not a man to offend, not even in the best of times. And these were certainly not the best of times.

Nazhreen was relieved to see his cousin smile broadly, as Anindais leaned in and placed his arm around the Emperor's shoulder. 'Ah, cousin, you came so close to victory. It was a brave gamble and I honour you for it. But times change, needs change.'

Nazhreen was about to answer when he saw the firelight glint from the dagger blade. There was no time to struggle or to scream, and the blade plunged in between his ribs, cutting through his heart.

There was no pain, only release as he slumped sideways, his head resting on Anindais's shoulder. The last feeling he experienced was of Anindais stroking his hair.

It was soothing . . .

Anindais pushed the body from him and stood. A figure shuffled from the shadows, an old woman in a wolfskin cloak. Kneeling by the body, she dipped her skeletal fingers into the blood and licked them. 'Ah, the blood of kings,' she said. 'Sweeter than wine.'

'Is that enough of a sacrifice?' Anindais asked.

'No – but it will suffice as a beginning,' she said. She shivered. 'It is cold here. Not like Mashrapur. I think I shall return there when this is over. I miss my house.'

'How will you kill him?' asked Anindais.

She glanced up at the general. 'We shall make it poetic. He is a Ventrian nobleman, and the sign of his house is the Bear. I shall send Kalith.'

Anindais licked his dry lips. 'Kalith is just a dark legend, surely?'

'If you want to see him for yourself I can arrange it,' hissed the Old Woman.

Anindais fell back. 'No, I believe you.'

'I like you, Anindais,' she said softly. 'You do not have a single redeeming virtue – that is rare. So I will give you a gift, and charge nothing for it. Stay by me and you will see the Kalith kill the Ventrian.' She stood and walked to the cliff-face. 'Come,' she called and Anindais followed. The Old Woman gestured at the grey rock and the wall became smoke. Taking the general's hand, she led him through.

A long dark tunnel beckoned and Anindais shrank back. 'Not a single redeeming feature,' she repeated, 'not even courage. Stay by me, general, and no harm will befall you.'

The walk was not long, but to Anindais it stretched on for an eternity. He knew they were passing through a world that was not his own, and in the distance he could hear screams and cries that were not human. Great bats flew in a sky of dark ash, and not a living plant could be seen. The Old Woman followed a slender path, and took him across a narrow bridge that spanned an awesome chasm. At last she came to a fork in the path, and moved to the left towards a small cave. A three-headed dog guarded the entrance, but it backed away from her and they passed through. Within was a circular room stacked with tomes and scrolls. Two skeletons were hanging from hooks in the ceiling, their joints bound with golden wire. A cadaver lay across a long table, its chest and belly cut open, the heart lying beside the body like a grey stone about the size of a human fist.

The Old Woman lifted the heart and showed it to Anindais. 'Here it is,' she said, 'the secret of life. Four chambers and a number of valves, arteries and veins. Just a pump. No emotions, no secret storehouse for the soul.' She seemed disappointed. Anindais said nothing. 'Blood,' she went on, 'is pumped into the lungs to pick up oxygen, then distributed through the atria and the ventricles. Just a pump. Now, where were we? Ah yes, the Kalith.' She sniffed loudly and threw the heart back towards the table; it hit the cadaver, then fell to the dusty floor. Swiftly she rummaged through the books on a high shelf, pulling one clear and flicking through the yellowed pages. Then she sat at a second desk and laid the book on the table. The left-hand page bore a neat script, the letters tiny. Anindais could not read, but he could see the picture painted on the right-hand page. It showed a huge bear, with claws of steel, its eyes of fire, its fangs dripping venom.

'It is a creature of earth and fire,' said the Old Woman, 'and it will take great energy to summon it. That is why I need your assistance.'

'I know no sorcery,' said Anindais.

'You need to know none,' she snapped. 'I will say the words, you will repeat them. Follow me.'

She led him further back into the cave, to an altar stone surrounded by gold wire fastened to a series of stalagmites. The stone sat at the centre of a circle of gold, and she bade Anindais step over the wires and approach the altar, upon which was a silver bowl full of water.

'Look into the water,' she said, 'and repeat the words I speak.'

'Why do you stay outside the wire?' he asked.

'There is a seat here and my old legs are tired,' she told him. 'Now let us begin.'

5

Oliquar was the first of the Immortals to see Druss striding down the hill. The soldier was sitting on an upturned barrel darning the heel of a sock when the axeman appeared. Laying the worn garment aside, Oliquar stood and called out Druss's name. Several of the soldiers sitting nearby looked up as Oliquar ran to meet him, throwing his brawny arms around Druss's neck.

Hundreds of other warriors gathered round, craning to see the Emperor's champion, the famed axeman who fought like ten tigers. Druss grinned at his old comrade. 'There are more grey hairs in that beard than I remember,' he said.

Oliquar laughed. 'I earned every one. By the Holy Hands, it is good to see you, friend!'

'Life has been dull without me?'

'Not exactly,' answered Oliquar, gesturing towards the walls of Resha. 'They fight well, these Naashanites. And they have a champion too: Michanek, a great warrior.'

The smile left Druss's face. 'We'll see how great he is,' he promised.

Oliquar turned to Sieben and Eskodas. 'We hear that you did not need to rescue our friend. It is said he slew the great killer Cajivak, and half the men of his fortress. Is it true?'

'Wait until you hear the song,' Sieben advised.

'Aye, there are dragons in it,' put in Eskodas.

Oliquar led the trio through the silent ranks of warriors to a tent set up near the river's edge. Producing a jug of wine and several clay goblets, he sat down and looked at his friend. 'You are a little thinner,' he said, 'and your eyes are tired.'

283

'Pour me a drink and you'll see them shine again. Why the black cloaks and helms?'

'We are the new Immortals, Druss.'

'You don't look immortal, judging by that,' said Druss, pointing to the bloodstained bandage on Oliquar's right bicep.

'It is a title – a great title. For two centuries the Immortals were the Emperor's hand-picked honour guard. The finest soldiers, Druss: the elite. But twenty or so years ago the Immortal general, Vuspash, led a revolt, and the regiment was disbanded. Now the Emperor has re-formed them – us! It is a wondrous honour to be an Immortal.' He leaned forward and winked. 'And the pay is better – double, in fact!'

Filling the goblets, he passed one to each of the newcomers. Druss drained his in a single swallow and Oliquar refilled it. 'And how goes the siege?' asked the axeman.

Oliquar shrugged. 'This Michanek holds them together. He is a lion, Druss, tireless and deadly. He fought Bodasen in single combat. We thought the war would be over. The Emperor offered two hundred wagons of food, for there is starvation in the city. The wager was that if Bodasen lost, the food would be delivered, but if he won then the city gates would be opened and the Naashanites allowed to march free.'

'He killed Bodasen?' put in Eskodas. 'He was a great swordsman.'

'He didn't kill him; he put him down with a chest wound, then stepped back. The first fifty wagons were delivered an hour ago and the rest go in tonight. It will leave us short on rations for a while.'

'Why didn't he strike the killing blow?' asked Sieben. 'Gorben could have refused to send the food. Duels are supposed to be to the death, aren't they?'

'Aye, they are. But this Michanek, as I said, is special.'

'You sound as if you like the man,' snapped Druss, finishing the second goblet.

'Gods, Druss, it's hard not to like him. I keep hoping they'll surrender; I don't relish the thought of slaughtering such bonny fighters. I mean, the war's over – this is just the last skirmish. What point is there in more killing and dying?'

'Michanek has my wife,' said Druss, his voice low and cold. 'He tricked her into marrying him, stole her memory. She does not know me at all.'

'I find that hard to believe,' said Oliquar.

'Are you calling me a liar?' hissed Druss, his hand snaking round the haft of his axe.

'And I find *this* hard to believe,' said Oliquar. 'What is the matter with you, my friend?'

Druss's hand trembled on the haft, and he snatched it clear and rubbed at his eyes. Taking a deep breath, he forced a smile. 'Ah, Oliquar! I am tired, and the wine has made me stupid. But what I said was true; it was told to me by a priest of Pashtar Sen. And tomorrow I will scale those walls, and I will find Michanek. Then we will see how special he is.'

Druss levered himself to his feet and entered the tent. For a while the three men sat in silence, then Oliquar spoke, keeping his voice low. 'Michanek's wife is called *Pahtai*. Some of the refugees from the city spoke of her. She is a gentle soul, and when plague struck the city she went to the homes of the sick and dying, comforting them, bringing them medicines. Michanek adores her, and she him. This is well-known. And I say again, he is not the man to take a woman by trickery.'

'It doesn't matter,' said Eskodas. 'It is like fate carved into stone. Two men and one woman; there must be blood. Isn't that right, poet?'

'Sadly you are correct,' agreed Sieben. 'But I can't help wondering how she will feel when Druss marches in to her, drenched in the blood of the man she loves. What then?'

Lying on a blanket within the tent, Druss heard every word. They cut his soul with knives of fire.

Michanek shielded his eyes against the setting sun and watched the distant figure of the axeman walk down towards the Ventrian camp, saw the soldiers gather round him, heard them cheer.

'Who is it, do you think?' asked his cousin, Shurpac.

Michanek took a deep breath. 'I'd say it was the Emperor's champion, Druss.'

'Will you fight him?'

'I don't think Gorben will offer us the chance,' answered Michanek. 'There's no need – we can't hold for long now.'

'Long enough for Narin to return with reinforcements,' put in Shurpac, but Michanek did not reply. He had sent his brother out of the city with a written request for aid, though he knew there would be no help from Naashan; his one purpose had been to save his brother.

And yourself. The thought leapt unbidden from deep within him. Tomorrow was the first anniversary of his marriage, the day Rowena had predicted he would die with Narin on one side of him, Shurpac on the other. With Narin gone, perhaps the prophecy could be thwarted. Michanek squeezed shut his tired eyes. It felt as if sand was lodged under the lids.

The mining under the walls had stopped now and soon, when the winds permitted, the Ventrians would fire the timbers in the tunnel. He gazed out over the Ventrian camp. At least eleven thousand warriors were now gathered before Resha, and the defenders numbered only eight hundred. Glancing to left and right, Michanek saw the Naashanite soldiers sitting slumped by the battlements. There was little conversation, and much of the food that had just been carried up from the city was left untouched.

Michanek moved to the nearest soldier, a young man who was sitting with his head resting on his knees. His helm was beside him; it was split across the crown, dislodging the white horsehair plume.

'Not hungry, lad?' asked Michanek.

The boy looked up. His eyes were dark brown, his face beardless and feminine. 'Too tired to eat, general,' he said.

'The food will give you strength. Trust me.'

The boy lifted a hunk of salted beef and stared down at it. 'I'm going to die,' he said, and Michanek saw a tear spill to his dust-stained cheek.

The general laid his hand on the boy's shoulder. 'Death is merely another journey, lad. But you won't be walking that road alone – I'll be with you. And who knows what adventures wait?'

'I used to believe that,' said the soldier sadly, 'but I've seen so much death. I saw my brother die yesterday, his guts spilling out. His screams were terrible. Are you frightened of dying, sir?'

'Of course. But we are soldiers of the Emperor. We knew the risks when we first strapped on the breastplate and greaves. And what is better, lad, to live until we are toothless and mewling, our muscles like rotted string, or to face down our enemies in the fullness of our strength? We are all destined to die one day.'

'I don't want to die; I want to get out of here. I want to marry and father children. I want to watch them grow.' The boy was openly weeping now and Michanek sat beside him, taking him in his arms and stroking his hair.

'So do I,' he said, his voice barely above a whisper.

After a while the sobbing ceased and the boy drew himself up. 'I'm sorry, general. I won't let you down, you know.'

'I knew that anyway. I've watched you, and you're a brave lad: one of the best. Now eat your ration and get some sleep.'

Michanek rose and walked back to Shurpac. 'Let's go home,' he said. 'I'd like to sit in the garden with *Pahtai* and watch the stars.'

Druss lay still, his eyes closed, allowing the buzz of conversation to drift over him. He could not remember feeling so low – not even when Rowena was taken. On that dreadful day his anger had been all-consuming, and since then his desire to find her had fuelled his spirit, giving him a strength of purpose that bound his emotions in chains of steel. Even in the dungeon he had found a way to fend off despair. But now his stomach was knotted, his emotions unravelling.

She was in love with another man. He formed the words in his mind, and they ground into his heart like broken glass in a wound.

He tried to hate Michanek, but even that was denied him. Rowena would never love a worthless or an evil man. Druss sat up and stared down at his hands. He had crossed the ocean to find his love, and these hands had killed, and killed, and killed in order that Rowena could be his once more.

He closed his eyes. Where should I be? he asked himself. In the front rank as they storm the walls? On the walls defending Rowena's city? Or should I just walk away?

Walk away.

The tent entrance flapped as Sieben ducked under it. 'How are you faring, old horse?' asked the poet.

'She loves him,' said Druss, his voice thick, the words choking him.

Sieben sat alongside the axeman. He took a deep breath. 'If her memories were taken, then what she has done is no betrayal. She does not know you.'

'I understand that. I bear her no ill-will – how could I? She is the most . . . beautiful . . . I can't explain it, poet. She doesn't understand hatred, or greed, or envy. Soft but not weak, caring but not stupid.' He swore and shook his head. 'As I said, I can't explain it.'

'You're doing fine,' said Sieben softly.

'When I'm with her there is no . . . no fire in my mind. No anger. When I was a child I hated to be laughed at. I was big and clumsy – I'd knock over pots, trip over my own big feet. But when people laughed at my clumsiness I wanted to . . . I don't know . . . crush them. But I was with Rowena one day on the mountainside, and it had been raining. I lost my footing and fell headlong into a muddy pool. Her laughter was bright and fresh; I sat up, and I just laughed with her. And it was so good, poet, it was so good.'

'She's still there, Druss. Just across the wall.'

The axeman nodded. 'I know. What do I do – scale the wall, kill the man she loves and then march up to her and say, "Remember me?" I cannot win here.'

'One step at a time, my friend. Resha will fall. From what I gathered from Oliquar, Michanek will fight to the end, to the death. You don't have to kill him, his fate is already sealed. And then Rowena will need someone. I can't advise you, Druss, I have never truly been in love and I envy you that. But let us see what tomorrow brings, eh?'

Druss nodded and took a deep breath. 'Tomorrow,' he whispered.

'Gorben has asked to see you, Druss. Why not come with me? Bodasen is with him – and there'll be wine and good food.'

Druss stood and gathered Snaga to him. The blades glittered in the light from the brazier burning at the centre of the tent. 'A man's best friend is said to be a dog,' said Sieben, stepping back as Druss lifted the axe.

The axeman ignored him and stepped out into the night.

Rowena stood by with a long robe as Michanek stepped from the bath. Smiling, she brushed two rose petals from his shoulder, then held the robe open. Michanek slid his arms into the sleeves, then tied the satin belt and turned towards her. Taking her hand he led her into the garden. Rowena leaned in towards him and he stopped and took her into his arms, kissing the top of her head. His body was rich with the smell of rose oil and she put her arms around him, snuggling in to the soft robe. Tilting back her head, she looked up into his dark brown eyes. 'I love you,' she said.

Cupping her chin he kissed her, lingeringly. His mouth tasted of the peaches he had eaten while lazing in the bath. But there was no passion in the kiss and he drew away from her.

'What is wrong?' she asked. He shrugged and forced a smile.

'Nothing.'

'Why do you say that?' she chided. 'I hate it when you lie to me.'

'The siege is almost over,' he said, leading her to a small circular bench beneath a flowering tree.

'When will you surrender?' she asked.

He shrugged. 'When I receive orders to do so.'

'But the battle is unnecessary. The war is over. If you negotiate with Gorben he will allow us to leave. You can show me your home in Naashan. You always promised to take me to your estates near the Lakes; you said the gardens there would dazzle me with their beauty.'

'So they would,' he told her. Slipping his hands around her waist he stood and lifted her swiftly, lightly kissing her lips.

'Put me down. You'll tear the stitches – you know what the surgeon said.'

He chuckled. 'Aye, I listened to him. But the wound is almost healed.' Kissing her twice more, he lowered her to the ground and

289

they walked on. 'There are matters we must discuss,' he said, but when she waited for him to continue he merely glanced up at the stars and the silence grew.

'What matters?'

'You,' he said at last. 'Your life.' Rowena looked at him, saw the lines of tension on his moonlit face, the tightening of the muscle in his jaw.

'My life is with you,' she said. 'That's all I want.'

'Sometimes we want more than we can have.'

'Don't say that!'

'You used to be a seer – a good one. Kabuchek charged two hundred silver pieces for a single reading from you. You were never wrong.'

'I know all this, you have told me before. What difference does it make now?'

'All the difference in the world. You were born in the lands of the Drenai, you were taken by slavers. But there was a man ...'

'I don't want to hear this,' she said, pulling away from him and walking to the edge of the tiny lake. He did not follow, but his words did.

'The man was your husband.' Rowena sat down by the water's edge, trailing her fingers across the surface, sending ripples through the moon's reflection.

'The man with the axe,' she said dully.

'You remember?' he asked, walking forward and sitting beside her.

'No. But I saw him once – at the house of Kabuchek. And also in a dream, when he lay in a dungeon.'

'Well, he is not in a dungeon now, *Pahtai*. He is outside the city. He is Druss the Axeman, Gorben's champion.'

'Why are you telling me this?' she asked him, turning to face him in the bright moonlight.

His white robe shimmered, and he looked ghostly, almost ethereal. 'Do you think I want to?' he countered. 'I'd sooner fight a lion with my hands than have this conversation. But I love you, *Pahtai*. I have loved you since our first meeting. You were standing with Pudri in the main corridor of Kabuchek's home, and you told my future.'

'What did I tell you?'

He smiled. 'You told me I would wed the woman I loved. But that is not important now. I think soon you will meet your ... first ... husband.'

'I don't want to.' Her heart was beating fast and she felt faint. Michanek put his arms around her.

'I don't know much about him, but I do know you,' he said. 'You are Drenai; your customs are different from ours. You were not high-born, therefore it is likely you married for love. And think on this: Druss has followed you across the world for seven years. He must love you deeply.'

'I don't want to talk about this!' she said, her voice rising as panic flooded her. She tried to rise, but he held her close.

'Neither do I,' he whispered, his voice hoarse. 'I wanted to sit here with you and watch the stars. I wanted to kiss you, and to make love.' His head dropped, and she saw tears in his eyes.

Her panic disappeared and the cold touch of fear settled on her soul. She looked up into his face. 'You talk as if you are going to die.'

'Oh, I will some day,' he said with a smile. 'Now I must go. I am meeting Darishan and the other officers to discuss tomorrow's strategy. They should be in the house now.'

'Don't go!' she pleaded. 'Stay with me a little while ... just a little while?'

'I'll always be with you,' he said softly.

'Darishan will die tomorrow. On the walls. I saw it; it was a vision. He was here today and I saw him die. My Talent is coming back. Give me your hand! Let me see our future.'

'No!' he said, rising and moving back from her. 'A man's fate is his own. You read my future once. Once was enough, *Pahtai*.'

'I predicted your death, didn't I?' she said, but it was not a question for she knew the answer even before he spoke.

'You told me about my dreams, and you mentioned my brother, Narin. I don't remember much of it now. We'll talk later.'

'Why did you mention Druss? You think that if you die I will just go to him, and take up a life I know nothing of? If you die, I will

291

have nothing to live for.' Her eyes locked to his. 'And I will not live,' she said.

A figure moved out of the shadows. 'Michi, why are you keeping us all waiting?' Rowena saw her husband flinch and glanced up to see Narin striding towards them.

'I sent you away,' said Michanek. 'What are you doing here?'

'I made it as far as the hills, but the Ventrians are everywhere. I came in through the sewers; the guards there recognised me, thank the gods. What is the matter with you? Are you not pleased to see me?'

Michanek did not answer. Turning to Rowena he smiled, but she saw the fear in his eyes. 'I'll not be long, my love. We'll talk again later.'

She remained on the seat as the two men walked away. Closing her eyes she thought of the axeman, picturing the pale blue eyes and the broad, flat face. But even as she pictured him, another image came to her:

The face of a terrible beast, with talons of steel and eyes of fire.

Gorben leaned back on his couch and watched with appreciation the sword jugglers before the huge fire, the five razor-sharp blades spinning in the air between the two men. It was a display of rare skill as the jugglers deftly caught the swords, before sending them soaring back across the open ground. The men were clad in loincloths, their skin shone red-gold in the firelight. Around them sat more than five hundred Immortals, enjoying the martial display.

Beyond the dancing flames of the campfire Gorben could see the walls of Resha, and the few defenders there. It was all but over. Against all the odds he had won.

Yet there was no sense of joy in his heart. The years of battle, the stresses and the fears had taken their toll on the young Emperor. For every victory he had seen childhood friends cut down: Nebuchad at Ectanis, Jasua in the mountains above Porchia, Bodasen before the gates of Resha. He glanced to his right where Bodasen was lying on a raised bed, his face pale. The surgeons said he would live, and they had managed to re-inflate his collapsed lung. You are like my

Empire, thought Gorben, wounded almost unto death. How long would it take to rebuild Ventria? Years? Decades?

A great roar went up from the watching men as the sword jugglers completed their performance. The men bowed to the Emperor. Gorben rose and tossed them a pouch full of gold pieces. There was great laughter when the first of the jugglers reached out and failed to catch the pouch.

'You are better with blades than coins,' said Gorben.

'Money has always slipped through his fingers, Lord,' said the second man.

Gorben returned to his seat and smiled down at Bodasen. 'How are you feeling, my friend?'

'My strength is returning, Lord.' The voice was weak, his breathing ragged as Gorben reached out and patted his shoulder. The heat of the skin and the sharpness of the bone beneath his hand almost made him recoil. Bodasen's eyes met his. 'Do not concern yourself about me, Lord. I'll not die on you.' The swordsman's eyes flickered to the left, and he smiled broadly. 'By the gods, there's a sight to gladden the eyes!'

Gorben turned to see Druss and Sieben walking towards them. The poet dropped to one knee, bowing his head. Druss gave a perfunctory bow.

'Well met, axeman,' said Gorben, stepping forward and embracing Druss. Turning, he took Sieben's arm and raised him to his feet. 'And I have missed your talents, saga-master. Come, join us.'

Servants brought two couches for the Emperor's guests, and golden goblets filled with fine wine. Druss moved to Bodasen. 'You look as weak as a three-day kitten,' he said. 'Are you going to live?'

'I'll do my best, axeman.'

'He cost me two hundred wagons of food,' said Gorben. 'I blame myself for believing him to be unbeatable.'

'How good is this Michanek?' asked Druss.

'Good enough to leave me lying here scarce able to breathe,' answered Bodasen. 'He's fast, and he's fearless. The best I ever met. I tell you truly, I wouldn't want to face him again.'

Druss turned to Gorben. 'You want me to take him?'

'No,' said Gorben. 'The city will fall in the next day or two – there is no need for single combat to decide the issue. The walls are undermined. Tomorrow, if the wind is good, we will fire them. Then the city will be ours and this ghastly war will be over. Now, tell me about your adventures. I hear you were held captive?'

'I escaped,' Druss told him, then drained his goblet. A servant ran forward to refill it.

Sieben laughed. 'I will tell you, Lord,' he said, and launched into a richly embroidered account of Druss's time in the dungeons of Cajivak.

The huge campfire was burning low and several men moved forward to throw logs upon it. Suddenly the ground heaved beneath one of them, pitching him to the earth. Gorben looked up, and watched the man struggle to rise. All around the fire the seated men were scrambling back. 'What is happening?' asked Gorben, rising and striding forward. The ground lurched beneath him.

'Is it an earthquake?' he heard Sieben ask Druss.

Gorben stood still and gazed down. The earth was writhing. The campfire suddenly flared, sending bright sparks into the night sky. The heat was intense and Gorben moved back from it, staring into the flames. Logs exploded out from the blaze and a huge shape appeared within the fire, a beast with outspread arms. The flames died and Gorben found himself staring at a colossal bear, more than twelve feet tall.

Several soldiers carrying spears ran at the creature, plunging their weapons into the great belly. The first of the spears snapped on impact. The beast roared, a deafening sound like captured thunder. One of the mighty arms swept down, steel talons ripping through the first soldier, cutting him in half at the waist.

Surging from the fading fire, the beast leapt towards Gorben.

As the creature of fire appeared Sieben, who was sitting alongside Bodasen, found all sensation of time and reality slipping away from him. His eyes fastened on the beast, and an image flew from the halls of his memory, linking what he could see in terrifying life to a still, small moment three years ago in the main Library at Drenan.

Researching for an epic poem, he had been scanning the ancient leather-bound books in the archives. The pages were dry and yellow, and much of the ink and paint had faded from them, but on one page the colours were still vibrant, fierce hues – glowing gold, savage crimsons, sun-bright yellows. The figure painted there was colossal, and flames sprouted like blooms from its eyes. Sieben could still picture the carefully painted letters above the painting ...

The Kalith of Numar

Beneath the heading were the words:

The Chaos Beast, the Stalker, the Hound of the Invincible, whose skin no blade of man shall pierce. Where he walks, death follows.

As Sieben recalled the night of the monster in later days, he would wonder anew at the lack of fear he experienced. He watched men die horribly, saw a beast from the depths of Hell tear human limbs asunder, disembowelling warriors, ripping their lives from them. He heard the ghastly howling and smelt the stench of death on the night breeze. Yet there was no fear.

A dark legend had come to life and he, the saga-master, was on hand to witness it.

Gorben was standing stock-still, rooted to the spot. A soldier Sieben recognised as Oliquar threw himself at the beast, slashing at it with a sabre; but the blade clanged against the creature's side, and the sound that followed was like the dim tolling of a distant bell. A taloned paw swept down, and Oliquar's face and head disappeared in a bloody spray of shattered bone. Several archers shot arrows, but these either shattered on impact or ricocheted away. The creature advanced on Gorben.

Sieben saw the Emperor flinch, then hurl himself to his right, rolling to his feet smoothly. The enormous beast turned ponderously, the glowing coals of its eyes seeking out Gorben.

Loyal soldiers, showing incredible bravery, threw themselves into the path of the beast, stabbing at it ineffectually. Each time the talons slashed down, and blood sprayed across the campsite. Within a few heartbeats there were at least twenty dead or maimed soldiers. The Chaos Beast's talons ripped into a soldier's chest, lifting him from his feet and hurling him across the dying fire. Sieben heard the man's ribs snap, and saw his entrails spill out like a tattered banner as the corpse sailed through the air.

Druss, axe in his hand, strode out towards the creature. Soldiers were falling back before it, but still they formed a wall between the beast and the Emperor. Looking tiny and insubstantial against the colossal frame of the Kalith, Druss stepped into its path. The moon was bright in the night sky, shining from his shoulder-guards and glinting on Snaga's terrible blades.

The Chaos Beast paused and seemed to stare down at the tiny man before it. Sieben's mouth was dry, and he could feel the hammering of his own heart.

And the Kalith spoke, voice deep and rumbling, words slurred by its foot-long tongue.

'Step aside, brother,' it said. 'I have not come for you.'

The axe began to glow as red as blood. Druss stood his ground, with Snaga held in both hands.

'Step aside,' repeated the Kalith, 'or I must kill you!'

'In your dreams,' said Druss.

The creature lunged forward, one great paw sweeping in towards the axeman. Druss dropped to one knee and swung the blood-red axe, the blade striking the beast's wrist and cleaving through. As the taloned paw fell to the ground beside the axeman, the Kalith reeled back. No blood issued from the wound, but an oily smoke pumped out into the air, billowing and growing. Fire blazed from the creature's mouth and it lunged again at the mortal before it. But instead of jumping back Druss leapt in to meet it, swinging Snaga high over his head and bringing the weapon down in a lethal arc that clove into the Kalith's chest, smashing the sternum and ripping a wound from throat to groin.

Flames exploded from the beast, engulfing the axeman. Druss staggered – and the Kalith fell back, and as the huge form struck the ground even Sieben, some thirty feet away, felt the tremor of the earth. A breeze blew up, the smoke disappearing.

And there was no sign of the Kalith ...

Sieben ran to where Druss stood. The axeman's eyebrows and beard were singed, but he bore no marks of burns. 'By the gods, Druss,' Sieben shouted, slapping his friend's back. 'Now that'll make a song to bring us both fame and riches!'

'It killed Oliquar,' said Druss, shrugging off Sieben's embrace and letting fall the axe.

Gorben moved alongside him. 'That was nobly done, my friend. I'll not forget – I owe you my life.' Bending his body, he lifted the axe. It was now black and silver once more. 'This is an enchanted weapon,' whispered the Emperor. 'I will give you twenty thousand in gold for it.'

'It is not for selling, my Lord,' said Druss.

'Ah, Druss, and I thought you liked me.'

'I do, laddie. That's why I'll not sell it to you.'

A cold wind swirled around the cave. Anindais felt the chill and swung from the altar, looking back to see the Old Woman rise from her seat outside the golden circle. 'What is happening?' he asked. 'The axeman has killed the beast. Can we send another?'

'No,' she told him. 'But he did not kill it, he merely sent it back to the Pit.'

'Well, what now?'

'Now we pay for the services of the Kalith.'

'You said the payment would be the blood of Gorben.'

'Gorben did not die.'

'Then I do not understand you. And why is it so cold?'

A shadow fell across the Naashanite, who swung round to see a huge shape rearing above him. Talons flashed down, slicing into his chest.

'Not even intelligence,' repeated the Old Woman, turning her back on his screams. Returning to her apartments, she sat back in an old wicker chair. 'Ah, Druss,' she whispered, 'perhaps I should have let you die back in Mashrapur.'

6

Rowena opened her eyes and saw Michanek sitting at her bedside. He was wearing his ceremonial armour of bronze and gold, the helm with the red crest, and the enamelled cheek-guards, the moulded breastplate covered in sigils and motifs.

'You look very handsome,' she said sleepily.

'And you are very beautiful.'

Rubbing her eyes, she sat up. 'Why are you wearing that today? It is not as strong as your old breastplate of iron.'

'It will lift morale among the men.' Taking her hand he kissed her palm, then rose and moved towards the door. At the doorway he paused and spoke without looking back. 'I have left something for you – in my study. It is wrapped in velvet.'

And then he was gone.

Within minutes Pudri appeared, bearing a tray which he laid down beside her. There were three honey-cakes and a goblet of apple juice. 'The Lord looks very magnificent today,' said the little man, and Rowena saw that his expression was sorrowful.

'What is wrong, Pudri?'

'I don't like battles,' he told her. 'So much blood and pain. But it is even worse when the reasons for battle have long been overtaken by events. Men will die today for no reason. Their lives will be snuffed out like midnight candles. And for why? And will it end here? No. When Gorben is strong enough he will lead a vengeance invasion against the people of Naashan. Futile and stupid!' He shrugged. 'Maybe it is because I am a eunuch that I do not understand such matters.'

'You understand them very well,' she said. 'Tell me, was I a good seeress?'

'Ah, you must not ask me this, my lady. That was yesterday, and it has flown away into the past.'

'Did the Lord Michanek ask you to withhold my past from me?'

He nodded glumly. 'It was for love that he asked this of me. Your Talent almost killed you and he did not wish for you to suffer again. Anyway, your bath is prepared. It is hot and steaming, and I managed to find some rose oil for the water.'

An hour later Rowena was walking through the garden when she saw that the window to Michanek's study was open. This was unusual, for there were many papers here and the summer breezes would often scatter them around the room. Moving inside, she opened the door and pulled shut the small window. Then she saw the package on the oak desk. It was small and, as Michanek had said, was wrapped in purple velvet.

Slowly she unwrapped the velvet to find a small, unadorned wooden box with a hinged lid, which she opened. Within lay a brooch which was simply, even crudely, made of soft copper strands surrounding a moonstone. Her mouth was suddenly dry. A part of her mind told her the brooch was new to her, but a tiny warning bell was ringing in the deep recesses of her soul.

This is mine!

Her right hand dropped slowly towards the brooch, then stopped, the fingers hovering just above the moonstone. Rowena drew back, then sat down. She heard Pudri enter the room.

'You were wearing that when I first saw you,' he said gently. She nodded, but did not answer. The little Ventrian approached and handed her a letter, sealed with red wax. 'The Lord asked me to give you this when you had seen his . . . gift.'

Rowena broke the seal and opened the letter. It was written in Michanek's bold, clear script.

Greetings, Beloved.

I am skilled with the sword, and yet, at this moment, I would sell my soul to be as skilful with words. A long time ago, as you lay dying, I paid three sorcerers to seal your Talents deep within you. In doing so they closed also the doorways of memory.

299

The brooch was, they told me, made for you as a gift of love. It is the key to your past, and a gift for your future. Of all the pain I have known, there is no suffering greater than the knowledge that your future will be without me. Yet I have loved you, and would not change a single day. And if, by some miracle, I was allowed to return to the past and court you once more, I would do so in the same way, in full knowledge of the same outcome.

You are the light in my life and the love of my heart.

Farewell, Pahtai. *May your paths be made easy, and your soul know many joys.*

The letter fell from her hands, floating to the floor. Pudri stepped forward swiftly and placed his slender arm around her shoulders. 'Take the brooch, my lady!'

She shook her head. 'He's going to die.'

'Yes,' admitted the Ventrian. 'But he bade me urge you to take the brooch. It was his great wish. Do not deny him!'

'I'll take the brooch,' she said solemnly, 'but when he dies, I shall die with him.'

Druss sat in the near-deserted camp and watched the attack on the walls. From this distance it seemed that the attackers were insects, swarming up tiny ladders. He watched bodies topple and fall, heard the sound of battle horns and the occasional high-pitched scream that drifted on the shifting breeze. Sieben was beside him.

'The first time I've ever seen you miss a fight, Druss. Are you mellowing in your old age?'

Druss did not answer. His pale eyes watched the fighting and saw the smoke seeping out from under the wall. The timber and brushwood in the tunnels were burning now, and soon the foundations of the wall would disappear. As the smoke grew thicker the attackers fell back and waited.

Time passed slowly now in the great silence that descended over the plain. The smoke thickened, then faded. Nothing happened.

Druss gathered his axe and stood. Sieben rose with him. 'It didn't work,' said the poet.

'Give it time,' grunted Druss and he marched forward, Sieben following until they were within thirty yards of the wall. Gorben was waiting here with his officers around him. No one spoke.

A jagged line, black as a spider's leg, appeared on the wall, followed by a high screeching sound. The crack widened and a huge block of masonry dislodged itself from a nearby tower, thundering down to crash on the rocks before the wall. Druss could see defenders scrambling back. A second crack appeared ... then a third. A huge section of wall crumbled and a high tower pitched to the right, smashing down on the ruined wall and sending up an immense cloud of dust. Gorben covered his mouth with his cloak, and waited until the dust settled.

Where moments before there had been a wall of stone, there were now only jagged ruins like the broken teeth of a giant.

The battle horns sounded. The black line of the Immortals surged forward.

Gorben turned to Druss. 'Will you join them in the slaughter?'

Druss shook his head. 'I have no stomach for slaughter,' he said.

The courtyard was littered with corpses and pools of blood. Michanek glanced to his right where his brother Narin was lying on his back with a lance jutting from his chest, his sightless eyes staring up at the crimson-stained sky.

Almost sunset, thought Michanek. Blood ran from a wound in his temple and he could feel it trickling down his neck. His back hurt, and when he moved he could feel the arrow that was lodged above his left shoulder-blade gouging into muscle and flesh. It made holding the heavy shield impossible, and Michanek had long since abandoned it. The hilt of his sword was slippery with blood. A man groaned to his left. It was his cousin Shurpac; he had a terrible wound in his belly, and was attempting to stop his entrails from gushing forth.

Michanek transferred his gaze to the enemy soldiers surrounding him. They had fallen back now, and were standing in a grim circle. Michanek turned slowly. He was the last of the Naashanites still standing. Glaring at the Immortals, he challenged them. 'What's the matter with you? Frightened of Naashanite steel?' They did not move. Michanek staggered and almost fell, but then righted himself.

All pain was fading now.

It had been quite a day. The undermined wall had collapsed, killing a score of his men, but the rest had regrouped well and Michanek was proud of them. Not one had suggested surrender. They had fallen back to the second line of defence and met the Ventrians with arrows, spears and even stones. But there were too many, and it had been impossible to hold a line.

Michanek had led the last fifty warriors towards the inner Keep, but they were cut off and forced down a side road that led to the courtyard of Kabuchek's old house.

What were they waiting for?

The answer came to him instantly: *They are waiting for you to die.*

He saw a movement at the edge of the circle, the men moving aside as Gorben appeared – dressed now in a robe of gold, a seven-spiked crown upon his head. He looked every inch the Emperor. Beside him was the axeman, the husband of *Pahtai*.

'Ready for another duel . . . my Lord?' called Michanek. A racking cough burst from his lungs, spraying blood into the air.

'Put up your sword, man. It is over!' said Gorben.

'Do I take it you are surrendering?' Michanek asked. 'If not, then let me fight your champion!'

Gorben turned to the axeman, who nodded and moved forward. Michanek steadied himself, but his mind was wandering. He remembered a day with *Pahtai*, by a waterfall. She had made a crown of white water lilies which she placed on his brow. The flowers were wet and cool; he could feel them now . . .

No. Fight! Win!

He looked up. The axeman seemed colossal now, towering above him, and Michanek realised he had fallen to his knees. 'No,' he said, the words slurring, 'I'll not die on my knees.' Leaning forward he tried to push himself upright, but fell again. Two strong hands took hold of his shoulders, drawing him upright, and he looked into the pale eyes of Druss the Axeman.

'Knew ... you would ... come,' he said. Druss half carried the dying warrior to a marble bench at the wall of the courtyard, laying him gently to the cool stone. An Immortal removed his own cloak and rolled it into a pillow for the Naashanite general.

Michanek gazed up at the darkening sky, then turned his head. Druss was kneeling alongside him, and beyond the axeman the Immortals waited. At an order from Gorben they drew their swords and held them high, saluting their enemy.

'Druss! Druss!'

'I am here.'

'Treat ... her ... gently.'

Michanek did not hear his answer.

He was sitting on the grass by a waterfall, the cool petals of a water lily crown against his skin.

There was no looting in Resha, nor any organised slaughter amongst the population. The Immortals patrolled the city, having first marched through to the centre past cheering crowds who were waving banners and hurling flower petals beneath the feet of the soldiers. In the first hours there were isolated outbursts of violence, as angry citizens gathered in mobs to hunt down Ventrians accused of collaborating with the Naashanite conquerors.

Gorben ordered the mobs dispersed, promising judicial inquiries at a later date to identify those who could be accused of treason. The bodies of the slain were buried in two mass graves beyond the city walls, and the Emperor ordered a monument built above the Ventrian fallen, a huge stone lion with the names of the dead carved into the base. Above the Naashanite grave there was to be no stone. Michanek, however, was laid to rest in the Hall of the Fallen, below the Great Palace on the Hill that stood like a crown at the centre of Resha.

Food was brought in to feed the populace, and builders began work, removing the dams that had starved the city of water, rebuilding the walls and repairing those houses and shops damaged by the huge stones of the ballistae that had hurtled over the walls during the past three months.

303

Druss had no interest in the affairs of the city. Day by day he sat at Rowena's bedside, holding to her cold, pale hand.

After Michanek had died Druss had sought out his house, the directions supplied by a Naashanite soldier who had survived the last assault. With Sieben and Eskodas he had run through the city streets until at last he had come to the house on the hill, entering it through a beautiful garden. There he saw a small man, sitting weeping by an ornamental lake. Druss seized him by his woollen tunic, hauling him to his feet. 'Where is she?' he demanded.

'She is dead,' wailed the man, his tears flowing freely. 'She took poison. There is a priest with the body.' He pointed to the house, then fell to weeping again. Releasing him, Druss ran in to the house and up the curved stairs. The first three rooms were empty, but in the fourth he found the priest of Pashtar Sen sitting by the bedside.

'Gods, no!' said Druss as he saw the still form of his Rowena, her face grey, her eyes closed. The priest looked up, his eyes tired.

'Say nothing,' urged the priest, his voice weak and seemingly far away. 'I have sent for a . . . a friend. And it is taking all my power to hold her to life.' He closed his eyes. At a loss, Druss walked to the far side of the bed and gazed down on the woman he had loved for so long. It was seven years since last he had laid eyes on her, and her beauty tore at his heart with talons of steel. Swallowing hard, he sat at the bedside. The priest was holding to her hand; sweat was flowing down his face, making grey streaks on his cheeks, and he seemed mortally weary. When Sieben and Eskodas entered the room Druss waved them to silence, and they sat and waited.

It was almost an hour before another man entered: a bald, portly man with a round red face and comically protruding ears. He was dressed in a long white tunic, and carried a large leather bag slung from his shoulder by a long gold-embroidered strap. Without a word to the three men he moved to the bedside, placing his fingers against Rowena's neck.

The priest of Pashtar Sen opened his eyes. 'She has taken *yasroot*, Shalitar,' he said.

The bald man nodded. 'How long ago?'

'Three hours, though I have prevented most of it from spreading through the blood. But a minute part has reached the lymphatic system.'

Shalitar clicked his teeth, then delved into the leather bag. 'One of you fetch water,' he ordered. Eskodas stood and left the room, returning moments later with a silver jug. Shalitar told him to stand close to the head of the bed, then from the bag he produced a small packet of powder which he tipped into the jug. It foamed briefly, then settled. Delving into the bag again, he pulled clear a long grey tube and a funnel. Reaching down, he opened Rowena's mouth.

'What are you doing?' stormed Druss, grabbing the man's hand.

The surgeon was unperturbed. 'We must get the potion into her stomach. As you can see, she is in no condition to drink, therefore I intend to insert this tube in her throat and pour the potion in through the funnel. It is a delicate business, for I would not want to flood her lungs. It would be hard for me to do it correctly with a broken hand.'

Druss released him, and watched in silent anguish as the tube was eased into her throat. Shalitar held the funnel in place and ordered Eskodas to pour. When half of the contents of the jug had vanished, Shalitar nipped the tube between thumb and forefinger and withdrew it. Kneeling by the bed, he pressed his ear to Rowena's breast.

'The heartbeat is very slow,' he said, 'and weak. A year ago I treated her for plague; she almost died then, but the illness left its mark. The heart is not strong.' He turned to the men. 'Leave me now, for I must keep her circulation strong, and that will involve rubbing oil into her legs, arms and back.'

'I'll not leave,' said Druss.

'Sir, this *lady* is the widow of the Lord Michanek. She is well loved here – despite being wed to a Naashanite. It is not fitting for men to observe her naked – and any man who causes her shame will not survive the day.'

'I am her husband,' hissed Druss. 'The others can go. *I stay.*'

Shalitar rubbed his chin, but looked ready to argue no further. The priest of Pashtar Sen touched the surgeon's arm. 'It is a long story, my friend, but he speaks truly. Now do your best.'

'My best may not be good enough,' muttered Shalitar.

* * *

Three days passed. Druss ate little and slept by the bedside. There was no change in Rowena's condition, and Shalitar grew ever more despondent. The priest of Pashtar Sen returned on the morning of the fourth day.

'The poison is gone from her body,' said Shalitar, 'yet she does not wake.'

The priest nodded sagely. 'When first I came, as she was sinking into the coma, I touched her spirit. It was fleeing from life; she had no will to live.'

'Why?' asked Druss. 'Why would she want to die?'

The man shrugged. 'She is a gentle soul. She first loved you, back in your own lands, and carried that love within as something pure in a tarnished world. Knowing you were coming for her, she was ready to wait. Her Talents grew astonishingly swiftly and they overwhelmed her. Shalitar, and some others, saved her life by closing the pathways of that Talent, but in doing so they also took her memory. So here she woke, in the house of Michanek. He was a good man, Druss, and he loved her – as much as you love her. He nursed her to health, and he won her heart. But he did not tell her his greatest secret – that she had, as a seeress, predicted his death . . . one year to the day after he was wed. For several years they lived together, and she succumbed to the plague. During her illness and, as I have said, with no knowledge of her life as a seeress, she asked Michanek why he had never married her. In his fear at her condition, he believed that a marriage would save her. Perhaps he was right. Now we come to the taking of Resha. Michanek left her a gift – this gift,' he said, passing the brooch to Druss.

Druss took the delicate brooch in his huge hand and closed his fingers around it. 'I made this,' he said. 'It seems like a lifetime ago.'

'This was the key which Michanek knew would unlock her memory. He thought, as I fear men will, that a return of memory would help her assuage her grief at his passing. He believed that if she remembered you, and that if you still loved her, she would have a safe future. His reasoning was flawed, for when she touched the brooch what struck her most was a terrible guilt. *She* had asked Michanek to marry her, thus assuring – as she saw it – his death. *She*

306

had seen you, Druss, at the house of Kabuchek, and had run away, frightened to find out her past, terrified it would destroy her new-found happiness. In that one moment she saw herself as a betrayer, and as a harlot and, I fear, as a killer.'

'None of it was her fault,' said Druss. 'How could she think it was?'

The priest smiled, but it was Shalitar who spoke. 'Any death produces guilt, Druss. A son dies of plague, and the mother will berate herself for not taking the child away to somewhere safe before the disease struck. A man falls to his death, and his wife will think, "If only I had asked him to stay home today." It is the nature of good people to draw burdens to themselves. All tragedy could be avoided, if only we knew it; therefore when it strikes we blame ourselves. But for Rowena, the weight of guilt was overpowering.'

'What can I do?' the axeman asked.

'Nothing. We must just hope she returns.'

The priest of Pashtar Sen seemed about to speak, but instead stood and walked to the window. Druss saw the change in the man. 'Speak,' he said. 'What were you about to say?'

'It doesn't matter,' he said softly.

'Let me be the judge of that, if it concerns Rowena.'

The priest sat down and rubbed his tired eyes. 'She hovers,' he said at last, 'between death and life, her spirit wandering in the Valley of the Dead. Perhaps, if we could find a sorcerer, we could send his spirit after her to bring her home.' He spread his hands. 'But I do not know where to find such a man – or woman. And I don't think we have the time to search.'

'What about your Talent?' asked Druss. 'You seem to know of this place.'

The man's eyes swung away from Druss's gaze. 'I . . . I do have the Talent, but not the courage. It is a terrible place.' He forced a smile. 'I am a coward, Druss. I would die there. It is no place for men of little spirit.'

'Then send me. I'll find her.'

'You would have no chance. We are talking of a . . . a realm of dark magic and demons. You would be defenceless against them, Druss; they would overwhelm you.'

'But you could send me there?'

'There is no point. It would be madness.'

Druss turned to Shalitar. 'What will happen to her if we do nothing?'

'She has maybe a day . . . perhaps two. Already she is fading.'

'Then there are no choices, priest,' said Druss, rising and moving to stand before the man. 'Tell me how I reach this Valley.'

'You must die,' the priest whispered.

A grey mist swirled, though there was no discernible breeze, and strange sounds echoed eerily from all around him.

The priest was gone now, and Druss was alone.

Alone?

Around him shapes moved in the mist, some huge, some low and slithering. 'Keep to the path,' the priest had said. 'Follow the road through the mist. Under no circumstances allow yourself to be led from the road.'

Druss glanced down. The road was seamless and grey, as if it had been created from molten stone. It was smooth and flat and the mist held to it, floating and swaying in cold tendrils that swirled around his legs and lower body.

A woman's voice called to him from the side of the road. He paused and glanced to his right. A dark-haired woman, scarce more than a girl, was sitting on a rock with legs apart, her right hand stroking her thigh. She licked her lips and tossed her head. 'Come here,' she called. 'Come here!'

Druss shook his head. 'I have other business.'

She laughed at him. 'Here? You have other business here?' Her laughter rang out and she moved closer to him, but he saw that she did not set foot upon the road. Her eyes were large and golden but there were no pupils, merely black slits in the gold. When her mouth opened a forked tongue darted between her lips, which Druss now saw were grey-blue. Her teeth were small and sharp.

Ignoring her he walked on. An old man was sitting in the centre of the road with shoulders hunched. Druss paused. 'Which way, brother?' asked the old man. 'Which way do I go? There are so many paths.'

'There is only one,' said Druss.

'So many paths,' repeated the other man. Again Druss moved on, and behind him he heard the woman's voice speaking to the old man. 'Come here! Come here!' Druss didn't look back, but only moments later he heard a terrible scream.

The road moved ever on through the mist, level and straight as a spear. There were others on the road, some walking tall, others shuffling. No one spoke. Druss moved through them silently, scanning their faces, seeking Rowena.

A young woman stumbled from the path, falling to her knees. Instantly a scaled hand caught at her cloak, dragging her back. Druss was too far back to help, and he cursed and moved on.

Many pathways merged with the road and Druss found himself travelling with a multitude of silent people, young and old. Their faces were blank, their expressions preoccupied. Many left the path and wandered through the mist.

It seemed to the axeman that he had walked for many days. There was no sense of time here, nor any fatigue, nor hunger. Gazing ahead, he could see vast numbers of souls wending their way through the mist-enveloped road.

Despair touched him. How would he find her among so many? Ruthlessly he pushed the fear from his mind, concentrating only on scanning the faces as he moved ever on. Nothing would ever have been achieved, he thought, if men had allowed themselves to be diverted by the scale of the problems faced.

After a while Druss noted that the road was rising. He could see further ahead, and the mist was thinning. There were no more merging pathways now; the road itself was more than a hundred feet wide.

On and on he moved, forcing his way through the silent throng. Then he saw that the road was beginning to diverge once more, into scores of pathways leading to arched tunnels, dark and forbidding.

A small man in a robe of coarse brown wool was moving back through the river of souls. He saw Druss and smiled. 'Keep moving, my son,' he said, patting Druss's shoulder.

'Wait!' called the axeman as the man moved past him. Brown Robe swung back, surprised. Stepping to Druss, he gestured him to the side of the road.

'Let me see your hand, brother,' he said.

'What?'

'Your hand, your right hand. Show me the palm!' The little man was insistent. Druss held out his hand and Brown Robe grasped it, peering intently at the calloused palm. 'But you are not ready to pass over, brother. Why are you here?'

'I am looking for someone.'

'Ah,' said the man, apparently relieved. 'You are the despairing heart. Many of you try to pass through. Did your loved one die? Has the world treated you savagely? Whatever the answer, brother, you must return whence you came. There is nothing for you here – unless you stray from the path. And then there is only an eternity of suffering. Go back!'

'I cannot. My wife is here. And she is alive – just like me.'

'If she is alive, brother, then she will not have passed the portals before you. No living soul can enter. You do not have the coin.' He held out his own hand. Nestling there was a black shadow, circular and insubstantial. 'For the Ferryman,' he said, 'and the road to Paradise.'

'If she could not pass the tunnels, then where could she be?' asked Druss.

'I don't know, brother. I have never left the path and I know not what lies beyond, save that it is inhabited by the souls of the damned. Go to the Fourth Gateway. Ask for Brother Domitori. He is the Keeper.'

Brown Robe smiled, then moved away to be swallowed up by the multitude. Druss joined the flow and eased his way through to the Fourth Gateway where another man in a brown, hooded robe stood silently by the entrance. He was tall and round-shouldered, with sad, solemn eyes. 'Are you Brother Domitori?' asked Druss.

The man nodded, but did not speak.

'I am looking for my wife.'

310

'Pass on, brother. If her soul lives you will find her.'

'She had no coin,' said Druss. The man nodded and pointed to a narrow, winding path that led up and around a low hill.

'There are many such,' said Domitori, 'beyond the hill. There they flicker and fade, and rejoin the road when they are ready, when their bodies give up the fight, when the heart ceases.'

Druss turned away, but Domitori called out to him. 'Beyond the hill the road is no more. You will be in the Valley of the Dead. Best you arm yourself.'

'I have no weapons here.'

Domitori raised his hand and the flow of souls ceased to move through the Gateway. He stepped alongside Druss. 'Bronze and steel have no place here, though you will see what appear to be swords and lances. This is a place of Spirit, and a man's spirit can be steel or water, wood or fire. To cross the hill – and return – will require courage, and so much more. Do you have faith?'

'In what?'

The man sighed. 'In the Source? In yourself? What do you hold most dear?'

'Rowena – my wife.'

'Then hold fast to your love, my friend. No matter what assails you. What do you fear most?'

'Losing her.'

'What else?'

'I fear nothing.'

'All men fear something. And that is your weakness. This place of the Damned and the Dead has an uncanny talent for bringing a man face to face with what he fears. I pray that the Source will guide you. Go in peace, brother.'

Returning to the Gateway he lifted his hand once more, and the entrance opened, the grim, silent flow of souls continuing without pause.

'You gutless whoreson!' stormed Sieben. 'I should kill you!'

The surgeon Shalitar stepped between Sieben and the priest of Pashtar Sen. 'Be calm,' he urged. 'The man has admitted to lacking

311

courage and has no need to apologise for it. Some men are tall, some short, some brave, others not so brave.'

'That may be true,' conceded Sieben, 'but what chance does Druss have in a world of enchantment and sorcery? Tell me that!'

'I don't know,' Shalitar admitted.

'No, but he does,' said Sieben. 'I have read of the Void; a great many of my tales are centred there. I have spoken to Seekers and mystics who have journeyed through the Mist. All agree on one point – without access to the powers of sorcery a man is finished there. Is that not true, priest?'

The man nodded, but did not look up. He was sitting beside the wide bed upon which lay the still figures of Druss and Rowena. The axeman's face was pale, and he did not seem to be breathing.

'What will he face there?' insisted Sieben. 'Come on, man!'

'The horrors of his past,' answered the priest, his voice barely audible.

'By the gods, priest, I tell you this: If he dies, you will follow him.'

Druss had reached the brow of the hill and gazed down into a parched valley. There were trees, black and dead, silhouetted against the slate-grey earth, as if sketched there with charcoal. There was no wind, no movement save for the few souls who wandered aimlessly across the face of the valley. A little way down the hill he saw an old woman sitting on the ground with head bowed and shoulders hunched. Druss approached her.

'I am looking for my wife,' he said.

'You are looking for more than that,' she told him.

He squatted down opposite her. 'No, just my wife. Can you help me?'

Her head came up and he found himself staring into deep-set eyes that glittered with malice. 'What can you give me, Druss?'

'How is it you know me?' he countered.

'The Axeman, the Silver Slayer, the man who fought the Chaos Beast. Why should I not know you? Now, what can you give me?'

'What do you want?'

'Make me a promise.'

312

'What promise?'

'You will give me your axe.'

'I do not have it here.'

'I know that, boy,' she snapped. 'But in the world above you will give me your axe.'

'Why do you need it?'

'That is no part of the bargain. But look around you, Druss. How will you begin to find her in the time that is left?'

'You can have it,' he said. 'Now, where is she?'

'You must cross a bridge. You will find her there. But the bridge is guarded, Druss, by an awesome warrior.'

'Just tell me where it is.'

A staff lay beside the old woman and she used it to lever herself to her feet. 'Come,' she said, and began to walk towards a low line of hills. As they walked, Druss saw many new souls wandering down into the valley.

'Why do they come here?' he asked.

'They are weak,' she told him. 'Victims of despair, of guilt, of longing. Suicides, mostly. As they wander here their bodies are dying – like Rowena.'

'She is not weak.'

'Of course she is. She is a victim of love – just as you are. And love is the ultimate downfall of Man. There is no abiding strength in love, Druss. It erodes the natural strength of man, it taints the heart of the hunter.'

'I do not believe that.'

She laughed, a dry sound like the rattling of bones. 'Yes, you do,' she said. 'You are not a man of love, Druss. Or was it love that led you to leap upon the decks of the corsair ship, cutting and killing? Was it love that sent you over the battlements at Ectanis? Was it love that carried you through the battles in the sand circles of Mashrapur?' She halted in her stride and turned to face him. 'Was it?'

'Yes. Everything was for Rowena – to help me find her. I love her.'

'It is not love, Druss; it is perceived need. You cannot bear what you are without her – a savage, a killer, a brute. But with her it is

313

a different story. You can leach from her purity, suck it in like fine wine. And then you can see the beauty in a flower, smell the essence of life upon the summer breeze. Without her you see yourself as a creature without worth. And answer me this, axeman: if it was truly love, would you not wish for her happiness above all else?'

'Aye, I would. And I do!'

'Really? Then when you found that she was happy, living with a man who loved her, her life rich and secure, what did you do? Did you try to persuade Gorben to spare Michanek?'

'Where is this bridge?' he asked.

'It is not easy to face, is it?' she persisted.

'I am no debater, woman. I only know that I would die for her.'

'Yes, yes. Typical of the male – always look for the easy solutions, the simple answers.' She walked on, cresting the hill, and paused, resting on her staff. Druss gazed down into the chasm beyond. Far, far below a river of fire, at this distance a slender ribbon of flame, flowed through a black gorge. Across the gorge stretched a narrow bridge of black rope and grey timber. At the centre stood a warrior in black and silver with a huge axe in his hands.

'She is on the far side,' said the old woman. 'But to reach her you must pass the guardian. Do you recognise him?'

'No.'

'You will.'

The bridge was secured by thick black ropes tied to two blocks of stone. The wooden slats that made up the main body of the structure were, Druss judged, around three feet long and an inch thick. He stepped out on to the bridge, which immediately began to sway. There were no guiding ropes attached by which a man could steady himself and, looking down, Druss felt a sick sense of vertigo.

Slowly he walked out over the chasm, his eyes fixed to the boards. He was halfway to the man in black and silver before he looked up. Then shock struck him like a blow.

The man smiled, bright teeth shining white against the black and silver beard. 'I am not you, boy,' he said. 'I am everything you could have been.'

314

Druss stared hard at the man. He was the very image of Druss himself, except that he was older and his eyes, cold and pale, seemed to hold many secrets.

'You are Bardan,' said Druss.

'And proud of it. I used my strength, Druss. I made men shake with fear. I took my pleasures where I wanted them. I am not like you, strong in body but weak in heart. You take after Bress.'

'I take that as a compliment,' said Druss. 'For I would never have wanted to be like you – a slayer of babes, an abuser of women. There is no strength in that.'

'I fought men. No man could accuse Bardan of cowardice. Shemak's balls, boy, I fought armies!'

'I say you were a coward,' said Druss. 'The worst kind. What strength you had came from that,' he said, pointing to the axe. 'Without it you were nothing. Without it you are nothing.'

Bardan's face reddened, then grew pale. 'I don't need this to deal with you, you weak-kneed whoreson. I could take you with my hands.'

'In your dreams,' mocked Druss.

Bardan made as if to lay down the axe, but then hesitated. 'You can't do it, can you?' taunted Druss. 'The mighty Bardan! Gods, I spit on you!'

Bardan straightened, the axe still in his right hand. 'Why should I lay aside my only friend? No one else stood by me all those lonely years. And here – even here he has been my constant aid.'

'Aid?' countered Druss. 'He destroyed you, just as he destroyed Cajivak and all others who took him to their hearts. But I don't need to convince you, Grandfather. You know it, but you are too weak to acknowledge it.'

'I'll show you weakness!' roared Bardan, leaping forward with axe raised. The bridge swayed perilously, but Druss leapt in under the swinging axe, hammering a ferocious punch to Bardan's chin. As the other man staggered, Druss took one running step and leapt feet first, his boots thudding into Bardan's chest to hurl him back. Bardan lost his grip on the axe and teetered on the edge.

315

Druss rolled to his feet and dived at the man. Bardan, recovering his footing, snarled and met him head-on. Druss smashed a blow to the other man's chin, but Bardan rolled with the punch, sending an uppercut which snapped the axeman's head back. The power in the blow was immense and Druss reeled. A second blow caught him above the ear, smashing him to the boards. Rolling as a booted foot slashed past his ear, he grabbed Bardan's leg and heaved. The warrior fell heavily. As Druss pushed himself upright, Bardan launched himself from the boards, his hands circling Druss's throat. The bridge was swaying wildly now and both men fell and rolled towards the edge. Druss hooked his foot into the space between two boards, but he and Bardan were hanging now over the awesome drop.

Druss tore himself free of Bardan's grip and thundered a punch to the warrior's chin. Bardan grunted and toppled from the bridge. His hand snaked out to grab Druss's arm – the wrenching grasp almost pulled Druss over the edge.

Bardan hung above the river of fire, his pale eyes looking up into Druss's face.

'Ah, but you're a bonnie fighter, laddie,' said Bardan softly. Druss got a grip on the other man's jerkin and tried to pull him up on to the bridge.

'Time to die at last,' said Bardan. 'You were right. It was the axe, always the axe.' Releasing his hold, he smiled. 'Let me go, boy. It's over.'

'No! Damn you, take my hand!'

'May the gods smile on you, Druss!' Bardan twisted up and hit out at Druss's arm, dislodging his grip. The bridge swayed again and the black and silver warrior fell. Druss watched him fall, spinning down, down, until he was just a dark speck swallowed up by the river of fire.

Pushing himself to his knees he glanced at the axe. Red smoke swirled from it to form a crimson figure – the skin scaled, the head horned at the temples. There was no nose, merely two slits in the flesh above a shark-like mouth.

'You were correct, Druss,' said the demon affably. 'He was weak. As was Cajivak, and all the others. Only you have the strength to use me.'

'I want no part of you.'

The demon's head lifted and his laughter sounded. 'Easy to say, mortal. But look yonder.' At the far end of the bridge stood the Chaos Beast, huge and towering, its taloned paws glinting, its eyes glowing like coals of fire.

Druss felt a swelling of despair and his heart sank as the axe-demon stepped closer, his voice low and friendly. 'Why do you hesitate, Man? When have I failed you? On the ship of Earin Shad, did I not turn away the fire? Did I not slip in Cajivak's grasp? I am your friend, Mortal. I have always been your friend. And in these long and lonely centuries I have waited for a man with your strength and determination. With me you can conquer the world. Without me you will never leave this place, never feel the sun upon your face. Trust me, Druss! Slay the beast – and then we can go home.'

The demon shimmered into smoke, flowing back into the black haft of the axe.

Druss glanced up to see the Chaos Beast waiting at the far end of the bridge. It was even more monstrous now: massive shoulders beneath the black fur, saliva dripping from its huge maw. Stepping forward, Druss gripped the haft of Snaga, swinging the blades into the air.

Instantly his strength returned, and with it a soaring sense of hatred and a lust to cleave and kill. His mouth was dry with the need for battle, and he moved towards the flame-eyed bear. The beast waited with arms at its sides.

It seemed to Druss then that all the evil of the world rested in the creature's colossal frame, all the frustrations of life, the angers, the jealousies, the vileness – everything that he had ever suffered could be laid upon the black soul of the Chaos Beast. Fury and madness made his limbs tremble and he felt his lips draw back in a snarl as he lifted high the axe and ran at the creature.

The beast did not move. It stood still, arms down and head drooping.

Druss slowed in his charge. Kill it! Kill it! Kill it! He reeled with the intensity of his need to destroy, then looked down at the axe in his hand.

'No!' he shouted, and with one tremendous heave hurled the axe high in the air and out over the chasm. It spun glistening towards the ribbon of flame, and Druss saw the demon spew from it, black against the silver of the blades. Then the axe struck the river of fire. Exhausted, Druss turned back to face the beast.

Rowena stood alone and naked, her gentle eyes watching him.

He groaned and walked towards her. 'Where is the beast?' he said.

'There is no beast, Druss. Only me. Why did you change your mind about killing me?'

'You? I would never hurt you! Sweet Heaven, how could you think it?'

'You looked at me with hate and then you ran at me with your axe.'

'Oh, Rowena! I saw only a demon. I was bewitched! Forgive me!' Stepping in close he tried to put his arms around her, but she moved back from him.

'I loved Michanek,' she said.

He sighed and nodded. 'I know. He was a good man – perhaps a great one. I was with him at the end. He asked me . . . urged me to look after you. He didn't need to ask that of me. You are everything to me, you always were. Without you there was no light in my life. And I've waited so long for this moment. Come back with me, Rowena. Live!'

'I was looking for him,' she said, tears in her eyes, 'but I couldn't find him.'

'He's gone where you cannot follow,' said Druss. 'Come home.'

'I am both a wife and widow. Where is my home, Druss? Where?'

Her head drooped and bright tears fell to her cheeks. Druss took her in his arms, drawing her in to him. 'Wherever you choose to make your home,' he whispered, 'I will build it for you. But it should be where the sun shines, and where you can hear the birdsong, smell the flowers. This place is not for you – nor would Michanek want you here. I love you, Rowena. But if you want to live without me I will bear it. Just so long as you live. Come back with me. We'll talk again in the light.'

'I don't want to stay here,' she said, clinging to him. 'But I miss him so.'

*The words tore at Druss, but he held her close and kissed her hair.
'Let's go home,' he said. 'Take my hand.'*

Druss opened his eyes and drew in a great gulp of air. Beside him
Rowena slept. He felt a moment of panic, but then a voice spoke.
'She is alive.' Druss sat up, and saw the Old Woman sitting in a chair
by the bedside.

'You want the axe? Take it!'

She chuckled, the sound dry and cold. 'Your gratitude is overwhelming, axeman. But no, I do not need Snaga. You exorcised the
demon from the weapon and he is gone. But I shall find him. You
did well, boy. All that hatred and lust for death – yet you overcame
it. What a complex creature is Man.'

'Where are the others?' asked Druss.

Taking up her staff, she eased herself to her feet. 'Your friends
are sleeping. They were exhausted and it took little effort to send
them deep into dreams. Good luck to you, Druss. I wish you and
your lady well. Take her back to the Drenai mountains, enjoy her
company while you can. Her heart is weak, and she will never see
the white hair of a human winter. But you will, Druss.'

She sniffed and stretched, her bones creaking. 'What did you want
with the demon?' asked Druss as she made her way to the door.

She turned in the doorway. 'Gorben is having a sword made – a
great sword. He will pay me to make it an enchanted weapon. And
I shall, Druss. I shall.'

And then she was gone.

Rowena stirred and woke.

Sunlight broke through the clouds and bathed the room.

Book Four

Druss the Legend

Druss took Rowena back to the lands of the Drenai, and, with the gold presented to him by a grateful Gorben, bought a farm in the high mountains. For two years he lived quietly, struggling to be a loving husband and a man of peace. Sieben travelled the land, performing his songs and tales before princes and courtiers, and the legend of Druss spread across the continent.

At the invitation of the King of Gothir Druss travelled north, and fought in the Second Campaign against the Nadir, earning the title *Deathwalker*[*]. Sieben joined him and together they travelled through many lands.

And the legend grew.

Between campaigns Druss would return to his farm, but always he would listen for the siren call to battle and Rowena would bid him farewell as he set off, time and again, to fight what he assured her would be his last battle.

Faithful Pudri remained at Rowena's side. Sieben continued to scandalise Drenai society and his travels with Druss were usually undertaken to escape the vengeance of outraged husbands.

In the east the Ventrian Emperor, Gorben, having conquered all his enemies, turned his attention to the fiercely independent Drenai.

* From the second chronicles of Druss the Legend.

Druss was forty-five, and once more had promised Rowena there would be no more journeying to distant wars.

What he could not know was, this time, the war was coming to him.

Druss sat in the sunshine, watching the clouds glide slowly across the mountains, and thought of his life. Love and friendship had been with him always, the first with Rowena, the latter with Sieben, Eskodas and Bodasen. But the greater part of his forty-five years had been filled with blood and death, the screams of the wounded and dying.

He sighed. A man ought to leave more behind him than corpses, he decided. The clouds thickened, the land falling into shadow, the grass of the hillside no longer gleaming with life, the flowers ceasing to blaze with colour. He shivered. It was going to rain. The soft, dull, arthritic ache had begun in his shoulder. 'Getting old,' he said.

'Who are you talking to, my love?' He turned and grinned. Rowena seated herself beside him on the wooden bench, slipping her arm around his waist, resting her head on his shoulder. His huge hand stroked her hair, noting the grey at the temples.

'I was talking to myself. It's something that happens when you get old.'

She stared up into his grizzled face and smiled. 'You'll never get old. You're the strongest man in the world.'

'Once, princess. Once.'

'Nonsense. You hefted that barrel of sand at the village fair right over your head. No one else could do that.'

'That only makes me the strongest man in the village.'

Pulling away from him, Rowena shook her head, but her expression, as always, was gentle. 'You miss the wars and the battles?'

'No. I . . . I am happy here. With you. You give my soul peace.'

'Then what is troubling you?'

'The clouds. They move in front of the sun. They cast shadows. Then they are gone. Am I like that, Rowena? Will I leave nothing behind me?'

'What would you wish to leave?'

'I don't know,' he answered, looking away.

'You would have liked a son,' she said, softly. 'As would I. But it was not to be. Do you blame me for it?'

'No! No! Never.' His arms swept around her, drawing her to him. 'I love you. I always have. I always will. You are my wife!'

'I would have liked to have given you a son,' she whispered.

'It does not matter.'

They sat in silence until the clouds darkened and the first drops of rain began to fall.

Druss stood, lifting Rowena into his arms, and began the long walk to the stone house. 'Put me down,' she commanded. 'You'll hurt your back.'

'Nonsense. You are as light as a sparrow wing. And am I not the strongest man in the world?'

A fire was blazing in the hearth, and their Ventrian servant, Pudri, was preparing mulled wine for them. Druss lowered Rowena into a broad-backed leather armchair.

'Your face is red with the effort,' she chided him.

He smiled and did not argue. His shoulder was hurting, his lower back aching like the devil. The slender Pudri grinned at them both.

'Such children you are,' he said, and shuffled away into the kitchen.

'He's right,' said Druss. 'With you I am still the boy from the farm, standing below the Great Oak with the most beautiful woman in the Drenai lands.'

'I was never beautiful,' Rowena told him, 'but it pleased me to hear you say it.'

'You were – and are,' he assured her.

The firelight sent dancing shadows on to the walls of the room as the light outside began to fail. Rowena fell asleep and Druss sat silently watching her. Four times in the last three years she had collapsed, the surgeons warning Druss of a weakness in her heart.

The old warrior had listened to them without comment, his ice-blue eyes showing no expression. But within him a terrible fear had begun to grow. He had forsaken his battles and settled down to life in the mountains, believing that his presence nearby would hold Rowena to life.

But he watched her always, never allowing her to become too tired, fussing over her meals, waking in the night to feel her pulse, then being unable to sleep.

'Without her I am nothing,' he confided to his friend Sieben the Poet, whose house had been built less than a mile from the stone house. 'If she dies, part of me will die with her.'

'I know, old horse,' said Sieben. 'But I am sure the princess will be fine.'

Druss smiled. 'Why did you make her a princess? Are you poets incapable of the truth?'

Sieben spread his hands and chuckled. 'One must cater to one's audience. The saga of Druss the Legend had need of a princess. Who would want to listen to the tale of a man who fought his way across continents to rescue a farm girl?'

'Druss the Legend? Pah! There are no real heroes any more. The likes of Egel, Karnak and Waylander are long gone. Now they were heroes, mighty men with eyes of fire.'

Sieben laughed aloud. 'You say that only because you have heard the songs. In years to come men will talk of you in the same way. You and that cursed axe.'

The cursed axe.

Druss glanced up to where the weapon hung on the wall, its twin silver steel blades glinting in the firelight. Snaga the Sender, the blades of no return. He stood and moved silently across the room, lifting the axe from the brackets supporting it. The black haft was warm to the touch, and he felt, as always, the thrill of battle ripple through him as he hefted the weapon. Reluctantly he returned the axe to its resting place.

'They are calling you,' said Rowena. He swung and saw that she was awake and watching him.

'Who is calling me?'

'The hounds of war. I can hear them baying.' Druss shivered and forced a smile.

'No one is calling me,' he told her, but there was no conviction in his voice. Rowena had always been a mystic.

'Gorben is coming, Druss. His ships are already at sea.'

'It is not my war. My loyalties would be divided.'

For a moment she said nothing. Then: 'You liked him, didn't you?'

'He is a good Emperor – or he was. Young, proud, and terribly brave.'

'You set too much store by bravery. There was a madness in him you could never see. I hope you never do.'

'I told you, it is not my war. I'm forty-five years old, my beard is going grey and my joints are stiff. The young men of the Drenai will have to tackle him without me.'

'But the Immortals will be with him,' she persisted. 'You said once there were no finer warriors in the world.'

'Do you remember all my words?'

'Yes,' she answered, simply.

The sound of hoofbeats came from the yard beyond, and Druss strode to the door, stepping out on to the porch.

The rider wore the armour of a Drenai officer, white plumed helm and silver breastplate, with a long scarlet cloak. He dismounted, tied the reins of his horse to a hitching rail and walked towards the house.

'Good evening. I am looking for Druss the Axeman,' said the man, removing his helm and running his fingers through his sweat-drenched fair hair.

'You found him.'

'I thought so. I am Dun Certak. I have a message from Lord Abalayn. He wonders if you would agree to ride east to our camp at Skeln.'

'Why?'

'Morale, sir. You are a legend. The Legend. It would boost the men during the interminable waiting.'

'No,' said Druss. 'I am retired.'

'Where are your manners, Druss?' called Rowena. 'Ask the young man to come in.'

Druss stepped aside and the officer entered, bowing deeply to Rowena.

'It is a pleasure to meet you, my lady. I have heard so much about you.'

'How disappointing for you,' she replied, her smile friendly. 'You hear of a princess and meet a plump matron.'

'He wants me to travel to Skeln,' said Druss.

'I heard. I think you should go.'

'I am no speechmaker,' growled Druss.

'Then take Sieben with you. It will do you good. You have no idea how irritating it is to have you fussing around me all day. Be honest, you will enjoy yourself enormously.'

'Are you married?' Druss asked Certak, his voice almost a growl.

'No, sir.'

'Very wise. Will you stay the night?'

'No, sir. Thank you. I have other despatches to deliver. But I will see you at Skeln . . . and look forward to it.' The officer bowed once more and backed away towards the door.

'You will stay for supper,' ordered Rowena. 'Your despatches can wait for at least one hour.'

'I'm sorry, my lady, but . . .'

'Give up, Certak,' advised Druss. 'You cannot win.'

The officer smiled and spread his hands. 'An hour then,' he agreed.

The following morning, on borrowed horses, Druss and Sieben waved farewell and headed east. Rowena waved and smiled until they were out of sight, then returned to the house, where Pudri was waiting.

'You should not have sent him away, lady,' said the Ventrian sadly. Rowena swallowed hard, and the tears began to flow. Pudri moved alongside her, his slender arms encircling her.

'I had to. He must not be here when the time comes.'

'He would want to be here.'

'In so many ways he is the strongest man I have ever known. But in this I am right. He must not see me die.'

'I will be with you, lady. I will hold your hand.'

'You will tell him that it was sudden, and there was no pain – even if it is a lie?'

'I will.'

Six days later, after a dozen changes of mount, Certak galloped into the camp. There were four hundred white tents set in unit squares in the shadow of the Skeln range, each housing twelve men. Four thousand horses were picketed in the surrounding fields, and sixty cookfires were blazing under iron pots. The odour of stew assailed him as he reined in outside the large red-striped tent used by the general and his staff.

The young officer handed over his despatches, saluted and left to rejoin his company at the northern edge of the camp. Leaving his lathered mount with a groom, he removed his helm and pushed aside the tent flap of his quarters. Inside his companions were dicing and drinking. The game broke up as he entered.

'Certak!' said Orases, grinning and rising to meet him. 'Well, what was he like?'

'Who?' asked Certak innocently.

'Druss, you moron.'

'Big,' said Certak, moving past the burly blond officer and throwing his helm to the narrow pallet bed. He unbuckled his breastplate, letting it drop to the floor. Freed of its weight, he took a deep breath and scratched his chest.

'Now don't be annoying, there's a good fellow,' said Orases, his smile fading. 'Tell us about him.'

'Do tell him,' urged the dark-eyed Diagoras. 'He's been talking about the axeman non-stop since you left.'

'That's not true,' muttered Orases, blushing. 'We've all been talking about him.' Certak slapped Orases on the shoulder, then ruffled his hair.

'You get me a drink, Orases, and then I'll tell you all.'

As Orases fetched a flagon of wine and four goblets, Diagoras moved smoothly to his feet and pulled up a chair, reversing it before sitting opposite Certak, who had streched out on the bed. The fourth man, Archytas, joined them, accepting a goblet of light honey mead wine from Orases and draining it swiftly.

'As I said, he is big,' said Certak. 'Not as tall as the stories claim, but built like a small castle. The size of his arms? Well, his biceps are as long as your thighs, Diagoras. He is bearded and dark, though there is some grey in his hair. His eyes are blue, and they seem to look right through you.'

'And Rowena?' asked Orases eagerly. 'Is she as fabulously beautiful as the poem says?'

'No. She is nice enough, in a matronly sort of way. I suppose she would have been lovely once. It's hard to tell with some of these older women. Her eyes are gorgeous, though, and she has a pretty smile.'

'Did you see the axe?' asked Archytas, a wand-slender nobleman from the Lentrian border.

'No.'

'Did you ask Druss about his battles?' asked Diagoras.

'Of course not, you fool. He may be only a farmer now, but he's still Druss. You don't just march up and ask how many dragons he's downed.'

'There are no dragons,' said Archytas loftily.

Certak shook his head, staring at the man through narrowed eyes.

'It was a figure of speech,' he said. 'Anyway, they invited me to join them for supper and we chatted about horses and the running of the farm. He asked my opinion about the war, and I told him I thought Gorben would sail for Penrac Bay.'

'It's a safe bet,' said Diagoras.

'Not necessarily. If it's that safe, how come we're stuck here with five regiments?'

'Abalayn is over-cautious,' answered Diagoras, grinning.

'That's the trouble with you westerners,' said Certak. 'You live so long with your horses that you start to think like them. Skeln Pass is a gateway to the Sentran Plain. If Gorben took that we would starve during the winter. So would half of Vagria, for that matter.'

'Gorben is no fool,' offered Archytas. 'He knows Skeln can be defended forever with two thousand men. The pass is too narrow for the numbers of his army to be of any real use. And there's no other way through. Penrac makes more sense. It's only three hundred miles from Drenan and the countryside around is as flat as a lake. There his army could spread and cause real problems.'

'I don't particularly care where he lands,' said Orases, 'as long as I'm close by to see it.'

Certak and Diagoras exchanged glances. Both had fought the Sathuli and had seen the true, bloody face of battle, and watched the crows peck out the eyes of dead friends. Orases was a newcomer who had urged his father to buy him a commission in Abalayn's lancers when news of the invasion fleet reached Drenan.

'What about the Cuckold King?' asked Archytas. 'Was he there?'

'Sieben? Yes, he arrived for supper. He looks ancient. I can't see the ladies swooning over him any longer. Bald as a rock and thin as a stick.'

'You think Druss will want to fight alongside us?' asked Diagoras. 'That would be something to tell the children.'

'No. He's past it. Tired. You can see it in him. But I liked him. He's no braggart, that's for sure. Down-to-earth. You'd never believe he was the subject of so many songs and ballads. They say Gorben has never forgotten him.'

'Maybe he sailed the fleet just for a reunion with his friend Druss,' said Archytas, with a sneer. 'Perhaps you should put that idea to the general. We could all go home.'

'It's an idea,' admitted Certak, biting back his anger. 'But if the regiments separate, we'd be deprived of your delightful company, Archytas. And nothing is worth that.'

'I could live with it,' said Diagoras.

'And I could do without being forced to share a tent with a pack of ill-bred hounds,' said Archytas. 'But needs must.'

'Well, woof woof,' said Diagoras. 'Do you think we've been insulted, Certak?'

'Not by anyone worth worrying about,' he replied.

'Now that is an insult,' said Archytas, rising. A sudden commotion from outside the tent cut through the gathering drama. The flap was pulled aside. A young soldier pushed his head inside.

'The beacons are lit,' he said. 'The Ventrians have landed at Penrac.'

332

The four warriors leapt to their feet, rushing to gather their armour.

Archytas turned as he buckled his breastplate.

'This changes nothing,' he said. 'It is a question of honour.'

'No,' said Certak. 'It is a question of dying. And you'll do that nicely, you pompous pig.'

Archytas grinned mirthlessly back at him.

'We'll see,' he said.

Diagoras pulled down the earflaps of his bronze helmet and tied them under his chin. He leaned conspiratorially close to Archytas.

'A thought to remember, goat-face. If you kill him – which is extremely doubtful – I shall cut your throat while you're sleeping.' He smiled pleasantly and patted Archytas's shoulder. 'You see, I'm no gentleman.'

The camp was in uproar. Along the coast the warning beacons were blazing from the Skeln peaks. Gorben, as expected, had landed in the south. Abalayn was there with twenty thousand men. But he would be outnumbered at least two to one. It was a hard five days' ride to Penrac and the orders were being issued at speed, the horses saddled, and the tents packed away. Cooking fires were doused and wagons loaded as men scurried about the camp in seeming chaos.

By morning only six hundred warriors remained in the mouth of Skeln Pass, the bulk of the army thundering south to bolster Abalayn.

Earl Delnar, Warden of the North, gathered the men together just after dawn. Beside him stood Archytas.

'As you know, the Ventrians have landed,' said the Earl. 'We are to stay here in case they send a small force to harry the north. I know many of you would have preferred to head south, but, to state the obvious, someone has to stay behind to protect the Sentran Plain. And we've been chosen. The camp here is no longer suitable for our needs and we will be moving up into the pass itself. Are there any questions?'

There were none and Delnar dismissed the men, turning to Archytas.

'Why you have been left here I do not know,' he said. 'But I don't like you at all, lad. You are a troublemaker. I would have thought your skills would have been welcome at Penrac. However, be that as it may. You cause any trouble here and you will regret it.'

'I understand, Lord Delnar,' replied Archytas.

'Understand this also: As my aide I will require you to work, passing on my instructions exactly as I give them to you. I am told you are a man of surpassing arrogance.'

'That is hardly fair.'

'Perhaps. I cannot see that it should be true, since your grandfather was a tradesman and your nobility is scarce two generations old. You will find as you grow older that it is what a man does that counts, and not what his father did.'

'Thank you for your advice, my lord. I shall bear it in mind,' said Archytas stiffly.

'I doubt that you will. I do not know what drives you, but then I don't care overmuch. We should be here about three weeks and then I'll be rid of you.'

'As you say, my lord.'

Delnar waved him away, then glanced beyond him to the edge of the trees bordering the field to the west. Two men were walking steadily towards them. Delnar's jaw tightened as he recognised the poet. He called Archytas back.

'Sir?'

'The two men approaching yonder. Go out to meet them and have them brought to my tent.'

'Yes, sir. Who are they, do you know?'

'The large one is Druss the Legend. The other is the saga poet Sieben.'

'I understand you know him very well,' said Archytas, barely disguising his malice.

'It doesn't look much of an army,' said Druss, shading his eyes against the sun rising over the Skeln peaks. 'Can't be more than a few hundred of them.'

Sieben didn't answer. He was exhausted. Early the previous day Druss had finally tired of riding the tall gelding borrowed in Skoda.

He had left it with a stock breeder in a small town thirty miles west, determined to walk to Skeln. In a moment – in which Sieben could only consider he had been struck by transient and massive stupidity – he had agreed to walk with him. He seemed to remember thinking that it would be good for him. Now, even with Druss carrying both packs, the poet stumbled wearily alongside, his legs boneless and numb, his ankles and wrists swollen, his breathing ragged.

'You know what I think?' said Druss. Sieben shook his head, concentrating on the tents. 'I think we're too late. Gorben has landed at Penrac and the army's gone. Still, it's been a pleasant journey. Are you all right, poet?'

Sieben nodded, his face grey.

'You don't look it. If you weren't standing here beside me I'd think you were dead. I've seen corpses that looked in better health.' Sieben glared at him. It was the only response his fading strength would allow. Druss chuckled. 'Lost for words, eh? This was worth coming for.'

A tall young officer was making his way towards them, fastidiously avoiding small patches of mud and the more obvious reminders of the horses picketed in the field the night before.

Halting before them, he bowed elaborately.

'Welcome to Skeln,' he said. 'Is your friend ill?'

'No, he always looks like this,' said Druss, running his eyes over the warrior. He moved well, and handled himself confidently, but there was something about the narrow green eyes and the set of his features that nettled the axeman.

'Earl Delnar asked me to conduct you to his tent. I am Archytas. And you?'

'Druss. This is Sieben. Lead on.'

The officer set a fast pace which Druss made no effort to match on the last few hundred paces uphill. He walked slowly beside Sieben. The truth of it was that Druss himself was tired. They had walked most of the night, both trying to prove they still had a claim to youth.

Delnar dismissed Archytas and remained seated behind the small folding table on which were strewn papers and despatches. Sieben, oblivious of the tension, slumped to Delnar's narrow bed. Druss lifted a flagon of wine to his lips, taking three great swallows.

'He is not welcome here – and, therefore, neither are you,' said Delnar, as Druss replaced the flagon.

The axeman wiped his mouth with the back of his hand. 'Had I been sure you were here, I would not have brought him,' he said. 'I take it the army has moved on.'

'Yes. They travelled south. Gorben has landed. You may borrow two horses, but I want you gone by sundown.'

'I came to give the men something to think about besides waiting,' said Druss. 'They won't need me now. So I'll just rest here for a couple of days then head back to Skoda.'

'I said you're not welcome here,' said Delnar.

The axeman's eyes grew cold as he stared at the Earl. 'Listen to me,' said Druss, as softly as he could. 'I know why you feel as you do. In your place I would feel the same. But I am not in your place. I am Druss. And I walk where I will. If I say I will stay here then I shall. Now I like you, laddie. But cross me and I'll kill you.'

Delnar nodded and rubbed his chin. The situation had gone as far as he could allow it. He had hoped Druss would leave, but he could not force him. What could be more ludicrous than the Earl of the North ordering Drenai warriors to attack Druss the Legend? Especially since the man had been invited to the camp by the Lord of Hosts. Delnar did not fear Druss, because he did not fear death. His life had been ended for him six years before. Since then his wife, Vashti, had shamed him with many more affairs. Three years ago she had delivered to him a daughter, a delightful child he adored, even if he doubted his part in her conception. Vashti had run away to the capital soon after, leaving the child at Delnoch. The Earl had heard his wife was now living with a Ventrian merchant in the rich western quarter. Taking a deep, calming breath, he met Druss's eyes.

'Stay then,' he said. 'But keep him from my sight.'

Druss nodded. He glanced down at Sieben. The poet was asleep.

'This should never have come between us,' said Delnar.

'These things happen,' said Druss. 'Sieben always had a weakness for beautiful women.'

336

'I shouldn't hate him. But he was the first I knew about. He was the man who destroyed my dreams. You understand?'

'We will leave tomorrow,' said Druss wearily. 'But for now let's walk in the pass. I need some air in my lungs.'

The Earl rose and donned his helm and red cape, and together the two warriors walked through the camp and on up the steep rocky slope to the mouth of the pass. It ran for almost a mile, narrowing at the centre to less than fifty paces, where the ground dropped away gently in a rolling slope down to a stream that flowed across the valley floor, angling towards the sea some three miles distant. From the mouth of the pass, through the jagged peaks, the sea glittered in the fragmented sunlight, glowing gold and blue. A fresh easterly wind cooled Druss's face.

'Good place for a defensive battle,' said the axeman, scanning the pass. 'At the centre any attacking force would be funnelled in and numbers would be useless.'

'And they would have to charge uphill,' said Delnar. 'I think Abalayn was hoping Gorben would land here. We could have sealed him in the bay. Left his army to starve, and brought the fleet round to harry his ships.'

'He's too canny for that,' said Druss. 'A more wily warrior you will not find.'

'You liked him?'

'He was always fair with me,' said Druss, keeping his tone neutral. Delnar nodded. 'They say he's become a tyrant.'

Druss shrugged. 'He once told me it was the curse of kings.'

'He was right,' said Delnar. 'You know your friend Bodasen is still one of his top generals?'

'I wouldn't doubt it. He's a loyal man, with a good eye for strategy.'

'I should think you are relieved to miss this battle, my friend,' commented the Earl.

Druss nodded. 'The years I served with the Immortals were happy ones, I'll grant that. And I have other friends among them. But you are right, I would hate to come up against Bodasen. We were brothers in battle, and I love the man dearly.'

'Let's go back. I'll arrange some food for you.'

337

The Earl saluted the sentry at the mouth of the pass and the two men made their way up the slope to the camp. Delnar took him to a square white tent, lifting the flap for Druss to enter first. Within were four men. They leapt to their feet as the Earl followed Druss inside.

'Stand easy,' said Delnar. 'This is Druss, an old friend of mine. He'll be staying with us for a while. I'd like you to make him welcome.' He turned to Druss. 'I believe you know Certak and Archytas. Well, this black-bearded reprobate is Diagoras.' Druss liked the look of the man; his smile was quick and friendly, and the gleam in his dark eyes bespoke humour. But more than this he had what soldiers call 'the look of eagles' and Druss knew instantly he was a warrior born.

'Nice to meet you, sir. We've heard a lot about you.'

'And this is Orases,' said Certak. 'He's new with us. From Drenan.'

Druss shook hands with the young man, noting the fat around his middle and the softness of his grip. He seemed pleasant enough, but beside Diagoras and Certak he seemed boyish and clumsy.

'Would you like some food?' asked Diagoras, after the Earl had departed.

'I certainly would,' muttered Druss. 'My stomach thinks my throat's been sliced.'

'I'll get it,' said Orases swiftly.

'I think he's a little in awe of you, Druss,' said Diagoras as Orases raced from the tent.

'It happens,' said Druss. 'Why don't you ask me to sit down?'

Diagoras chuckled and pulled up a chair. Druss reversed it and sat. The others followed suit and the atmosphere eased. The world is getting younger, thought Druss, wishing he had never come.

'May I see your axe, sir?' asked Certak.

'Certainly,' said Druss, pulling Snaga smoothly from the oiled sheath. In the older man's hands the weapon seemed almost weightless, but as it passed to Certak the officer grunted.

'The blade that smote the Chaos Hound,' whispered Certak, turning it over in his hands, then returning it to Druss.

'Do you believe everything you hear?' said Archytas, sneering.

'Did it happen, Druss?' said Diagoras, before Certak could answer.

'Yes. A long time ago. But it scarce pierced its hide.'

'Was it true they were sacrificing a princess?' asked Certak.

'No. Two small children. But tell me about yourselves,' said Druss. 'Wherever I go people ask me the same questions and I get very bored.'

'If you're that bored,' said Archytas, 'why do you take the poet with you on all your adventures?'

'What does that mean?'

'Quite simply that it seems strange for a man as modest as you seem to be to take a saga-master with him. Although it proved very convenient.'

'Convenient?'

'Well, he created you, didn't he? Druss the Legend. Fame and fortune. Surely any wandering warrior with such a companion could have been boosted into legend?'

'I suppose that's true,' said Druss. 'I've known a lot of men in my time whose deeds are forgotten, but who were worthy of remembrance in song or tale. I never really thought of it before.'

'How much of Sieben's great saga is exaggerated?' asked Archytas.

'Oh do shut up,' snapped Diagoras.

'No,' said Druss, lifting his hand. 'You've no idea how good this is. Always people ask me about the stories, and whenever I tell them they are – shall we say – rounded, they disbelieve me. But it's true. The stories are not about me. They are based on the truth, but they have grown. I was the seed; they have become the tree. I never met a princess in my life. But to answer your first question. I never took Sieben on my quest. He just came. I think he was bored and wanted to see the world.'

'But did you slay the werebeast in the mountains of Pelucid?' said Certak.

'No. I just killed a lot of men in a lot of battles.'

'Then why do you allow the poems to be sung?' asked Archytas.

'If I could have stopped them I would,' Druss told him. 'The first few years of my return were a nightmare. But I've got used to it since. People believe what they want to believe. The truth rarely makes a difference. People need heroes, and if they don't have any, they invent them.'

Orases returned with a bowl of stew and a loaf of black bread. 'Have I missed anything?' he asked.

'Not really,' said Druss. 'We were just chatting.'

'Druss has been telling us that his legend is all lies,' said Archytas. 'It's been most revealing.'

Druss chuckled with genuine humour and shook his head. 'You see,' he told Diagoras and Certak, 'people believe what they want to believe, and hear only what they wish to hear.' He glanced across at the tight-lipped Archytas. 'Boy, there was a time when your blood would now be staining the walls of this tent. But I was younger then, and headstrong. Now I get no delight from killing puppies. But I am still Druss, so I tell you this, walk softly around me from now on.'

Archytas forced a laugh. 'You cause me no concern, old man,' he said. 'I don't think . . .'

Druss rose swiftly and backhanded him across the face. Archytas hurtled backwards over his chair to lie groaning on the tent floor, his nose smashed and leaking blood.

'No, you don't think,' said Druss. 'Now give me that stew, Orases. It must be getting cold.'

'Welcome to Skeln, Druss,' said Diagoras, grinning.

For three days Druss remained at the camp. Sieben had woken in Delnar's trent, complaining of chest pains. The regimental surgeon examined him and ordered him to rest, explaining to Druss and Delnar that the poet had suffered a serious spasm of the heart.

'How bad is it?' asked Druss.

The surgeon's eyes were bleak. 'If he rests for a week or two he could be fine. The danger is that the heart might cramp suddenly – and fail. He's not a young man, and the journey here was hard for him.'

'I see,' said Druss. 'Thank you.' He turned to Delnar. 'I am sorry, but we must stay.'

'Do not concern yourself, my friend,' responded the Earl, waving his hand. 'Despite what I said when you arrived, you are welcome. But, tell me, what happened between you and Archytas? It looks like a mountain fell on his face.'

'His nose tapped my hand,' grunted Druss.

Delnar smiled. 'He's a somewhat loathsome character. But you had better watch out for him. He's stupid enough to challenge you.'

'No, he won't,' said Druss. 'He may be foolish, but he's not in love with death. Even a puppy knows to hide from a wolf.'

On the morning of the fourth day, as Druss sat with Sieben, one of the lookout sentries came running headlong into the camp. Within minutes chaos reigned as men raced for their armour. Hearing the commotion, Druss walked from the tent. A young soldier ran by. Druss's arm snaked out, catching the man's cloak and wrenching him to a stop.

'What's going on?' asked Druss.

'The Ventrians are here!' shouted the soldier, tearing himself loose and running towards the pass. Druss swore and strode after him. At the mouth of the pass he halted, staring out over the stream.

Standing in armoured line upon line, their lances gleaming, were the warriors of Gorben, filling the valley from mountainside to mountainside. At the centre of the mass was the tent of the Emperor, and around it were massed the black and silver ranks of the Immortals.

Drenai warriors scurried past him as Druss made his slow way to Delnar's side.

'I told you he was cunning,' said Druss. 'He must have sent a token force to Penrac, knowing it would draw our army south.'

'Yes. But what now?'

'You're not left with many choices,' said Druss.

'True.'

The Drenai warriors spread out across the narrow centre of the pass in three ranks, their round shields glinting in the morning sun, their white horsehair-crested helms flowing in the breeze.

'How many here are veterans?' asked Druss.

'About half. I've placed them at the front.'

'How long will it take a rider to reach Penrac?'

'I've sent a man. The army should be back in about ten days.'

'You think we've got ten days?' asked Druss.

341

'No. But, as you say, there aren't too many choices. What do you think Gorben will do?'

'First he'll talk. He'll ask you to surrender. You'd better request a few hours to make up your mind. Then he'll send the Panthians in. They're an undisciplined bunch but they fight like devils. We should see them off. Their wicker shields and stabbing spears are no match for Drenai armour. After that he'll test all his troops on us . . .'

'The Immortals?'

'Not until the end, when we're weary and finished.'

'It's a gloomy picture,' said Delnar.

'It's a bitch,' agreed Druss.

'Will you stand with us, axeman?'

'Did you expect me to leave?'

Delnar chuckled suddenly. 'Why shouldn't you? I wish I could.'

In the first Drenai line Diagoras sheathed his sword, wiping his sweating palm on his red cloak.

'There are enough of them,' he said.

Beside him Certak nodded. 'Masterly understatement. They look like they could run right over us.'

'We'll have to surrender, won't we?' whispered Orases from behind them, blinking sweat from his eyes.

'Somehow I don't think that's likely,' said Certak. 'Though I admit it's a welcome thought.'

A rider on a black stallion forded the stream and galloped towards the Drenai line. Delnar walked through the ranks, Druss beside him, and waited.

The rider wore the black and silver armour of a general of the Immortals. Reining in before the two men, he leaned forward on the pommel of his saddle.

'Druss?' he said. 'Is that you?'

Druss studied the gaunt features, the silver-streaked dark hair hanging in two braids.

'Welcome to Skeln, Bodasen,' answered the axeman.

'I'm sorry to find you here. I was meaning to ride for Skoda as soon as we took Drenan. Is Rowena well?'

'Yes. And you?'

'As you see me. Fit and well. Yourself?'

'I'm not complaining.'

'And Sieben?'

'He's asleep in a tent.'

'He always knew when to avoid battles,' said Bodasen, forcing a smile. 'And that's what this is looking like unless common sense prevails. Are you the leader?' he asked Delnar.

'I am. What message do you bring?'

'Merely this. Tomorrow morning my Emperor will ride through this pass. He would consider it a courtesy if you could remove your men from his path.'

'We will think on it,' said Delnar.

'I would advise you to think well,' said Bodasen, turning his mount. 'I'll be seeing you, Druss. Take care!'

'You too.'

Bodasen spurred the stallion back towards the stream and on through the Panthian ranks.

Druss beckoned Delnar aside, away from the men. 'It's pointless standing here all day staring at them,' he said. 'Why don't you order them to stand down and we'll send half of them back to bring up some blankets and fuel?'

'You don't think they'll attack today?'

'No. Why should they? They know we'll not be reinforced tonight. Tomorrow will come soon enough.' Druss tramped back to the camp, stopping in to see the poet. Sieben was asleep. Druss pulled up a chair and stared down at the poet's lined face. Uncharacteristically he stroked the balding head. Sieben opened his eyes.

'Oh, it's you,' he said. 'What's all the fuss about?'

'The Ventrians tricked us. They're on the other side of the mountain.'

Sieben swore softly. Druss chuckled. 'You just lie here, poet, and I'll tell you all about it once we've sent them running.'

'The Immortals are here too?' asked Sieben.

'Of course.'

'Wonderful. A nice little outing you promised me. A few speeches. And what do we get? Another war.'

'I saw Bodasen. He's looking well.'

'Marvellous. Maybe after he's killed us we can have a drink together and chat about old times.'

'You take things too seriously, poet. Rest now, and later I'll have some men carry you up to the pass. You'd hate to miss the action, now, wouldn't you?'

'Couldn't you get them to carry me all the way back to Skoda?'

'Later,' grinned Druss. 'Anyway, I must be getting back.'

The axeman walked swiftly up the mountain slopes and sat on a boulder at the mouth of the pass, gazing intently at the enemy camp.

'What are you thinking about?' asked Delnar, moving up to join him.

'I was remembering something I told an old friend a long time ago.'

'What was that?'

'If you want to win, attack.'

Bodasen dismounted before the Emperor and knelt, pressing his forehead to the earth. Then he rose. From a distance the Ventrian looked as he always had, powerful, black-bearded and keen of eye. But he could no longer stand close inspection. His hair and beard showed the unhealthy sheen of heavy, dark dye, his painted face glowed with unnatural colour and his eyes saw treachery in every shadow. His followers, even those like Bodasen who had served him for decades, knew never to stare into his face, addressing all their remarks to the gilded griffin on his breastplate. No one was allowed to approach him bearing a weapon, and he had not granted a private audience to anyone in years. Always he wore armour – even, it was said, when he slept. His food was tasted by slaves, and he had taken to wearing gloves of soft leather, in the belief that poison might be spread on the outside of his golden goblets.

Bodasen waited for permission to speak, glancing up swiftly to read the expression on the Emperor's face. Gorben was staring moodily.

'Was that Druss?' he asked.

'Aye, my lord.'

'So even he has turned against me.'

'He is a Drenai, my lord.'

'Do you dispute with me, Bodasen?'

'No, sire. Of course not.'

'Good. I want Druss brought before me for judgement. Such treachery must be answered with swift justice. You understand?'

'Yes, sire.'

'Will the Drenai give us the way?'

'I think not, sire. But it will not take long to clear the path. Even with Druss there. Shall I order the men to stand down and prepare camp?'

'No. Let them stay in ranks for a while. Let the Drenai see their power and their strength.'

'Yes, sire.'

Bodasen backed away.

'Are you still loyal?' asked the Emperor, suddenly.

Bodasen's mouth was dry. 'As I have always been, lord.'

'Yet Druss was your friend.'

'Even though that is true, sire, I will see him dragged before you in chains. Or his head presented to you, should he be slain in the defence.'

The Emperor nodded, then turned his painted face to stare up at the pass.

'I want them dead. All dead,' he whispered.

In the cool of the pre-dawn haze the Drenai formed their lines, each warrior bearing a rounded shield and a short stabbing sword. Their sabres had been put aside, for in close formation a swinging longsword could be as deadly to a comrade standing close as to an enemy bearing down. The men were nervous, constantly rechecking breastplate straps, or discovering the bronze greaves protecting their lower legs were too tight, too loose, too anything. Cloaks were removed and left in tight red rolls by the mountain wall behind the ranks. Both Druss and Delnar knew this was the time a man's courage was under the greatest strain. Gorben could do many things. The dice were in his hands. All the Drenai could do was wait.

'Do you think he'll attack immediately the sun comes up?' asked Delnar.

Druss shook his head. 'I don't think so. He'll let the fear work for about an hour. But then again – you can never tell with him.'

The two hundred men in the front rank shared the same emotions now, with varying intensity. Pride, for they had been singled out as the best; fear, for they would be the first to die. Some had regrets. Many had not written home for weeks, others had left friends and relatives with bitter words. Many were the thoughts.

Druss made his way to the centre of the first line, calling for Diagoras and Certak to stand on either side of him.

'Move away from me a little,' he said. 'Give me swinging room.' The line shuffled apart. Druss loosened his shoulders, stretching the muscles of his arms and back. The sky lightened. Druss cursed. The disadvantage for the defenders – apart from the numbers of the enemy – was that the sun rose in their eyes.

Across the stream the black-skinned Panthians sharpened their spears. There was little fear among them. The ivory-skins facing them were few in number. They would be swept away like antelope before a veldt blaze. Gorben waited until the sun cleared the peaks, then gave the order to attack.

The Panthians surged to their feet, a swelling roar of hatred rising from their throats, a wall of sound that hurtled up into the pass, washing over the defenders.

'Listen to that!' bellowed Druss. 'That's not strength you hear. That's the sound of terror!'

Five thousand warriors raced towards the pass, their feet drumming a savage beat on the rocky slopes, echoing high into the peaks.

Druss hawked and spat. Then he began to laugh, a rich, full sound that brought a few chuckles from the men around him.

'Gods, I've missed this,' he shouted. 'Come on, you cowsons!' he yelled at the Panthians. 'Move yourselves!'

Delnar, at the centre of the second line, smiled and drew his sword.

With the enemy a bare hundred paces distant, the men of the third line looked to Archytas. He raised his arm. The men dropped their shields and stooped, rising with barbed javelins. Each man had five of them at his feet.

The Panthians were almost upon them.

'Now!' yelled Archytas.

Arms flew forward and two hundred shafts of death hurtled into the black mass.

'Again!' bellowed Archytas.

The front ranks of the advancing horde disappeared screaming, to be trampled by the men behind them. The charge faltered as the tribesmen tripped and fell over fallen comrades. The mountain walls, narrowing like an hour-glass, slowed the attack still further.

Then the lines clashed.

A spear lunged for Druss. Blocking it with his axe blades, he dragged a backhand cut that sheared through the wicker shield and the flesh beyond. The man grunted as Snaga clove through his ribcage. Druss tore the weapon clear, parried another thrust and hammered his axe into his opponent's face. Beside him Certak blocked a spear with his shield, expertly sliding his gladius into a gleaming black chest. A spear sliced his upper thigh, but there was no pain. He counter-thrust, and his attacker fell across the growing pile of corpses in front of the line.

The Panthians now found themselves leaping upon the bodies of their comrades in their desperation to breach the line. The floor of the pass became slippery with blood, but the Drenai held.

A tall warrior threw aside his wicker shield and hurdled the wall of dead, spear raised. He hurtled towards Druss. Snaga buried itself in his chest, but the weight of the man bore Druss back, tearing his axe from his hands. A second man leapt at him. Druss turned aside the thrusting spear with his mail-covered gauntlets, and smashed a cruel punch to the man's jaw. As the warrior crumpled Druss grabbed him by the throat and groin and hoisted the body above his head, hurling him back over the corpse wall into the faces of the advancing warriors. Twisting, he wrenched his axe clear of the first man's body.

'Come on, my lads,' he bellowed. 'Time to send them home!'

Leaping up on the corpses, he cut left and right, opening up a space in the Panthian ranks. Diagoras couldn't believe his eyes. He swore. Then leapt to join him.

The Drenai advanced, clambering over the Panthian dead, their swords red, their eyes grim.

At the centre the tribesmen struggled first to overcome the madman with the axe, then to get back from him, as other Drenai warriors joined him.

Fear flashed through their ranks like a plague.

Within minutes they were streaming back across the valley floor.

Druss led the warriors back into position. His jerkin was stained with blood, and his beard spotted with crimson. Opening his shirt, he removed a towel and wiped his sweating face. Doffing his helm of black and silver, he scratched his head.

'Well, lads,' he called out, his deep voice echoing in the crags, 'how does it feel to have earned your pay?'

'They're coming again!' someone shouted.

Druss's voice cut through the rising fear. 'Of course they are,' he bellowed. 'They don't know when they're beaten. Front rank fall back, second rank stand to. Let's spread the glory!'

Druss remained with the front line, Diagoras and Certak alongside him.

By dusk they had beaten off four charges for the loss of only forty men – thirty dead, ten wounded.

The Panthians had lost over eight hundred men.

It was a macabre scene that night as the Drenai sat around small campfires, the dancing flames throwing weird shadows across the wall of corpses in the pass, making it seem as if the bodies writhed in the darkness. Delnar ordered the men to gather all the wicker shields they could find and recover as many javelins and spears as were still usable.

Towards midnight many of the veterans were asleep, but others found the excitement of the day too fresh, and they sat in small groups, talking in low tones.

Delnar walked from group to group, sitting with them, joking and lifting their spirits. Druss slept in the tent of Sieben, high in the mouth of the pass. The poet had watched part of the day's action from his bed, and fallen asleep during the long afternoon.

Diagoras, Orases and Certak sat with half a dozen other men as Delnar approached and joined them.

'How are you feeling?' asked the Earl.

The men smiled. What answer could they give?

'Can I ask a question, sir?' asked Orases.

'Certainly.'

'How is it that Druss has stayed alive so long? I mean, he has no defence to speak of.'

'It's a good point,' said the Earl, doffing his helm and running his fingers through his hair, enjoying the cool of the night. 'The reason is contained in your question. It is because he has no defence. That terrible axe rarely leaves a man with a non-mortal wound. To kill Druss you have to be prepared to die. No, not just prepared. You would have to attack Druss in the sure knowledge that he will kill you. Now, most men want to live. You understand?'

'Not really, sir,' admitted Orases.

'Do you know the one kind of warrior no one wants to face?' asked Delnar.

'No, sir.'

'The baresark, sometimes called the berserker, a man whose killing frenzy makes him oblivious to pain and uncaring about life. He throws his armour away and attacks the enemy, cutting and killing until he himself is cut to pieces. I saw a baresark once who had lost an arm. As the blood spewed from the stump he aimed it in the faces of his attackers and carried on fighting until he dropped.

'No one wants to fight such a man. Now, Druss is even more formidable than the berserker. He has all the virtues, but his killing frenzy is controlled. He can think clearly. And when you add the man's awesome strength he becomes a veritable machine of destruction.'

'But surely a chance thrust amid the melee,' said Diagoras. 'A sudden slip on a pool of blood. He could die as well as any other man.'

'Yes,' admitted Delnar. 'I do not say that he won't die in such a way; only that the odds are all with Druss. Most of you saw him today. Those who fought alongside him had no time to study his technique, but others of you caught a glimpse of the Legend. He's always balanced, always moving. His eyes are never still. His peripheral vision is incredible. He can sense danger even amid chaos. Today a very brave Panthian warrior hurled himself on the axe, dragging it from Druss's hand. A second warrior followed. Did anyone see it?'

'I did,' said Orases.

'But you didn't really learn from it. The first Panthian died to remove Druss's weapon. The second was to engage him while the others breached the line. Had they come through then, our force might have been split and pushed back into the walls of the mountain. Druss saw that instantly. That's why, although he could have just knocked his attacker senseless and retrieved his axe, he hurled the man back into the breach. Now think on this: in that instant Druss had seen the danger, formulated a plan of action, and carried it out. More even than this. He retrieved the axe and took the battle to the enemy. That's what broke them. Druss had judged exactly the right moment to attack. It's the instinct of the born warrior.'

'But how did he know we would follow him?' asked Diagoras. 'He could have been cut to pieces.'

'Even in this he was confident. That's why he asked you and Certak to stand alongside him. Now that's a compliment. He knew you would respond, and that others who might not follow him would follow you.'

'He has told you this?' asked Certak.

The Earl chuckled. 'No. In a way Druss would be as surprised to hear it as you are. His actions are not reasoned. As I said, they are instinctive. If we live through this you will learn much.'

'Do you think we will?' asked Orases.

'If we are strong,' lied Delnar smoothly, surprised at himself.

The Panthians came again at dawn, creeping up through the pass as the Drenai waited, swords drawn. But they did not attack. Under the bewildered eyes of the defenders, they hauled away the bodies of their comrades.

It was a bizarre scene. Delnar ordered the Drenai back twenty paces to make room for the work, and the warriors waited. Delnar sheathed his sword and moved alongside Druss in the front line.

'What do you think?'

'I think they're preparing the ground for chariots,' said Druss.

'Horses will never attack a solid line. They'll pull up short,' the Earl pointed out.

'Take a look yonder,' muttered the axeman.

On the far side of the stream, the Ventrian army had parted, making way for the gleaming bronze chariots of the Tantrians. With their huge wheels bearing sickle blades, serrated and deadly, each chariot was drawn by two horses and manned by a driver and a spear carrier.

For an hour the clearing of bodies continued, while the chariots formed a line in the valley below. As the Panthians withdrew, Delnar ordered forward thirty men carrying the wicker shields retrieved from the battle the day before. The shields were spread in a line across the pass and doused with lantern oil.

Delnar placed his hand on Druss's shoulder. 'Take the line fifty paces forward, beyond the shields. When they attack, break formation left and right and make for the cover of the rocks. Once they are through we will fire the shields. Hopefully that will stop them. The second rank will engage the chariots while your line holds the following infantry.'

'Sounds good,' said Druss.

'If it doesn't work we won't try it again,' said Delnar.

Druss grinned.

Along the line of chariots the drivers were pulling silken hoods over the eyes of the horses. Druss led his two hundred men forward, hurdling the wall of wicker shields, Diagoras, Certak and Archytas beside him.

The thunder of hooves on the valley floor echoed through the crags as two hundred charioteers whipped their horses into the gallop.

With the chariots almost upon them Druss bellowed the order to break ranks. As men raced to the safety of the mountain walls on either side, the enemy thundered on towards the second line. Flaming torches were flung upon the wall of oil-soaked wicker shields. Black smoke billowed instantly, followed by dancing flames. The breeze carried the smoke towards the east, burning the flaring nostrils of the hooded horses. Whinnying their terror, they tried to turn, ignoring the biting whips of the charioteers.

Instantly all was confusion. The second line of chariots tore into the first, horses falling, vehicles overturning, hurling screaming men to the jagged rocks.

And into the milling chaos leapt the Drenai, hurdling the dying flames to fall upon the Ventrian spearmen, whose lances were useless at such close quarters.

Gorben, from his vantage point a half-mile away, ordered a legion of infantry into the fray.

Druss and the two hundred Drenai swordsmen re-formed across the pass, locking shields against the new attack, presenting a glittering wall of blades to the silver-armoured infantry.

Crushing the skull of one man and gutting a second, Druss stepped back, casting a lightning glance to left and right.

The line held.

More Drenai fell in this attack than on the previous day, but their numbers were few compared with the losses suffered by the Ventrians.

Only a handful of chariots burst back through the Drenai front line, there to crash and cut a path through their own infantry in their desire to be free of the pass.

Hour upon bloody hour the battle continued, savagely fought by both sides, with no thought of quarter.

The silver-clad Ventrian infantry continued to press their attack, but by dusk their efforts lacked conviction and weight.

Furious, Gorben ordered their general forward into the pass.

'Lead them hard, or you'll beg to be allowed to die,' he promised.

The general's body fell within the hour, and the infantry slunk back across the stream in the gathering gloom of twilight.

* * *

Ignoring the dancing troupe performing before him, Gorben lay back on the silk-covered couch, conversing in low tones with Bodasen. The Emperor wore full battle-dress, and behind him stood the massively muscled Panthian bodyguard who for the last five years had been Gorben's executioner. He killed with his hands, sometimes by strangling his victims slowly, at other times gouging his thumbs through the eye sockets of the hapless prisoners. All executions were performed before the Emperor, and scarcely a week passed without such a grisly scene.

The Panthian had once killed a man by crushing his skull between his hands, to the applause of Gorben and his courtiers.

Bodasen was sickened by it all, but he was caught within a web of his own making. Through the years, naked ambition had driven him to the heights of power. He now commanded the Immortals and was, under Gorben, the most powerful man in Ventria. But the position was perilous. Gorben's paranoia was such that few of his generals survived for long, and Bodasen had begun to feel the Emperor's eyes upon him.

Tonight he had invited Gorben to his tent, promising him an evening of entertainment, but the king was in a surly, argumentative mood, and Bodasen trod warily.

'You thought the Panthians and the chariots would fail, did you not?' asked Gorben. The question was loaded with menace. If the answer was yes, the Emperor would ask why Bodasen had not stated his view. Was he not the Emperor's military advisor? What was the use of an advisor who gave no advice? If the answer was no, then his military judgement would prove to be lacking.

'We have fought many wars over the years, my lord,' he said. 'In most of them we have suffered reverses. You have always said "Unless we try we will never know how to succeed".'

'You think we should send in my Immortals?' asked Gorben. Always before the Emperor had called them *your* Immortals. Bodasen licked his lips and smiled.

'There is no doubt they could clear the pass swiftly. The Drenai are fighting well. They are disciplined. But they know they cannot withstand the Immortals. But that decision is yours alone, my lord.

Only you have the divine mastery of tactics. Men like myself are mere reflections of your greatness.'

'Then where are the men who can think for themselves?' snapped the Emperor.

'I must be honest with you, sire,' said Bodasen quickly. 'You will not find such a man.'

'Why?'

'You seek men who can think as rapidly as you yourself, with your own penetrating insight. Such men do not exist. You are supremely gifted, sire. The gods would visit such wisdom on only one man in ten generations.'

'You speak truly,' said Gorben. 'But there is little joy in being a man apart, separated from his fellows by his god-given gifts. I am hated, you know,' he whispered, eyes darting to the sentries beyond the tent entrance.

'There will always be those that are jealous, sire,' said Bodasen.

'Are you jealous of me, Bodasen?'

'Yes, sire.'

Gorben rolled to his side, eyes gleaming. 'Speak on.'

'In all the years I have served and loved you, lord, I have always wished I could be more like you. For then I could have served you better. A man would be a fool not to be jealous of you. But he is insane if he hates you because you are what he never can be.'

'Well said. You are an honest man. One of the few I can trust. Not like Druss, who promised to serve me, and now thwarts my destiny. I want him dead, my general. I want his head brought to me.'

'It shall be done, sire,' said Bodasen.

Gorben leaned back, gazing around him at the tent and its contents. 'Your quarters are almost as lavish as my own,' he said.

'Only because they are filled with gifts from you, sire,' answered Bodasen swiftly.

Faces and armour blackened by dirt mixed with oil, Druss and fifty swordsmen silently waded the narrow stream under a moonless sky.

Praying the clouds would not part, Druss led the men single file towards the eastern bank, axe in hand, blackened shield held before him. Once ashore Druss squatted at the centre of the small group, pointing towards two dozing sentries by a dying fire. Diagoras and two others ghosted from the group, approaching the sentries silently, daggers in hand. The men died without a sound. Removing torches hastily constructed from the wicker shields of Panthian warriors, Druss and the soldiers approached the sentries' fire.

Stepping over the bodies, Druss lit his torch and ran towards the nearest tent. His men followed suit, racing from tent to tent, until flames leapt thirty feet into the night sky.

Suddenly all was chaos, as screaming men burst from blazing canopies to fall before the swords of the Drenai. Druss raced ahead, cutting a crimson path through the confused Ventrians, his eyes fixed on the tent ahead, its glowing griffin outlined in the towering flames. Close behind came Certak and a score of warriors bearing torches. Wrenching open the flaps, Druss leapt inside.

'Damn,' he grunted, 'Gorben's not here! Curse it!'

Setting torch to silk, Druss shouted for his men to regroup, then led them back towards the stream. No concerted effort was made to stop them, as Ventrians milled in confusion, many of them half-clothed, others filling helmets with water, forming human chains to battle the fierce inferno racing on the wings of the wind throughout the Ventrian camp.

A small group of Immortals, swords in hand, collided with Druss as he raced towards the stream. Snaga leapt forward, braining the first. The second died as Diagoras backhanded a slash across his throat. The battle was brief and bloody, but the element of surprise was with the Drenai. Bursting through the front line of swordsmen, Druss crashed his axe through one man's side before reversing a slashing swipe across another's shoulder.

Bodasen ran from his tent, sword in hand. Swiftly gathering a small group of Immortals, he raced past the flames towards the battle. A Drenai warrior loomed before him. The man aimed a thrust at Bodasen's unprotected body. The Ventrian parried and launched a devastating riposte that tore open the man's throat. Bodasen stepped over the body and led his men forward.

Druss killed two men, then bellowed for the Drenai to fall back.

The pounding of feet from behind caused him to swivel and face the new force. With the fire behind them Druss could not make out faces.

Nearby Archytas despatched a warrior, then saw Druss standing alone.

Without thinking, he raced towards the Immortals. In that instant Druss charged. His axe rose and fell, shearing through armour and bone. Diagoras and Certak joined him, with four other Drenai warriors. The battle was brief. Only one Ventrian broke clear, hurling himself to the right and rolling to his feet behind Archytas. The tall Drenai turned on his heel and engaged the man. Archytas grinned as their swords met. The man was old, though skilful, and no match for the young Drenai. Their swords glittered in the firelight: parry, riposte, counter, thrust and block. Suddenly the Ventrian seemed to trip. Archytas leapt forward. His opponent ducked and rolled to his feet in one flowing movement, his sword ramming into Archytas's groin.

'You live and learn, boy,' hissed Bodasen, dragging his blade clear. Bodasen turned as more Immortals ran forward. Gorben wanted Druss's head. Tonight he would give it to him.

Druss wrenched his axe from a man's body and sprinted for the stream and the relative sanctuary of the pass.

A warrior leapt into his path. Snaga sang through the air, smashing the man's sword to shards. A backhand cut shattered his ribs. As Druss passed him, the man reached out, grabbing his shoulder. In the gleam of the flames, the axeman saw it was Bodasen. The dying Immortal general gripped Druss's jerkin, trying to slow him. Druss kicked him aside and ran on.

Bodasen fell heavily and rolled, watching the burly figure of the axeman and his companions fording the stream.

The Ventrian's vision swam. He closed his eyes. Weariness settled on him like a cloak. Memories danced in his mind. He heard a great noise like the crashing of the sea, and saw again the corsair ship bearing down upon them, gliding out of the past. Once more he raced with Druss to board her, carrying the fight to the aft deck.

Damn! He should have realised Druss would never change.

Attack. Always attack.

He opened his eyes, blinking to clear his vision. Druss was safely on the other side of the stream now, leading the warriors back to the Drenai line.

Bodasen tried to move, but agony lanced him. Carefully he probed the wound in his side, his sticky fingers feeling the broken ribs and the rush of arterial blood from the gaping gash.

It was over.

No more fear. No more insanity. No more bowing and scraping to the painted madman.

In a way he was relieved.

His whole life had been an anticlimax after that battle with Druss against the corsairs. In that one towering moment he had been alive, standing with Druss against ...

They brought his body to the Emperor in the pink light of dawn.

And Gorben wept.

Around them the camp was a shambles. Gorben's generals stood beside the throne, uneasy and silent. Gorben covered the body with his own cloak and dried his eyes on a white linen towel. Then he turned his attention to the man kneeling before him, flanked by Immortal guards.

'Bodasen dead. My tent destroyed. My camp in flames. And you, you pathetic wretch, were the officer of the guard. A score of men invade my camp, killing my beloved general, and you still live. Explain yourself!'

'My lord, I sat with you in Bodasen's tent – by your order.'

'So now it is my fault the camp was attacked!'

'No, sire ...'

'No, sire,' mimicked Gorben. 'I should think not. Your sentries were sleeping. Now they are dead. Do you not think it fitting for you to join them?'

'Sire?'

'Join them, I say. Take your blade and slice your veins.'

The officer drew his ornamental dagger, reversed it, then plunged the blade into his belly. For a moment there was no movement. Then

357

the man began to scream and writhe. Gorben drew his sword, slashing the blade through the man's neck.

'He couldn't even do that right,' said Gorben.

Druss entered Sieben's tent and hurled his axe to the floor. The poet was awake, but lying silently watching the stars when Druss arrived. The axeman sat down on the floor, his great head slumped to his chest, staring at his hands, clenching and unclenching his fists. The poet sensed his despair. He struggled to sit up, the ache in his chest becoming a stabbing pain. He grunted. Druss's head came up, his back straightened.

'How are you feeling?' asked Druss.

'Fine. I take it the raid failed?'

'Gorben was not in his tent.'

'What is wrong, Druss?'

The axeman's head slumped forward and he didn't answer. Sieben climbed from the bed and made his way to Druss, sitting beside him.

'Come along, old horse, tell me.'

'I killed Bodasen. He came at me out of the hadows and I cut him down.'

Sieben put his arm on Druss's shoulder. 'What can I say?'

'You could tell me why – why it had to be me.'

'I can't tell you that. I wish I could. But you did not travel across the ocean, seeking to kill him, Druss. He came here. With an army.'

'I only ever had a few friends in my life,' said Druss. 'Eskodas died in my home. I've killed Bodasen. And I've brought you here to die for a pile of rock in a forgotten pass. I'm so tired, poet. I should never have come here.'

Druss rose and left the tent. Dipping his hands in the water barrel outside, he washed his face. His back was painful, especially under the shoulder-blade where the spear had cut him so many years before. A swollen vein in his right leg nagged at him.

'I don't know if you can hear me, Bodasen,' he whispered, staring up at the stars, 'but I am sorry it had to be me. You were a good friend in happier days, and a man to walk the mountains with.'

Returning to the tent, he found Sieben had fallen asleep in the chair. Druss lifted him gently and carried him to his bed, covering him with a thick blanket. 'You're worn out, poet,' he said. He felt for Sieben's pulse. It was ragged but strong. 'Stay with me, Sieben,' he told him. 'I'll get you home.'

As the dawn's rays bathed the peaks Druss walked slowly down the rocky slope to stand again with the Drenai line.

For eight terrible days Skeln became a charnel house, littered with swelling corpses and the foul stench of putrefaction. Gorben threw legion after legion up into the pass, only to see them stumble back defeated and dejected. The dwindling band of defenders was held together by the indomitable courage of the black-garbed axeman, whose terrifying skill dismayed the Ventrians. Some said he was a demon, others a god of war. Old tales were recalled.

The Chaos Warrior walked again in the stories told around Ventrian campfires.

Only the Immortals stayed aloof from the fears. They knew it would fall to them to clear the pass, and they knew it would not be easy.

On the eighth night Gorben at last gave in to the insistent demands of his generals. Time was running out. The way had to be taken tomorrow lest the Drenai army trap them in this cursed bay.

The order was given and the Immortals honed their swords.

At dawn they rose silently, forming their black and silver line across the stream, staring stonily ahead at the three hundred men who stood between them and the Sentran Plain.

Tired were the Drenai, bone-weary and hollow-eyed.

Abadai, the new general of the Immortals, walked forward and lifted his sword in silent salute to the Drenai, as was the Immortal custom. The blade swept down and the line moved forward. To the rear three drummers began the doleful marching beat, and the Immortals' swords flashed into the air.

Grim were the faces as the cream of Ventria's army slowly marched towards the Drenai.

Druss, bearing a shield now, watched the advance, his cold blue eyes showing no expression, his jaw set, his mouth a tight line. He stretched the muscles of his shoulders, and took a deep breath.

This was the test. This was the day of days.

The spear-point of Gorben's destiny against the resolution of the Drenai.

He knew the Immortals were damned fine warriors, but they fought now for glory alone.

The Drenai, on the other hand, were proud men, and sons of proud men, descended from a race of warriors. They were fighting for their homes, their wives, their sons, and sons yet unborn. For a free land and the right to make their own way, run their own lives, fulfil the destiny of a free race. Egel and Karnak had fought for this dream, and countless more like them down through the centuries.

Behind the axeman, Earl Delnar watched the nearing enemy line. He was impressed by their discipline and, in a strangely detached way, found himself admiring them. He transferred his gaze to the axeman. Without him they could never have held this long. He was like the anchor of a ship in a storm, holding the prow into the wind, allowing it to ride clear and face the might of the elements without being broken upon the rocks or overturned by the power of the sea. Strong men drew courage from his presence. For he was a constant in a world of shifting change – a colossal force that could be trusted to endure.

As the Immortals loomed ever nearer, Delnar could feel the fear spreading among the men. The line shifted as shields were gripped more firmly. The Earl smiled. Time for you to speak, Druss, he thought.

With the instinct of a lifetime of war, Druss obliged. Raising his axe he bellowed at the advancing Immortals.

'Come in and die, you whoresons! I am Druss and this is death!'

Rowena was picking flowers in the small garden behind the house when the pain struck her, cutting beneath her ribs through to her back. Her legs collapsed beneath her and she toppled into the blooms. Pudri saw her from the meadow gate and ran to her side, shouting for help. Sieben's wife, Niobe, came running from the meadow and between them they lifted the unconscious woman and carried her into the house. Pudri forced a little foxglove powder into her mouth, then poured water into a clay goblet. Holding it to her lips, he pinched her nostrils, forcing her to swallow.

But this time the pain did not pass, and Rowena was carried upstairs to her bed while Niobe rode to the village for the physician.

Pudri sat by Rowena's bedside, his lined leathery face sunken and filled with concern, his large dark eyes moist with tears.

'Please do not die, lady,' he whispered. 'Please.'

Rowena floated from her body and opened her spirit eyes, gazing down with pity at the matronly form in her bed. She saw the wrinkled face and greying hair, the dark rings below the eyes. Was this her? Was this tired, worn-out shell the Rowena that had been taken to Ventria years before?

And poor Pudri, so shrunken and old. Poor devoted Pudri.

Rowena felt the pull of the Source. She closed her eyes and thought of Druss.

On the wings of the wind, the Rowena of yesterday's dreams soared above the farm, tasting the sweetness of the air, enjoying the freedom of those born to the sky. Lands swept below her, green and fertile, dappled with the gold of cornfields. Rivers became satin ribbons, seas rippling lakes, cities peopled with insects scurrying without purpose.

The world shrank until it became a plate studded with gems of blue and white, and then a stone, rounded as if by the sea, and finally a tiny jewel. She thought of Druss once more.

'Oh, not yet!' she begged. 'Let me see him once. Just once.'

Colours swam before her eyes, and she fell, twisting and spinning through the clouds. The land below her was gold and green, the cornfields and meadows of the Sentran Plain rich and verdant. To the east it seemed as if a giant's cloak had been carelessly thrown on to the land, grey and lifeless, the mountains of Skeln merely folds in the cloth. Closer she flew until she hovered over the pass, gazing down on the embattled armies.

Druss was not hard to find.

He stood, as always, at the centre of the carnage, his murderous axe cutting and killing.

Sadness touched her then, a sorrow so deep it was like a pain in her soul.

'Goodbye, my love,' she said.

And turned her face to the heavens.

The Immortals hurled themselves on the Drenai line, and the clash of steel on steel sounded above the insistent drums. Druss hammered Snaga into a bearded face, then sidestepped a murderous thrust, disembowelling his assailant. A spear cut his face, a sword-blade ripped a shallow wound in his shoulder. Forced back a pace, Druss dug his heel into the ground, his bloody axe slashing into the black and silver ranks before him.

Slowly the weight of the Immortals forced back the Drenai line.

A mighty blow to Druss's shield split it down the middle. Hurling it from him, the axeman gripped Snaga with both hands, slashing a red swathe through the enemy. Anger turned to fury within him.

Druss's eyes blazed, power flooding his tired, aching muscles.

The Drenai had been pushed back nearly twenty paces. Ten more and the pass widened. They would not be able to hold.

Druss's mouth stretched in a death's-head grin. The line was bending like a bow on either side of him, but the axeman himself was immovable. The Immortals pushed towards him, but were cut down with consummate ease. Strength flowed through him.

He began to laugh.

It was a terrible sound, and it filled the veins of the enemy with ice. Druss lashed Snaga into the face of a bearded Immortal. The man was catapulted into his fellows. The axeman leapt forward, cleaving Snaga into the chest of the next warrior. Then he hammered left and right. Men fell back from his path, opening a space in the ranks. Bellowing his rage to the sky, Druss charged into the mass. Certak and Diagoras followed.

It was suicidal, yet the Drenai formed a wedge, Druss at the head, and sheared into the Ventrians.

The giant axeman was unstoppable. Warriors threw themselves at him from every side, but his axe flashed like quicksilver. A young soldier called Eericetes, only accepted into the Immortals a month before, saw Druss bearing down on him. Fear rose like bile in his throat. Dropping his sword he turned, pushing at the man behind him.

'Back,' he shouted. 'Get back!'

The men made way for him, and the cry was taken up by others, thinking it was an order from the officers.

'Back! Back to the stream!' The cry swept through the ranks and the Immortals turned, streaming towards the Ventrian camp.

From his throne Gorben watched in horror as his men waded into the shallow stream, disorganised and bewildered.

His eyes flicked up to the pass, where the axeman stood waving Snaga in the air.

Druss's voice floated down to him, echoing from the crags.

'Where is your legend now, you eastern sons of bitches?'

Abadai, blood streaming from a shallow cut in his forehead, approached the Emperor, dropping to his knees, head bowed.

'How did it happen?' demanded Gorben.

'I don't know, sire. One moment we were pushing them back, and then the axeman went mad, charging our line. We had them. We really had them. But somehow the cry went up to fall back, and then all was chaos.'

In the pass Druss swiftly honed the dulled blades of his axe.

'We beat the Immortals,' said Diagoras, slapping Druss on the shoulder. 'By all the gods in Missael, we beat the damned Immortals.'

'They'll be back, lad. And very soon. You'd better pray the army is moving at speed.'

With Snaga razor-edged once more, Druss looked to his wounds. The cut on his face stung like the devil, but the flow of blood had ceased. His shoulder was more of a problem, but he strapped it as best he could. If they survived the day, he would stitch it that night. There were several smaller cuts to his legs and arms but these had congealed and sealed themselves.

A shadow fell across him. He looked up. Sieben stood there, wearing breastplate and helm.

'How do I look?' asked the poet.

'Ridiculous. What do you think you're doing?'

'I'm getting into the thick of it, Druss old horse. And don't think you can stop me.'

'I wouldn't dream of it.'

'You're not going to tell me I'm stupid?'

Druss stood and grabbed his friend's shoulders. 'These have been good years, poet. The best I could have wished for. There are few treasures in a man's life. One of them comes with the knowledge that a man has a friend to stand beside him when the hour grows dark. And let's be honest, Sieben . . . It couldn't get much darker, could it?'

'Now you come to mention it, Druss my dear, it does seem a tiny bit hopeless.'

'Well, everybody has to die sometime,' said Druss. 'When death comes for you, spit in his eye, poet.'

'I'll do my best.'

'You always did.'

The drums sounded again and the Immortals massed. Fury was in their eyes now, and they glared balefully at the defenders. They would not be turned back. Not by Druss. Not by the pitiful two hundred facing them.

From the first clash the Drenai line was forced back. Even Druss, needing room to swing his axe, could find space only by retreating a pace. Then another. Then another. He battled on, a tireless machine, bloody and bloodied, Snaga rising in a crimson spray and falling with pitiless efficiency.

Time and again he rallied the Drenai. But ever on came the Immortals, striding across the bodies of their dead, their eyes grim, their mood resolute.

Suddenly the Drenai line broke, and the battle degenerated in moments to a series of skirmishes, small circles of warriors forming shield rings amid the black and silver sea filling the pass.

The Sentran Plain lay open to the conqueror.

The battle was lost.

But the Immortals were desperate to erase the memory of defeat. They blocked the pathway to the west, determined to kill the last of the defenders.

From his vantage point on the eastern hill Gorben threw down his sceptre in fury, turning on Abadai.

'They have won. Why are they not pushing on? Their bloodlust leaves them blocking the pass!'

Abadai could not believe his eyes. With time a desperate enemy waiting to betray them, the Immortals were unknowingly continuing the work of the defenders. The narrow pass was now gorged with warriors as the rest of Gorben's army jostled behind them, waiting to sweep through to the plain beyond.

Druss, Delnar, Diagoras and a score of others had formed a ring of steel by a cluster of jutting boulders. Fifty paces to the right Sieben, Certak and thirty men were surrounded and fighting furiously. The poet's face was grey and terrible pain grew in his chest. Dropping his sword he scrambled atop a grey boulder, pulling his throwing knife from its wrist sheath.

Certak parried one thrust, but a spear punched through his breastplate, ripping into his lungs. Blood welled in his throat and he fell. A tall Ventrian leapt to the boulder. Sieben hurled his blade. It took the man through the right eye.

A spear flashed through the air, lancing Sieben's chest. Strangely, far from causing him pain, it released the agony from his cramped heart. He toppled from the rock, to be swallowed by the black and silver horde.

Druss saw him fall – and went berserk.

Breaking from the shield ring, he launched his giant frame into the massed ranks of the warriors before him, cutting them aside like wheat before a scythe. Delnar closed the ring behind him, disembowelling a Ventrian lancer and locking shields with Diagoras.

Surrounded now by Immortals, Druss hammered his way forward. A spear took him high in the back. He swung round, braining the lancer. A sword bounced from his helm, gashing his cheek. A second spear pierced his side, and a clubbing blow from the flat of a sword thundered into his temple. Grabbing one assailant, he hauled him forward, butting him viciously. The man sagged in his grip. More enemies closed in around the axeman. Using the unconscious Ventrian as a shield, Druss dropped to the ground. Swords and spears slashed at him.

Then came the sound of bugles.

Druss struggled to rise, but a booted foot lashed into his temple and he fell into darkness.

*　　*　　*

He awoke and cried out. His face was swathed in bandages, his body wracked with pain. He tried to sit, but a hand pushed gently on his shoulder.

'Rest, axeman. You've lost a lot of blood.'

'Delnar?'

'Yes. We won, Druss. The army arrived just in time. Now rest.'

The last moments of battle surged back into Druss's mind. 'Sieben!'

'He is alive. Barely.'

'Take me to him.'

'Don't be a fool. By rights you should be dead. Your body was pierced a score of times. If you move, the stitches will open and you'll bleed to death.'

'Take me to him, damn you!'

Delnar cursed and helped the axeman to his feet. Calling an orderly who took the weight on the left side, he half-carried the wounded giant to the back of the tent and the still, sleeping form of Sieben the Saga-master.

Lowering Druss into a seat by the bedside, Delnar and the orderly withdrew. Druss leaned forward, gazing at the bandages around Sieben's chest, and the slowly spreading red stain at the centre.

'Poet!' he called softly.

Sieben opened his eyes.

'Can nothing kill you, axeman?' he whispered.

'It doesn't look like it.'

'We won,' said Sieben. 'And I want you to note that I didn't hide.'

'I didn't expect you to.'

'I'm awfully tired, Druss old horse.'

'Don't die. Please don't die,' said the axeman, tears causing him to blink furiously.

'There are some things even you cannot have, old horse. My heart is almost useless. I don't know why I've lived this long. But you were right. They have been good years. I wouldn't change anything. Not even this. Look after Niobe and the children. And make sure some saga-master does me justice. You'll do that?'

'Of course I will.'

'I wish I could be around to add to this saga. What a fitting climax.'

'Yes. Fitting. Listen, poet. I'm not good with words. But I want to tell you . . . I want you to know you've been like a brother to me. The best friend I ever had. The very best. Poet? Sieben?'

Sieben's eyes stared unseeing at the tent ceiling. His face was peaceful and looked almost young again. The lines seemed to vanish before Druss's eyes. The axeman began to shake. Delnar approached and closed Sieben's eyes, covering his face with a sheet. Then he helped Druss back to his bed.

'Gorben is dead, Druss. His own men slew him as they ran. Our fleet has the Ventrians bottled up in the bay. At the moment one of their generals is meeting with Abalayn to discuss surrender. We did it. We held the pass. Diagoras wants to see you. He made it through the battle. Can you believe it, even fat Orases is still with us! Now, I'd have laid ten to one odds he wouldn't survive.'

'Give me a drink, will you,' whispered Druss.

Delnar came back to his side, bearing a goblet of cool water. Druss sipped it slowly. Diagoras entered the tent, carrying Snaga. The axe had been cleaned of blood and polished to shine like silver.

Druss gazed at it, but did not reach out. The dark-eyed young warrior smiled.

'You did it,' he said. 'I have never seen the like. I would not have believed it possible.'

'All things are possible,' said Druss. 'Never forget that, laddie.'

Tears welled in the axeman's eyes, and he turned his head away from them. After a moment he heard them back away. Only then did he allow the tears to fall.

Acknowledgements

My thanks to my editor John Jarrold, copy-editor Jean Maund, and test readers Val Gemmell, Stella Graham, Edith Graham, Tom Taylor and Vicki Lee France. Thanks also to Stan Nicholls and Chris Baker for bringing Druss to life in a new way.

About the Author

David Gemmell's first novel, *Legend*, was published in 1984. He has written many bestsellers, including the Drenai saga, the Jon Shannow novels and the Stones of Power sequence. Widely acclaimed as Britain's king of heroic fantasy, David Gemmell died in 2006.

Find out more about David Gemmell and other Orbit authors by registering for the free monthly newsletter at www.orbitbooks.net

WOLF IN SHADOW

David Gemmell

It is three hundred years since the world toppled on its axis, and civilisation was destroyed. In this savagely reshaped world ruled by brigads and war-makers, a rider seeks a lost city. Pursuing a dream to calm the violence in his soul, Jon Shannow, the brigand slayer, desires only peace.

But from the Plague Lands emerges a fresh terror. The Lord of the Pit and his Hellborn army seek to plunge mankind into a new Satanic ers. Seemingly invincible, they make a fatal mistake. They take Shannow's woman for blood sacrifice.

And find themselves facing the deadliest warrior of the new age. Jon Shannow – the Jerusalem Man.

'The mood that Gemmell weaves is compelling . . . This powerful, harsh fantasy examines our assumptions about good, evil and nature of quests . . . Immense'
Locus

www.orbitbooks.net

LION OF MACEDON

David Gemmell

He is Parmenion. A hated outsider, he must fight the hardened heroes of Sparta.

He will survive. Dark forces have marked out his destiny as the most fearsome warlord the world has known.

He is the Lion of Macedon. The man called Death of Nations will reshape the glory of Greece before he faces the wrath of hell . . .

'*Lion of Macedon* delivers everything if promises: a muscular and expertly plotted adventure, a real feeling for Ancient Greece, its myths, magic and politics. All in all, a wonderful excursion back to the Ages of Heroes'
Robert Holdstock

'Sweeping historical fantasy . . . the glory and magic of ancient Greece live again in Gemmell's *Lion of Macedon*'
Locus

'Book of the year . . . an important book for both the writer and the historical fantasy genre'
GMI

'An enduring and compulsive epic . . . nobody writes better fantasy'
Starbust

orbit

www.orbitbooks.net